PLAY THE
RED QUEEN

Also by the author

The Trudeau Vector
Red Flags

PLAY THE
RED
QUEEN

JURIS JURJEVICS

SOHO
CRIME

Published by Soho Press, Inc.
227 W 17th Street
New York, NY 10011

Library of Congress Cataloging-in-Publication Data
Jurjevics, Juris, 1943–2018.
Play the Red Queen / Juris Jurjevics.

ISBN 978-1-64129-137-8
eISBN 978-1-64129-138-5

1. United States. Army—Officers—Fiction.
2. Female assassins—Vietnam (Republic)—Fiction. 3. Americans—Vietnam
(Republic)—Fiction. 4. Ho Chi Minh City (Vietnam)—Fiction.
5. Vietnam (Republic)—History—Coup d'état, 1963—Fiction.
PS3610.U76 P55 2020 | DDC 813/.6—dc23

Interior design by Janine Agro, Soho Press, Inc.

Printed in the United States of America

10 9 8 7 6 5 4 3 2 1

In memory of
Jānis Ivars Rozēns
Ralph Gold
and
Charles Thanhauser.

War is a racket.

—MAJOR GENERAL SMEDLEY BUTLER, USMC,
TWICE AWARDED THE MEDAL OF HONOR
BY THE UNITED STATES CONGRESS

Our society had been a kleptocracy of the
highest order, the government doing its best to
steal from the Americans, the average man doing
his best to steal from the government, the worst
of us doing our best to steal from each other.

—VIET THANH NGUYEN, *THE SYMPATHIZER*

PROLOGUE

On 24 August 1963, the newly arrived American ambassador to South Viet Nam, Henry Cabot Lodge, received a cable from Washington. A few days earlier, the South Vietnamese government had conducted brutal raids on Buddhists throughout the country. Washington instructed Ambassador Lodge to inform South Viet Nam's president, Ngo Dinh Diem, that he must immediately remove his younger brother, Ngo Dinh Nhu, whose police and Special Forces had carried out the beatings, arrests, and killings, from power. Many in Saigon and Washington feared Nhu was already running the government nominally headed by Diem.

"If, in spite of all your efforts, Diem remains obdurate and refuses," the cable read, "then we must face the possibility that Diem himself cannot be preserved."

SAIGON

OCTOBER

1963

CHAPTER ONE

The dead American major lay faceup on the sidewalk in his stocking feet. His khaki shirtfront gleamed with blood, a sizable pool now spreading toward the gutter. A stray dog, weighing the odds of sampling some, cringed when a waiter clouted it with a broom. Street hustlers with pointy sideburns cackled as their leader mimicked the mutt's lapping tongue.

Two plainclothes Vietnamese dicks were chatting up some military police in green fatigues with QC in white letters on their black helmet liners. The tallest of the army cops stood bareheaded in an open jeep, forearms leaning on the bar of red flashers that ran along the top of the windshield. Our own Air Force military police were in khakis and black boots, MP emblazoned in white on their sleeve brassards and helmets. One sergeant took 35-millimeter photographs of the major while another readied a body bag.

Saigon municipal police—who everyone called "white mice" both for their all-white uniforms and their cowardly inclinations—busied themselves waving away vehicles streaming past the cordon. The higher ranks stood in the shade and made a bored show of checking their wristwatches, as it was nearly time for their *ngu trua*, the long midday break the Vietnamese took during the worst of the heat. Another American getting himself murdered had them acting even more inconvenienced than usual.

As agents of the Army's Criminal Investigation Division, me and Robeson had jurisdiction over the victim; the Viets, over the killer. I flipped open my spiral notebook and entered *11:28 hours, 16 October 1963.* Then the basics: *Staff Sergeant Ellsworth Miser and Sergeant Clovis Auguste Robeson, CID investigators at scene. One entry wound, upper torso.*

From the damage, it looked like the round might've flattened as it struck, smacking into his chest like a quarter driven by a pickaxe. Sergeant Robeson turned the body partway but found no obvious exit wound. The slug was lodged somewhere in the corpse.

In the first incident, a week and a half ago, the shooter had aimed for body mass on an American army captain and let the bullet do its work. Six days later she'd gone for a head shot on a major. "Hit 'im straight between his running lights," Freddie Crouch had announced to the office on returning from the scene.

Lying in front of us, her third kill was much less messy. Perfect placement: straight to the heart. Struck in the breast pocket, the major had been slammed right out of his shoes. The shot bordered on impossible, given the moving motorbike on which the sharpshooter had balanced, firing from behind the driver.

We approached the closest witness to the killing, a staff sergeant like me, three gold chevrons on his sleeve above a single rocker. He stopped teeter-tottering his café chair midair and lowered the front legs to the sidewalk.

"Can you describe the assailant?" I said, ready to take notes.

He reared up again on the back legs of the chair. The cap of his lighter *ching*ed open and clicked shut over and over as he spoke.

"Drop-dead gorgeous, you might say." He smiled faintly at his lame joke. "Way better-looking than my broad. Otherwise typical: no knockers, not much ass. Coal-black hair way past her shoulders. Slender as a sparrow."

"Wearing?" Robeson said.

The sergeant didn't so much as glance Robeson's way. He looked straight at me like I'd asked the question. "An *ao dai*. White. Loose dark pants underneath."

"Head covered?" I asked.

He nodded. "Cone hat tied under her chin."

"Height?"

"No idea. Little. Course they're all little. One cute baby-san, I tell ya. My Fifth ARVN guys iced some female VCs last week out in the boonies, but they were nothin' to look at compared to this kid."

"Kid? What age?"

"Maybe twenty, tops." He clicked his Zippo shut and laid it on the pack. I read the sentiment etched into its side:

I LOVE THE

FUCKING ARMY

AND THE ARMY

LOVES FUCKING ME

"She have the piece in a bag before she produced it?"

The sergeant lit a Lucky Strike and inhaled deeply. "Had it in this red silky scarf. Slipped away as the barrel came up. She fired as soon as she had the gun raised and nested."

"Could you make out the weapon?"

"Looked to be a forty-five."

A .45 pistol had a lot of stopping power but wasn't everyone's weapon of choice. The piece was a lot to lift—three pounds—and its iron sights sucked. The recoil from the large-caliber bullet was notoriously hard to handle. Harder still to hit anything at all with a .45, much less while balanced on the back of a moving vehicle. But smacking into you at high velocity, the stubby slugs could dislocate your shoulder if they so much as struck a finger. Like reaching up and catching a cannonball, our firearms instructors liked to boast. A .45 could knock you upside down if it struck low, or toss you backward like a puppet, as it had the major.

"She had no problem handling the kick?"

"None. One shot. No hesitation. Hit 'im dead center and flung 'im."

"Standard issue forty-five?"

"Looked to be standard," he said, "except the finish was lighter."

"Shiny, you mean? Plated like?"

"No. Just not blued. And the grips . . . they could've been light too."

"Pearl."

"Not pimp grips, no. Not sparkly. More like bone."

"Ivory?"

"Like that, yeah. Sort of grayish-yellow."

Sweat dripped down my chin. I brushed it away.

"How is it you saw the grips," Robeson interjected, "if she was clutching the piece?"

Again, the sergeant answered me. "She took it by the slide right after the discharge. Held it at her side like a hammer. Had a finger through the trigger guard riding away."

"How far was she when she fired? Ten feet? Fifteen?"

"I'd say twenty-five to thirty."

"Jesus. No mean feat."

"She oughta shoot for their Olympic team, if the zips ever get their act together to have one."

"You get a look at the motorbike driver?"

"Not a motorbike. A scooter. Young stud. Dark pants, red and black short-sleeve shirt. Plaid, like yours."

Robeson and me had on our civvies: tan desert boots from the base exchange, beige socks, drip-dry pants. No underwear. CID credentials rode in the breast pockets of our short-sleeve shirts, left untucked to cover our holstered revolvers.

I glanced across the black macadam, trying to imagine the scene just before the shot. "The major, was he sitting when he got hit?"

"He had just stood up. The poor bastard was smiling."

"He was leaving?" Robeson said.

"Don't think so," the sarge said to me. "Just got up."

"Why, if he wasn't leaving?"

"No idea."

"And you said he was smiling?"

"Yeah. The major said something as the weapon popped up."

"What exactly?"

The sergeant frowned. "I wasn't paying no mind. The gun had my full attention."

"Who did he say it to?"

"Maybe the pro who had planted herself at his table. I'm not sure."

"She still here?"

"No. When the little lady got splashed, she wailed and bolted."

"And were you socializing with a tea girl too?"

"Yeah." He nodded to where she stood, quaking.

I let the sergeant retreat to another table and went to talk to the tea girl who'd been sitting next to him during the attack. She was wearing white, as decreed by the Diem regime's morality laws. The laws also forbade hostesses to consume alcohol, but a waiter was plying her with liquor after what she'd seen. "Lousy VC numba ten," was the extent of her English. I took down her name from her hostess ID for our office interpreter to follow up, but I wasn't expecting much from that quarter.

I blotted my eyes with my sleeve. "Lady Death," the Saigon press had dubbed the shooter. At the shop we called her "the Red Queen" because a playing card bearing a red female figure in a cone hat and *ao dai* had been left at each of the first two shootings, a detail our boss had held back from the press. Though they'd have it soon enough: Saigon was a sieve.

Our military press was lucky to report on it at all. The new Armed Forces Radio broadcasts were censored both by the Vietnamese and by us in solidarity with our ally's restricted news accounts. Also in keeping with our commanding general's morale directive—no lurid shit. Our service rag wasn't much better. Most days *Stars and Stripes* read like a small-town weekly filled with photo spreads of Saigon's orphan boys learning "simple trades and civic responsibility" at the local Lions Club.

What it didn't have was hard military news about Green Berets arming Montagnard tribesmen in the highlands and building fortified mountain camps for them along the border with Laos. Not a thing about our secret air bases in Thailand flying missions against VC supply lines running south down through Cambodia. Nada about the black-op coastal raiders launching out of Da Nang into North Viet Nam's waters.

Instead we got the "landslide" victory of the Vietnamese president's party in a country that practically outlawed opposition, alongside stirring stories about American ground crews servicing choppers in the blazing sun and guys getting care packages from home. I could hardly wait for this year's Christmas piece on Santa's sleigh taking fire over Bien Hoa. But today there had been a rare short article—barely two inches of type—about the two previous attacks by the deadly damsel. No names or details, just a quick cautionary tale meant to warn uniformed advisors off Saigon's streets, from its swank boulevards to its narrow stinking alleys.

An American MP brought over the major's wallet and dog tags. James Calvin Furth, blood type A, Presbyterian. Officer and gentleman by Act of Congress, career concluded three thousand leagues from home. Back there it was a little before midnight, his kids asleep, his wife drifting off. Dreaming. Or maybe jarred awake by terrible dread like people bullshitted about in movies.

CHAPTER TWO

Trucks, sedans, and overloaded buses rolled past the newly dead body at speed. Among the mass of vehicles jamming the boulevard rode women on bicycles, scooters, and the benches of pedal rickshaws, their long hair trailing behind them. Most of the younger ones were dressed just like the Red Queen in white *ao dais* and woven cone hats, their eyes flitting over us from beneath black bangs. The gauzy silk tunics billowed as the women floated by.

The street cops' white uniforms blazed as they went through the motions of searching for the expended shell casing among the automobiles and motorbikes darting around them like spooked fish. They weren't exactly busting ass, but you could hardly blame them. There was no mystery as to who had killed the major or why. It's what we did—hostiles and friendlies. It's what we were there to do to each other. Any so-called evidence wasn't going to tell you much more than that. This wasn't a crime of passion or common murder. It was a skilled assassination, a stranger coming upon a stranger and cutting him down. Nothing personal.

A QC sergeant found the red silk scarf she'd used to cloak the pistol and turned it over to me. I got a whiff of gardenia and gun oil. Righting the major's café chair, I sat down at his table, still feeling kind of hollow from a touch of fever the week prior. Something crackled underfoot—looked like pieces of windshield glass and bits of chalky stucco. I leaned down to see what it was. Pinned beneath a leg of the major's chair was a torn wedge of paper—a corner of an astrological chart, common as candy in Saigon. I piled the debris on the paper scrap and lifted it onto the table. "Well, I'll be," I muttered. Bleached bones from the skeleton of a small creature, maybe a tiny bat. A miniature fang stuck to my thumb. The glassy fragments were broken mirror.

"Might've been getting his fortune read when he bought it," I called out to Robeson. He came over to examine my collection, then went to check with our witness, who looked mighty pissed at being questioned by Robeson on his own. The staff sergeant was lucky we were outside in broad daylight. If this had gone down in a bar after hours, whitey might have ended his night picking glass out of his skull.

"You were right," Clovis called over to me. "The sergeant here says an astrologer was squatting next to the major when he bought it." A fortune-teller poring over small mirrors and bones, divining the American's destiny. The Year of the Cat hadn't lined up so good for Major Furth.

Robeson joined me at the table. "You think this dude gave Furth a break on the price when he saw how little work it was gonna take to lay out the guy's future?"

A Vietnamese police captain, in gray slacks and snappy white shirt with black epaulettes, fanned himself with his hat and called his men out of the road. They sidled to the curb, exhausted. Come evening, they'd be dragging themselves to second jobs, the lucky ones at hotels and businesses, the others doing hard-ass manual labor. Elite nabobs and shitbags lived well in Saigon but even ranking soldiers and police struggled, doing menial work far beneath them just to get by. Which had Vietnamese cops like these forever fishing for bribes, and threatening shopkeepers with raids if they came away empty-handed. The more ambitious ones saved up to buy promotions. Higher rank would let them extort more and work less, like their bosses and the plainclothesmen standing in the shade.

One of the street cops handed me what looked like a face card, but not any of the sixteen cards in the standard Vietnamese deck. I took it by its edges: a female figure in a black *ao dai* beneath a black cone hat, with a red skull for a face and empty black eye sockets. Instead of a suit symbol, a yellow Communist star gleamed in the upper corner.

"She's using revenge cards," Robeson said. "Same as our side." He reminded me about the rumors that some of our guys had started marking their kills with an ace of spades stuffed in the victim's mouth or wounds. "It's like she's mocking us, tossing it right back in our faces."

My buck sergeant was good. Robeson ground it out, working the details until they talked. I liked to think I didn't have the patience. More likely his kind of smarts is what I didn't have. Not that he needed them. The fucker had family money. He'd gone to college for a couple of semesters and had kicked back in places like Paris and Morocco. He could read music, speak some French and do arithmetic in his head. He knew things that weren't in Army manuals.

I slipped the card into my breast pocket without touching the face or back. "The bystanders give you anything useful about her driver?"

"Mostly no one remembers a whole lot more than hearing

the gunshot. One of the waiters said a male in his twenties, on a pale green Vespa."

Vespa motor scooters puttered all around Saigon, humming like hornets. A few red, the rest a watery pea-soup green. "Some getaway vehicle," I said, peeved at the humiliation. "Fleeing on a two-stroke lawn mower engine."

A waiter delivered us each a small aperitif. I sipped the blond liqueur and sifted through the contents of the major's wallet. Pictures of two kids, the wife, a pickup truck and a Ford Falcon parked in the driveway of a sprawling white Victorian with a wraparound porch. A wallet-size hand-tinted photo showed a pink-cheeked ARVN ranger in a beret. In a tiny insert next to him, a tinier paratrooper rappelled down a rope. In another black-and-white, a properly shy Vietnamese girl in a tight, high-collared, long-sleeved *ao dai* stood next to the major. In with the piasters in the bill compartment was a condom packet that had raised a permanent round impression in the leather.

The Virginia driver's license had him at age forty, nine years older than me. I groped my pants pocket for my mentholated Newports and examined his tiny bank-card calendar. Three months left to mark off from his tour of duty. He'd be home earlier than expected, Glad-bagged inside a crate, his personal effects in a ditty pouch between his knees, his body seen off by an honor guard from the Army of the Republic of Viet Nam, the ARVN troops he had come such a long way to instruct in the art of war. Never mind that they'd been soldiering since before the baby Jesus drew breath.

Judging from his starched khakis and MAAG shoulder patch, Major Furth was more likely a Saigon warrior, a REMF: Rear Echelon Motherfucker. Even so, unarmed and ambushed on a city street by a woman in civvies was no way for any soldier to go.

In '62, fifty-three Americans had gone home in flag-draped boxes, yet the embassy kept insisting we all were non-combatants. Though five thousand of us were in the field, Washington insisted all sixteen thousand US military in-country were "advisors." Whether we bore arms or wielded pens, flew missions or desks, didn't seem to matter. We were paying the price for taking a stand alongside the South Vietnamese. As we closed in on the last two months of '63, the casualty toll was already double last year's and rising as the Red Queen trawled the streets, adding her kills to the total.

Before the Red Queen showed up, weeks had gone by without shots being fired. We had explosions in town—bombs, plastique—and restaurants had started to put up latticework grills to keep out tossed grenades, but gunplay was rare. Your chances were still far better of getting killed by a barstool than a bullet.

Until now, Americans in Saigon had rarely been targeted. And never their dependents, like the kids in the stateside yellow bus passing in front of us, carting students home from their half day at the unairconditioned American Community School, the older boys in the back puffing on Bastos, impressed with themselves 'cause they could buy beer and smokes anywhere in the city or bum them from the armed GI on board. The boys stared at the body, the girls mostly looked away. All of them worried it might be somebody they knew.

Guerillas were embedded in Saigon's Chinese district and encamped in swampy wetlands within sight of the city, yet poor and posh alike denied that the Viet Cong were at the gates. The terrifying executions took place *out there*. Whenever violence erupted locally, the regime blamed "bandits." But last month, during a crowded matinee of *Lady and the Tramp* at the theater leased for American use, a bomb had smashed the ladies' room. And across town in Cholon, a thirty-foot section of the wall surrounding General Harkins's headquarters had gotten blown out. These incidents made everybody edgy with the thought that the VC had something new in mind for US personnel that might even include their families. Nevertheless we'd carried on like everything was normal—until these slayings.

Not that there was much we could do if Viet Cong assassination teams started targeting unarmed American advisors. We lived and worked in locations scattered across the city. Being dispersed allegedly made us less noticeable and safer than if we were concentrated. At least that was the official bullshit the brass put out. The simple truth: there wasn't any huge, impregnable base to take shelter in. Tasked with our well-being, the US Navy didn't have the manpower to secure the bus lines, the dispensary, the American library, the brand-new naval hospital, the bowling alley, the swimming pool in Cholon, the USO, the motor pools and commissaries, the mess halls, or the big base exchange where everyone shopped. Much less our widespread workplaces or the villas and apartments throughout the city the Navy leased for service members and their families. Security at our bachelors' quarters was only slightly better.

I drained the aperitif, letting the chilled alcohol drench my tongue and glide down my throat. An MP collected the major's dog tags and wallet, slipping them into an olive-drab drawstring bag. Two other MPs hoisted the stretcher with the body onto a small Army truck, HANG LOOSE WITH THE DEUCE stenciled on the bumper.

Pedestrians stepped around the waiters sluicing blood off

the sidewalk. A siren announced high noon, the beginning of the three-hour siesta. The Vietnamese cops scattered.

I squinted against the stabbing flashes of light as we got back into our jeep. A pang turned into pain in my hips. A recent bout of dengue revisiting the scene.

Me and Robeson went over the little we knew from Freddie Crouch, our voices raised over the engine and the hot air streaming past us in the open jeep. Two Americans had been cut down in the street in quick daylight attacks, the first shot dead near a flower market, the next a few days later at a food kiosk. "She's in and out lightning fast," Crouch had said, "improvising targets on the fly." And now this third blitz attack curbside at a café, using the same shoot-and-scoot tactic. The drivers varied, the shooter didn't.

"She's always the button—and deserves to be. She doesn't miss," I said.

"You think this is one of Madame Nhu's paramilitary broads? She puts her sharpshooters up in contests against guys."

True, the president's pain-in-the-ass sister-in-law had created her own women's paramilitary corps. But much as she loved attacking America in the press, I doubted she'd have the balls to start ordering hits on us herself. If you asked me, she just liked having 20,000 uniformed women saluting her for the cameras. But this was how Robeson covered all bases, casting a wide net before he circled back toward simpler possibilities.

"If the Dragon Lady was sending a message the shooter would have been wearing the corps' blue jumpsuit and regulation dark lipstick. She acts like her ladies' militia's a force to be reckoned with but they're mostly for show. Her 'little darlings' may be decent enough at target practice, but they couldn't pull off shots like this."

"Yeah, our girl's got some serious skills."

I leaned toward him. "I'd say a decade's worth."

"So maybe she's a Viet Minh veteran?"

"No," I objected. "Too damn young. If she's twenty, she would've been, what?—ten or eleven back when the Viet Minh were kicking French ass up north." The independence fighters had recruited some awfully young teens, but that still seemed like a stretch.

"She got herself trained real good by somebody somewhere." Robeson wiped his brow. "The North's got Chinese and Russian advisors. There's gotta be some decent pistol instructors among 'em."

I shook my head. "Taking down a *live* target from the back of a moving scooter—she didn't learn that on no VC firing range or live-fire course up north."

"Point taken," Robeson agreed. "She got thrown in the shit."

Robeson navigated us expertly through the sea of vehicles. Saigon traffic was a chaotic mix of hand-drawn carts, oxcarts, bicycles, three-wheeled *cyclo-pousse* rickshaws, overloaded scooters, motorcycles, Renault taxis, buses, and military vehicles like ours. Vietnamese drivers could buy their licenses whether or not they could drive. In an accident, the foreigner was always in the wrong—and would be expected to pay to make it right. The army was known to shell out up to a thousand bucks, so accidents were not always so accidental.

We cruised down a street lined with eateries that specialized in snake dishes, then passed under a long canopy of flame trees. I swiped at the sweat stinging my eyes, grateful for the shade. Saigon had hardly a traffic light to slow our progress. At intersections, vehicles never stopped or slowed, but passed between each other at right angles like synchronized drill teams.

The heavy air was muzzy with exhaust fumes. A derelict villa loomed over the road, barely visible through creepers growing upward along its façade, its roof slowly being lifted off by vines. The purple and red flowers smelled great but couldn't hide the aroma of raw sewage in the street. Saigon was like a booby prize. The Vietnamese had surrendered it to the French a century ago hoping they'd be devoured by the mosquitoes. The colonists brought in mosquito netting and built four thousand kilometers of canals to protect themselves. The French had planned for half a million residents. Four times that many had flooded the town for protection and profit, overwhelming the roads and plumbing. Saigon's sewers were bursting. The poorer neighborhoods—like the shantytowns on the outskirts and the sampan slums on the canals—had none. No running water, no electricity either.

Robeson sang to himself as we rolled. "*Oh mama don't you weep and moan/Uncle Sam he got your man and gon'.*" On a traffic island, sentries dozed in shaded hammocks while their fortified pillbox stood empty. On the sidewalks, vendors slept beside their covered wares or atop their outdoor counters. I wondered where the Red Queen had tucked herself away for the noontime siesta after her morning's success.

CHAPTER THREE

The Headquarters Support Activity Saigon office was an aging French villa covered with wisteria and sandbags. HSAS was a bastard unit with a few agents from each of the different investigative agencies of the armed forces: OSI, ONI, AIC, and us, the Army's Criminal Investigation Division. CID was on the second floor, across the hall from the Office of Naval Intelligence. Our work space was a large room with metal desks, a fake fireplace, and French doors that looked out over rue Pasteur.

On the floor above us were the offices of the provost. Three gentlemen lawyers were the total Judge Advocate presence in Saigon, which meant all court-martial proceedings had to be held in Okinawa. Our operation was nearly as small, usually just six of us CID investigators. We had no police lab or even so much as a legitimate jail in-country, only a jury-rigged brig near the baseball diamond at Pershing Field, out by the airport. But me and Robeson were content, happy to be out of the boonies. No more rice paddies, forests, mountains, or jungles. We were comfortably posted in the capital of the eight-year-old half-a-nation we'd come to save from the red tide of Communism that was leaching down from its northern half in support of VC insurgents in the south. Taa fucking raa.

On our first tours, the two of us had advised a Vietnamese

battalion of about four hundred men. Robeson ran an ambush academy, training troops in combat assaults, shoot-and-scoot patrolling, pincer movements, and bracketing with mortars. Me, I taught basic commo: radio discipline, Morse code, and how to transmit commands for directing small-unit maneuvers. Our instruction was barely tolerated and largely ignored. Hot pursuit of the enemy wasn't a popular subject either, when we took the training into the field. You could bed down in a dicey night position with an entire ARVN company and wake up all by your lonesome if they didn't care for you or your advice. Turns out they weren't interested in engaging the enemy. All the South Vietnamese wanted were the goodies we could deliver and for us to shut the fuck up.

Viet Nam was nothing like Korea, where the US commanded both the American and Korean troops, and everyone was dropped into the crap together. Here we were strictly outsiders—guests—making suggestions our hosts happily spurned. Dealing with ARVN was like trying to nail Jell-O to the wall. Me and Robeson grew weary of the struggle to get Buddhist troops fired up about battling Communists on behalf of their abusive and unloved Catholic government. We both got real tired of jungle rot, biting bugs and ground leeches, the foul dysentery that vacuumed you out and the heatstroke and tropical fevers that stewed the gray matter in your brainpan. One day we concluded that the longer we stayed out in the woods with the unhappy lads of the ARVN, the worse our odds got of going the distance in this non-war.

So we'd both grabbed at the chance for military police training at Fort Gordon, Georgia. Half a year later we came back to Viet Nam as newly minted "Sidneys," Criminal Investigation Division agents. We didn't have to worry anymore about motivating badly served Asian troops or playing hide-and-seek in the woods. Our jurisdiction was strictly limited to American soldiers in-country. Granted, these numbered in the thousands, with few of us "Sids" to police them. But the mostly small-time lawlessness that accompanied the undeclared conflict suited us both. We lived on the cheap and tax-free, most everything expensed, and we didn't have to sweat about who was winning and who wasn't.

Our office interpreter, Xanh Lan Hoa—Blue Orchid—sat at her Underwood in a lavender *ao dai*, her long black hair cinched in a French braid. She was a young widow whose husband had perished in a skirmish in the highlands years ago. "Missy Blue" had a thing for Robeson. One day when some Vietnamese had jeered at them walking together in the street, Missy had pointed to the small brown birthmark on her right cheek and touched Robeson's wrist. "Same-same," she'd said, and giggled. "We same." Robeson had tried his best not to be moved, but he was. I'm not sure what their relationship was doing for her English, but it had certainly done wonders for his Vietnamese.

"*Đại úy* want you both," she said, her soft brown eyes fixed on Robeson.

Our boss, an MP captain, was a mustang—an up-from-the-ranks enlisted man who caught a field promotion in Korea that put an officer's butter bar on his helmet. We trudged dutifully into his lair, formerly a large wardrobe closet.

"'Bout time, gents," Captain Deckle said, sounding none too happy. Captain Deckle told us he was just back from briefing his superior, an obnoxious major half his age, a ping-pong-playing super soldier with custom-made boots we lovingly referred to as "Major Asshole."

"Sir," I said, as Deckle waved us into the chairs facing his antique desk. Rent on the office was next to nothing but renting the furnishings cost plenty. Go figure. In one of the endless twists of Vietnamese law, income from rents was heavily taxed, income from leasing furniture was not. So renting out cheap places expensively furnished was one of the many schemes the Saigonese employed to hold on to their money, not that many Vietnamese paid taxes at all.

We filled the captain in on the latest killing. He listened, then said he was taking Crouch off the case for good. "Henceforth you two are officially in charge of this death-dame business."

I could tell from Robeson's expression that he was thinking the same as me: if Freddie Crouch wasn't such a fuckup, he might have gotten somewhere on the first two killings, and our frustrated captain wouldn't have dumped the third killing—and now the whole case—in our laps. Robeson sighed, making no secret of being put out.

Deckle glared at him. "The three men she's gunned down are *our* people, and the locals aren't showing much interest in catching her," the captain stressed. "So don't look so damn disgruntled, Agent Robeson."

"Yes, sir," Robeson said, "but how do *we* protect *our* people from random street attacks?"

"Sounds like a personal problem. Did you hear me ask for questions?"

"No, sir."

"Captain, he has a point. How do we interdict this broad? She's got the run of the city. Anywhere she spots an American uniform and the glint of an officer's insignia, she's got a target. How do we possibly stop that?"

Captain Deckle eased back in his chair. "We might have caught a break."

He handed over a sheet of foolscap on which he'd scribbled the name and holding location of a Viet Cong who'd recently deserted, using one of the new safe-conduct passes regularly scattered across the countryside to tempt the half-starved guerillas into switching sides. This one had surrendered himself to a Psy Ops advisor in Da Nang. Looking for favors during his debriefing, the VC had nervously brought up the Commie heroine who'd started zapping Americans in the capital.

Deckle said, "The deserter, Tam, swears he doesn't know the lady's name or so much as her nom de guerre, but claims the Viet Cong command holds her in very high regard. Says her prowess battling ARVN made such a big impression on the commissars, they've put her in charge of Unit Eight."

"Sweet Jesus," Robeson mumbled. "Another kid in charge of Unit Eight."

The captain nervously tapped the desktop. "Yeah, yeah. Your witness says she's barely twenty but old before her time and commanding our favorite local terror cell."

"Kids making war on American officers," I said.

"The defector also claims the Committee of the South recently gave their bad girl an additional objective—liquidation of a major player. Says he doesn't know who or when. Just that it's soon. But maybe the right questions haven't been put to him. Go see if this *hoi chanh* can give you a line on her and who the honcho is they've added to her to-do list."

I said, "This bigwig she's been assigned. Do we at least know whether he's American or South Vietnamese?"

"Not clear." Captain Deckle fired up a Salem. "'*Cáo già*' was the quote."

"'Old fox,'" Robeson said. "She's going after an 'old fox'?"

"Miss Blue's translation too," Deckle said, impressed. "The Red Queen's unit is likely after someone pretty senior. Remember a year ago last May? The brat in charge of Unit Eight before her tried to take down our esteemed secretary of defense."

Robeson nodded. "A sweet-lookin' sapper boy trying to blow up McNamara."

"And when the charge didn't go off," I said, "he switched to grenades. We got him with, what, fifteen strapped to his chest?"

"That sweet-looking boy," said Captain Deckle, "had already killed eight Vietnamese and was drawing a bead on a member of President Kennedy's cabinet."

"Does Counselor Nhu still want him in front of a firing squad?"

"Badly."

Ngo Dinh Nhu, President Diem's loathed and feared younger brother, had nearly limitless power. He was effectively the country's attorney general, head of its FBI, Secret Service and CIA, the secretary of state, and speaker of the House for good measure. Oh, and he controlled all the newspapers, too. Tall and gaunt, Nhu was the physical opposite of his squat older brother. Gary Cooper on a bad day. For my money, Diem was nuts and Mr. and Mrs. Nhu were evil shits who ran the country for their own benefit, lining the pockets of the business guys and generals who backed them, at the expense of everyone else. Brother Nhu squashed his political opponents like bugs. If he wanted the sapper killed, the kid was already as good as dead.

"Except if the kid's executed," Deckle was saying, "the Viet Cong will reciprocate and kill an American prisoner they're holding." He handed us travel orders for Da Nang. "Check out the late Major Furth's effects while he's still with us. Then get yourselves to Da Nang and shake this collaborator. Do it somewhere private; wring the guy out. He's the only lead we've got."

"Should we haul him back here when we're done, sir," I said, "or take him over to the Vietnamese turncoat program?"

"We can't keep him, no way. So be fast, be thorough. I doubt you'll get a second go at Tam once the Vietnamese take charge of him." The captain fixed us with his *hombre* stare. "Our betters are already in a twist about this Red Queen. If she manages to take out somebody prominent, that will really ratchet their knickers. They want the lady dealt with before she gets that chance. Questions?" he said, pointedly looking at Robeson.

"Our orders, sir?"

"Find her and do her—quick."

"Detain her, you mean?" Robeson said, even though he knew damn well what Deckle meant.

The captain absently rubbed his slight paunch. "She's in civilian clothes," he said, "killing unarmed US soldiers in uniform. That ain't legal. She's not playing by the rules. You're within your rights to shoot the bitch where she stands. Got it?"

Robeson looked uneasy. "We ain't one of Counselor Nhu's death squads, captain."

I put a hand on his shoulder. Times like these, I remembered how many years I had on him, especially the three in Korea.

"The laws of war say she's not a lawful combatant," Deckle said slowly. "If you *detain* her, it's gonna be the same dragged-out business as her predecessor: arguments about her tender age, threats of retaliation. *Und so weiter.* So do unto her before she does any more of ours." He paused to look us each in the eye. "I want this woman off my planet. *Verstehen?*"

We exited Deckle's closet and pulled Crouch's meager file on Lady Death. The details didn't make for light reading, especially the color pictures. The body of the second officer she'd killed looked like a white-chocolate Easter bunny with raspberry filling, its hollow head chomped open.

I rummaged around in the file drawer on Crouch's side of the desk for the ammo box where he kept the envelope with the first two Red Queen cards, the scarves, and spent shell casings. I carefully added the third card and took possession of the box. So much for forensics. It wasn't like any of the JAG lawyers upstairs would ever be taking this to court.

CHAPTER FOUR

"Number one rue Catinat," Robeson announced as we pulled up. "Home from the fields." I lashed down the radio antenna. Robeson chained the steering wheel while he haggled with the street kids who controlled the curbside spot outside our hotel over the price for guarding the jeep to make sure our tires didn't get slashed or stolen, our gasoline didn't get siphoned off. Wherever we went, Robeson drew Vietnamese kids to him. To them he was a wonder with his Bazooka bubbles and African skin. Not so to their elders, who kept their distance, even though they could see how respectful he was, knowing not to touch the tops of the children's heads where the sacred energy entered and evil spirits could suck out your soul.

We got regular complaints from the hotel manager about paying the young hustlers protection money, but I didn't care. With the street kids on the job, our vehicle wouldn't get stripped, go AWOL, or get booby-trapped. Besides, extortion was necessary training for the boys' criminal futures if they were going to survive the tough straits they'd gotten themselves born into. Their other options were few: the overcrowded schools turned away more kids than they accepted.

We finished raising the canvas roof so they'd have some

shade, and took in the glistening Saigon River just across the street from the hotel. The tide was out, the pylons exposed on the concrete dock that paralleled the shore. A couple of sampans lay on the bank, their owners asleep beneath makeshift lean-tos.

The Hotel Majestic was curved like a boomerang, with the entrance at the bend where its two wings hinged. The ground floor of the stucco building was reddish-brown, topped by four pale-yellow stories. Turquoise awnings shaded the balconies and the ground floor's tall arched windows, five on either side of the identically arched front door.

Robeson breathed a sigh of relief as we entered the dim, high-ceilinged lobby. The Majestic wasn't luxurious, but from our point of view, it couldn't be better: the hotel hadn't been commandeered by the Navy and remained privately run. We were some of its few military residents. That the Majestic was overstaffed suited Clovis Auguste Robeson perfectly. He came from one of the richest black families in the state of Louisiana and liked being waited on. Great-grandfather Robeson had started a small undertaking and burial business that made his descendants wealthy. By the time he took up final residence in his own cemetery, his was the largest black funeral business in the county and second-biggest in the state. His great-grandson Clovis should have been back at Shaw University in Raleigh, finishing his studies in funeral management so he could take it over. But the young man wasn't partial to the field and had quit school to escape into the army. Same as me, except for the college part and the fat-cat money.

Me, I spent my seventeenth summer with my bachelor uncle on his Pennsylvania farm, dipping live chickens and turkeys upside down into a metal funnel that worked like a garbage disposal to lop off their heads. In my senior year of high school, he started talking about my going into his poultry business. I joined up on my eighteenth birthday and got sent to the "police action" in Korea.

The air-conditioning cut out as we plodded across the dark marble floor to collect our keys at the long front desk. As Saigon brownouts went, this was a short one: in a minute, the lights flickered back on and the ceiling fans above the club chairs resumed stirring the heavy air. Still, we were taking our chances stepping into the cage elevator. The printed daily schedules of brownouts and blackouts were completely unreliable. One second you had juice, the next you didn't. We could easily find ourselves stranded between floors, sleeping standing up. But we were both too punked to make the climb, and grateful when the white-jacketed lift operator got us to the third floor. I did my best to ignore the insecticide smell in the hall as we dragged ass toward our rooms.

"You all right?" Robeson inquired, lighting a joint and passing it over. "Still feeling feverish?"

"Fucked up but functioning." I took a hit and passed it back.

Robeson unlocked his door and disappeared. I let myself into 302, hurrying to the big tiled bathroom to piss. Another Majestic bonus: the Western toilet worked. As did the bidet and the shower, although a mama mouse and her babies liked to keep me company whenever I stepped under the enormous brass showerhead.

Like the mice, our aged barefoot housemaid Mama-san Kha went about her business as though I wasn't there, and thought nothing of popping in no matter how undressed I might be. She'd raise the toilet seat and climb up on the pedestal to squat and relieve herself while I shaved, or use the bidet to pee if I was on the throne. She had shooed away the other chamber-maids to claim us, but otherwise stayed strictly in her zone: shining shoes, changing sheets, making the bed, doing my washing in an aluminum basin, hanging my drip-dry shirts and slacks in the shower. To keep away mold, she kept the electric light burning in the armoire, and left me a daily bottle of potable water for brushing my teeth or rinsing the city's grit out of my eyes. Clovis and I loved our irascible Mama-san. By garrison standards, she had us living like kings.

The hit of dope had melted the muscles in my neck and shoulders. I hung my dog tags and room key on a hook and threw open the balcony doors. Across the narrow three-hundred-yard waist of the Saigon River stood warehouses and grubby facto-ries. Beyond them nothing but marsh. Downriver to the right, the smokestacks and bridge of a departing ship passed into the Long Tau channel that snaked south along the edge of the huge tidal marsh all the way to the sea. The river's edge was dotted with wooden shacks, their backs propped on stilts. Small boats lay stranded on mud and sewage; the tide had borne most of the raw waste toward the bayou. High tide would carry it back.

I must have drifted off because Robeson's loud knocking woke me. I stumbled over an armchair to let him in. After I showered, we headed for a local food counter on the street where a small sign advertised MÓN ĂN ĐẶC BIỆT —"special dish," meaning grilled dog meat on skewers. Mama-san Kha had urged us to try it. Yellow dog tasted best, she insisted, especially the ones with speckled tongues. She was right.

We squatted on low stools under a tarp while the proprietor turned strips of frog meat and threw the ugliest water creature I'd ever seen onto the grill. Elephant-ears fish, he called it. Swear to God, looked like a piranha with dentures, but it tasted great.

Robeson swatted away flies while I ordered us cold bottles of Coke. He winced at the first sip. "Damn knock-off. Tastes like cough medicine." I downed half my bottle. I couldn't tell the difference anymore.

The overcast sky blackened and opened with a rare flash of lightning. My bum knee hurt. The end of Saigon's monsoon season was just about upon us. Warm rain bucketed down, pelting the tarp. A stream hit my back and raced for my ass crack, which actually felt good. The quick downpour weakened and stopped. The ground steamed, making the air thick as a sauna's.

"This Red Queen situation is choice," Robeson said. "A city the size of Saigon and we don't have even a rough idea where she's gonna strike next, much less a real police force to go after her with."

"And suppose we knew and were there waiting for her? We'd stand out way too much. She sees us, she just rides on by and hits somebody else somewhere else."

"No wonder Crouch dropped this mess on us." Robeson exhaled his exasperation.

Freddie Crouch was a Class-A prick. Whenever he got drunk we had to hear about the VC he "almost" got when he was out in the field advising. Except the truth was the kid had hauled ass bare-assed, leaving behind only his pants. What a battle— what a victory. We even heard the Charlie's Mama-san hit Crouch in the face with some cow shit. More power to her.

"Motherfuckin' Crouch," I said, and we clinked bottles. "While we're here drinking somebody's half-assed idea of a Coke you can bet the Red Queen's commissars are toasting her with the good stuff."

"You gotta give it to her. She's gutsy, that woman, going after targets in public places." Robeson blotted his wet hair with a napkin. "She don't seem to worry about anybody drawing down on her."

I set down my bottle. "The government may not like us walking around their capital strapped, but for damn sure a lot of guys are gonna carry from here on. Things might not go so smooth for her next time."

"But you'd have to see her coming," Robeson said. "Small chance of that. *Bang* and she's gone. No time to react. Even if some onlooker gets his piece out in time, she picks crowded streets. No way to fire without hitting bystanders."

"We need to find her before she rolls up on her next target."

"And we ain't got the manpower to flood a block, much less a whole district."

He was right, of course. The odds of us finding her in Saigon were less than lousy.

"Remind me to leave some cow shit in Crouch's desk," I said.

FULL AND LAZY, we flagged a Lambretta for the short ride to the hotel. The elevator operator let Robeson off on three but I felt restless and continued up to the partially enclosed saloon-restaurant on the roof terrace.

The sun was burning into the canals and marshes to the west. Speckled turquoise geckos were congregating around the sconce lights on the wall, working on their first course. At the far end of the bar a bunch of raucous Aussie construction men were knocking back martinis and tossing olives into one another's mouths. A dark-skinned brunette and a pale young thing with fiery red hair sat on either side of the junior banker who lived on four. Both round-eyes were lookers.

I took a stool next to Lieutenant Nick Seftas and ordered a

rum and Coke, but had to settle for a Sarsi sarsaparilla and rum. Seftas wasn't staying long, he said. He needed to be fresh for the morning's planeload of congressmen he was welcoming on behalf of General Harkins, MAAG's commanding officer.

General Harkins lived in what Seftas liked to call the Hawaiian Room: a happy can-do state, completely out of touch, that caused you to insist against all indications that everything was swell and getting sweller. Paul Harkins was personally convinced the recent Viet Cong surges would subside, and that he'd be sending a thousand American boys home by Christmas. He'd promised the same thousand-man hump a year ago last May. Said we'd *all* be out of Viet Nam by *last* Christmas. Head in the sand, hell. Harkins would need a Rome plow to pull his head out of his ass.

Meanwhile Nick Seftas spent his days playing tour guide for VIP visitors: mayors seeking out local boys among the advisors and support detachments, governors eyeing higher office, senators and their staffs searching for insights on the guerilla war at hidden brothels and underground clubs.

"They're pouring in from everywhere," Seftas said. "Congress, the Pentagon, Pacific Command in Tokyo and Honolulu, the goddamn Peoria Chamber of Commerce."

"Peoria? Sounds like hazardous duty. You putting in for the extra pay?" I enjoyed busting his chops.

"This guerilla war's a boondoggle. It's fucking *Fantasia*: they never stop coming. The lefties opine that we're helping Diem oppress the Buddhist protesters and prolonging colonialism. The right-wingers wonder why we're not bombing China with nukes and Bibles. And don't get me started on the actual Bible-thumpers. Got word today Cardinal 'Moneybags' Spellman of New York is coming to spend another Christmas with the troops and encourage his favorite altar boy—Diem—in his fight against the godless enemy."

"He came every Christmas I was in Korea," I said. "Never heard him called 'Moneybags,' though."

"Seems His pain-in-the-ass Worship has the second-most valuable coin collection in the whole fucking world."

"Oh, yeah? He travel with any of it? I've been thinking of taking up coin collecting. Might be nice to pick up a starter set on the cheap."

"No problemo. I'm sure he keeps it bedside right next to his tiara."

I ordered another round as Del Shannon hit the high notes on "Runaway," spun on the 45-rpm turntable by the cash box in open defiance of Madame Nhu's music ban.

"While the Dragon Lady's away, the mice will play rock 'n' roll," Seftas said.

"Madame Nhu? What's she up to now?"

"She's been speechifying across the States, roasting President Kennedy every chance she gets. Left town with strict orders not to make any public pronouncements, but you know they haven't invented the muzzle yet that would keep that woman quiet. The White House is doing its best to ignore her, but the Republicans are loving her up. I hear her return's gonna be delayed by a stopover in Beverly Hills for a little plastic surgery around the eyes." Seftas yawned and slid off his stool. "Gotta shine my brass and hit the rack," he said, and settled up.

I looked around for my other regular drinking buddies but the patio was empty except for the banker, who had maneuvered the brunette and redhead to a table close to my perch and was working hard to impress them with his worldly understanding of Saigon.

"The whole system's corrupt," he announced. "Every government department is its own little gift shop. Anyone with a rubber stamp and a little authority has his hand out for 'gratitude.'"

"How frightful," said the redhead, all exaggerated and breathy. "I simply had no idea." He didn't notice she was having him on. The banker and the brunette were obviously into each other, so Red got up to leave, and—surprise—parked herself on the stool alongside mine. She ordered a vodka and tonic. "With ice, please."

I tipped toward her. "Wouldn't do that."

"Do what?"

"Ice," I said. "There's a cholera outbreak."

"Neat, then. Tonic back." Her accent was flawless Brit with just the tiniest hint of something else.

I signaled the barman to give her a chilled shot glass from the short fridge under the bar.

She knocked back her shot and said, "Guess my line of work and you win a drink."

I didn't take her for a pro. Not a professional do-gooder either. More like some oil honcho's flashy secretary.

"Reporter?" I said. Sexier sounding than "flack for a petroleum company."

She shook her head but looked pleased. "Nadja Kowalska," she said, extending her hand. A wide silver bracelet shackled her wrist. "I do for the ICC."

"International Control Commission."

"Quite."

Her slightly snooty vowels went nicely with her bare-shouldered summer dress, held up by the thinnest straps. Gone tropical, I noticed with a thrill. No bra. What a coincidence, I wanted to say, suddenly reminded that I wasn't wearing underwear either.

CHAPTER FIVE

"Ellsworth Miser," I said, and put out my hand. "Delighted." We shook.

"ICC, eh?" I said. The International Control Commission was the referee for the various Geneva Accords that spelled out every country's proper behavior in partitioned Viet Nam, rules paid plenty of lip service all around but obeyed by no one.

She nodded and knocked back her second vodka. Impressed, the barman set up another iced glass. The electricity failed; the lights and music died. The barman pulled extra candles from beneath the bar and lit them. Across the river, a chandelier flare split apart a mile or two out. As each blazing section floated down, the trembling white light made the terrain dance.

"That happen much?" Nadja said, indicating the flare.

"Not this side of the river." I told her how the roof terrace had been my front-row seat last year for the attempted coup that had destroyed the old presidential palace. "Two South Vietnamese bombers swooped in, low and slow," I said, tracing their flight path with a finger drawn across the dark sky behind us. "Twin-engine Skyraiders, red devils painted on their tails, wing guns blazing. First bomb landed in President Diem's bedroom."

"I say. That must have been a bit of a wake-up."

"Would've been if it had gone off. Diem got lucky. He'd gotten up early and was reading in his study. Hightailed it to his bomb shelter as soon as he saw what was happening."

"And you witnessed the whole attack from here?" Nadja said.

"Yes, ma'am. The second fighter sprayed the palace with its wing guns. For days afterward, kids at the Cercle Sportif were diving to the bottom of the pool to bring up expended shell casings. The pilots came back around to rocket the place. One of the rockets overshot and took out the dining room of the Lycée principal's house. Then the palace itself caught fire."

"It must have been terrifying," Nadja said. "I mean, inside the palace. Was anyone killed?"

"The Nhus' Chinese governess got crushed by a falling beam. And a reporter who'd climbed out on a roof to see the action fell to his death. Diem's brother—the archbishop—and the Nhus and their kids all made it safely to shelter with Diem in the basement. Madame Nhu got pretty banged up when the floor caved in under her and she fell two stories. They lost everything, including Madame Nhu's treasured stack of highland tiger pelts, all personally shot by her husband."

Nadja's eyes widened. "And yet the coup fizzled," she said.

"Definitely not Diem's first reveille. Just one of a long list of attempts that've tanked, yeah. But I doubt they're done trying."

Less than a decade ago, after the Saigonese voted their absentee emperor Bao Dai off the throne, Diem had installed himself as the new republic's first president. The Saigonese had cast two hundred thousand more votes for Diem than there were voters. But eight years later, especially after six bloody months of vicious attacks on the Buddhists, not many Diem loyalists were left.

I ordered us another round. "Where exactly are you from?" I said, wondering about the accent underneath the British I still couldn't place.

"Vorsaw."

"Poland?"

"Yes." She laughed. "That Vorsaw."

"And what's your job at ICC?"

"I am the new appointments secretary and general dogsbody for the first deputy to the Polish commissioner." She pointed over her shoulder. "My lovely friend there, she works for the Indian commissioner, who is the ICC chairman at the moment."

I glanced at her pal. The junior banker was gone and the brunette was flirting with the *Der Stern* photographer from 316. "What brings you to my part of town?" I said.

"Trying to secure better lodging than the pantry closet I'm currently in. Unfortunately, according to the manager, all forty-four of the Majestic's rooms are currently occupied."

"Actually, I happen to know there's a guy leaving in the morning."

"A vacancy? Really?"

"Yup. On the fourth floor. Facing the river."

"So the room stays cool?"

"No," I said, "but the godawful smell off the river at low tide helps you forget the heat. And the wall lizards do a pretty good job of tamping down the insects."

"Sounds promising." Nadja smiled, her perfect teeth like pearls. She ordered us each another shot of vodka. "Is there someone upon whom I should bestow my . . . gratitude to obtain this room?"

"No bribe, no. You just need to win someone over, someone with juice."

"Juice?"

"Clout. Pull."

"Ah, influence. Who would you suggest?"

"Mathieu Franchini, the owner. Local legend. Arrived in Viet Nam a cabin boy, retired to Paris a wealthy man. A shady guy gone sort of legit."

"Mr. Franchini. Italian?"

"Corsican. Restaurants, bars—most everything here in District One is owned by Corsicans. Franchini leased the Majestic from the government after the war. His son Philippe runs it for him now."

"So it's young Philippe I ask for this juice?"

I shook my head. "Dad's in town for a visit. Every day, before lunch, the Corsicans get together at the sidewalk terrace café of the Continental Hotel—the 'Continental Shelf.' I'm sure you'll find him there tomorrow. Sought out by a beautiful redhead in distress while jawing with a platoon of his cronies? He'll be in heaven."

"Very well." She beamed. "I'll have a go."

"No need to, ah, mention my name, though."

She looked at me, amused. "I shan't, then." She rested a sleek elbow on the bar and cupped her porcelain chin. "May I trouble you for a tad more advice?"

"Shoot."

"You weren't wrong when you guessed I was a reporter. I'm actually hoping to write a human-interest piece, a feature of sorts. For a magazine."

"No kidding." I tried to appear impressed.

"If I could land an exclusive interview with a Viet Cong guerilla fighter, a British mag might well pick it up. Or better yet, a huge German newsweekly." She tipped her head in the

direction of the *Stern* photographer. "Truth be told"—she made
a face—"I'm hesitant about venturing into the countryside.
There's all the expense: driver, interpreter, car, camera, portable
recorder."

Undertaker, casket, shipping costs home, I thought, and
nodded, real polite.

"Are you acquainted with any proper journalists you might
introduce me to?"

Wishing like hell I could oblige, I shook my head. "The
print reporters mostly come on short assignments, happy to
cover the action from their barstools. Apart from the wire services, the *New York Times* is the only big American paper with
a correspondent here full time. But the likes of me and them
don't fraternize."

"You being . . . ?"

"An army cop."

"Really?" she said, "how exciting." But she didn't sound the
least bit excited.

I was interested in keeping her interested, so I fed her sec-
ondhand gossip about the young newshounds, how covering
the Diem regime had grown steadily riskier since May, when the
huge Buddhist protests had broken out. For years, Diem's fellow Catholics had enjoyed favoritism in everything. Resentment
over the bald-faced discrimination had finally boiled over, setting off huge demonstrations, which were put down with lethal
force only to spring up again, along with a wave of fiery suicides
protesting the prejudiced treatment. In August, with the old
American ambassador on his way home and the new American
ambassador not yet arrived, Nhu and Diem saw their chance
to crush the resisters, especially the monks, and ordered their
Special Forces—trained and paid directly by Uncle Sam—to

raid the temples. The Red Berets arrived with rifles, grenades, tear gas, fixed bayonets. The Buddhists got beat bad, trashed just like protesting Negroes back in the States. Some of the Buddhists got killed. Thousands got arrested.

"To justify the raids, the government planted arms and VC leaflets, then claimed the Buddhist pagodas were housing bordellos. They said they'd found stashes of women's underwear, pornography, love letters. That the monks were getting it on with virgins."

"Did anyone believe that tripe?" she asked.

"Not for a minute. People just got angrier. The protests got bigger, the cops nastier." I didn't add that it hadn't made us Americans so popular, either, when hundreds of teenage protestors had been hauled off to detention camps in trucks painted with USAID's clasped-hands logo. A clear message that we were working hand in hand with the Buddhist-beaters. "The reporters who tried to cover the raids and protests got seriously roughed up. Their stories got censored—you couldn't say 'raids.' It had to be 'searches.' The situation couldn't be 'dramatic' or the country 'troubled.' Violators got flat-out blocked. The main post office 'misplaced' their wire transmissions. Journalists who somehow managed to file articles critical of the regime found themselves on Madame Nhu's 'I'd-be-delighted-if-they-died' blacklist, accused of being pinko fellow-travelers or outright Communists."

"Well, in my case . . ." she said, laughing. She insisted she still wanted to try reporting. That she wouldn't be fazed by the current atmosphere. I wasn't sure she understood how bad things had gotten. Even senior newshounds were getting hassled.

"*Newsweek*'s man got expelled from the country for taking a bite out of President Diem's live-in sister-in-law."

"The shrew who acts like she's his wife."

"The very one. Acting First Lady for her bachelor brother-in-law. Rides roughshod over Diem and her husband both. Diem's got a sign outside his office forbidding women to enter. But that doesn't keep the Dragon Lady out. The second he shows the slightest sign of letting up on the Buddhists, she yells, throws a tureen of soup at him, calls him a jellyfish and a coward."

"Arrogance personified," Nadja said.

"She's a hellion, all ninety pounds of her. Picks candidates for the National Assembly like she's buying accessories. If they don't vote exactly as she instructs, she threatens them with exile. She once actually slapped the vice president in public."

Nadja winced. "I've heard Madame Nhu says power is wonderful and total power is totally wonderful."

"When the Pope dared to question the treatment of the Buddhists, she questioned the infallibility of the Pope. Her advice on how to handle the protestors? 'Beat them three times harder.' The woman makes people want to bring down the government around her beautiful ears."

"My boss says when Madame Nhu was growing up she had her own rickshaw and coolie to carry her to school, and twenty servants waiting on her at home. Back when her cousin Bao Dai was emperor." She licked the vodka from her lips. "Did you know she and Nhu met while he was having an affair with her mother? She was fifteen, Nhu was thirty."

Nadja said perhaps she would try writing a feature about the Nhus. I made noises like I was listening, but the features that most interested me were hers. She was a seriously gorgeous University of Warsaw grad with two semesters at the London School of Economics. Nadja Kowalska of the flaming hair claimed she could trace her mother's family back to grand rabbis in the Middle Ages. I boasted I could trace my immediate ancestors to Shunk Street in South Philly and a Saturday night dance chaperoned by the Norbertine Fathers at St. Monica's.

Nadja spoke Polish, Russian, French, and English fluently, and several more languages passably. I bragged that I could speak American without a Philadelphia accent and occasionally made my gestures understood by Vietnamese waiters, even when drunk. I could also make her laugh. She looked great when she did, and she did it a lot.

Red was a happy, gold-tipped-cigarette-smoking Communist. Go figure. Most of 'em were deadpan stiffs. She had been allowed to study abroad and travel outside her sealed Communist homeland—the officially trusted daughter and granddaughter of rabidly anti–Nazi Party members who had spent the war years in Moscow and returned to Poland to rise in a society not so friendly to Jews.

Folks that tough had to be smart, I thought. I needed to be likewise. Partying with a daughter of the Party wasn't the best idea. If my major got wind of it, I could kiss my clearances and job goodbye. Retreat now, I told myself. But her beautiful eyes flashed, her perfectly corrected teeth sparkled. She was a privileged child of the proletariat who shopped at hard-currency stores and saw Western-trained dentists. I regretted my own crooked canines as she talked. Though I had a few years on this kid and was nothing to write home about, a sudden longing settled in my gut.

She sipped and licked her lips again. "I'm also considering writing an article about the first monk who immolated himself last June," she said.

"You mean Venerable Quang Duc."

"Yes. Did you see it?"

"No, I went on duty late that day. Traffic everywhere was at a standstill, Vietnamese standing all over the roadways weeping and pointing at the sky where they'd seen Buddha's face appear in the clouds." I tapped out a fresh cigarette. "Madame Nhu said she'd supply the gasoline for the next 'barbecue' and bring the matches herself—especially if American journalists would volunteer to roast themselves alongside the monks."

"Good Lord!" Nadja shuddered. Artillery flashed and thundered over the marshes.

"*Trống chiến*," said the barman. War drums.

Tracers floated along the horizon and crisscrossed in the distance: ours red, theirs green. A slow stream of reds ricocheted and shot upward like sparklers.

"Enchanting," she said.

"Yeah. Not so much when they're comin' at you."

"Exciting too, I imagine. Boys get to have all the fun."

I signaled the bartender for the tab and took out my wallet. The red scarf came with it.

"Aha," Nadja said with a sly grin. "You're already seeing another."

"It ain't like that," I stammered.

She lifted the scarf to her face. "Mmm. Lovely fragrance; gardenia," she said, and handed it back. "It's over between us," she teased.

The lights flickered momentarily. I invited her to my room to judge for herself if she'd like the accommodations and the view. We never made it to the balcony. Landed instead on the bed, panting. She was shameless and sensational, even more beautiful naked. We coupled like minks, flesh sliding against flesh. I felt myself caught by her hips, angled down expertly. She arched suddenly, making a sound like something wounded, and clamped me inside her.

Sensation pulled the air from my lungs and plunged hard into the center of me. I'd been done before but not like this. After the third go-round, we lay bathed in sweat, gulping air, spent. I gave in to the softest sleep.

When I snapped awake the geckos were silent but something shifted in the dark on the balcony. I reached for the small automatic resting in the fold of mosquito netting tucked under the mattress and squinted at the figure. Nadja, naked as a newborn, smoking a cigarette and absently scratching the underside of a beautiful breast as she peered through my notebook by the light of the moon and a lone flare.

CHAPTER SIX

When Nadja heard me stir, she quickly slipped under the mosquito net, into bed. I pounced on her. Sex in the silky tropical night changed to gasps, groans. Nick Seftas knocked on the common wall to shut us up. "No more frolic and rollick," Nadja murmured, her face flushed, and passed out.

She was still fast asleep when I left for breakfast on the roof terrace. Too late I remembered Mama-san Kha would be arriving soon. I figured she would ignore Nadja the same way she ignored me and simply go about her business. I didn't bother going back down.

Up on the roof, I ran into Seftas decked out in gold-rimmed aviator sunglasses and a perfectly creased khaki uniform, fresh as the morning. His black dress shoes gleamed, brass insignia shone like gold. Within the hour he'd be greeting junketing bigwigs dropping by our splendid little war. Their pale faces flushed pink, they'd stumble down a roll-up aluminum staircase onto the tarmac, drained by the bumpy six-hour flight from Manila and the merciless, thick, humid Saigon air that would make them struggle to catch their breath.

The tide was coming in. Out on the river a rusty freighter reached the turning basin upstream and began the slow pivot to reverse direction before steaming back to dock on our side of the river. A blast of the freighter's horn announced the maneuver. Small ferries and barges veered out of the way. The horn blared once more, stabbing my hungover brain.

"Gee," Seftas said, "sounds like you last night. You having Korea combat dreams or bedding a noisy broad?"

"Noisy and nosey."

"Anyone I know?"

"That redhead from last night."

"Oh, yeah, yeah." Seftas brushed a dead fly off the table. "Hair on fire. Great fuselage."

"Caught her going through my stuff."

"You got to stop fraternizing with those high-class all-night ladies."

"She wasn't a pro. And she wasn't thieving. More like snooping. Going through my case notes. I should report it."

"Don't be crazy."

"She's a foreign national," I said, "from an Iron Curtain country."

Seftas frowned. "Hey, we're all foreign nationals in this place. Don't go talking it up or you'll get thrown to the counter-intel wolves. You don't need that kind of grief." He set down his napkin. "What could she want with your notes anyway?"

"A story. She wants to be a journalist."

"Ah," Seftas said. "Or at least that's her story."

"See? I ought to at least run it by my captain."

He shook a finger at me. "You're not listening. Way too tempting for the security freaks. They'll jump on you for the exercise, blow it all out of proportion."

"Shit. They'll jam me up for falling into a honeypot."

"It's not like your cop notes contain earthshaking military secrets. You'll get yourself fucked up for nothing."

"You got a point, Sef. Never happened." I saluted him with tamarind juice, hoping he was right. After last night, it was a chance I was willing to take.

Sometime in the night a cruise ship with a huge seahorse logo on its funnel had tied up at the mooring across from the hotel for a two-day port call. Passengers crowded the gangway, cautiously disembarking for a little war tourism. Toward evening they'd drift back, wearing peasant hats and black pajama tops, the wives carting vases made from fired artillery shells. Shiny drilled-out bullets strung on lanyards would drape their husbands' necks, souvenirs that would cost them a hundred and forty piasters apiece—one dollar, a day's pay for a local.

Seftas pushed back his chair and stood up. "I look okay?"

"Absolutely STRAC, Lieutenant." Strategic, Tough, Ready Around the Clock!

He raised a victory fist. "Where you headed today?"

"Graves Registration out at Tan Son Nhut."

"Need a lift?"

"Thanks, but I got a chore to take care of first," I said, and headed downstairs to the fourth floor to rap on McClutchen's door.

McClutchen's day job was constructing reinforced concrete revetments that protected parked aircraft. Evenings he hosted high-stakes card games catered with first-class dope and booze.

"It's me, Miser," I said loudly.

A crack opened. I stepped inside to warn McClutchen that word on the street was that the Corsicans intended to put him out of business in a very permanent way.

"Damn, damn, damn," he muttered, groggy and still a bit stoned. "Man, I gotta sky outta here. Put some miles between me and them mafia motherfuckers."

He couldn't stop thanking me as he threw his stuff into a B-4 bag. Going around the room with a brown plastic tote, he pulled his stash from its various hiding places: a four-pound bag of fine Cambodian Red, some hash, skag, amyl nitrate poppers, red pills, blue pills, and wads of the little aluminum foil packets of French downers sold at every Saigon pharmacy. The tote would be easy to ditch if necessary. In the meantime, it was currency.

He laid half a kilo of pure Laotian horse on me and a sealed carton of Park Lane cigarettes filled with tobacco marinated in opium. I wished him luck and let myself out. Downstairs, I left the cigs and the smack with my favorite bellman to put in the safe. He informed me Robeson had left word I should fetch him out by Tan Son Nhut, where he'd gone in the wee hours for some late-night loving.

I snagged one of the small blue-and-cream Renault cabs at the front door but was immediately sorry when I had to sit with my feet on either side of a sizeable hole in its badly rusted floor as the pavement sped by beneath me. Before picking up Robeson, I stopped at the Army Procurement office for a consult with Sergeant Major Pamelle. Better to do that alone, as sweet, down-home "Pammy" didn't exactly care for black soldiers, especially ones making rank fast for hazardous duty. I'd seen Pammy turn surly and snake-eyed at the mention of the civil-rights struggles back in the States.

Pamelle was in the last months of his final enlistment, about to retire after thirty years. He sat at his steel desk, pencils knife-sharp and forms at the ready, his heavy white coffee mug filled with diesel. Miss October reclined on the bulletin board behind him, big *X*s marking off the days.

The linoleum was buffed, the shelves empty—dusted every

hour from the look of them. The only personal item was the framed presentation pistol he had won a few years back in the Army's annual All-Pacific competition. The sarge knew his guns.

"Counting down, Sergeant Major?"

"Seventy-six more sunsets and a wake up. How the hell are ya?"

I told him I was hoping he might help identify our shooter's unusual weapon. He nodded as I read him the notes. Right off he said, "It's a Vis Radom."

"Never heard of it."

"Pistol manufactured in Radom, Poland, for their army officers."

He pulled a book out of his drawer and flipped it open to a weapon that sure looked like a .45 automatic in silhouette.

"Single action, nine-millimeter. Seven rounds to the magazine. Low muzzle blast. The Wehrmacht took 'em off captured Polish officers and traded or sold them to Luftwaffe pilots. The kraut flyboys liked 'em. Carved their own grips out of trashed cockpit windshields."

"Meaning they're clear?"

"The grips? Yeah, yeah. Kinda pale yellow."

"Any of these Radoms ever forty-five caliber?"

"Some, yeah."

"A good piece?"

"Yup. Lots of velocity. Real accurate and stable. Tear ya right up."

He handed me the book so I could take a closer look. I pointed to a black-and-white photo of a German pilot leaning against a dive-bomber, showing off his Iron Cross. "What's with the picture?"

"The Krauts slid 'em under the grips. I seen some with

snapshots of sweethearts in one-piece bathing suits or starlets flashin' their gams. Most GIs who got hold of Radoms left the Nazi pictures in place."

I handed back the book. "Thanks, Sergeant Major."

"Anytime, chief. So, is the scuttlebutt true? She hit 'im from the back of a moving motorcycle fifteen feet out?"

"It was a goddamn motor scooter and more like thirty feet."

"Whoa. That's some fancy marksmanship."

"Takes down each target with a single shot."

"Fucking Calamity Jane." He gave me a wary look and nodded toward the black steel revolver holstered on my hip. "I see you're still totin' that heavy Japanese .38."

"I like my Miroku."

"Don't go to anythin' smaller, y'hear me? Or you'll think you're packin' a pellet gun when you get into it with her. Me, I'd get a damn Magnum."

Amazingly, the rusted-out hack had waited for me. I retrieved Robeson where he'd shacked up in Soul Alley with the Malaysian beauty who loved him only for himself and two dollars, plus a little extra for her poor mama's tuberculosis treatments.

"Jesus," he said, straddling the holes.

"You got a problem?"

"It ain't got no floor."

"No shocks either, from what I can tell."

"You see the plate number on this wreck?" he said, his voice rising to falsetto. "Z666."

"Maybe it's an omen. A warning not to be disrespecting Missy." I glanced over at him. "You on the outs with Miss Blue?"

"Sweetness was indisposed," Robeson said. "Besides, you're

to blame for keeping me awake with all that caterwaulin'. That love racket got me so stoked I couldn't sleep. Took for*ever* going through all the checkpoints after curfew. Was damn sure worth the bother, though."

"Soon as we get to the office, I'm going to tell Missy you've been stepping out on her. Maybe she'll finally come round to appreciating my charms."

"You best not tamper with her affections if you don't want to disappear out the bottom of this cab. She's still my *yobo*."

GRAVES REGISTRATION WAS a ten-man tent abutting a Quonset hut on the military side of the airfield. A refrigerator truck piped in cold air to keep the heavy heat from the plain wood coffin sitting on sawhorses. The Specialist-5 who had prepped and processed Furth said, "He's good to go," and asked if we wanted to see the body. We said no but he un-bagged the major anyway so we could admire his handiwork. "Stitched him perfect," he bragged.

Future funeral director Robeson was unimpressed. Major Furth looked a little ashen against the white shroud he'd travel in. Stateside, the cheeks would get colored pink and he'd get fitted for a perfect green uniform, the medals and insignia exact.

"Thanks, Specialist," I said. "You can wrap him back up."

A corporal brought us Furth's personal effects to voucher. We spread them across the top of his pine box. Wallet, immunization card. Gold wedding ring, Esterbrook fountain pen, Seiko wristwatch, and a large framed photograph of the family with both sets of grandparents.

Robeson held up a college ring. "University of Chicago, class of forty-five."

A footlocker and duffel held his uniforms, fatigues, an

Emerson transistor radio, two cartons of Marlboros, boots, dress shoes stuffed with rolled socks, underwear, stationery, saved letters, and one mink hat bought at the base exchange, most likely a Christmas present for the wife. A hardcover book about economics, two paperback novels, a 35-millimeter Konica. No film in the camera, no notes in the margins of the books.

The wallet picture of the parachutist was there but the photo of the major with the Vietnamese girl was gone. No condom either, just the circular impression in the worn leather. I took off my dog tags, removed my lucky grenade-pin ring from the chain, and slipped it into the raised circle. Close enough. Robeson returned everything to the personal effects bag and signed the form releasing the major's possessions.

A sweating honor guard led the pallbearers who slow-marched the pine box onto the tarmac, halting long enough for a Vietnamese military delegation to place a wreath of red and yellow flowers atop the American flag covering the coffin. The honor guard saluted as their five-piece Air Force band played a dirge. A pair of mechanics on the flight line and a passing courier stopped work to give a hand salute.

Robeson and I went to get the wound-and-ballistics report. The doc presented us with an envelope containing the slug he'd removed. I tipped it into my palm.

"The hollow tip mushroomed as it spun," the doctor said. "Bullet increased size to a much larger caliber by the time it punched its way in." He slid his glasses to the top of his head. "Brutal wound."

"How much bigger a caliber?"

"Maybe sixty."

Standing on end, the deformed bullet looked like a

miniature soufflé, discolored by the explosion that blasted it out of the muzzle.

"Hollow point, you say."

"Yep, with a concave puckered tip. Soft as a lover's kiss. Hit him like a train."

"Damn illegal ammo," Robeson said, indignant.

The doc frowned. "Nobody here's paying any mind to such niceties, son. Not them with their souped-up bullets and nail bombs, or punji-stick booby traps laced with feces. Not us with our phosphorous artillery rounds and napalm. Same-same."

The man was right. No whistle, no foul. The Viet Cong wanted us gone, just like the French colonials who'd stomped their dicks for a hundred damn years until Ho Chi Minh's army returned the favor in '54. The French had conceded the north. Now Uncle Ho wanted Uncle Sam gone from the south and the two halves rejoined, as had been agreed. Sounded simple.

We had to wait for a tandem of electric carts to pass, each carrying a ten-foot-long napalm canister to the flight line, BURN IN HELL chalked along the flanks of both pods. Toasting at thirty-six hundred degrees, the canisters would certainly crackle and pop like they were in Hades. Our new war toys would be rolled out and tested, young officers blooded, the dinks saved from Communism. Easy as pie if they'd only let us bring in American combat units to sweep away the Commie infestation so the Vietnamese army could get back to fucking off.

CHAPTER SEVEN

The VC defector, Tam, was waiting to be questioned in Da Nang. It took the better part of the morning to cadge a flight on a noisy single-engine, six-seater STOL that took us up the coast, riding the thermals like a gull.

Below us, winter monsoon clouds poured out of mountain passes in a thick foam of black rain squalls. Our bright silver plane banked across the dark sky. My knee ached. Eighty-four miles south of the demilitarized border between North and South Viet Nam, we descended through the cloud layer to emerge over Da Nang City. Dredgers huffed smoke as we circled over the water in a slow spiral to sweep across Red Beach, the long wide curve of sandy shoreline split by the mouth of the Tourane River where it emptied into the bay.

Along the river's western bank stretched the city's wide streets and yellow houses topped by orange-tiled roofs. The eastern bank of the river continued, forming the flank of a peninsula that ended in a misshapen knob of land atop which hunched Monkey Mountain, home to the American air-traffic center. As we circled lower, government buildings, wooden barracks, and shacks with sheet-metal roofs sped by under our wings. Checkpoints bulged with layers of sandbags. We swooped over parked Vietnamese war planes and US Army helicopters, above bulldozers and backhoes lengthening runways, and finally touched down real gentle, coming to an immediate stop. The STOL could've set down in a backyard.

Despite the rain, Americans housed in the helicopter detachment at the edge of the flight line were cooking hotdogs and hamburgers on a smoky grill made from a fifty-five-gallon drum. A buck sergeant worked the tongs while an E-7 held an umbrella over him. With their birds grounded by weather, the younger soldiers were playing football. The quarterback spiraled a sharp pass into the extended arms of a soldier who dove to catch it and slid through the muck, whooping like a banshee.

A crew chief took pity on our sodden selves and offered dogs and burgers under their tarp. We gulped a hotdog each and accepted a short lift in their jeep to the Marine detention point, where we stepped into ankle-deep mud. A platoon of GIs was unspooling concertina wire around the outside of a freshly laid minefield in a section of the perimeter. A large, crudely lettered placard planted among the explosives read DON'T FEED THE ANIMALS. Dripping wet and innocent as angels, soldiers smirked as their lieutenant raged at their prank, far too dangerous now to undo.

A corpsman pointed us toward a plywood-sided structure topped with corrugated metal. The rain surged as we jogged into the rickety building, ignoring the posted instructions to clear our weapons in a barrel half-filled with drowned sand. Inside, two Marines in utilities and an Air Force MP in khakis worked diligently at desks facing into the spartan room. In the center, a holding cell made of cyclone fencing was empty. No Tam.

The Air Force MP said Rallier 57412 had been claimed by a detail of Vietnamese in military fatigues bearing a lot of official paper filled out in their native language. He showed us the stack of forms and apologized for the stains. "Fucking humidity's already rusted the fucking staples. The Marines on duty couldn't read them, and our translator wasn't around. The gestures came through loud and clear, though, so they handed him over."

This handover to Vietnamese military cops was odd. "Any chance the combat police were taking Tam to the Open Arms halfway house?" I wanted to know. The brand-new Open Arms program offered VC the chance to defect without penalty. Commie deserters like Tam were supposed to go directly to special low-security halfway houses where they'd get daily volleyball games and sympathetic talks on fitting back into South Vietnamese society.

The MP shrugged and gave us the use of their phone. But the local Chieu Hoi turncoat center had never heard of Tam or anybody designated 57412. Robeson cranked the phone again and called the ARVN field-police stockade, where the commanding officer claimed to know nothing either. Robeson tossed in some Vietnamese phrases to impress upon him our need to locate the man, but he'd already hung up.

A sudden burst of rain drummed the roof. The jarheads broke out some bourbon with warm cherry soda chaser to counter the damp. The combo tasted like mouthwash. While Robeson tried to find anything useful in the papers the MP had handed us, I nosed around and spotted a container of Sealtest frozen concentrated milk. Neither of us had seen nearly real milk in a while and happily downed a cup each.

The Marines' interpreter arrived and confirmed Robeson's assessment that the stack of rusty paper might as well have been last week's *Stars and Stripes* for all the good it would do us.

Plenty of official language saying they were taking charge of the prisoner. Zero about what they planned to do with him. We asked the interpreter to phone the field police lieutenant who'd taken Tam away. After a heated exchange, he finally ferreted out the information that a man who might perhaps have been 57412 had been transferred, again—taken this time by four national policemen.

"Transferred fucking where?" I said.

"To National Police station," the interpreter said, ear to the phone, "on way to prison."

The Saigon government didn't always recognize VC guerillas as legitimate soldiers. In the eyes of the South Vietnamese, neither the laws of war nor the Geneva Convention applied to captured Viet Cong. Legal niceties aside, the Viet Cong didn't take prisoners much either. Which meant most ARVN troops had lost someone to the Communists. With those scores to settle, they were known to take vengeance on any available VC POW. If they survived interrogation, the VC were interned in camps or stuck in one of Brother Nhu's prisons. But our guy Tam hadn't been captured. He'd quit, voluntarily surrendered to Americans. Number 57412 was a Viet Cong turncoat, not a prisoner of war. He should've been treated well, not hauled away to some hellhole.

But which hellhole? One of the forty-four official prisons we knew about that were scattered around the country? No way to know how many more were unmarked on our maps. All of them squalid, overflowing with Diem's own citizens who hadn't loved their president enough.

With the interpreter's help, I called the Da Nang Military Interrogation Center, a notorious local clink. No sign of Tam there either.

"This don't make a damn lotta sense," one of the Marines said. "Whaddya think got the guy jammed up?"

A fighter jet taking off nearby hit its afterburners, engines howling.

"You should ask Terwilliger," the other leatherneck shouted.

Captain Terwilliger was the US Psy Ops officer who'd brought Tam in and filed the initial report on what the *hoi chanh* had to say about our Saigon assassin. My call woke the captain from his afternoon nap.

"The Slop Chute in twenty," the *dai uy* said.

"The what, sir?"

"Officers' Club."

AS HEAD HONCHO of the Psy Ops shop in Da Nang, Captain Terwilliger advised the Viets on how to psych out their enemy. The man looked the part: black hair, black glasses, black stateside boots, black captain's bars on the lapel of his fatigue shirt and on his baseball cap. His call sign was Head Case.

"How did Tam end up here, sir?" Robeson asked.

"I was testing the detachment's thousand-watt loudspeakers one evening around dusk, beaming this out over the perimeter wire."

He pressed play on a portable recorder the size of a brick and loosed a terrifying otherworldly howl, followed by the voice of a kid pleading for papa-san to come home, and finally a weird-sounding dude reciting something the captain translated from memory: "Disgrace and sorrow await your families. Come home. Come home before you die. Rally to the government and live a happy life forever."

The message was grim but Terwilliger sounded chipper. "What do you think?"

Robeson did his best down-home wail. "Whooeee. That is some bad shit, *dai uy*."

Captain Terwilliger was pleased. "We play it on the radio, too, along with the names and dates of their casualties when we have them. The North doesn't notify relatives. Bad for morale. So we try to inform their families whenever possible." He grinned. "Anyway, I was testing this tape at the perimeter, really blasting it, and this lone VC rises up out of the weeds on the other side, holding an Open Arms safe-conduct pass way over his head. Surrenders himself—to me."

"How would you describe him?"

"Nervous, thin as a rail, totally worn out. But personable. I liked him. We all did. I got him fed, took him for a physical. He had a tapeworm. We got him medicated and put him up in our compound. See for yourself." He passed over a Polaroid of him and Tam smiling over a meal. The bony Vietnamese looked like a possum caught in the headlights.

I asked if Tam had turned in his rifle. Defectors got serious bonus money for bringing in their weapons. The Viet Cong could forgive those who'd broken faith as long as they eventually returned to their comrades, but not if they'd surrendered their weapon when they defected. Terwilliger shook his head. Tam had not brought in his rifle. Meaning he knew he could go back.

"Made me wonder," Terwilliger said, "but he made up for any doubts with information and a cooperative attitude. Tam got nervous at any mention of the South Vietnamese eventually housing him, which of course was inevitable. When he sensed the end of his stay with us was approaching, he bought himself a little extra time by mentioning the Saigon lady assassin."

"And it worked," Robeson said.

"It did. He wasn't even being formally interviewed at the time. We were just having tea when Armed Forces Radio reported she had gunned down a second American officer."

"He understood the English?"

"Enough, yes."

"So this must've been last week?" I said.

"Exactly right. Given the importance of the intel," the captain said, "I was happy to let Tam stick around a day or two longer. After which I managed to talk the security detachment at the airfield into sheltering our guest until the Chieu Hoi Open Arms program was able to collect him."

"Did he say anything about the assassin's history?" I asked. "Like where she learned to shoot like that?"

"He'd been told she made her bones in Tay Ninh province, up by the Cambodian border. She'd stand on the side of the road in civilian clothes next to a smashed-up bicycle, and wave down lone ARVN trucks. The minute one stopped to help her, she'd shoot the driver dead—and anyone else in the cab. Her squad would take out anybody riding in the truck bed. She and her cadre did their thing in seconds. Stripped the vehicle. Twice made off with the entire rig."

"No prisoners," Robeson said with concern.

Terwilliger shook his head. "In recognition of her heroism, Tam said, the Capital Liberation Regiment sent her to Saigon to take over Unit Eight, the unit he was supposed to join."

"Any chance he gave you a current schematic of the unit? Any of their names or aliases?"

"No schematic. No names."

"Did you interrogate him in English or Vietnamese?"

"I mostly used our interpreter. But our last big conversation was in his broken English and my Simple-Simon Vietnamese."

"What did he know about her latest orders?"

"Said she was ordered to eliminate '*Mỹ cáo già*.'"

"His exact words?"

"We were mixing pidgin with Vietnamese. I asked him what *Mỹ cáo già* meant. He struggled to translate and finally said, 'old fox.'"

Robeson and I exchanged glances. In Vietnamese *Mỹ* meant American, as in the ever-popular Buddhist chant *Đả Đảo Mỹ Diệm* —Down with American Diem. Had Tam meant the Americans' old fox—Diem? Or did he mean an old American fox? Another attempt on McNamara? General Harkins? Ambassador Lodge?

"We need to have a conversation with Mr. Tam," I said.

Terwilliger looked from me to Robeson and back to me.

"I'm sorry I let him go," he said. "He was a *hoi chanh*. I thought he'd be safe."

WE CHECKED IN to the Grand Hotel de Tourane, a whitewashed colonial relic, flaking a bit on the outside but elegant on the inside. And we could sleep easy: a trio of off-duty Vietnamese soldiers from the military compound next door guarded the place at night in return for room and board for their families.

The rain had stopped so we strolled along the strand, past Mediterranean-style residences with pastel walls and fenced-in yards. Young American Air Force and Navy officers promenaded with nurses or huddled over drinks in cafés along the riverfront. The odor of wet mortar and mown grass mixed with the aroma of strong French coffee. It smelled like lazy afternoons everywhere, like peace.

The evening breeze off the water felt almost cool. Patrol boats motored up the river past skiffs and sampans. Every so often the Vietnamese infantrymen guarding the bridge shot at a floating object in case it was a buoy mine or a sapper using French underwater breathing apparatus to plant charges. Across the river, visible through a line of trees, bathers on China Beach were enjoying the glassy blue water of the open sea. An artillery shell struck the slope of Monkey Mountain, sending up a cloud of dirt and smoke. Nobody flinched.

We ate dinner on the hotel's terrace, and hashed the odds of finding Tam wherever he was being held. After a couple of bottles of wine, we decided to try flashing our credentials at the National Police headquarters, demanding the whereabouts of the man the field police had taken from the American detention cage. We got lucky. Nearly hysterical with fear, the ARVN captain on duty claimed total ignorance and pulled out a ream of paperwork, probably hoping we couldn't read Vietnamese and learn anything that might get him in trouble. Robeson missed the fine points but got the basic idea: Rallier 57412 had become Prisoner 94711, transported under guard to Con Son, a hundred-year-old French penal colony on an island five hundred miles to the south and fifty miles out to sea.

"Oh, that's fuckin' great," Robeson said. "They've hauled him off to Devil's Island."

CHAPTER EIGHT

From the air, Con Son looked like a caveman's idea of a moose. Contorted antlers bulged from the large head and mountainous ridges with two dramatic peaks rose along its back. The airstrip cut across its neck like a collar. A single road looped down its western flank and along the curve of its underbelly, where the town nested: all of two dozen houses in four rows. The lone road reappeared on the other side, leading to the large penal colony made up of five separate compounds, over a hundred buildings in all. At its heart squatted an ancient French fort right out of *Beau Geste*, circled by stone walls and parapets and facing a jetty. We banked, passing over a huge cemetery with so many markers it looked like a plague had hit the island.

We dropped down over coconut trees, skimming palms eighty feet high, and flew a half circle over the clearest water. A Pacific paradise.

A short, jaunty Vietnamese met us at the airstrip and attempted to engage us in French. Robeson smiled and nodded but the man saw I didn't understand and switched instantly to bad English. He was the warden, come personally to drive us to his office.

"Who lives there?" Robeson asked as we drove past the hamlet abutting the town.

"Several hundred civil servant. Seventy-six guard. All work in prison. Six hundred militia defend Con Son from attack. One dozen army officer command mens."

The warden was in no hurry. He asked if we wished to stop at the gift shop in the miniature town to see the swagger sticks and other souvenirs the prisoners made in their carpentry workshop. We declined. Apparently quite proud of his slammer, he offered us a tour of its vegetable gardens and Catholic chapel. We declined those, too.

No weapons were permitted in the prison. Guards and administrative personnel went unarmed. As we surrendered our sidearms, Robeson grew visibly edgy. He peppered the warden with questions: What crimes had the inmates committed? How many were hardcore Communists?

"Over four thousand guest," the warden said. "Few make crime, many politic detainee. No worry. Not manys here do . . ." he pantomimed a weapon against his shoulder, trigger finger cocked.

"Understood," I said. "Only a few of your prisoners ever bore arms."

"Even so," Robeson said, "seventy-six guards? Man, that's an awful small detachment to cope with over four *thousand* inmates."

The warden shrugged. "Where is possible to go?" he said, adding something in French.

"It's eighty klicks to the mainland," Robeson translated. Meaning, the whole island was a prison. Geography made a larger force unnecessary.

The warden offered us a *café filtre* while his clerk began to pull out their records. Robeson puffed his cheeks at the height of the stack of ledgers filled with elegant penmanship, tens of thousands of names, probably going back to the days of the French. But when we described the circumstances of Prisoner 94711, the warden instantly knew who we had come for. Robeson translated the warden's explanation that all prisoners were given a classification of "easy," "questionable," or "stubborn," and that Tam had been classified as "stubborn." His orders had been to isolate the man in Compound Four, where the most uncooperative inmates were housed in a cellblock of what he called *cages à tigre*—tiger cages—punishment cells whose guards kept close watch from overhead through barred ceilings.

"Compound Four? So that's where we need to go to talk to him?" Robeson said. "Can you give us the map?"

The warden smiled. "We cannot make map. Communist obtain map, come liberate comrades."

"So you'll show us the way?"

He shook his head. "Not."

"Why not? You're not holding him in Compound Four? You housed him somewhere else? Against orders?" I asked.

"*Mais non.*" The warden raised both hands toward heaven. "*Il est mort.*" The prisoner had died before arriving, he explained, while attempting to escape from his escort.

"He was arriving by ship?" Robeson said.

"Aeroplane." The warden skimmed the air with his hand. "Die two kilometer from island, so to say."

Two klicks out from the island? No, two *over* Con Son— above. Up. He demonstrated.

"Vietnamese Air Force plane?" I said. "USA?"

"*Américain. Oui.*"

"Military aircraft? Civilian?"

"*Civil.*"

"Vietnamese soldiers brought him?"

"No, no." The warden stood with arms crossed. "Police in cloth of the street."

Vietnamese plainclothesmen in an American civilian aircraft were bringing Tam to the island when he tried to escape . . . from the plane, at altitude. Right.

Robeson asked if they had retrieved the body.

"*Oui, oui. Bien sûr.* I show."

The warden drove us to the enormous cemetery we'd seen from the air, thousands of markers crowding a long sloping hill overlooking the sea. He pointed to a fresh mound at the foot and stayed with his jeep while we hiked down. We found Tam's prisoner number on a slip of paper tacked to a white stick protruding from the ground.

Robeson gazed out to sea. "If they just wanted him dead, they could've taken care of that back in Da Nang." He gestured at the size of the cemetery. "The Vietnamese must like doin' it out here. You suppose it was an Air America plane that brought him?"

"What else? You figure the cops were questioning him at six thousand feet?"

"Air America pilots ain't likely to tell us, or talk about somebody deplaning early."

I agreed. The CIA had bought the Air America operation a bunch of years ago and manned it with soldiers of fortune from half a dozen countries. Whatever happened in the back of the aircraft was no concern of theirs. Just shut the door as you leave. Robeson called up to the warden: "You're sure this prisoner was Mr. Tam?"

"*Oui, oui. Sans aucun doute.*" No doubt about it, Robeson said.

We climbed back up to the car. "What did he look like, this Tam?" I asked the warden.

"*Homme de constitution ordinaire.*"

"A man of average build," Robeson translated. "An ordinary joe."

"When I see him," the warden went on, "he broken. Fall many far," he added, mournfully.

"Shit." I ran a hand down my face. We'd gone to a lot of trouble to interrogate a corpse.

THE WARDEN DROPPED us at the airport to get ourselves on the next outbound flight, which wouldn't be until sometime the day after tomorrow—maybe. It took nearly an hour on the Air Force radiophone to reach Vung Tau on the coast and get relayed from there to Saigon so I could bring Captain Deckle up to speed.

Deckle paused. "What's your read? You think they've still got the guy and are deliberately hiding him from you?"

"Could well be, yes sir. We could be getting shammed while he disappears deeper."

"Well, either way, the scrot is not available to question."

Deckle agreed to do some digging at his end, and we'd do some on ours. With luck we'd be back at CID in forty-eight hours. By which time he or we might know more.

Robeson and I passed on the hostel in town and went for the more isolated of the two inns on the beach. I talked Robeson into a deluxe cottage at the water's edge: a thatched shelter on a platform, with mats for beds and no plumbing or mosquito nets. But it did come with stubby US Army entrenching tools to manage the shallow cooking pit, and an incredible ocean view.

"Not so much as a rubber lady to bed down on," Robeson complained.

"You've been at the Majestic too long. You're getting soft, soldier."

We dropped our gear and walked toward the surf. A few Americans—officers by the look of them—lay on the perfectly white sand, slathered with baby oil, toasting themselves. Parents busily herded their blond kids along the water's edge or helped them build sandcastles. A very pregnant woman with a toddler holding on to her finger waded in the ankle-deep water, seemingly unaware she was sharing the island with a notorious prison.

Robeson had never learned how to swim, but he kicked off his shoes, rolled up his pant legs, and let the waves lap at his feet. I walked out until the water was chest high, but didn't go any farther. Before Korea I had loved to swim. Now being under water spooked me. Sounds falling away, muted. The silence thick in your ears. It was haunted, a dead place where the ones I had wasted waited for me. I couldn't go there anymore.

I RETURNED TO the beach and found Robeson in conversation with Rafe, an airman who'd lucked out and pulled Con Son as his duty station. He was reading a paperback and wasn't due on duty until evening.

Robeson said, "VC ever attack the island?"

"Con Son?" Rafe's eyebrows arched in disbelief. "Never. There's no war here. Worst we see is when new prisoners arrive. They push 'em over the side manacled. They struggle like hell not to drown getting ashore. Not all of 'em make it. Wherever they've been, they can hardly walk. Knees the size of melons, some of 'em. They'll carry each other, or drag themselves out of the water on their backsides, like crabs." He dabbed zinc ointment on his nose. "Once they finally crawl up the beach they get the choice of *chanh dao*, the right path—the Diem way—or the bad-news Ho Chi Minh path through two lines of guards who beat them something awful. The prison guards are real liberal when it comes to applying their truncheons and real chary when it comes to supplying food. They'd much sooner beat 'em than feed 'em. Weak inmates are easier to control."

We told Rafe that we'd come to find a prisoner who died before getting the choice of the Diem way or the Ho Chi Minh way.

"From what I've seen, he's probably lucky."

I noticed colored patches on the uniforms of the prisoners who stood hip-deep in the surf, hauling in a fishing net. A lot of them seemed to have yellow badges with orange stripes. I asked Rafe if he knew what they meant.

Rafe pushed up his sunglasses. "Prisoners detained without trial. Red badges are politicals. VC, sympathizers, independent thinkers who criticized the regime. Sometimes a political's just a guy who dared to run against the 'approved' candidate or whose business got too successful and started eating into the profits of the province chief or his relatives."

"That's a hell of a way to eliminate the competition. And the green and red?"

"Military politicals. Small-time traitors. Encouraging desertion or otherwise engaging in anti-Diem activity. Green and yellow are military criminals, I think. The gents with plain yellow badges, they're civilian criminals."

"And some of the military and civilian criminals also get yellow armbands?"

"'Cause they're trustees. Orderlies. They pick the real hard-core guys and give 'em special privileges for keeping the others in line. They're much worse than the guards."

"So is this their version of a chain gang?" Robeson asked.

"This isn't so bad. They've got other crews on the island breaking rocks. These inmates do all the fishing for the prison. Run a sea-turtle farm too. Raise them for food, carve their shells into bowls. Plus they man this giant mortar that grinds coral and seashells into a lime powder that'll burn your eyes and skin real bad. Anybody in the cells gets out of line, and they douse him with it. Breathe it in and you cough up blood. Some of 'em even go blind."

"Ain't that self-sufficient," Robeson said. "Prisoners making do-it-yourself teargas for their own punishment."

The skeletal men working in the surf sang as they hauled.

"That their chain-gang work song?" Robeson said.

"A revolutionary chant." The airman rose up on an elbow. "They only take it up when the warders aren't close enough to hear."

"Singing about kicking our asses and fucking our women?" Robeson said.

"Nah. It's all glory and winning and shit like that. 'The enemy has bullets of steel, we have hearts of gold.' I wanted to tape-record them to send home, even offered them vitamins, but they wouldn't go for it."

Two small groups of prisoners clustered in the shallow water being lectured by one of their own. The leader of the bunch closer to us called out something and everyone tapped the shells they were holding in unison.

I recognized the dit dahs instantly. "He's teaching them Morse code."

Rafe smiled. "Ho Chi Minh University."

The other group was listening intently to a white-haired gent whose voice carried toward us as the wind shifted.

"So what's that course?" Robeson said.

The airman turned his head to look before placing fresh disks of cucumber on his eyes and lying back, face to the sun.

"Don't know, but the prof's Dr. Phan. Harvard grad. One-time rival of the president. Diem tossed him in some lockup in Saigon and had him tortured, after which he was sent here."

"Communist?" I said.

"Who knows? The guards like to brag that if the prisoners aren't when they get here, they will be when they're finished with them."

"Charming," Robeson said.

"You see the big cemetery yet?" Rafe said. "A lot of prisoners get sent to the island just for disposal. Easier here—no visitors. No fuss, no muss. They do it real quiet, the French way. Groups of thirty. Three men at a time blindfolded and made to kneel in front of a firing squad. Ten trios, ten volleys, and the guards are done for the day."

CHAPTER NINE

Watching the skin-and-bones inmates had made us both crazy hungry. In the village market Robeson bought us a snack of rice-and-pork pancakes, while I bargained for six cans of beer and some fresh fish to cook for supper. I waved away the lady pushing C-rations, instant coffee packets and Klim, the brownish-yellow shit alleged to be powdered milk. Soap and cigarettes we picked up at a tiny indoor market.

Back at the beach hut, we deepened the cooking pit with the green entrenching shovels, which doubled as our cooking utensils, and fired up some brush and wood to roast the fish on the spades. Wrapped in palm fronds, they cooked fast. We scarfed the white flesh with our fingers as the sun dropped, taking the light with it. Robeson lay back, patting his stomach. He sipped his beer, hummed for a bit, and absently sang: *"Big brunettes with long stelets / On the shores of Italee, / Dutch girls with golden curls / Beside the Zuyder Zee . . ."* Embers from the cooking pit zigged skyward.

On the side of the hut hung an Australian shower bag filled with water warmed by the day's sun. I wet down and lathered. Robeson sacked out on the sand. I rinsed off and lay in the hut to drift off to the sound of the surf.

When we got up, it was night. Low tide. We took off our

dog tags, put on olive-drab T-shirts, and cut the legs off our spare fatigues to make shorts. Clovis taped down his grandfather's gold bracelet so it wouldn't flash. I applied charcoal from the cooking pit to my face so I wouldn't glow in the dark. I streaked my bare ears, neck, arms and legs, and handed the charred stick to Robeson. He dabbed the tip of his nose. Big joke.

We slipped out of our hut and walked west through the surf. The faint ocean breeze cooled my sunburned neck, and my skin tingled with relief. The night was moonless so we cast no shadows. We were moving near blind except for starlight. A campfire flickered in the dunes beside a derelict French bunker made of concrete. A lone sentry slept on its roof under the riot of stars. More soldiers lay in hammocks inside the eroding structure, made visible by a lantern. We slipped by, fifty yards distant, keeping to the shallow surf, and pressed on for a few minutes before turning inland. We came upon a black-and-white sign on a post and used our red-lensed flashlight to read it: something-something *Cấm Vào* — entry prohibited.

Once we reached the tree line, the foliage made the dark so impenetrable we stumbled the whole way to the cemetery. Now there were four fresh graves at the bottom of the slope. We risked using the flashlight again to make sure the first in the row was the one marked as Tam's, and set to digging on our knees with our short shovels.

"Funeral directors do *not* dig graves personally, Sarge. If my granddaddy seen me doing this," Robeson panted, "he'd downright expire."

"Shh. You hear something?" I said.

Robeson paused. "I hear ocean is all. Stop fretting. Nobody here's stirring."

We resumed digging. "Granddaddy, he had this showroom full of fine wooden coffins. Me and my brother liked to play in there, and in the embalming room. Strictly forbidden to mess with the pumps and tubes and syringes. Did anyway, of course. Right in the middle of his showroom Granddaddy had this extra-fancy casket he kept filled with water, to demonstrate his boxes were tight as ticks. One time my brother and me dumped in these real ugly catfish we caught. Our Gramps opened the lid for some new widow and them fish set her to screamin' . . ."

We dug a foot deeper. The smell of decay grew stronger. Flesh rotted fast in the tropics. I pinched my nose shut. "Damn, he's ripe."

Robeson tied his green T-shirt over his nose and mouth. Our shovels soon dug into something unmistakably fleshy. Taking quick shallow breaths through our mouths, we scraped the dirt away from the corpse.

"Damnation," Robeson said, holding his nose. "No legs, no arms."

"What the fuck," I said. "No head."

Robeson shone the red light over the body. We'd uncovered the putrid diseased carcass of a hellish-looking pig.

Robeson said, "I'm gonna throw up or dump a deuce." He made a retching noise and disappeared with his shovel into the dark. Robeson was very particular about what he called bathroom etiquette.

I backed away from the grave to get upwind of the rotting flesh and lay on the ground, wishing I could light a cigarette against the stench. The breeze blowing in from the sea chilled the sweat along my back.

"Dừng lại!"

A light blinded me. Not five feet away stood a scrawny beanpole of a sentry, shouting. Eyes huge and barking orders in Vietnamese, he leveled his rifle at the crazy grave robber.

Did he want me to stand up? Raise my arms? I sat up slowly. He screamed louder, wailing like a banshee, clutching the rifle stock tight against his shoulder.

"Easy, easy," I said, heart pounding. I extended my hands toward him so he'd see they were empty, but that only aggravated him. Whatever he wanted, he was furious I wasn't giving it to him.

"Đụ má mày," he growled—motherfucker.

A *thunk*, metal on bone, knocked him to his knees. A second blow from Robeson's shovel flattened him. If the little fuck's head hadn't been attached, Clovis would've knocked it right out of the park.

"Holy Hannah," he said, down on his hands and knees, sucking wind. "Where the hell did he come from?"

I crawled over to the prostrate guard, grabbed his rifle, and groped him for other weapons.

"Goddamn." Robeson drew a shaking arm across his sweaty face.

The sentry's eyes had gone moon-white inside his head. I felt his neck artery to check his pulse.

Robeson gulped air. "We'd better ease on outta here before he comes to."

"No rush," I said.

Robeson slid to his knees. "What—? No," he pleaded, in a whisper. "He ain't."

"Yeah."

"Jesus. I killed him?"

"Looks like."

"What are we gonna do? We gotta report this."

"No way."

"But I'm a cop."

"Fucking right you're a cop. You wanna bunk down in that crap-hole of a prison and grind turtle shells into teargas until somebody gets around to dealing with us? If the inmates or the guards don't do it first? Give me a hand."

We rolled the dead sentry into the grave on top of the pig, tossed his rifle in after him, and replaced the dirt, making sure to scatter any extra bulges and blur our footprints. Breathing rapidly, we snuck back down to the shoreline, angling our tracks into the surf like we were headed in the opposite direction. Once in the water, we turned around and waded along the beach, past the French bunker, back to our patch.

We sat on the shallow floor of the South China Sea under the huge starlit sky, driving the spades into the sand to scrape away the stench, then tossed them toward the fire pit. I retrieved our bar of soap and we bobbed in the surf, scrubbing ourselves clean.

"Better get in the hut," I said to Robeson as we staggered out of the water. "They're bound to start looking."

Robeson slumped on the sand and didn't answer.

"Clovis," I said, "we can't be out here all night. We gotta sleep."

"I can't, man." Robeson's voice wavered. "I . . . I can't."

"What's your problem? You got sand in your pussy or some-thing? Move your hind end, damn it."

I pulled him to his feet, marched him to our hut, and shoved him inside. We stripped off our wet clothes and hung them on pegs. I ate some of the fish we'd cooked and lay down, totally punched out. Robeson slouched in the doorway, looking out into the night.

"Be strong in the Lord," he said, "in the power of His might. Put on the whole armor of God, that ye may stand against the wiles of the Devil."

"You're worryin' me, Clovis," I said.

"The fear of you and the dread of you shall be upon every beast of the earth."

"You talking about me?"

"Only if your name's God."

CHAPTER TEN

We spent most of the morning sitting on the tarmac at the airstrip, hoping hard for aircraft—any aircraft—going to the mainland. Nothing arrived, nothing left. The waiting was driving Robeson nuts. Did I think they'd found him. Did I think they were looking for us. He grew increasingly convinced we'd be arrested any minute. I tried to calm him down but there wasn't much I could say. I recognized the demons circling his heart. There was no undoing what he'd done.

A chopper landed to pick up some tanned Navy officers humping scuba gear and we begged our way on board, volunteering to sit in the open doorway by the gunner. The pilots took us to nine thousand feet to cool their beer and we clutched ourselves, hands jammed into our armpits, trying to stay warm. They got us as far as Vung Tau on the coast, where we lucked into a jump to Saigon on a C-47 transport and landed at Tan Son Nhut just before three.

"Well, that was fuckin' productive," I grumbled, as we queued for a taxi outside the terminal.

"Productive? Shit, I killed a guy! I never killed anyone before. Ever."

"That was an accident. It just happened."

"It didn't 'just happen.' I bludgeoned him dead," he said loudly.

"Shut the fuck up," I snapped. "Don't say another word 'bout this—not goddamn ever."

"We don't tell Captain Deckle?"

"You lookin' for a court-martial? Stockade time? Booking into a first-class penitentiary?"

"They're gonna find him."

"So what?" I said. "Maybe you've noticed, this place is full of dead slopes."

"Just another yellow nigger, huh?"

He'd topped the guy but now he was pissy with me like I'd made him do it. I wanted to hammer him but thought better of it. He was scared and angry, skewered by guilt.

"Listen," I said. "At some point in the future you'll mean to do somebody. That sentry wasn't it. You weren't looking to kill him. You were saving my ass. The shovel hit something that shorted out his head, is all. Now shut up about it or we'll both be in deep shit."

Robeson crossed his arms, chin on his chest, unconvinced. A taxi took us on a silent ride to our boss, to report our progress—or lack thereof. I shot Robeson a don't-you-say-a-fucking-thing look as we got out, but as soon as we sit down in front of the captain, he immediately spills his guts about the cemetery and the sentry, like the man was a priest.

"Holy Mary, Mother of God." Deckle leapt to his feet. "You did not—you did *not* just confess to that. Fuckin' A."

Deckle's career was swirling down the crapper before his eyes.

"Whatta we do?" I said, watching mine swirl away with his.

"Nothing," Deckle shot back and stood over me. "You damn

well do nothing. You say nothing, you seen nothing." He bent low to get in my face, hands on his knees. "You hear me?"

"Yes, sir."

He turned to Robeson. "Stick it back in the tube. Got it?"

Robeson sat silent, eyes downcast.

"*Verstehe,* Sergeant?"

Robeson's chin rose slowly. "Yes. Yes, sir." Deckle kept his eyes fixed on Robeson—hard.

"You get a line on our missing boy, Cap?" I said, trying to get Deckle off Robeson's case. I flipped open my notebook.

Deckle returned to his chair behind his carved desk and consulted his notes. "On the phone you said Tam was delivered by Air America. So I called the Assistant Director at the USAID Office of Public Safety, who refers me to the Vietnamese Directorate of Rehabilitation, which sends me to their Director of Corrections, who . . ."

"How did you keep all that straight, sir?" Robeson said, composing himself a little.

"Wasn't supposed to," the captain muttered. "Finally the Director of Corrections passes me off to his American babysitter," Deckle said. "A guy I actually knew. So I thought I'd finally lucked out. He manages to trace Tam from military field police over to municipal police in Da Nang, and finally to CIO, their Central Intelligence Organization. Who also claimed to know nothing."

"Flamin' hell," I said. "What a fucking runaround. Where have they stashed this dude?" I sure as shit hoped Tam hadn't ended up in one of Diem's prisons that specialized in tying detainees in impossible positions with barbed wire, or burying them up to their necks in sand as the tide was coming in. Those wardens weren't going to be offering tours of any vegetable gardens you wanted to know about.

"No telling." The captain seemed resigned. "He's one of theirs," he said. "A Vietnamese national. We can't do anything about that. They could have him squirreled away anywhere."

I was beginning to get the picture. "Tam's got something the Vietnamese need to know real bad, or something they're hot for us not to know."

Deckle popped a pill and swallowed it dry. This wasn't territory he was comfortable messing with. I eyed him.

"No matter who's holding him," I said, "we need whatever they got out of the guy about the Red Queen and Unit Eight."

"Hah," Deckle groused. "Don't hold your breath."

"We got an important question for the man, sir."

I broke the news to our boss about the language dilemma. Was her likely target the old American Fox or the Americans' Old Fox?

"Jesus," Deckle said. "The Americans' Old Fox has got to be Diem. But who's the old American Fox? If they wanted another shot at McNamara, they had their chance when he was here 'fact-finding' last month."

"And given the less-than-encouraging facts, I doubt he's coming back anytime soon." I knew this would piss off Deckle, but I was too tired to care. "Harkins is about the only one who thinks the war is 'well in hand.'"

"What about Harkins, then?" Robeson asked. "Our senior military advisor would make a helluva prize."

"The VC approach to Harkins seems to run more toward plastique," I said, reminding him about the blown-out wall at Harkins's HQ.

Deckle agreed. "General Harkins would be a much tougher close-range target, even for her. Lodge is new, he's the top American in-country, and he can't stop himself from parading around in public. If it's an Old American Fox she's after, my money's on Lodge. So which Old Fox is she more likely to be after—our ambassador or their president?"

Robeson bit his lip. "You'd think with potential targets like their president or our new ambassador they'd welcome our help instead of playing keep-away with the only informant."

"They don't share," I said. "The VBI's only too happy to have our bulletproof vests and lie detectors and riot guns, and brag about the state-of-the-art crime lab CIA built for them. But ask 'em for information and they're quick to tell you to fuck off, they're a *sovereign* nation."

Deckle sighed. He might not like my saying all this out loud but he knew it was true. He didn't bother to contradict me. "If Counselor Nhu thinks the Red Queen is lining up on Diem, he'll suck every drop of information from this Tam. But if it's Lodge she's after, he may be happy to leave us ignorant while she plots on undisturbed."

"Let her go after Lodge? Don't it matter we're allies?" Robeson protested.

Deckle said, "Things are looking rocky on that score. Lodge has been sent from Washington to deliver the tough message that the Nhus have got to go, and Diem has to make the reforms he promised or he'll be joining them."

I said, "So could be Nhu is sending back a message of his own."

The captain nodded. "And your Red Queen is a pretty convincing messenger."

Robeson said, "If the CIO goons have Tam and are under orders not to help us, how the hell are we gonna find out what he's spilled?"

Deckle rocked in his swivel chair. "Calls for some major

juju." The captain scribbled a message by hand and shouted for a courier.

"Yes, sir," I said. "Have we got anybody with that kind of juice, Captain?"

Captain Deckle emptied his ashtray into the wastebasket. "We'll find out tomorrow. You've got a breakfast meeting in the morning at oh eight hundred. At the Cercle Sportif."

I blanched. The Cercle Sportif Saigonnais was an exclusive club set inside a thirty-acre park, right across from the new presidential palace rising slowly from the ashes of the bombed-out ruin. I'd only been to the club a few times when I'd driven the provost's wife to her every-second-Monday meeting of the American Women's Association of Saigon.

"Captain," I said, "they don't exactly appreciate the likes of us enlisted at the Cerc."

"Not 'us,' Staff Sergeant Miser. Just you." No Robeson. The Cerc appreciated black enlisted even less.

"Yes, sir. Who am I meeting?"

"The old American Fox himself. Our new ambassador." He shoved a dossier across his desk. "So leave your goddamn attitude at home. And for Chrissake, put on some underwear."

CHAPTER ELEVEN

Back at the Majestic, we cracked open a bottle of Jim Beam. Robeson checked his watch and switched on the shortwave to the English newscast from Manila. A British voice was giving a rundown on "Freedom Day" in Selma. Days earlier, three hundred and fifty Negroes had baked in the Alabama sun for hours, waiting to register to vote. Students trying to bring them food and water had got beat with clubs, shocked with cattle prods. The BBC could have been describing Nhu's Red Berets and police descending on Buddhist protesters. Same-same.

Robeson took a healthy belt of whiskey as the broadcast continued. Elsewhere in the South, cops were swinging truncheons with abandon and sheriffs were setting dogs on uppity Commie-inspired blacks and white "outside agitators." Clovis switched to the new Armed Forces radio station broadcasting out of the Rex Hotel. The announcer reported the third street attack on an American officer in Saigon and cautioned all US personnel to be vigilant.

The mellow voice slid right from murder into the weather: a hundred percent humidity and clammy hot. Right on cue the air turned liquid, pouring down on the balcony in a solid sheet. I massaged my aching leg.

Robeson shut off the radio and took up Crouch's lame

excuse for case notes on the previous killings, looking for anything that might point to her next kill zone or high-value target. I rifled through the broadside on Lodge from the embassy's information officer, along with the much less puffy Agency profile.

> *Subject: Henry Cabot Lodge.*
> *Major General, US Army Reserve.*
> *US Senator, Vice Presidential Candidate,*
> *UN Ambassador, Ambassador to South Viet Nam.*

Lodge came from old New England money and had bounced on Teddy Roosevelt's knee as a kid. Silver spoon? Hell, the guy was born with a whole fucking place setting. Surprisingly, he hadn't chosen a gentleman's war. Africa in tanks, then liaison with the French in Europe until the armistice.

JFK and Henry Cabot Lodge were both sons of big-time Boston clans. Lodges had entertained George Washington and made the family's first fortune as privateers—a polite name for pirates the new revolutionary government licensed to operate against its enemies on the high seas. The Cabots, on the other hand, made their fortune in the opium business.

Well, well. Not so different from his rival's old man. Papa Kennedy had made his dough smuggling the best hooch during Prohibition. He clinched his reputation as a stud banging Hollywood starlets while fathering a horde of kids with his wife, Rose. Young Jack was following close in daddy's footsteps. Gossip about his womanizing had reached all the way to Indochina.

I turned the page. Henry Cabot Lodge had followed his grandfather into the Senate, but neglected his own re-election while managing General Eisenhower's campaign for the White House. Ike won, Lodge lost—to young congressman Jack Kennedy. Seven years later Lodge lost to Senator Jack Kennedy again, this time as Dick Nixon's running mate. It seemed like the ambassador might soon return the favor by challenging President Kennedy in next year's election.

His fierce debates with Soviet envoys as UN Ambassador had fired up his popularity. Accepting the dangerous posting in Viet Nam added further kindling. Henry Cabot Lodge was looking like presidential timber about to burn bright. Especially if he succeeded in his present assignment. Maybe Diem's wasn't the only presidency at stake in Southeast Asia.

"You done with those?" Robeson said, setting down the file he'd been reading. "All three officers she's zapped," he announced, "were from Military Assistance Advisory Group."

"So? Most everyone in Saigon is MAAG."

"True, but all three MAAG officers she tapped were G-5s."

"Civil affairs? Three kills and she hasn't managed to hit a field advisor yet?"

"Nope. All administrators. Captain Edward Victor, a fancy numbers-cruncher advising in the Vietnamese comptroller's office. Reserve Major Henderson LaValle, economist, called up to hand-hold Diem's assistant secretary at their Economy Directorate. Target three, Major James Furth, master's degree from Harvard Business School, oversaw import licenses for USAID in a STEM office, whatever that is."

"Saigon commandos in the rear with the beer."

Robeson yawned and I realized how bone-tired I was. Neither of us had slept much on Con Son. I left Robeson nursing the Jim Beam and went to my room to rack out. We both slept until dark, when we staggered up to the roof for dinner. Across the river, a couple of forty-pound parachute flares floated down like smoking suns.

"*Une nuit blanche*," said the barman. A white night.

We knocked back cocktails and dined on oysters, fried noodles, and cutlets washed down with cold beer. I was feeling no pain and Robeson seemed to be recovering from the shock of what he'd done to the sentry.

"This ain't makin' a whole lotta sense," he said, wiping his mouth with a linen napkin.

"Which part?"

"The woman's dressed as a civilian and murdering advisory personnel, so we get the assignment. I understand that."

"So what don't you get?" I said, sipping my beer.

"Why our CIA agents and their badass counter-terrorist trainees haven't taken over the job of chasin' down lovely Lady Death. Given what's on the line, I mean. Big-shot targets. So why ain't serious measures being taken? If she's aiming to grease our esteemed ambassador, CIA ought to take the reins, no? Likewise if she's looking to put our client's head of state in the ground. There's American spooks across Saigon who are tight with the regime. The CIA's tutoring our Asian pals in the dark arts, training and advising Nhu's gestapo outfits. Their people are totally plugged into all the National Police forces."

"So you think the spooks should be out front, taking point."

"This spook says *exactement*. Eyes everywhere. Resources galore. But do you see any sneaky petes on CIA payrolls invitin' us to confer with their Vietnamese counterintelligence contacts?"

"So you'd be happier if our spooks and their informants would just get together to do their back-alley shit?"

"And leave us the hell out of it, yes. Those good old boys

take pride in their unsung deeds. Let them take it all, go for the glory. Instead they're leaving all two of us out front to take whatever heat is coming. I don't even particularly want to be in the caboose on this fucker. Or maybe you're thinking we're the lead investigators 'cause they hold us to be such splendid GI detectives? That based on our heretofore stellar work on PX pilfering cases they somehow decided we should be the ones to crack an assassination ring?"

"Listen, if Diem's her target there's no way Brother Nhu is sitting this out. CIO, VBI, all his secret police and our CIA gotta be looking for her, too; they're just doing it under the radar."

"Maybe so," said Robeson, "but I'm thinking our red, white, and blue-blooded finest are deliberately keeping to the weeds."

"You might be right, especially if she's after Lodge. Maybe the CIA is okay with Lodge being in her sights."

The local gossips had been saying for months there was no love lost between Lodge and the CIA. From day one, Ambassador Lodge had thought the CIA station chief was far too chummy with the Ngo clan, Brother Nhu in particular. Lodge had wanted Jocko Richardson gone, but Langley refused to recall him. The White House neither. Out of nowhere, a two-bit DC paper reveals that Jocko Richardson is Agency. Smears Richardson as a rogue spymaster and accuses him of sharing closely held information with Nhu, the man behind the murderous attacks on the Buddhists. Then the rest of the press joins in. Pictures of Richardson run next to shots of a protesting Buddhist monk melting in a bubble of fire, gulping flames into the round black hole of his mouth.

"Lodge played nasty," I said. "Maybe Richardson's faithful are paying him back, dragging their feet on the Red Queen."

"I don't give a goddamn why they're doing it," Robeson said, looking worried. "I just don't want to be holding the claim check when whatever happens happens."

He had a point. If she popped either bigwig before we found her, we would be the first ones held to account.

"We're strictly 'use and toss' in this," he said. "Handy-dandy if they need some fools to catch the blowback when she plants the next dude. Especially if it's an Old Fox. Me, I don't wanna land some payback assignment to the ass end of nowhere. You get what I'm saying, Sarge?"

I did. It was all too easy to picture the STRAC information officers at a bullshit afternoon press briefing, khakis starched, demo boards up on easels, reciting rote crap about Free World Forces. They'd flip through charts of our failings, their pointers indicating exactly at which junctures Sergeants Miser and Robeson had gone disastrously wrong.

CHAPTER TWELVE

The blue-and-white seersucker jacket I'd borrowed from Robeson was too big in the shoulders and too small at the waist. I could carry it off as long as I left it unbuttoned. The matching slacks hadn't fit me at all so I grabbed my plain tan trousers. At oh seven thirty, I hailed a blue-and-cream Renault taxi to take me to the Cercle Sportif, where Ambassador Henry Cabot Lodge liked to swim his morning laps in the outdoor pool. He'd only been in-country a few months, but his daily routines were common knowledge.

The city was already in motion. Citizens had risen out of their comfortable cots in doorways and up from improvised pallets on the bare sidewalks, where parents and kids squatted to relieve themselves. Ever since the Buddhist protests and government crackdown, a lot of them had made a point of doing their business on the rear wall of the secret-police headquarters near the bloodstained Xa Loi pagoda.

The hack let me off in the parkland among stately trees and flowering bougainvillea. The red of the flame trees was brilliant; the shrubbery the deepest green, some of it groomed in the French style in the shape of animals. A couple of giggling American girls trotted by on small Asian horses, their ponytails bouncing in time with their butts.

Reaching the back of the stucco pavilion, I climbed the outside stairs to the elevated pool, where jacketed waiters were serving coffee and croissants to half-clad young Frenchmen and Corsican girls in the tiniest bathing suits. I walked around the pool's tiled apron, which was lined with Greek columns, trying to spot Lodge. He wasn't in the water.

I scanned the throng in reclining chairs and at poolside tables. The Cercle Sportif was an aging piece of colonial luxury enjoyed by Western swells, including our Republican Yankee ambassador, invisible at the moment. The Cerc had become popular with Americans and their families, but was still dominated by the French: bankers, merchants, *Le Monde* correspondents, Gaullist doctors, plantation owners, and all their privileged sons and bikini-clad daughters. From what I could see, they'd been joined by a smattering of the Vietnamese elite who'd previously been denied membership, and by senior Vietnamese military; many had served under the French and held both passports.

Behind some potted palms, a gang of French teens, happily taunting a pair of American boys, suddenly spat in their faces. I wanted to smack the little frog shits but didn't think getting ejected from the Cerc was what Deckle had in mind.

I surveyed the tennis courts and the large gingerbread clubhouse beyond that contained the bar, the club's dining hall, and a mahogany-paneled library where white-haired gents kicked back in armchairs after breakfast, heads nodding over foreign newspapers. Tables on the huge porch were already being set for their lunch; its gold railing glinted in the sun.

Between the pool and the clubhouse the ten clay tennis courts were all in use. Surprisingly fit American officers in middle age rallied with paunchy Asian men and thin Vietnamese military types with close-cropped hair. All wore regulation whites, a strict club rule. I easily spotted Ambassador Lodge serving in the farthest court, all six-foot-four of him.

Lodge's court seemed a bit more private than the others, but still plenty risky. Two US Marines in short-sleeve khaki uniforms and garrison caps stood at either end, girded with white pistol belts and holsters, each packing a .45 Army automatic, their backs to the game. I wondered if they'd noticed the light flashing off a lens in an upstairs window of the clubhouse, because Lodge was doing almost nothing to protect himself. Luckily, a sniper's scope wouldn't produce that kind of reflection. But someone was watching Lodge's game through binoculars or a camera lens.

I descended to the wide path between the paired courts. An unfortunate-looking Vietnamese general in fatigues stood hatless near the net, arms folded. A gun butt stuck out from his worn leather shoulder holster. The closer I got the worse he looked, the flashing black eyes in the large smooth head as hard as the metal stars on his collar. Not a face you wanted to get to know better. Next to him a stiletto-thin captain with a Sten gun leaned on the net post. He was no Miss Congeniality either.

Cabot Lodge could hit the ball but he was panting for air, sweat dripping from his chin. His fleet-footed tennis partner, "Fatty" to his friends, was two hundred pounds easy. Almost six feet tall, "Big" Minh was the country's most popular general. When he and Lodge finished their joust and came to the net to shake hands, Big Minh flashed his famous toothless smile. Japanese interrogators had broken off all but one of his teeth during the war, and he often didn't wear his dentures. He preferred to display his ruined mouth like a badge of honor,

especially when meeting Tokyo dignitaries, happily recounting
the story of how he'd strangled his Japanese warder and escaped.

A graduate of the General Staff School at Fort Leavenworth,
these days Minh served as "special advisor" to President Diem.
Translation: he was out of favor, a field commander without
troops, smiled upon but suspected. He'd been benched, but
not because he was Buddhist when the clique at the top calling
all the shots were Catholics. And not because one of his brothers was said to be a Communist general, or because the
Americans liked him too much, although that didn't help.
What made him odd man out was his success in the field,
which had turned him into a national hero. Worried that Fatty
could easily rouse his many admirers among the officers and
enlisted men to mount a coup, Diem had assigned Big Minh
to desk duty, allowing the general plenty of time for his orchids
and mah-jongg and Japanese doll collection, but keeping him
far from his men. No surprise that Big Minh had not stirred
himself from his hobbies to help his president during the last
two coup attempts.

President Diem had similarly mothballed a number of the
better ARVN field commanders to keep them from temptation.
Nor did he trust any single officer with the authority of
supreme command. Instead, he divvied up that authority
among a few loyalists, keeping the position of defense minister
for himself. The few he allowed field commands were forbidden
to maneuver their battalions without his personal okay. Just to
keep his commanders off-balance, he'd regularly bypass them
to personally deploy their men by radio from the palace.

With Buddhist protesters still regularly rioting and demon-
strating, President Diem had brought a whole division up from
the Delta to just across the river from Saigon—close enough

to protect him, but not so near as to endanger him if subverted by a rebelling commander. The Reds took full advantage of this division's absence from the field, but for Diem, fighting the Communist enemy was taking a back seat to foiling plots against his regime. Saigon buzzed with speculation about who might be conspiring against the unpopular president, his loathed brothers, and his much-hated sister-in-law. Lodge's tennis partner, General Big Minh, led the list.

When Lodge and the general parted, the frog-faced general and gnarly captain trailed after Minh. Lodge draped a towel around his neck and mopped his brow while instructing me on what he wanted for breakfast. Even sweaty, Lodge looked the distinguished statesman. Handing over his club ID, the ambassador pointed me toward the pool pavilion to order and wait while he showered. *Membre actif*, his card read, next to a photo of his mandarin face, stately and confident.

Making my way to a shaded table, I slipped off the pebbly seersucker jacket and draped it over the back of my chair. At the next table, two tan young American officers in civvies and black Army dress shoes, hair crudely whitewalled, were tucking into a hearty breakfast, one devouring *jambon à la moutarde* on rounds of French bread, washing it down with Coke and grenadine. The other shavetail was having dinner at eight in the morning: grilled beefsteak, giant French fries and a glass of red wine with ice. They paused over their food to watch a French beauty eel into the pool. Water streamed across her bare shoulders as she swam.

A white-jacketed waiter approached and bowed. I ordered oatmeal with fruit for the ambassador, a *café filtre* and madeleines for me. Along with the menu came bilingual lists of club facilities on offer. It gladdened my heart to learn that my betters were maintaining their physiques and morale with fencing runs, a bicycle track, table tennis, judo instruction, fucking lawn bowling, water polo, badminton, basketball, soccer, billiards, and swimming lessons from Monsieur Vatin.

Lodge reappeared, natty in white shirt, lightweight beige suit and yellow silk tie. On his feet, gray suede loafers with pale lavender socks. I started to rise but he waved me back into my seat.

"No need, Sergeant Miser. Relax. We're off duty at the moment. Just two gents grabbing a quick bite."

"Yes, sir. How was your game with General Minh? I've heard he's a natural athlete."

"So General Taylor warned me. I should have listened." Lodge frowned. "I'm afraid the General has had far too much leisure time to work on his strokes."

If the coup rumors were true, Minh was planning to be more fully occupied soon. "I didn't recognize the two-star standing by the net."

"Major General Xuan," Lodge said, looking past me for the waiter. "The other fellow, with the machine gun, was Captain Nhung, Minh's longtime bodyguard."

"That's Captain Nhung?"

"You've heard of him?"

"Yes, sir. Stone-cold assassin. Keeps score with notches on some French knife he carries. The tally is supposed to be nearing forty."

"Well, well," Lodge said. "In that case, I'm going to assume I needn't worry about General Minh's safety."

His oatmeal arrived, topped with the thinnest slices of banana. Pineapple bits filled a tiny bowl on the side. My madeleines came with perfect coffee. An almost invisible gesture instantly summoned a waiter to Lodge's side. He ordered mineral water and took the oatmeal on board.

"This VC woman," he said, "you think she's after my scalp?"

"Seems highly likely."

Our waiter appeared with ice-cold mineral water and poured two glasses.

"God, she'll have to get in line. Plots against my life are all I've heard since the day we arrived. And you require something urgently from our Vietnamese friends to help you locate her, is that right?" Lodge lifted the chilly glass to his lips.

I told him we needed to know whatever information Vietnamese interrogators had obtained about the female assassin from a recent Communist defector. "And any intel on the Viet Cong cell she leads," I added. "If Nhu's operators will part with it."

"I take it the local authorities haven't been of any help?"

"Less than zero."

"Why am I not surprised? My staff can't get so much as an updated chart of the Viet Cong's Order of Battle from their Central Intelligence Organization, even though our CIA has been instrumental in setting it up and supporting it."

"There's not much the slopes want us knowing."

"We mustn't denigrate our hosts, Sergeant," he said, spooning pineapple on his oatmeal.

"Sorry, sir."

"Who should be approached on your behalf?"

"I suppose Counselor Nhu's office."

"Because he commands the gendarmerie," Lodge said, spoon poised.

"That he does, sir. Runs the municipal police, the National Police, the military security service, and half a dozen secret police forces. Whichever police group is holding the deserter, they all work for Nhu."

Lodge looked amused. "You're refreshingly candid. Let me be candid in kind. I understand it would be logical to go to Counselor Nhu, given all the law enforcement agencies he runs. And yet . . . I might prefer not to."

"You mean, because Nhu hates you like poison and wishes you dead?"

Lodge cocked his head. "You're referring to the vehemence of his feelings because I've made it clear to Diem that Washington's continued support is contingent on Nhu's removal?"

"No, sir. I meant that Nhu's been making noises about assassinating you."

Lodge dabbed at his dish a few times before he glanced up. "How is it you're so well-informed?"

"I tune in to Radio Catinat. The only way to keep abreast."

"Radio Catinat? An English language broadcast?"

"No, sir. It's a string of rumor mills—bars, cafés—up and down rue Catinat."

"Radio Catinat seems to be right on the money." Lodge pinched the bridge of his nose. "Last week, CIA informed me that before she left the country for her tour of the US, Madame Nhu urged her husband to invade the embassy. The plan is to incite university students against Americans, and me in particular. Then student 'demonstrators'—most likely Special Forces in disguise and armed youths from the Republican Guards—will storm the embassy, seize the Buddhist dissidents I'm harboring, and kill me on their way out. Some of my staff think Nhu sent his wife out of the country so she'd be far from the event when it happens—and any repercussions. Which, of course, makes it awkward to approach Counselor Nhu for help in finding this Communist femme fatale."

"I can see that, sir."

Lodge drew a long breath. "I already have the First Lady of Viet Nam and her husband plotting my demise. Now the Communists have put their lovely sharpshooter on the job. General Harkins advises me not to take any of it personally." He smiled grimly. "We'd better get you the information you need."

The springboard sounded as a diver knifed into the water. Lodge consulted his watch.

"I've got a security briefing at the embassy in thirty minutes. I'd like you to sit in."

"Yes, sir."

Lodge wiped his lips and fingertips on his napkin. "I assume I can take you into my confidence." He clapped me on the shoulder as we rose.

"Never a good idea in Saigon, Ambassador."

CHAPTER THIRTEEN

The little American flags fluttering on the hood signaled the ambassador was aboard. Two Marines in khakis rode up front, and we sat in the padded interior behind a glass partition. The air-conditioning chilled me to the bone. The steel Checker limo had no visible armor but had bulletproof windows and rode heavy. It must have weighed several tons.

Security sucked everywhere in-country. Reinforced limousine aside, the ambassador's personal protection was more ceremonial than real. I didn't doubt the Marines' assault training but they weren't professional bodyguards and only carried .45 pistols.

Our Marine driver was steering an erratic course to the embassy, turning off the broad boulevard into a narrow street festooned with yellow and orange propaganda banners strung from building to building overhead. Normally a roundabout route would be a wise move, but it made me antsy that we couldn't maneuver on the tight one-way street. I'd have stayed with the wide avenue.

Traffic slowed. Two boys bore a rectangular table across the road in front of us, a tall teenager in front, his much shorter kid brother in back. The skirt board hid the head of the younger boy, making it look as though the table's back end had grown human legs.

The Checker came to a dead halt, stuck behind a water truck. A lady squatting by the curb picked at her bare feet and stared up at a woman in toreador pants standing alongside, her toenails painted a glistening red.

An iceman pedaled by, the glacier on the back of his bicycle covered in burlap. A nun, wearing black glasses and the full black habit of the Sisters of Mercy, abandoned her taxi and marched away on foot, an ancient leather briefcase under her arm. A regal elderly woman in a gray *ao dai* and darker gray pants glided past us, holding an English umbrella to protect her ivory skin from the intense light.

Someone on the sidewalk recognized Lodge and loudly announced his presence. People gathered, applauding, excited by the sight of him. Lodge waved, smiling. The door on his side clicked open.

"Jesus H. Christ," the Marine driver exclaimed. "He's getting out."

The gyrene pulled on the handbrake. His partner leapt out after the ambassador. Lodge pressed ahead. The Marine and I struggled to follow. The closer we got to Lodge the thicker the throng grew until he was entirely hemmed in, smiling and leaning down to listen respectfully to Vietnamese elders speaking French. The man definitely had the touch. If Vietnamese could vote in an American election, he'd win, hands down. But if a Viet Cong happened to be in this knot of Saigonese . . .

"We gotta go, sir," the Marine escort said real loud.

"Of course we do."

Lodge bid the assembly goodbye, extricated himself and returned to the Checker. Traffic restarted, only to stop again half a block later. The Marine guard in the front passenger seat mopped his brow. Lodge shifted against the gray upholstery, impatient.

Ignoring the heat, spiffy young men with bushy haircuts hustled cameras and showed off the watches on both their wrists. Children stepped into the street bearing trays of cakes, hawking them to drivers and passengers trapped in vehicles going nowhere. Vendors selling sugarcane, noodle soup, and rice cakes signaled their wares by clapping bamboo sticks, snapping scissors, or banging on small drums. A lady selling soda pop shook a necklace of bottle caps at us. A boy tapped on our window, startling the jumpy Marines. The grinning youngster held up the loose cigarettes he was selling and vanished in a cloud.

The explosion yanked the oxygen away hard before punching my eardrums and chest as the air rushed back with a thunderclap. A dense column of asphalt and shards geysered skyward. A small truck crashed to earth, its tires and driver on fire. Debris and spent shrapnel rained down on the limo, drumming the roof. The bulletproof windshield had cracked but held. The tiny flagpoles on the hood were twisted and bare. Our Marine driver cranked the ignition. Nothing. The steel-framed Checker had saved us but wasn't going anywhere.

"We need to get out of here," I shouted, pushing open my door. The punctured steel panel bled sand. Dust and smoke filled the air, soured by nitrates and vaporized aluminum powder. The smell of oil mixed with hot metal and ruined flesh.

Lodge and I tumbled out into the haze, coughing. The blown truck belched thick dark smoke, the orange flames driving it upward. Patriotic banners and tree branches burned. All was silent. Dazed, our driver leaned against the car, gun drawn, blood trickling from his ear. A mist of white particles swirled around us as in a snow globe. Casualties lay limp in the gutter, their clothes smoldering. The concussed staggered in circles, shirts and pants ripped, gums bleeding. The second Marine flopped out from the shotgun seat and dropped to his knees. A lamppost toppled into the road, bringing wires down onto a tree that immediately burst into flame.

Deafened by the blast, the lance corporal yelled, "Get back in the car. We gotta protect the ambassador until help arrives."

"Bad idea," I shouted back, leading Lodge forward by his elbow. "The first explosion's usually a diversion." I leaned close to his ear, not sure whether he could hear me or how loud I was yelling. "We've got to move in case there's another."

Lodge nodded, breathing through his mouth.

I could see no sign of a CIA tail or anyone else. Lodge's shadows remained in the shadows or were down themselves. I yelled at the corporal, "We gotta get the ambassador the fuck outta here."

"Our orders—"

"Screw orders."

"Aye, sir," he yelled.

Our driver slumped back into the limo. The gyrene and I flanked the ambassador and the three of us set off at a trot down a perpendicular street, passing an Indian fabric store, its dazed proprietor still holding out a sample of his wares. Shots popped somewhere nearby. Midway down the block we found a pedal-powered trishaw. I pushed Lodge onto its bench in front of the driver and jumped in beside the ambassador. Ambulance klaxons howled. A second explosion went off behind us. Maybe a car's gas tank, more likely a second dose of explosives.

"Ham Nghi thirty-nine," Lodge called up to the driver

seated behind us, who was wearing the telltale fatigues of an ARVN veteran. Lodge calmly repeated the address in French, using the older name of the street, Boulevard de la Somme.

A man ran up to us shouting, arms flailing, frightened out of his wits. My .38 froze him. I waved him away as the coolie pumped the pedals for all he was worth. The lance corporal jogged alongside, his tailored khakis streaked with grime and sweat, pistol swinging like a baton. As we picked up speed, he fell behind.

"A first for me, a getaway tricycle," Lodge said, smiling, as he slapped dust from his shoulder with a trembling hand. "Think that was our girl taking a crack at me?"

"Not her style." I pinched a bit of my sleeve to wipe the grit from my eyes. "Too sloppy." I squeezed my nostrils shut and tried to clear my ringing ears. "She wouldn't have missed."

"My security's certainly a bit primitive," Lodge said, brushing powdery debris from his hair.

"That it is. Yes, sir."

He turned toward the passing traffic. "If I followed my instinct for self-preservation, I'd put you in charge of my security on the spot. But . . . that would hamper your investigation. I need you to find this woman before she brings down her next target, whether or not it's me." He looked back at the smoky air behind us. "But whenever you feel it's warranted, I want you to speak up. I'd like to make it home to my wife in one piece."

"Yes, sir." My bones ached. My lungs felt thick. "You're aware CIA could give you a damn sight better protection than what you've got," I said.

"Everything I do would be easier if I could trust our CIA agents. They've grown too close to their Vietnamese counterparts and have their own ideas about what our stance toward the regime should be. I can't have CIA operatives working at cross-purposes from mine. When their station chief was recalled, they got a clear warning to step back from their local contacts, or else. Yet they still maintain their old private channels."

"Can't say I blame them."

Lodge stiffened. "How not?"

"They've spent years cozying up to Vietnamese officials and generals—exactly like they were told. Of course they got close. They aren't about to flush those relationships because this month the suits in Washington want to dump Diem's brother in the crapper, maybe Diem too. They don't want to see all their risks and hard work go for nothing. And they want to shield old friends who are afraid for their lives, afraid for their families." He had to know all this, but he'd asked me to speak up, so I told him.

"Fair enough. But it means I can't trust them. Nor they me."

"Too bad," I said. "They're the ones with the manpower, the resources, the hidden assets it would take to protect you."

His eyes narrowed. "Hidden agendas too. You don't, Sergeant. There's nothing opaque about you. You didn't study Machiavelli at Harvard. Your father wasn't in the Skull and Bones at Yale, or an OSS recruit."

"Got an uncle who's a Mason."

He laughed. "Splendid. Just like George Washington." Lodge dabbed his neck with a handkerchief. "We have a good deal in common, Sergeant. I'm not much of a team player either. I can't imagine that frank attitude of yours makes life in the military easy."

We hit a pothole and the trishaw lurched. My stomach, too. Lodge went pale. I felt pale.

"By the way, Sergeant, my wife isn't aware of the threats on my life. I'd appreciate you not mentioning any of this if you meet."

"Course, sir."

"Or this tremor in my hand."

"Probably just adrenaline."

"It's visited off and on since Africa. Embarrassing. Maybe just age. You'll keep my secret, I trust, even if—as you've pointed out—no one in Saigon is to be trusted."

"Not if you have future plans, Ambassador."

We turned onto the broad, tree-lined boulevard and rolled toward the seedy six-story office building that passed for the US Embassy. The route was too direct. I had the trishaw driver go around the block. We hung a right and a left, followed by another left at the British Embassy, approaching our destination at the rounded corner, where white mice lounged in the open back of a parked armored personnel carrier.

I threw our driver a handful of piasters and helped Lodge out of the trishaw. We wobbled unsteadily past the white concrete-filled barrels into the skimpy barbed-wire funnel. Several Marine guards rushed out to escort us the last twelve feet to the front entrance. We'd made it.

Lodge quietly ordered their sergeant to see to the two Marines we'd left behind. Turning to me, he said, "Sergeant Miser."

"Yes, sir?"

"Your seersucker. It's smoldering."

CHAPTER FOURTEEN

The embassy's brand new air-conditioned conference room, Lodge explained, had become the temporary living quarters of the *bonze* who had led the Buddhist uprising and several of his brother monks. Ignoring all official demands to surrender them, Lodge had granted the monks indefinite sanctuary. So the morning's security briefing would have to make do with an older room on the fourth floor. Paint peeled and flaked from the shabby walls. The cracked ceiling dripped plaster.

Lodge handed his jacket off to someone to have it sponge-cleaned and went into the meeting in shirtsleeves, primping his hair with his hand. I took off Robeson's jacket, doused it with a glass of water and dropped it into a metal rubbish bin. We got odd looks from the group seated around a scuffed oval table, but nobody said a word as Lodge introduced me to a guy from embassy security and "Donald" from CIA.

The ambassador gave a brief after-action report about our close shave, shrugging off the idea that he had been the target. The others in the room seemed less convinced. The security officer reviewed new safety precautions and said the chancery was henceforth closed to all Vietnamese nationals. Access to non-Americans would be limited to the USAID offices in the annex next door.

Lodge turned to his gatekeeper and personal assistant, who

had slipped into the chair just behind the ambassador: blue-eyed, black-haired Colonel Mike Dunn, a seriously decorated artillery officer. Mike Dunn was known to like his fellow Catholic, President Diem, but he also toed the official line drawn by his boss.

"Mike, have a warning issued immediately to all US officers at all ranks. Authorize the discreet carrying of personal weapons."

"The regime won't like our people going around the city armed," he said.

"Let's set that nicety aside until this Communist agent is dealt with." Lodge turned to Donald CIA. "Should I worry about President Diem's safety? How good is his protection?"

"Massive. Although we have new intelligence of some unusual surveillance going on."

"Of Diem?"

"Of his personal secretary."

Lodge peered over his reading glasses. "Viet Cong agents are following the president's secretary?"

"No, sir. Nhu's secret police are."

"Why would Nhu have the poor man followed? Hasn't he been the president's trusted secretary for years?"

"Nhu suspects everyone," said Donald. "And the secretary recently pleaded with one of our foreign-service officers to save Diem by getting rid of Nhu."

"Just as Washington is urging."

"Yes, sir. But once Nhu got wind of that, he'd have his snoops watching the guy every waking moment."

Mike Dunn weighed in. "They're coming apart over in the palace, panicking that the end is nigh."

Donald said, "Cao Xuan Vy is also being followed."

Lodge raised an eyebrow. "Mr. Vy being who?"

Donald CIA sucked his cigarette. "One of the president's longtime personal bodyguards. Vy also heads Brother Nhu's armed youth militia."

"The Republican Guard," Mike Dunn added. "Nhu's answer to Hitler Youth."

Lodge looked to Donald. "Does Counselor Nhu believe the Communist assassin might be able to persuade Mr. Vy to betray the president?"

"Any close-range attempt on President Diem would have to go through Mr. Vy. Nhu's worried he may've been turned."

"By the Communists."

"No, sir."

"Who then?"

"By us."

The ambassador sat back. "Please elaborate."

"Last month, the chief of Special Police made a public claim that CIA has marked Diem for assassination. Turning his secretary or bodyguard would be the most direct route."

Lodge inhaled deeply. "Donald, please assure me there's nothing to this fear of theirs but paranoia."

Donald raised three fingers in a scout's-honor gesture and everybody laughed.

Lodge rubbed his left shoulder, flexing it a little. The trembling left hand stayed out of sight, under the table. He turned to the blonde taking the minutes.

"Send an alert to the palace. Say that until the assassin has been apprehended, we urge their highest officials and general officers to take appropriate precautions. Assure them we have genuine concern for their safety."

Lodge explained to the room that I needed to obtain an interrogation report from the National Police that might provide some leads about the Viet Cong newcomer who'd been killing Americans and was possibly now targeting Diem.

"I've got a solid contact in Counselor Nhu's office," Donald from CIA volunteered. "Why don't I mosey over to the palace after the meeting and fetch the report?"

"No," Lodge snapped. "Keep to my directive. No one moseys over or makes a casual phone call. No one makes drinks dates. No one accepts an invitation to dinner or so much as attends a christening without my express approval."

Which wouldn't be forthcoming, I thought. Lodge's easy public style won over the ordinary citizens in the street. But with his staff, Lodge behaved more like a shit-kicking interrogator in a Senate committee than a genteel Yankee ambassador.

"Nothing is to be conveyed," Lodge went on, "none of our positions are to be softened—or hardened—other than by me. No intelligence goes to the palace, either, and most certainly not about any South Vietnamese opposition to the president."

Like Nhu, Lodge seemed not to trust anyone. Rumors had it that no classified communications were transmitted from the embassy to Washington except by Lodge. I'd heard he even typed some communiqués himself. Likewise, incoming cables came only to him. Lodge had blacked out his own staff, even General Harkins, cabling Washington about the military situation in Viet Nam without bothering to consult the commanding four-star general. Harkins and Diem liked each other, which was enough to make the general untrustworthy in Lodge's eyes.

Maybe back in Washington they were having trouble making up their minds where they stood on Diem, but Lodge showed no signs of indecision. If Diem and Nhu wished to communicate with the American government they'd have to come to him, appropriate reforms in hand. And Nhu's exit still topped that list.

Donald from CIA shrank back, reprimanded. "Understood, sir. You talk to the regime. No one else."

"Good," Lodge said. "I also want all relevant intelligence on this lady assassin to be made available to Investigator Miser and his associate, ah—" He looked to me.

"Sergeant Clovis Robeson."

"Agent Robeson, yes. Henceforth CIA will avail Agents Robeson and Miser of all classified intelligence materials relating to her. Am I clear?"

"Yes, sir," everyone chimed.

"Do you have any questions concerning my instructions?"

"Several, sir," said the CIA man. "How do I carry them on the access list? I mean, there's the question of clearances and—"

"I'll take responsibility for their clearances," Lodge said.

"Sir," Donald interrupted. "I'm not sure your regulations permit—"

"We've just formulated new ones," Lodge said, annoyed.

"Excuse me," I interrupted, hand half-raised like a grade-schooler. "My partner and I have clearances through Top Secret, and unlimited arrest authority on up through generals and GS-16s."

"But not ambassadors," said Lodge, wryly.

"No, sir. Though we're working on it."

That got a ripple of a smile, even from Donald. Lodge's eyes crinkled politely. He brought both hands up on the table. "All right. I suppose we need a contingency plan in case it's me at the top of her to-do list and she succeeds in her objective."

Donald CIA said, "Already in place, Mr. Ambassador."

"Ah. How diligent."

"Thank you, sir."

Lodge constructed a smile. "What exactly happens if she manages to rend me asunder?"

"The Seventh Fleet comes in, dependents go out. We stand by for instructions from the secretary of state"—Donald looked him dead in the eye—"and await the arrival of the next ambassador."

Lodge nodded. "Quite proportionate and proper. An effusive memorial service would be appropriate too."

Everybody laughed. Lodge rose and the room with him.

"Sir," Mr. CIA interrupted.

"Yes, Donald."

"One last thing. If the rumored rebellion against Diem actually materializes, the code word we'll transmit to announce it is *durian*, as in the fruit."

"Zombie fruit?" the security chief said, making a face. Vietnamese cooks made gorgeous desserts out of durian, but raw it smelled like rotting corpses.

"Durian," Lodge repeated. "Everyone got that? Very well. We're done, gentlemen."

Lodge summoned me to join him but Donald CIA blocked my path.

"Excuse me," I said, trying to slip past.

Donald smirked and stepped aside. "Mustn't keep the Man waiting."

I caught up with the ambassador and followed him to the elevator.

"Don't mind Donald," he said. "He's a tad resentful because he was close to former Station Chief Richardson. A lot of folks—including Donald—hold me responsible for Richardson's recall and tattered career." He glanced away. "As well they might."

CHAPTER FIFTEEN

Saigon had the largest American embassy staff in the world, so I expected Lodge's office to be grand, but the suite was barely ordinary. Unsafe too. Someone could practically step into his window from the terrace of the adjoining apartment building. A new embassy was badly needed.

"Sir." I nodded toward the neighboring balcony. "Even a crappy marksman could make easy work of you at that distance."

"True," Lodge agreed. "Which is why Mike Dunn had that building bought to ruin the sight lines into my office. Worse, he keeps insisting on closing my shutters no matter how hellishly hot it gets. And as you can see, I've been provided with personal weapons in case we're boarded."

He indicated a small side table where a Police Special .38 revolver sat next to a fat Dictaphone machine.

"It wouldn't discourage a real mob for very long, but it packs all the authority you can fit in a desk drawer. Fred Flott's in the adjoining office with a Schmeisser machine pistol, commandeered from the CIA's non-attributable weapons stash. It's an arms wonderland down there, Freddy says."

A half-eaten jar of baby food sat in the middle of the ambassador's desk. Ulcers, I wondered, or just an attack of the tropics?

I was surprised how quiet and empty the entire floor was.

Everyone had been cleared out to make room for the ambassador; his appointments secretary, Mrs. Lacey; and his two closest aides, Mike Dunn and Freddy Flott. Lodge had worked with Colonel Dunn at the Pentagon and brought him to Saigon as his ass-kicker. Flott, a former infantry officer and a friend of Lodge's son, was the ambassador's official French interpreter, not that he really needed one.

Lodge's classy secretary, Mrs. Lacey, appeared in the doorway. From the way Lodge groused about signing his correspondence and initialing the cables she spread in front of him, it was clear he wasn't the paperwork type. The scuttlebutt about Lodge looked to be true: that he'd gotten a taste for action in the tank corps in North Africa and felt shortchanged in most of his jobs since. Judging from his excited reaction to the street bombing, and given the two office pistols—the .38 Special and a .357 Magnum poking out from under a briefing book—I suspected the dangers of his new post were to his liking.

Mrs. Lacey reported the ambassador's Checker limo had been towed to the embassy motor pool, its front tires flat, one door completely misshapen. The Marine escorts looked the worse for wear, too, the driver hospitalized with concussion and ruptured eardrums, his partner already treated and released for limited duty.

"Anyone see the car arrive, Mrs. Lacey?" Lodge squinted. "Reporters, I mean."

"Only one or two."

"Good." Lodge slipped into his jacket. "Don't confirm my presence at the scene when they come snooping. No need to hand our adversaries a propaganda victory, however minor."

Mrs. Lacey nodded and reminded him of an upcoming meeting with Lucien Conein.

Lucien Conein —"Black Luigi"—featured in many a Radio Catinat legend. A former French legionnaire who had been in Viet Nam on and off since he parachuted into the country to battle the Japanese occupiers, he had briefly fought alongside Ho Chi Minh. He had a reputation as an expert OSS saboteur too. After the partition of the country in 1954, he'd rigged a surprise for the new Communist occupant of the Hanoi mansion where he'd been staying: a refrigerator full of hidden C3 explosives wired to detonate when the fridge got plugged in. The American consul had thoughtfully disarmed Black Luigi's booby trap before it could blow anybody up.

"Conein's CIA, isn't he?" I asked Lodge.

"Yes, but he reports directly to me."

From Lodge's expression, Conein was one of the few people he trusted besides his aides, Mike Dunn and Fred Flott. Maybe me, now. Lodge seemed to have isolated everyone else.

Lodge finally introduced me to Mrs. Lacey.

"Thanks to Sergeant Miser's quick thinking," he said, "we escaped the scene unscathed."

She brushed away a stray gray strand and smiled at me. "Well done, Sergeant. You're most certainly going on the Christmas card list this year."

THE GIVRAL BAKERY and café, the town's number-one rumor station, stood catty-corner from the National Assembly. Assembly members sometimes stopped in, as did attachés from the various embassies.

The shoeshine kid waved us into his shady parking spot and we did our customary negotiation over the fee to guard the jeep and our Prick-10 field radio. I liked the little mercenary. As soon as we agreed on the price, he tossed his polish and rags into an olive-green ammo can and piled in behind the wheel, joined quickly by his gang.

Café Givral had the hottest gossip and coldest air-conditioning in Saigon. "Ah, *climatisé*," Robeson sighed and licked his parched lips as we entered. The icy currents raised the sunburn on my neck.

Onetime legionnaire André Lebon was at his usual table, snowing German reporters with stories about how he'd lost his foot at Dien Bien Phu. At the next table, half a dozen Western ladies in summery Parisian blouses and chino skirts enjoyed ice creams and pastries. Across the room, a group of Catholic Relief Services women in open-toed shoes shared a dish of flan along with a bar of the blackest chocolate.

A few threadbare Frenchmen hid behind newspapers, nursing their coffees like boulevardiers, waiting to shop bits of information to intelligence operatives for a few bucks. So far the only one who'd found a taker was Jacques Rae, bending the ear of gents from the French SDECE and the Cambodian Deuxième Bureau. Next to them, a pair of retired French policemen were loudly giving it away to impress their CIA guest with their formerly hush-hush work in Indochina.

We took a table next to the duo of *Le Monde* correspondents—French Olivier and Italian Enrico—who practically lived at the Givral. Olivier was revisiting the rumor that Madame Nhu had personally set fire to a section of houses with wooden roofs to force through a law requiring metal ones, because she had recently purchased a factory that made galvanized metal sheets.

The waiter took our order, then spoke to Robeson in a speedy mix of French and Vietnamese I couldn't follow.

"He's curious where I'm from," Robeson explained. "*Nouvelle Orléans,*" he said to the waiter.

"*Ahhh, oui,*" the man said, "*le* jazz," and happily mimicked a clarinet.

"Got anything juicy?" I asked the journalists.

Olivier beckoned us closer. "An American general just flew his Korean mistress in from Seoul aboard his personal military transport."

The rest of the day's gossip concerned the going prices the wives of Saigon's ruling elite were negotiating for their husbands' latest government positions. Not bribes, of course, Olivier insisted sarcastically.

"The wives deal in 'gifts of esteem and gratitude,'" he said with panache. "Their men touch nothing. *Hót của*—harvesting the wealth—is woman's work."

Wives ran the family finances and came to "understandings" with their counterparts about their spouses' salaries and advancements, who got trade permits, whose children could get visas to go abroad, and whose sons could escape military service by leaving the country to study or getting a soft noncombatant's army posting somewhere civilized. Of course, at the very top of that hierarchy of "understandings" sat Diem's sister-in-law, Madame Nhu, receiving her cut and amassing a fortune.

"Gratitude flows ever upward in Saigon," Olivier said and sipped his coffee. "Entry visas, exit visas, passports. Business is brisk."

"In permissions to divorce too," said Enrico. "Except for Madame Nhu's sister—no sale there. She will not be let out of her marriage to run off with her French lover. The sister, she cuts her wrists after Madame Nhu says to her this news.

Howling and bleeding, she runs through the family quarters in the palace."

"Ah, the dramatic opera of the ruling classes," Olivier said. "Madame Nhu commands like an empress. She has far more the personality of a ruler than Diem or Nhu."

"No Nhus is good Nhus," Enrico quipped. Olivier came back with a joke about "Diemocracy."

Enrico turned serious. The latest Vietnamese official to land on Brother Nhu's shit list had just been posted to Dam Doi as punishment for protesting the mistreatment of peasants, he said. We all groaned. Few civil servants survived Dam Doi. The Viet Cong were hard on Saigon's lackeys in what they considered their territory. But the odds were even worse in Nhu's gulags, so the administrator had gratefully accepted the new job and was leaving the next day, right after finalizing his will.

"Nhu feeds another man of integrity to the enemy," Olivier said. "I suppose it saves him the trouble of imprisoning the poor fellow. His jails are entirely full, after all."

As the waiter delivered our Cokes and burgers, I asked for the latest word on possible coups.

"The twenty-sixth of this month, Independence Day," Enrico whispered. "I hear that is the leap on."

"Jump-off," Olivier corrected and dabbed his lips. "Perhaps because—as we are hearing it—Diem plans to reshuffle the generals' commands after Independence Day to break up their alliances. In the meantime the generals feed Diem false information about Viet Cong activity to justify moving troops where they will need them for the coup. But I understand the senior military men, like Big Minh and General Don, are still suffering from an excess of caution. The *je-ne-rals* frighten and back away. The younger officers are not so nervous. They are poised to strike immediately. So the crafty old horses of war keep ordering deployments that disrupt any schemes of coup d'état by the young Turks."

"Do any of 'em, young or old, really have the balls to take down their president?" Robeson said.

"Diem is ripe for the picking," Olivier said, "if they can bring themselves to trust their fellow officers. Of course, they'd need also the right assurances from your embassy."

"Enrico," Robeson said, "how many coups are cooking, at last count?"

"For sure six. Is possible now seven."

"Who's behind the latest one?" I said.

"Good you are sitting," Enrico whispered, and edged closer. "Brother of President Diem—Monsieur Nhu."

"No shit," Robeson said, and took a swig of Coke.

Enrico made a pinched face. "We think Nhu he spreads this rumor himself to draw real plotters to the *faux* coup and unmask them so he can purge them from the government, perhaps from the earth. He has done it before."

"And a *coup manqué* cleverly sows confusion," Olivier explained. "It makes officers worry about how genuine the conspirators are who invite them to join the next one."

Enrico shrugged. "Counselor Nhu, he likes everyone in the dark." He tented his fingers together. "One week he agrees to leave the government 'for his brother's sake and for the country.' The week that follows he recants and complains Diem is incompetent, not worthy to govern."

"So his coup could roll up conspirators," I said, "or roll up on his older brother. You think Supreme Leader Nhu's got plans that don't include Diem?"

Olivier tapped his lip. "He doesn't lack for ambition and

certainly has the ego. Nhu runs the show already from the wings, like your Wizard of Oz. He writes Diem's speeches and pronouncements, prepares his answers for press interviews. Nhu issues orders to Diem's ministers in meetings the president chairs. Put a question to Diem and Nhu answers." Olivier blotted his forehead. "Diem seems to know only what Nhu wants him to know."

Enrico speculated that Madame Nhu might want to make Nhu's unofficial presidency official. Perhaps she was looking to the lady assassin to make a martyr of her brother-in-law, catapulting her husband into the presidency on a wave of sympathy. What did I think?

I thought the only sure bet was that if a coup came, Vietnamese officers would die, shot for their loyalty or shot for their disloyalty, depending on who won. If the young studs seized power, for sure the senior generals and colonels would soon be locking horns with their juniors. If those crafty generals pulled it off first, the younger officers would grouse and plot against their jaded elders. Either way there'd be *beaucoup* coup attempts to follow, turmoil both the Viet Cong and Givral patrons would welcome.

A platinum blonde stopped by to chat with Enrico in Italian. Robeson and I turned back to our food.

"Uncle Sam owes you a seersucker jacket," I said to Robeson and quietly filled him in on the morning's events. He informed me that lunch at the Givral was on me, and that I'd probably be picking up the tab for the rest of the year.

Mouth full, Robeson said, "While you were busy hobnobbing with the higher-highers, I started thinking about the Red Queen making her bones with those road ambushes. Figured maybe ARVN or our advisors had done after-action reports on some of 'em."

"You found the reports?"

"Ask and ye shall receive. Actually, Missy Blue asked and she received. I got plenty to show you."

"Like what?" I said, stealing some of his fries.

Licking ketchup from his thumb, he glanced around at the clientele. "Not here."

I covered the bill and we got up to leave.

"You are hear this?" Enrico said, pointing to an attaché who had joined them. "The vehicle of your ambassador? Attacked not three hours ago. Good fortune, His Excellency was not within."

"Saints be praised," I said, easing past Robeson toward the door.

CHAPTER SIXTEEN

Robeson pulled color photographs from a manila folder and laid them out on his desk. "Take a look at these photos from three Tay Ninh after-action reports. Each picture here is of a different kill zone she set up."

The first shot showed a wrecked ARVN truck where it had stopped to aid the stranded young beauty, her disabled bicycle still propped upside down, tires in the air. Another ambush site showed a bike lying twisted and wrecked in a ditch. Red arrows on both photos indicated the directions from which the VC had attacked.

"Look at the arrows," Robeson said. "They never once struck from where you'd expect, not any of the likely places, like thick scrub or jungle. Mostly they attack from open ground."

"You're right," I said, sifting through the photos. "There's nothing by way of cover for the attackers."

Robeson went on. "Half the time comrades popped out of spider holes hidden in bare, hard earth. In this attack, from a produce stand sitting out in the open. And in this one, from behind a schoolhouse close to the road, books scattered across desks, maybe students inside when it all goes down. Can you imagine, VC cutting loose with automatic weapons from a classroom full of kids?"

"Total shock and little to no return fire."

"Exactly," he said. "These ambush schemes employed heavily prepared positions, clever camouflage and firing angles. Everything worked out in advance. The lone civilian who witnessed the last incident reported that the attack took seconds."

"Obviously well-prepped and planned," I agreed.

"Roger that. Being the underdog, they can't afford not to plan every detail. Somethin' you taught me back when we were advisors, Sarge. You said then the Viet Cong aren't partial to winging it."

If the southerners were the Italians of Indochina, the North Vietnamese were the Germans, made even more rigid by the Maoist hardliners who'd come to advise and train them. Over time they'd foisted this stick-up-the-ass approach on their southern Viet Cong brethren.

"Crouch assumed the Red Queen was improvising blitz attacks," Robeson continued.

"Making her unpredictable and just about impossible to interdict."

"With what we're lookin' at here, I'm convinced she don't do anything on the fly." Robeson opened a second manila envelope and pulled out black-and-white photographs. "The speed of the incidents don't mean the action's random."

"What are those?" I craned my neck to see.

"Pics from Crouch's crappy files on the previous two killings."

"We've seen them before," I said.

"Yeah, but look at the close-up of the ground at the first one." He lay the picture in front of me. "See the glints? The shiny bits? I don't think that's tinsel."

"Any closer shots?"

"They're pretty skimpy."

"Any close-ups from the second killing?"

"None that show anything useful."

"Crouch, did he remember what that was on the ground?"

"No. Looked at the picture and thought maybe chewing-gum foil."

"Crouch is full of shit."

"Me, I think it's bits and pieces of another astrologer's kit."

"You think an astrologer was at two scenes?"

"Maybe all three." Robeson spread the photos like a fan. "I'm thinking he's her spotter. Like you said, Crouch is full of shit. This young miss ain't flyin' by the seat of her pretty pantaloons. She don't just pick random targets, plug the first American officer she sees. Look how she ran her damsel-in-distress roadside number back in Tay Ninh. A team of hardcore hard-asses: painstaking, careful, disciplined as hell. That's how she'll be working in Saigon."

"So say the locations are picked way in advance. Places American officers frequent. All the locations right on the street. Easy way in, easy way out. At a prearranged time, the spotter marks a target and holds him in place for her until she arrives."

"She don't need to roam the streets looking for a clean shot at an American officer. She just has to roll by the appointed spot at the appointed time. She fires, she books. Everybody dives for cover, hugs the ground, and by the time they look up she's long gone."

"So what size operation are we looking at to pull this off?" I said. "There's her, there's the driver."

"Drivers," Robeson corrected. "Three of 'em: a young male in his twenties, a man in his forties, and an older guy north of fifty. Then there's the fortune-teller who bullseyes the poor soul, keeps him still until she shows."

"Most likely there's at least one comrade protecting her," I said. "Covering her back."

"Yeah," Robeson agreed. "That's one, maybe two more cadre. Easily hidden among the onlookers."

Captain Deckle emerged from his office and we laid out our thinking. He ticked off the headcount on his fingers. "Driver. Spotter. Plus, her rear guard. That's three. Four, if there's a second rear guard. Lady Death makes five."

"The other two drivers," I said, "totals seven."

Captain Deckle frowned. "Unless they're rotating as the backups in the crowd. That would keep it to five."

"She'd go with the lower headcount," Robeson said. "Less exposure."

"But if they're scouting locations ahead of time," Deckle said, "that gives us a chance to intercept her if we can crack her team. Who's the weak link?"

"The drivers?" Robeson suggested.

I shook my head. "I bet you she climbs on the Vespa at some corner where the driver's been told to wait, probably instructed not to turn around. She gets aboard, they go, his eyes glued to the road. Afterward, she hops off along the escape route and disappears. He never sees her full face. At most, just flashes of her over his shoulder."

"Makes sense," Deckle conceded. "Her commissars would want her to stay cloaked as long as possible. Minimum face-to-face contact. The longer she stays unidentified, the longer she stays in business."

Robeson bit his lip. "But if the other two drivers also double as her backup, mixed in with the crowd at the point of attack, they must get a good look at her while they're waiting for her entrance. I mean, they gotta be curious."

"How much of a look?" I argued. "She's got the hat on, she's behind the driver. The backups' job is to scan the crowd, stay alert for trouble."

"The fortune-teller." Robeson said. "He's got clear sight of her each time she rides up."

"He's gotta be busy distracting the target. But you may be right that he's our best bet."

"So how in hell do we find him?" Robeson said. "All we've got is bits of bone and mirror. Oh, and the torn paper from under Major Furth's chair with the astrological hocus-pocus and Chinese characters."

I took out the evidence box and brought the scrap of the chart to Miss Blue's desk to ask her to see what she could make of it. She nodded.

Deckle got a call and waved us over. Captain Ting of the National Police, VBI criminal investigations, was on the line, requesting our immediate presence at a crime scene.

CHAPTER SEVENTEEN

We tore over to Lam Son Square and pulled up alongside Ting's unmarked Renault outside the Continental, Franchini's other hotel. Vietnamese detectives were screeching to the curb in Black Marias, sirens braying like mules. Ting had said to meet him here, but there was no sign of him. No downed MAAG officer at the terrace café either. Confused, we followed the Vietnamese cops inside.

The Continental's Belgian manager stood in the lobby, wringing his hands. Captain Ting was upstairs, he said. The polished-wood birdcage elevator with its beveled mirrors was—as usual—out of order, so we rushed past the manager up the imposing staircase. Two surly Vietnamese Special Police challenged us on the landing, disappointed to hear we were there at the captain's summons. They would've liked nothing better than to get in our faces, things being more tense than usual between local law enforcement and us overpaid and under-cultured big-dog Americans. Another pair happily blocked a *Newsweek* journalist emerging from his office to see what the ruckus was about.

We found Captain Ting in the hallway, tugging back the cuff of his white shirt to consult the gold-filled Bulova on his wrist. Ting was a devoted fan of American and French films and in better times he'd liked to meet me at the movies when we needed to put our heads together someplace dark. As a Vietnamese, he wasn't allowed to patronize the new American theater, so we'd have a bite at Cheap Charlie's before going to his favorite tacky theater in Cholon. But I hadn't heard from him in weeks. Thanks to Nhu's suspicions about Americans' intentions toward Diem, no one in government could afford to be seen fraternizing with a long nose in public. The watchers were being watched. Everyone was scared and trying to keep clear of the regime as its end approached. I appreciated him reaching out in spite of it.

Since he'd called us in, I'd assumed the victim was a fourth MAAG officer, but Ting nudged open the door of a small suite where a Vietnamese general's khaki blouse lay neatly over the back of an armchair, his pants folded on the seat.

"*Le géneral Lang est mort*," Ting said.

I blanched. "Yeah, I'll say."

The room smelled like an abattoir. Black blood pooled on the floor. The ceiling fan was churning, but the Saigon heat was already doing its work on the body. The general lay on his back on the sagging bed, clearly naked beneath a sheet. The round base of a wineglass protruded from his chest, the stem buried deep between his ribs. Robeson pointed to the sodden red silk impaled on the glass spike. "Don't look like that came with the champagne."

Ting remained in the doorway, hands clasped behind his back. "Hotel linen only white." He nodded toward the bucket where a magnum rested in a pool of melted ice, a white serving cloth expertly knotted around its neck. Ting was careful to keep his distance from the corpse and any dripping surfaces, not wishing to soil his immaculate white shirt and pressed slacks—or disturb the man's ghost. "Bottle almost empty," he said. In his halting English, Ting explained he'd learned from the general's aide that a woman had shared the general's last hours. The victim had brought her to the hotel himself. A one-night stand, his aide assumed, since she wasn't the man's regular mistress. The lieutenant had discreetly avoided gazing at the young woman in the black *ao dai*, though he'd wanted to. She hadn't carried so much as a purse, just a thin red scarf.

"All that champagne in his system must've slowed him up," I said to Robeson. "That would have helped her get it done. Any reason to think it's not our girl?"

"Only if the Commies are fielding whole platoons of killer babes carrying red silk scarves." He cupped his nose against the smell and pointed to the swollen mass around the general's right eye socket. "Looks like she gave him a major shiner during the struggle." Robeson pushed aside the mosquito netting and lifted the sheet, revealing a soggy mess around the corpse.

While he examined the body, I slipped into the bathroom. Wet towels lay where she'd tossed them on the tiles of the stall shower. A blood-streaked hand towel hung on the rail, properly folded. Upside down in the drain of the sink was the crystal champagne flute she'd snapped off to make her weapon.

"She's one cool customer," I said to Robeson, returning to the carnage.

"A lot of guts," he agreed. "Taking on a stocky male like that in a locked room armed with nothing but stemware and surprise. Not a peaceful way to die, bleeding out, spraying like a fountain. He couldn't have gone easy."

I pointed at the crystal stem. "If that had hit a rib, she'd have been alone in a confined space with a wounded guy fearing for his life. She's always worked in the open where it's easy to get away quickly. She's got world-class skills with a gun. Why change tactics? Why change weapons?"

Robeson scratched an ear. "Say they cased him. Saw he had a weakness for the ladies. She exploits his need for privacy, comes at his invitation wearing nothing but an *ao dai* and a scarf. Harmless-looking young girl. She had to change weapons."

"Why take the risk? She could've gone with a smaller gun. Strapped it to her ankle under the pantaloons. Smuggled in a garrote, a blade. I mean, she's in here with no help. No good way to escape if things go wrong."

Robeson turned in a circle, surveying the room. "Her *ao dai* must've been smeared head to foot. What's she do for clean clothes? No overnight bag, no shoulder bag. She must have had an accomplice staying in the hotel or on staff."

"She didn't need a change of clothes," I concluded. "They weren't here to talk politics. She undresses in the bathroom. Hangs up the *ao dai*. Goes to him starkers, with the scarf hiding the broken-off stem."

"You thinking she did him before she did him?"

"Or when he was . . . most distracted."

"Man oh man. That's so cold it's hot."

"Then she goes and showers, washes off all the blood. Puts on her clean *ao dai*. Quietly slips away."

"Premeditated as hell," Robeson said. "Y'all see a picture card anywhere, Sarge?" He started going through the night table closest to the door.

I rifled the blank stationery on the small writing desk. *Punctilious service and social eminence,* read the hotel's ad card. *Favored by discriminating travelers.* And beautiful killers. No playing card. Nothing in the center drawer of the wooden secretary either. I pinched a hotel envelope, slipped in as much of the glass flute as

I could retrieve from the bathroom sink, folded it lengthwise and slid it gently into my shirt pocket.

Ting pretended not to notice that I was removing evidence. His department had a fancy crime lab thanks to generous US advisors, yet he clearly wanted me to have her prints, maybe to confirm her identity if either of us ever bagged her. Or . . . maybe he needed me to preserve the prints because officially nothing was going to be left of the scene: no photos, no evidence of what had happened. Witnesses would be warned off. The police captain's immediate concern would be concealing the circumstances of the general's demise, not finding the Red Queen.

Senior plainclothes dicks like Captain Ting of the new Vietnamese Bureau of Investigation were repackaged old-school Sûreté detectives trained by the French, coached and equipped for years by Michigan State University's policing experts, presently mentored by CIA operatives. Plainclothes VBI detectives weren't any less corrupt than their white mice colleagues, just better paid and more sophisticated in their extortions. Some, like Ting, showed some class, even a little reluctance. Meaning they might apologize if they ever had to squeeze your nuts or erase evidence.

"What branch of the army did the general belong to?" I said.

"General Nguyễn Văn Lang's post is at headquarter," Ting replied.

"What did he do at headquarter?"

"Work with Directorate of Supply. And at Ngân Hàng Quốc Gia also."

"What the fuck is that, Captain?"

"National Bank, Viet Nam."

The red scarf was cut away on Ting's orders. With great difficulty two policemen cocooned the body in two ponchos and lifted the general onto a litter. Messy work. The cops were smeared. Half the hotel must have heard by now; no matter how much Ting's bosses might wish or pretend, no way would all this stay secret.

"Unseemly business," Ting said, repeating a favorite expression he'd borrowed from a British war flick we'd seen together at the small Shell Theatre beneath the apartment building the oil company maintained for its employees. Ting added his customary, "Bad thing, very bad thing," his face somber. "General Lang have wife, many childrens." He warbled something showy in French that sounded like a poodle gargling.

I cocked an eyebrow at Robeson. "What's he sayin'?"

"*Il me semble parfois que mon sang coule à flots/Ainsi qu'une fontaine aux rythmiques sanglots . . . Fait pour donner á boire á ces cruelles filles,*" Robeson repeated. "My blood gushes like a fountain and is given to whores to drink."

I whistled. Ting allowed himself a sheepish grin. "Baudelaire," he said, a frog poet I knew he liked.

"'Tutti frutti, oh rooti,'" I said. "Beau de Little Richard."

The grin vanished. "*Assez vu,*" Ting announced. "Enough seen," Robeson whispered.

Captain Ting stepped into the hall to check on his men's progress. I followed. Ting's detectives had already questioned the room-service waiter, the doormen, clerks, and floor maids. Aside from the waiter who had delivered champagne, no one had seen the Red Queen or the general after they closeted themselves in his suite. The general's aide had talked the night manager into letting him sack out in the room of a Dutch journalist away on assignment. No one remembered seeing the heartbreakingly innocent young woman leave the hotel. Certainly no one had copped to helping her escape.

"Any chance she's still here," I said to Ting, "hidden in a room of her own?"

"Hotel not big," he said and flicked his hand. "She gone."

Robeson joined us. "No one saw her split, *Dai uy*? A boss fox like that?"

"Maybe she *qui*," Ting suggested. "Evil spirit."

"Is that right?" Robeson looked somber. He was church-raised but took supernatural doings real serious. He used to say his late granny had conversations with the dead while they lay in rest at the family funeral parlor.

Ting glanced around to make sure none of his men were near enough to see him pull out a handkerchief and extract a circular silvery medallion.

"What the fuck is that?" I said.

Ting grunted. "Found on body. You take."

He dropped the medallion back in the handkerchief and handed it to me. Robeson opened the cloth to get a closer look. Within the medallion's outer ring a hollow triangle framed an engraved lotus plant with a sword in the foreground, its blade raised. Sitting underneath the medallion was a familiar playing card: the death figure in an *ao dai*, red skull for a face and gold star in the upper corner.

"*La carte de vengeance de la Belle Dame Sans Merci.*"

Robeson translated: "He says it's the revenge card of the beautiful dame—"

"—without mercy. I get it, I get it."

Something was scrawled in Vietnamese across the card's face. We hadn't seen that before.

"What's this mean?" Robeson said to Ting, pointing to the writing: *Trừ gian.*

"Say, 'exterminate traitor.'" Using his manicured pinky nail,

Ting pointed to a tiny hole in the card and the bloody pin on the back of the medallion. "She pin card to General with needle."

"Pin where?" I said.

Ting brought his index finger up to his face. "Through cover of eye." He leaned in. "No say I say."

Pinned to his eyelid and pushed right into the eyeball.

"You careful, yes? *Dangereuse*," Ting whispered in French. He repeated it in Vietnamese: "*Tồi tệ*." Ting turned and strolled down the corridor to check on the men wrestling the stretcher down the rear stairs.

"Well, that's a first," Robeson said, "Ting inviting us to investigate where we've got no jurisdiction."

I rewrapped Ting's evidence. "And coming that close to the general's corpse. Meaning he's more scared of his superiors than of hungry ghosts."

A South Vietnamese general stabbed to death in Saigon would have Ting's bosses gnawing on his bones and demanding the impossible, even as they tried to cover it up. So he needed our help. He couldn't openly investigate a murder they wanted buried, the very fact of it erased. Yet they'd also insist he solve it, having ordered him to destroy evidence, silence witnesses, and make their compromised general vanish along with the true circumstances of his death.

MISS BLUE RECOGNIZED the medallion immediately as a badge of the Cao Dai religious sect's private army. She mimicked its central position on their tan berets by holding it up against her beautiful head of hair. I didn't tell her it had recently been tacked through a dead man's eye.

"What exactly is Cao Dai?" Robeson said.

"Special religion," Blue said. "Big temple in Tây Ninh City."

"And it has an army?"

She shook her head. "Years ago, yes. Big army. Battalion of mens and womens both."

"I hope the Baptists don't get wind of this," her boyfriend joked.

"Diệm finish Cao Đài army," Missy Blue said. "Army no more. Cao Đài soldier no more."

I removed the envelope from my pocket, carefully lifted the bloody thumbprint from the largest piece of glass, and taped it to a white card. I wrapped the flute fragments in a page of *Stars and Stripes*, then placed them, the calling card, the medallion, and the tape with the thumbprint in the ammo box padded with cardboard. Not much of an evidence collection: three red scarves, two shell casings and three other vengeance cards. I snapped the fasteners closed.

"What's buggin' you?" Robeson asked.

"Just mulling the lady's handiwork at the Continental. I wonder if getting close to her victims is something she's done before. Remember that wallet photo of the girl with Major Furth? What if that was her? What if it's not the astrologer who picks them out? What if she's already met her ambush victims?"

"Major Furth got to his feet as she was approaching the café."

I nodded. "Maybe because he was waiting for her."

"Christ almighty. So they don't just pick the location and the time, they find an officer who's looking for female company, and set him up on a date with Lady Death?"

I needed someone to do a little discreet snooping. I couldn't trust Crouch, so I called over the captain's clerk, Corporal Magid, and told him to check into the first two dead officers' personal lives, to see if they'd taken up with a respectable young lady of university age in the weeks before they died.

CHAPTER EIGHTEEN

Robeson and Blue were back on again, so I was solo for the evening and called Nadja to invite her up to the bar on the Majestic's rooftop terrace. Neither of us had remembered to eat, so we were quickly and happily drunk.

She needed the buzz, she said, to subdue the headache she'd gotten that morning trying to sort out all the in-country American agencies for her boss.

"I can't imagine why you were confused," I said, and explained that the Vietnam Task Force was replacing the Vietnam Working Group, which had fused with the Southeast Asia Task Force. "Meanwhile MAAG-V is phasing out and the brand-new MAC-V is phasing in. MAAG supplied and subsidized the French, MAC-V will aid and advise the South Vietnamese."

She covered her ears. "It should be set to music, made into a patter song." Nadja took a long, deep drag on her cigarette. "It's all horribly knotty," she said, smoke punctuating her words.

"Naughty?"

"No, knotty. Knotty." She mimicked tying a bow. "You're as bad as the Russians, with their directorates and groups and departments, changing names ad nauseam. The Vietnamese have taken to imitating you, creating new agencies for MAC-V to advise just to keep your noses out of their affairs."

"You think they're making up departments for us to advise that don't actually do anything?"

"Very nearly. Their job is to agree with you and say, 'Yes, yes. You numba one!' And collect your largesse."

"We duck and dodge our superiors too, come to that. Have to. There's a dozen contrary US generals and admirals in-country and nowhere near enough soldiers and sailors to make all those brass heads happy, moving us around like poker chips."

Our top military honchos and the new ambassador were like ants riding down the Saigon River on a turd, each of them convinced he was the commodore.

"Viet Nam is just a piece of it," I said. "We've got arms cached in trouble spots on several continents, along with military-assistance missions, prepping for Communist revolutions."

"Yes," she said. "People's wars." She raised her glass. "The old imperialism is done for. Dollar imperialism and Red imperialism are the coming thing."

"And us? You and me? Where are we in all that?"

"Unnoticed, I hope."

"Why's your boss interested in our alphabet soup anyway?"

"He didn't say. He's flying to Hanoi tonight and asked me what I knew."

"Hanoi, as in North Viet Nam?"

"It's nothing special," she said, pleased by my surprise. "He flies up at least once a month on the Commission's ancient Boeing Stratoliner. Always at night. There aren't as many fighter aircraft aloft after dark, you see."

"What's he go to Hanoi for?"

"To make the diplomatic rounds. He's trying to back-channel a settlement of this darling bush war of yours. He's young and dashing and wants ever so much to help craft a ceasefire and get awarded the Order of Lenin along with a Nobel Peace Prize."

"How's that going?"

"He's making progress, he says. He insists the North Vietnamese are genuinely interested in avoiding all-out civil war."

"You ever go along?" I said. "To Hanoi?"

"Only once. It's fairly gloomy. They're not having a good year. There's a major drought and assistance has been slow coming because Moscow and Peking are squabbling. Besides, I am a cowardly flier, and that plane is a fright, decades old . . . Mind you, it's not as bad as a Soviet death ship. At least it has four working engines. Still, I am not particularly anxious to explore another Marxist society. Too many Russians hanging around Hanoi, glowering at the Communist Chinese advisors whilst playing out their intramural rivalries. Comrades those comrades are not."

"You're gonna find yourself hanging around a salt mine talking like that."

Nadja arched her eyebrows. "They will do what they will do, and always badly. Back in Poland every job has eight workers doing it. All eight desperately bored and depressed because there's not enough work to share and no pleasure in it. There's nothing to purchase with your earnings either, other than *wodka*. Gray is the prevailing hue, and everybody's always chuntering.

"In any case," she went on, "the Stratoliner's got thirty seats, most of them empty. If you'd like a lost weekend, I'm sure I could arrange it." The vixen in Nadja appeared as she broke into a smile.

A Hanoi holiday. I shot her a look.

"No, no." She giggled at my expression and actually snorted. "You misunderstood. I'm not inviting you to Hanoi. The Stratoliner stops off next door in Cambodia and Laos to pick up and drop off diplomats. You would love Vientiane City. Much wilder than Saigon, a rogues' gallery of Russian spies, French and Corsican mafiosi, Pathet Lao agents and Red Chinese operatives, all mixing it up with Laotian royalists. We could deplane there, or Phnom Penh if you prefer, and have some time to ourselves away from this place. We'd fly back on its return leg. What say you, Ellsworth Miser?"

I had spent a week in Vientiane at Lulu's brothel, and at the Green Lantern where I'd tried Lao opium for the first time. A wild town. One streetlight, countless dives. Opium was their only money crop. Bales of it lay in the street. I spent the next week in Phnom Penh getting high on soups spiced with the Cambodians' favorite herb—marijuana. Lieutenant Seftas loved to escort official visitors there and encourage unsuspecting cheeseheads from Wisconsin to get blasted on bowls of *somlah machoo.*

"You're on," I kidded her, "and then when your boss negotiates a settlement we can give Hanoi a try."

A weekend with Nadja could really broaden my horizons, though I doubted my captain or the major would see it that way. How long could I keep them from finding out about us?

"You know," she slurred, as we each downed another shot of *wodka,* "I set out this morning to be knotty—I mean naughty." The way she looked at me as she said it, I no longer cared who found out about us. "But Madame Nhu's blue laws make it strangely difficult to be naughty. Underwire bras—disallowed. Extravagant hairdos—illegal. Sentimental love songs—forbidden. And here I am *lusting* after a good weepy ballad."

"You think you got it bad? Brothels ain't legal," I said. "No more strip tease. Not even a beauty contest. Can't go to the track to bet the ponies. The Dragon Lady has nixed boxing matches and cockfights. You can't even buy a deck of cards for a game of solitaire, much less play games of chance at a casino. Here we are in Asia and opium dens are outlawed."

The things that offended the holier-than-thou First Lady were as endless as the absurd decrees President Diem issued at her behest.

Nadja licked her lips. "So what is there for sincere sinners to do by way of debauchery?"

"Less and less, I tell ya. No more blue movies or risqué magazines. No contraceptives either."

"Fine thing. Soldiers without contraceptives or pornography," she said. "Men without women. What is war coming to?"

"Necking in public, verboten. General Harkins's orders: soldiers rotating home can't so much as kiss their girlfriends goodbye."

"Well then, we'll just have to stay in."

I helped her down to her new room on four, where she abandoned her clothes a piece at a time. I followed, gathering them up. She passed out as soon as her naked flesh hit the sheets. I lowered the gauzy mosquito net and slipped in next to her in my clothes. A mosquito already under the net settled on her beautiful arm, ready to gorge. If it tipped its ass up to slip its syringe beak into her, I'd know it was a malaria carrier, and have to smack it hard enough to wake her. But if it lay flat while inserting its tiny hair needle—standard behavior of the non-malaria variety—I could let it be and let her sleep. Buddha would decide if the mosquito lived or died, if Nadja was going to awaken or sleep on. The mosquito raised its ass. Malaria.

But Nadja was snoring so sweetly, I took pity on her and pinched it off, smearing my thumb and index finger with a little of her blood. She awoke anyway, scratching the site.

"You like my room?" she said.

I wasn't sure if she was talking in her sleep. "Yes. And you're far better looking than the last occupant."

I eased back down beside her and kissed her eyes.

"You'd be cooler if you shed some clothing," she said, and worked at my belt while I stared at her pink nipples, set off against her white bosom. "I need skin," she said, suddenly energized, though her eyes were still closed. She pulled my belt and holster away, held back her flaming hair and lightly ran her tongue along my thighs. I groaned. Straddling me, she wove back and forth like a tipsy cobra.

"Why must Madame Nhu loathe the twist," she said, pouting. "I do love it so."

"If you've got the urge to twist, a GI combo jams every Tuesday at the Brink Hotel."

"I insist you take me to the brink right now."

"It's not Tuesday. You'll have to wait until tomorrow."

She giggled. "I didn't mean the hotel."

The thought of being out in the world with the assistant to a Communist boss on the International Control Commission made my heart skip. Being in bed with her sent it racing.

"Why are you here, Nadja Kowalska?" I asked as she rolled off to lie beside me.

"With you, illegally naked?"

"In Saigon."

Nadja slid her hand between my thighs, smiling at my reaction. "Ah, well. I would have preferred a posting in the West, but anything that got me out of Poland qualified as irresistible. In a way, Saigon is perfect. To prove myself as a journalist, this is the place. If I could latch onto a magazine or wire service, that would be splendid."

"Your government would let you do that?"

"I wasn't planning to ask for permission," she said as she stroked me.

"You'd defect?"

"I prefer to think of it as slipping away and not looking back."

"Your parents wouldn't get in trouble?"

"My reputation for irreverence is well established. And I made sure Papa had nothing to do with my getting assigned to the ICC here."

"You'd be okay with not seeing your folks again?"

"My father loves me too much, my mother not at all. She and I have never gotten along. His affection for me drove her mad with jealousy. I couldn't bear the way she punished him with her scorn. When I left for university papa wept. My dear *mamusia* did a crossword puzzle. I never lived with them again, which pleased her immensely."

I turned her over, curled around her lovely rump to nuzzle her ear and cop a feel.

"At least you'll never have to worry about the craziest law Madame Nhu and His Holiness ever dreamt up."

"What law is that?" she said, hoarse with passion, her pale flesh trembling.

"Banning falsies."

She gasped, either at the ludicrous idea or my fondling her. "You can't be serious."

"Luckily they've been talked out of it."

"What a pity. The police would have adored enforcing it."

She opened herself to me and her breath kept catching as I touched her. "I've heard a story about a brothel in Saigon," she said, "where the women are suspended from the ceiling . . . in seated postures . . . and lowered onto their clients until they're . . . joined. The ladies are . . . spun. I'd give quite a lot to—"

The room phone rang. Somehow she managed to answer it. Robeson had tracked me down. Had I heard the news?

"What news?"

"The report of General Nguyen Van Lang's death."

Vietnamese radio, Blue had told him, was announcing the valiant general's heroic death fighting off a Viet Cong ambush in the marshes west of the city. He had died instantly, struck in the chest, a large-bore hole now blown in him where the crystal spike had protruded.

CHAPTER NINETEEN

I arrived at CID a half hour late the next morning.

"Robeson call for you," Missy Blue said as I walked in. "Better go there."

"Where is there?"

She handed me an address for the Special Technical and Economic Mission. I recognized it as the late Major Furth's duty post. "Hurry," she said.

I rushed over. On the building's second floor a plywood door hung off its hinges. A pissed-off major stood staring at overturned office equipment and the row of emptied filing cabinets that lined the far wall. He kept running a hand back and forth across his crew cut. The name plate on his khaki blouse said KLETT.

I identified myself as CID and said, "No guard on the place?"

"An ARVN corporal and private were on last night. No sign of either one this morning. Gone AWOL, their captain says. So much for round-the-clock protection from our hosts."

"Anybody see the break-in?" I asked, as Robeson approached us from the far end of the room.

Major Klett shoved his hands into his back pockets. "A couple of shopkeepers across the street who live above their businesses."

"Did they recognize the burglars as locals?"

"Didn't sound like the neighborhood layabouts, no." Klett nodded at the shambles. "Bastards didn't take much of anything saleable. Left the typewriters, the adding machines. They sure trashed everything, though. That, over there, they ransacked real good."

He pointed to a steel desk, its crappy lock busted open.

"I called my boss when I saw that," he said. "And he called you."

"It's Major Furth's," Robeson explained.

The desk was gutted, its contents spilled on the floor. Labeled file folders lay empty. Robeson asked about Furth's work.

"Jim chaperoned a USAID program called CIP."

"CIP?" I said. "Cows, Insecticide, and Pigs?"

"Commodity Import Program. It's like the aid we laid on Europe after the war."

"The Marshall Plan," Robeson said.

"Pretty much, yeah. Day-to-day Major Furth signed off on new import licenses the South Vietnamese government issues to businessmen and processed the paperwork on the procured goods. He also handled the paper on USAID's civilian giveaways."

"He was the CIP watchdog?"

Klett shook his head. "More like a rubber stamp. Whatever they asked for, we gave them. When the embassy started making noises that they were planning to bring Diem around by shutting down American aid for commodity imports, our overseers asked Jim to take stock. Work up a report."

"Was their thinking the requests Furth was getting weren't legit? They want him to check for suspicious activity?"

"No, quite the contrary. The hope was he'd give the program

high marks and a glowing review that would convince the embassy of its importance, so the ambassador wouldn't turn CIP off for too long—and risk driving Diem closer to negotiations with Hanoi. Jim had the idea to do an audit while he was at it. The first ever. He was looking to see if the program could be run more efficiently, make it even more appealing. Soon as he began, though, Jim started complaining it was shameful, a total disgrace."

"What was a disgrace?" I said.

"The amount of fraud and larceny in CIP. The rampant theft of USAID shipments arriving in port. Lifted straight off the ships even before they dock, rustled from storehouses on the docks, dipped into whenever any of it moves by truck."

"Tapped at every step."

Klett nodded. "If it's in transit, it's in play. The pilfering's so bad, Jim said, we're constantly buying back our own supplies to compensate for the losses."

"What's going missing?" I said.

"Whatever the Vietnamese are hot to have. Rice, sugar, concrete, paper, all the luxury goods . . . at least half of every shipment disappears. He mentioned cash recently too."

"Dollars?"

"No." Klett blinked. "Local currency. Lots of it."

Robeson made a quizzical face. "Sir, what exactly was he referring to?"

"I'm sorry. I was engaged elsewhere. I never got a chance to ask for the details."

"But he kept you abreast of his findings?"

"Only in general terms. But for sure he had found more than the garden variety horseshit that passes for normal in this place."

Robeson said, "Normal horseshit like GIs buying back our own stolen goods in the street markets at three times the PX price?"

"Not just that. The Viets have a genius for rackets." Major Klett beckoned us to the window that overlooked the building's courtyard. "The city's electrical grid is crap, right?" he said. We nodded.

He pointed to a portable generator running full-out. "Practically the minute we got our own generator up and running," Klett said, "city officials showed up with our Vietnamese counterparts and insisted we connect it to the building's meter. Said we had to pay for the electricity *we* were generating. Threatened to evict us if we didn't. I balked. But my CO told me to pay."

"What do you think they'd have done if he'd backed you and you said no?" Robeson asked.

"Complain and whine until they got me and him transferred, swapped out for more compliant advisors. Failing that, they'd make our lives as miserable as possible until our tours were up, then send us off with nasty write-ups about our uncooperative attitudes." He looked out beyond the buildings. "Jim was starting to see this place as one big scam."

I said, "How far along was he with his report?"

Klett sucked air between clenched teeth, his face pained. "Close to finished."

"And this is where he kept it?" I pointed to the rifled desk.

"No, no. Major Furth kept his baby under wraps, locked away in our office safe. Ledgers, notes, the latest working draft. The supporting data too, pages numbered and dated. He was meticulous about security."

"Where's the safe where Furth kept the report?" I said.

Klett grimaced and pointed to a heavy French antique in

the far corner of the room. The dented front suggested the thieves had attempted to bust it open, without success.

"We'll need to see the contents," I said. "We have the clearances."

"A squad from MAAG headquarters showed up the day after Major Furth was killed. I thought they might be coming to protect us. They demanded I open the safe, cleaned it out, sealed it all up and took it away. All ordered by General Harkins— acting on orders from the Department of Defense."

Major Klett had the resigned calm of a man about to be engulfed in an unavoidable shitstorm.

"Who else might be privy to what's in the major's report?" Robeson asked.

"There's an American civilian who was helping him interpret the data. He and Jim socialized some. He just up and quit when he heard Jim got killed."

"Tell me about him."

"Fred Tuttle, economic counselor lent to Jim by USOM. He was advising three, four days a week. Some weekends too."

"Where is Mr. Tuttle?"

"Holed up in a hotel, waiting on a flight out."

"Which one?"

"Hotel Duc. Maybe a block or so from the old bombed-out palace."

"Corner of Cong Ly and Tran Qui Cap," I said. "I know the place."

The major got called away by one of his men and gingerly made his way through the mess. Robeson squatted at Major Furth's trashed desk, poking underneath the gutted file drawer.

He smirked. "Ya oughta remember Hotel Duc," he said.

"You unburdened yourself of half a month's pay there—what?—two weeks ago."

"Do I bust your chops like that?" I bitched.

Robeson stopped rifling through the spilled files. "Jesus." He passed two empty file folders over his shoulder to me and kept rummaging. The label on one read *Victor, Edward*; the other, *LaValle, Henderson*—the first and second of the Red Queen's American kills. We called over to Major Klett to ask if he knew them. He didn't but thought they were economic advisors, old colleagues of Jim Furth's who'd been helping unofficially with his report. "Is it important?"

Me and Robeson exchanged a look. Whoever had tossed the office hadn't known Furth's report had already been seized. They'd still be after it, or anyone who might know its contents.

"The rest of your American personnel all accounted for?" I said.

"My people? Yeah. Except the civilian, Tuttle."

"Sir," Robeson said, "it might be advisable to arm yourselves."

"We already have." He patted his holster.

Out on the street, Robeson and I put our heads together. The three casualties were looking less and less like random ambush victims.

"These men had regular dealings over this report," I said. "A fact that seems to have escaped fuckin' Sergeant Crouch. We better get to the bean counter while he's still among the living."

CHAPTER TWENTY

Hotel Duc was all CIA. Their military friends might stay a night or two, but the Duc belonged to the Agency. Two uniformed white mice lolled on the corner next to their green-and-white police jeep, but the CIA knew they offered no protection, so Nungs in black guarded the hotel's front and back entrances. Tribal mercenaries, Nungs had no credos, no ideology—except fight like hell for whoever was paying.

The hotel had amenities: a good little bar, rec room, restaurant, small theater, its own liquor store, and fully polygraphed mama-sans to clean the fifty rooms and five apartments. Plus a swimming pool and a freestanding pool house where a poker game redistributed wealth nightly. As Robeson had been happy to remind me, I'd dropped a couple of hundred at that table betting a broken straight.

Hotel Duc was home to a hundred agents, and now to one Fred Tuttle. The duty officer wouldn't so much as speak his room number but had us escorted upstairs by a small graying American who wore a shoulder holster with a shiny .357 so big it made him look like he'd sprouted half a bosom. He took us to a room on the top floor where we banged on the door and announced ourselves. Silence. Our escort spoke up on our behalf and a voice inside demanded we hold our credentials up to the peephole. The door creaked open.

Fred Tuttle was short and balding and looked like the accountant he was, except for the .45 he held unsteadily behind his right leg. Tuttle sat down on the couch and indicated the armchairs across from him. Robeson slid into one. I slouched against the wall, arms akimbo, and made a friendly face, trying to put him at ease.

"How soon you out of here?" I said.

Tuttle dropped the pistol on the cushion beside him. His fingers shook a little as he lit up a Marlboro. "Eleven days and a wakeup."

"You must be happy to be going home."

He wiped the sweat from his upper lip. "I'll be happy when I'm at thirty thousand feet and still breathing."

"Yeah," I said. "You're wise to be cautious."

He huffed derisively. "Terrified is more like it. There are parties out there who'd like me not to leave the country with what I know." Tuttle clutched himself as if he was cold, though sweat stained his shirt. "Fuck," he said. "I hate hiding like this but who wants to be a dead hero? I'm putting as many air miles as I can between here and wherever."

"Your bosses okay with you quitting?" Robeson said, trying to distract Tuttle from his panic.

"My superiors weren't happy, no. Leaned on me hard. Couldn't stop me, legally speaking. I'm in breach of contract is all. I said I can walk and I did. But now I'm no longer eligible for government transport. And civilian flights are booked solid. I'd try going standby but I can't risk hanging around the airport for hours. So I'm flying commercial on my own dime, taking nothing through customs, walking straight onto the flight."

Robeson shone his pearly whites on Tuttle. "You and Jim Furth were friends, I understand. Was he involved with any local women? Keep a private apartment where they could meet, that sort of thing?"

"Why are you asking?" he said, instantly suspicious.

"We're wondering if he might have stashed a draft of his report somewhere outside the office."

"Jim inventoried everything like trial evidence. Everything dated and coded. Nothing left the premises. It's all in an ancient safe in the STEM office."

"Yeah," I said. "Except . . ."

"Except what?"

"All the research is gone, along with the report. Confiscated."

Tuttle paled and curled in on himself where he sat on the couch. You could see his fear reignite. I didn't want to lose him, and kept talking.

"Was there a new lady in Major Furth's life?"

"Always. The latest was a real Kewpie doll, way younger than him."

"You saw her?"

"Once. A sweet shy thing."

"This new friend, you recall a name? Anything about who she was, where they met?"

"He probably said, but I don't remember."

The room was messy, the bed unmade. Soiled dishes sat on a table alongside a near-empty bottle of Johnnie Walker. Tuttle caught me scoping the place.

"Yeah," he said, "it's, ah . . . a little scungy. I keep the maids out. Change rooms every day. Can't risk having the housekeepers coming through. They tell me everyone who works here is heavily screened, but . . ."

"You're afraid of the maids?" Robeson said.

"I'm afraid of whatever Lady Death might turn up as next. Look how she did in General Lang."

Robeson shot me a look. Tuttle's CIA hosts were clearly keeping current on the Red Queen.

"Did you know the other two G-5s she killed?"

Tuttle nodded. "Captain Victor and Major LaValle. We heard Ed died in a random VC attack. But LaValle's family was hard to track down, so his name was withheld. If Jim had known . . ." Tuttle looked like crap, rheumy and pasty.

"Victor and LaValle, what was their connection to Jim's work?"

"Jim enlisted their help when he started to grasp the extent of the corruption and outright thievery. After they saw what he'd already found, both of them volunteered incriminating information they'd become aware of independently."

"Did they know what was in the draft report?"

"Much of it, yes. They'd come in after hours when they could to review Jim's work, add their pieces to the growing puzzle."

"And did you ever have occasion to meet with General Nguyen Van Lang?"

"Never had the pleasure, but we certainly became aware of him as we proceeded."

"He had something to do with the National Bank," I said.

Tuttle snorted like I'd made a joke. "Yeah, a little something."

"And with the Commodity Import Program."

"Ah, yes," Tuttle said with disdain. "C-I-P. Jim said it stood for Corrupt Indochinese Pissants."

"Which particular pissants?"

"General Lang for one, and nearly all the elite South Vietnamese we dealt with in the Economic Directorate. Plus plenty of others we never laid eyes on—high up in the regime and out of sight. Clever, cunning, crooked as snakes. Venal shits getting rich from the program and the scams they spun off it."

"Whoa," Robeson said. "Back up if you will, please. CIP—what the hell is it exactly?"

"A program of US-supported import subsidies."

"Like the Marshall Plan," I volunteered, parroting what Robeson had said.

"Pretty much," Tuttle agreed. "The program kicked off right after Diem came to power eight years ago and has been running full-out ever since. Until one day Lodge shut it down without a word of warning to the Vietnamese. Just turned off the taps and let the realization of what that meant sink in."

"What does—did—CIP do?"

"Congress wanted to encourage the Vietnamese to import machinery for factories and farming, like we did with Europe. The idea was to help the Viets grow their manufacturing and consumer industries, improve their agriculture—like that. Build up their economy, give them a taste of free-market prosperity that would make their citizens look favorably upon the Diem government for bringing them luxuries they'd never had."

"Sounds like a good deal," Robeson said. "Must've made the civilians stateside happy too, to have a new market for their John Deeres and orange cheese."

"The surplus cheese, yeah. It was a condition they take the fucking cheese. Tractors, no. Turns out the Vietnamese didn't want tractors. Didn't want manufacturing equipment either. Just consumer goods. Water skis and record players. Bring 'em in and sell 'em, fast. In all the years CIP's been running, they've never produced much of anything. The more they import, the weaker the economy gets."

"Ass-backwards," I said. "How does this CIP thing actually work—when it's running?"

"Once Jim rubber-stamped the purchases, USAID transferred the dollar cost of the commodity into a special bank account at the National Bank of Viet Nam—administered by guess who."

"Uncle Lang again."

"Bingo. Whoever holds the license to import the desired commodity has the right to buy American dollar credits from the special account at a huge discount, use that money at face value to purchase the commodity overseas, then import it to Viet Nam and sell it."

"So the American manufacturers are happy," Robeson said.

"Sure. They're getting paid full market price."

"How much of a discount do the licensees get on those dollars?" I said.

"The importer gets each buck for, like, twenty-five cents."

"Two bits on the dollar," I said, thunderstruck. My mind reeled with the local investments I could make if my pay packet was juiced by their discount subsidy.

"So you can see where the licenses are an extremely valuable commodity," Tuttle said, with a wan smile.

"Licenses to breed money," I said.

Tuttle nodded. "So of course the licensees are happy to show their gratitude with gifts to Diem's clan. Each month the palace handpicks a fortunate two thousand from a huge pool of applicants, all of them bearing gifts, naturally. The favored few come away with the licenses."

"Bearing gifts, you mean they buy these licenses?" Robeson said.

"More like bid on them, but yeah, amounts to the same thing. Gold, cash, gems. Or contributions to Nhu's semi-secret political party, for which General Nguyen Van Lang also happened to serve as treasurer. Lang had his fingers deep in government cash and the Diem clan's personal funds—which can often seem interchangeable."

"Small world," Robeson said. "So for the right price, the palace issues a license, say, for importing shoes, or air conditioners or whatever."

"And then the licenses make the importers rich without even trying," I said. "They're like a guarantee of double and triple profits."

"Exactly," Tuttle said, loosening up. He lit a fresh cigarette from the end of the one he was already smoking. "You military guys"—he puffed—"you get your super-duper special rate of exchange on your pay. Higher than the phony official rate, but nothing like full value. Our government has you personally subsidizing the Vietnamese economy without ever asking you." Tuttle looked back and forth between me and Robeson. "Which is why I'm guessing you take your pay packets to the Indian moneychangers."

He was polite; he hadn't added "illegally."

"You got that right," I said, thinking being up-front with him might help us.

"They usually give us a hundred and forty piasters to the dollar, max," Robeson added, following my lead. "Last month we made out like bandits. Just about doubled our money. Got one hundred ninety P for our greenbacks."

"Sure," Tuttle said. "The dollar is a hot commodity right

now. Everybody wants money that won't wobble or crash if—
more likely when—the Diem government goes down. Still,
keeping the piaster pegged at a make-believe rate penalizes
in-country personnel and costs US taxpayers, all the while
making a shitload of Vietnamese importers damned well-off."

Robeson said, "They're makin' a friggin' windfall from every
fan and hair dryer."

Tuttle nodded. "The profit margins are spectacular. But even
so they're always asking, 'How can I exploit this further?' They
tease out even more by diverting goods to the black market."
Tuttle unzipped a new red-and-white pack of Marlboros and
resumed fumigating the room. His voice dropped to a whisper.
"LaValle told us the US Army is sitting on its own nasty reports.
Like one that says nine out of ten captured enemy rifles are
American, distributed to ARVN but found on dead and captured Viet Cong fighters. Yet strangely there's a chronic
shortage of weapons among the village militias. The South
Vietnamese like to pretend the arms intended for the militias
are just misplaced somewhere in the logistical shambles. They're
not about to own up to where they really ended up—or how
they got there."

"Black market," I said.

He shrugged. "Bought, stolen, captured," he said. "Take
your pick. I mean, think about it. Only *a tenth* of VC arms
come from the Communist bloc. Their mortars, explosives,
field dressings, grenades? Ours."

He poured himself a shot and knocked it back.

"Sounds like we're running a supply line for all comers,
friend and foe alike," I said.

"It gets worse. Diem's own officers sell ammunition to
nearby Communist forces. You're never going to hear, 'Thank

you for the bullets. Now we can go fight Communism for you.' They're too busy thinking, 'I could sell these bullets across the border, and I don't want to know who's buying.'"

"American bullets shot from American guns at American advisors."

Tuttle seemed to find my discomfort funny. "Diem's hard-ass brother, Can, the one who rules Hue like a dictator, he's selling rice to VC and the North."

"Diem's own brother is trading with the enemy?"

"When it comes to business, friend or enemy doesn't matter," Tuttle said.

"How do the Viet Cong and North Vietnamese come by enough cash to buy our mortars and Brother Can's rice?" Robeson asked.

"From their Russian comrades and the Chinese, I suppose. Plus, the VC collect tolls on all the trucking routes, of course. The shippers buy a window of immunity—maybe four hours—to drive the fifty miles from, say, Saigon to the Cambodian border unmolested. If you've paid up, the VC may take a few sacks or crates of what you're hauling, but that's all."

"And if you don't buy immunity?"

"The guerillas take whatever you've got on board. One way or another, everybody contributes to the VC cause. Vietnamese are notorious for not paying their taxes, but they all pay their 'love donations' to the VC, believe me. From little mom-and-pop shops right up to the big international corporations. Just the cost of doing business."

"Corporations? They pay cash?"

"Naturally. Can't have cancelled checks payable to Viet Cong fronts. If you run a coffee or tea plantation in the highlands, or a rubber plantation near Saigon, you slip the Viet Cong collector a cool million and your rubber trees are safe as gas pumps for another year."

"Gas pumps? You mean Western petroleum outfits pay the VC?"

"Damn right. Huge oil companies like Dutch Shell can't afford to have their tanker trucks or gas stations torched, or that huge depot downriver at Nha Be touched off. What's a million bucks to them? Petty cash. First of every month, the executives look away while a Vietnamese manager passes along the gratitude. No lousy piasters either. Strictly Swiss francs, US dollars, British pounds sterling."

"How much are these love donations?"

"Do the math. The monthly installment on a million dollars has gotta be eighty, eighty-five thou."

My brain was going *ka-ching*.

"Dream on." Tuttle read me right. "You don't want to fuck with these people. Diem and Nhu, Ho and the VC—you don't wanna get between any of these parties and their piggy banks . . . or their destiny. Mess with their little arrangements and you'll be doing the backstroke in a canal with your feet chained together and your wrists wrapped in barbed wire."

Tuttle slumped back into the couch. "The boys around the trough aren't exactly civil. The palace in particular isn't gentle about reprimanding deadbeats. Any fool who fails to remunerate the Ngo clan for his import privileges gets his goods repossessed and his ass thrown in jail. If Nhu is feeling generous or the guy's a relative his commodities might just get sold off. If not, it's goodnight, Irene."

CHAPTER TWENTY-ONE

Tuttle chewed a couple of aspirin, swigged some whiskey and took a deep drag on his cigarette while he weighed whether to say more. But we didn't have to push. He had a lot pent up. He was afraid but he was also angry as hell.

"CIP was supposed to do good," he said. "Supposed to fund the Vietnamese government, finance the military and police forces and civil service. The piasters the importers pay to buy the discounted dollars, they go right into the government's treasury account."

"At General Lang's National Bank," I said.

"Natch. Those piasters are the country's currency reserve. Hard to run a government—much less fight a war—if all you have are ridiculously low taxes you can't collect because the South Vietnamese won't pay. Millions of citizens, and maybe a few thousand shell out any taxes. CIP was intended to help their government get around that little problem. Which is why we didn't really care what they imported—scotch, Mercedes limos, baby food—just as long as the program was funneling currency into the war effort to make up for all those missing taxes. And it has. About forty percent of their economy comes from CIP piasters."

"Jesus. How much does our government pour into this Commodity Import Program?" I said.

"Two million a week and rising," Tuttle said, "until Lodge closed the tap."

Robeson whistled. "And the late General Lang was the honcho wrangling all this cash?"

"Yup. The dollars USAID put up to buy the credits, the piasters from the licensees for the discounted money. Nhu's political party treasury. The gratitude from the license winners. As well as receipts for various . . . other accounts."

Robeson gave him his best innocent look. "Other accounts?"

"Like port fees for all the merchant and military supply ships waiting weeks, sometimes months, for the port director to assign them a berth. First they make them wait, then they charge them for the privilege of waiting." Tuttle squinted against the smoke.

Robeson said, "How much are we talkin' about?"

"Something like three to seven grand for each supply ship waiting to be unloaded, Jim said. Then there's import tariffs on all the commodities rafting in here under CIP. Years ago it was eighteen piasters for every dollar's worth of goods. General Lang refused us access to the current figures."

"Even though these are tariffs on American goods financed with American money?" Robeson asked. "He actually said no dice?"

"Yep. 'Vietnamese government business,' not ours."

I stretched out my leg to relieve the dengue ache in my knee. "And all the money Furth was tracking went through General Lang, coming and going?"

Tuttle nodded. "Lang was the hub, Brother Nhu's bagman."

"Busboy for the fat cats' table," Robeson muttered.

"More like the family's personal banker. Who knows how much CIP money actually made it to the war effort and how much went straight into the Ngo family's accounts. When Madame Nhu wanted to go shopping for properties in Brazil and France, or pick up a rubber plantation or a coal mine, or buy the entire Saigon bus company, the Dragon Lady got her funds from General Lang. Her other brother-in-law, the archbishop? Turns out he likes to shop too. Tea plantations, coffee plantations, timber concessions. Plunked down four million dollars for the Charner department store, for God's sake. Lang provided the cash."

"Kee-rist," Robeson said. "They shoulda kept Lang protected around the clock, chauffeured everywhere in a mink-lined tank. You know, you make the Diem regime sound like the mob."

"Damn straight. This isn't some half-assed larceny," he said. "It's sophisticated and systemic. The regime doesn't just countenance corruption. Corruption is what keeps the treasury filled and the government fueled. Diem and Nhu and the rest of their clan? They're not so interested in prosecuting the war. But they sure as hell want the machinery of war to keep cranking so they can keep pocketing their profits. The regime's a fucking cartel that rents us their armed forces and this place to fuck up. In return, we permit our hosts to go through our pockets extracting every last dime, while we fill their government coffers and subsidize their luxury imports, send them advisors and pilots and police experts. Train their fliers, their security people, their soldiers. We send them free everything and look away as they pillage our supply line. We just tot up our losses and order more."

Tuttle took another drag. Ash fell across his front. "One day . . ." He hesitated. Long seconds passed. "We made a mistake."

"An accounting error?"

Tuttle sawed off more ash and glared at Robeson. "I wish. Major LaValle had a connection at the National Bank. He found large amounts of cash being deposited into a custodial account, piasters flooding in and gushing out. We're talking *billions* taken out of circulation in Viet Nam. Transported to General Lang's right-hand man in Hong Kong, a colonel posted there as an attaché, but somehow receiving this cash is his only responsibility. He channels it straight into a Crown Colony bank where it's deposited at half its value."

"You're not talking about wire transfers?" Robeson said.

"No. Actual physical piasters sucked out of the marketplace here and carried there. We're talking planeloads. A goddamn torrent of wholesaled Vietnamese money. A high-discount, high-volume business. So much pouring out of the country, there's a rolling risk of a currency drought."

I rubbed my forehead. "Planeloads of piasters regularly bucket out of Viet Nam into a British colony bank and nobody—no one in international business or banking—ever notices? Not even Viet merchants when they start running out of change in the till?"

Robeson looked at Tuttle, chin resting on his hand. "It's kinda incredible—so much local money leaving the country that it threatens to dry up circulation."

"You're right," said Tuttle. "There should've been noticeable shortages here. There was one—very briefly—in June of last year. But never since, because the wholesaled bricks of cash don't sit in Hong Kong long enough. They're sold on quickly."

I scratched at an ear. "The piaster isn't an international currency. Its only value is local. Exporting planeloads of it seems nuts. Who'd want to buy piasters?"

Tuttle laughed. "Exactly right. Which is why they're unloaded at fire sale prices. Each shipment goes immediately to a lone buyer"—Tuttle tapped the coffee table—"who brings it right back here."

Robeson's eyes sprang wide. "Who in the hell? The VC?"

Tuttle jiggled his foot nervously, aware it might be unwise to answer but unable to resist. "Nope," he said, grinning. "Uncle Sam."

"The United States government." I paced to the window. A couple frolicked with a beach ball in the swimming pool below. Alarm bells were going off in my head. "Treasury?"

"Nah," said Robeson. "The set-up's too hinky."

"CIA?"

"Bingo. The Agency buys up the piasters dirt cheap and hustles them straight into a huge walk-in refrigerator out by Tan Son Nhut." Tuttle lay back on the couch, forearm across his brow. "Nobody ever notices the drain because the dough gets transfused into the local economy real quick. Whatever CIA undertaking requires cash payment, which is all of them, the cash comes from that locker."

Robeson whistled. "Holy cow."

"Think about it," Tuttle said. "The Agency can't exactly issue checks. Agency paymasters and field agents go to the walk-in fridge and load up like it's the Big Rock Candy Mountain. Cash to make payroll for Montagnard mercenaries fighting Communists in the highlands, wages for sixty-five thousand village militiamen. Money for arms, for Agency informants, Nung guards, a quarter million a month for Colonel Tung's Red Berets guarding Diem at the palace." He brushed ash from his shirt with the back of his hand. "Marauders working secretly out of Da Nang, VC turncoats who need a cash stake to start over, farmers with accidentally slain livestock or destroyed crops. Bounties on VC weapons, stipends to ralliers, payouts to Vietnamese legislators we like who have enemies we don't like.

Some general or province governor whose goodwill we want to buy, who can't afford the going price for his next promotion. Tokens of appreciation for reporters and political activists we want to empower, delivered along with lists of groups we'd like to see them subvert. Propaganda pamphlets, rice, documentary films . . . It's all there for the taking."

"No accounting?" I said.

"None whatsoever. Totally unvouchered."

"We buy the laundered Viet money on the cheap," Robeson said, trying to get his head around what we were hearing. "After which we give it away again?"

"Takes some getting used to," Tuttle said. "You gotta admit, though, it's clever. The Agency gets lots of super cheap local cash to play with. Money they don't have to buy at the bullshit official rate. Keeps the gears oiled, the machinery humming. Keeps Washington happy because there's money flowing into the South Vietnamese economy that they didn't have to appropriate and explain to voters who don't like hearing about Buddhists being beaten in the streets and grade-school kids hauled off to detention camps in the countryside. Totally unappropriated cash that gives the Agency boys all the dough in the world to fund their covert schemes."

Robeson smiled ruefully. "Christ Almighty. You uncover the Agency's private cash cow, this giant slush fund, and you're hiding in a CIA billet. Man. Is it really safe for you to be here? Me, I would've gone elsewhere."

"Hey." Tuttle held up a hand. "They've given me shelter and protection, which is more than my employer did when I balked at staying after Jim was killed. They're cool. These boys are having the time of their lives training junior spooks, doing black ops. They're living the life, man: running liquidation units, hiring mercenaries, bedding dames. They toss money around like confetti, spy on the enemy, fuck over Communists—and sometimes the South Vietnamese if they get out of line."

He sat quiet for a moment, smiling to himself.

"You wouldn't believe the silly shit they get into. They produce movies to make Diem look good, slip in subliminal messages that the eye can't see but the brain absorbs. Put out astrology magazines that show the president's horoscope is always rosy. Finance rumors about Communist atrocities—like that they're amputating the arms of villagers inoculated by our medical teams—and mix 'em with real stories of the nasty executions the VC stage in the hinterlands. The other night the boys were boasting about driving the North Vietnamese crazy by parachuting ice men into North Viet Nam."

"Ice men?" Robeson said.

"Seems the Agency's program of inserting operatives into North Viet Nam is a total bust. Completely compromised. Commies grab up the agents as soon as they parachute in. Meaning we've got no agents in North Viet Nam. Zero. The Agency guys wanted payback. Got this ice maker in town to make half-size human figures they strap into parachutes and toss out over North Viet Nam. The ice men melt on the way down. The Commies find the chutes but can't find the spies. Drives 'em batshit."

"Talk about spies melting into the local population!" Robeson hooted. "But seriously, all that currency shit—Furth's report laid that out? No wonder there's folks upset with y'all."

Tuttle leaned back on the couch, hands laced behind his head, elbows splayed. "Jim Furth was painstaking, gradually fitting the pieces together. He got so damn excited when he could see the whole picture."

An argument broke out in the hall in rapid Vietnamese. Tuttle sat up, clutching his gun.

CHAPTER TWENTY-TWO

As the voices receded, Tuttle exhaled a long stream of smoke. Robeson said, "Did you and Major Furth ever talk about what shining the light of day on all this might bring down on y'all?"

Tuttle laughed uncomfortably, which made him cough. "Obviously not. Uncovering the mechanics had us stoked. We didn't think it might cause trouble for us personally." He took a pull on his cigarette and stubbed it out. "Hell, we're Americans. Who's going to mess with us?" Tuttle coughed again. "Besides, I didn't think for a second the higher-ups would ever let any of it surface." He tried to light a new cigarette with an unsteady hand.

"What do you mean?" I said.

"Jim sent a sample of what we'd collected over to USAID and a little way up the chain of command, sort of a test run. They'd asked for a report on CIP, after all."

"What happened?"

"Nobody so much as initialed the distribution list to acknowledge they'd seen it. No one wanted any part of what we found."

I extended my Zippo to his Marlboro. The tip flamed. Black circles ringed his eyes. He gave me an exhausted stare.

"Major LaValle predicted nobody would touch it. Not the can-do, ass-kissing brass in Saigon or the embassy suits. Not our supreme command enchiladas in Hawaii either, with all that gold braid on their hats. The politicians in Washington might hold some bullshit hearings. But they only want the Commie threat quashed. They don't care about sloppiness or skimming or the crony conspiracies running this place. Their eyes are on the Big Picture. The Big Prize."

"Holdin' back world Communism," Robeson said.

Tuttle laughed. "Fuck no. Re-election! The Congress and two presidents have carried Diem for eight years. They nip at him to change his ways but he's intractable. They need to cut him loose, but they don't want the kind of political blow-back that followed Mao's victory in China. Nobody wants to be seen as the ones who lost Indochina. No, sir. Damn the torpedoes and the corruption. Just keep on hammering them Commies."

We could hear people passing in the hall. Gun in hand, Tuttle went to peer out the peephole before turning back to us. He slipped his piece in the waistband of his trousers and paced, hands tucked in his armpits.

"Me, I told Jim I didn't think anything would splash back on us because all the clever scams we'd documented would never be made public. The report was going to get buried. No way our superiors would ever admit knowing about the regime's duplicity, much less admit they'd been cooperating with it for years." Tuttle reached for the bottle and drained the last of the scotch. "This so-called economy is a balloon, a bubble. Nothing's being produced in Viet Nam except rich Vietnamese and dead Vietnamese. We're bucketing guns and goods over here to keep up pretenses and buy loyalty." He lit up and sent a cloud of smoke toward the ceiling. "What a waste. The four of us were gagged by non-disclosures we'd signed long ago. All they had to do was quarantine the report, classify it Top Secret, Eyes Only and toss some wordy commendations into our files."

"What about Lodge?" I said. "He needs sweeping reforms from Diem. Your report would be a hell of a big stick."

"Don't kid yourself. Lodge is a loyal politician. He wouldn't do anything that would make our government look incompetent or complicit in propping up a criminal syndicate. He's not about to expose our South Vietnamese allies as venal war profiteers. No way he'd get caught holding the short end of that stick."

Robeson fixed Tuttle with a stare. "You said Major Furth felt differently about the report?"

"Jim was optimistic *somebody* would read the report and announce that there is no such thing as Vietnamese productivity, just products bought with the money we pump in here in every conceivable way. Plus our humanitarian supplies and free military equipment expropriated and *sold.*" Tuttle fell silent for a moment. "Jim toyed with the idea of sneaking the full report to the Comptroller General at the General Accounting Office, even though that would have meant the end of his reserve career."

Furth and the others had had no idea what kind of trouble this report could bring them. While they debated the possible reactions of our government and military command, they never saw the Red Queen coming. I wouldn't have either.

I asked Tuttle straight out. "Why would the VC want to squash a report that lays out such damning stuff about their enemy? Exposing what you found could topple the regime without them having to fire a shot. You'd think they'd want your report on billboards ten feet high."

"I can see why Nhu would want the report buried and to

shut the four of you up," Robeson agreed. "But why would the VC go after MAAG whistleblowers?"

Tuttle scanned our faces, pushed his ashtray aside and leaned closer. "Because like it or not, USAID and the ever-lovin' Commodity Import Program are completely enmeshed with Viet Cong needs. They rely on it. Our aid brings materiel into the country the VC wants for their own forces. Medicine, rice, gasoline, guns, explosives. As much as the South, the North needs our goods flowing in, markets operating full blast. Sure, the South Vietnamese want their fancy shampoo and air conditioners. But CIP also puts cash in the VC war chest from the black-market profit they're making on our stolen goods." Tuttle waited for this to sink in. "If you ask me, the ambassador should be watching his own ass. With CIP shut off, nothing's in the pipeline. That's bad news for both sides. If there's even a chance disposing of Lodge might impress Washington with the shaky state of things in Saigon and un-dam the aid dollars—turn the tap back on—I can think of a number of parties who wouldn't hesitate."

A soft knock at the door had Tuttle on his feet, gun in hand. An American voice announced that he would be changing rooms in twenty minutes.

"Guys," he said, "we're done."

We left the Hotel Duc, our heads reeling. Our jeep was boxed in by a pair of the high-powered Mitsubishi Colts the CIA favored, so we climbed over the open back and walked across the seats. Robeson dropped behind the wheel, put his hand to the ignition and looked relieved as the engine revved without blowing us up.

"You're antsy," I said.

"Hell yeah, I'm antsy." He backed us out. "Look what

happened to the first three guys who knew about this shit. Tuttle makes four, but he's locked up tight in Fort Knox. We're out here in an open jeep."

"Keep your shirt on and tell me how we piece this fucker together into something that makes sense."

"We don't," Robeson said. "We keep our damn noses out of the regime's commodity scams and the VC's black market. We forget about this CIP report. We go after the lady assassin," he said. "And try to keep her from bumping off the ambassador."

"Or President Diem."

Robeson shook his head. "Forget Diem. Lodge cutting off CIP sent the signal that Diem's gang wasn't our gang anymore. That move right there was the big green light for his generals to take over." He gave me a hard look. "You hearin' me?"

"Loud and clear," I said. "We concentrate on the broad."

Robeson wiped his forehead with the back of his sleeve. "Light me a cig, will ya?" he said, shifting from second into third. "All that high finance. My head's swimming."

I leaned below the dash to light two cigarettes. Something lay on the floorboard by my feet. I strained to pick it up.

Robeson saw the card in my hand, spanking new, the skull's teeth bared. He hunched over the wheel. "This your idea of a joke? Tell me you're putting me on. That one of the cards from Crouch's lockbox?"

I shook my head, then scanned the traffic. No sign of her, but any of the riders behind us could be one of her scouts.

"Fuckin' A, Ellie," Robeson said. "CID was supposed to be easy duty, not make us marked men. I wish we were back in the boonies advising again." He snuck another look at the death card as he drove. "I don't wanna know what I know."

"Too late to unknow it. She's already got eyes on us."

CHAPTER TWENTY-THREE

Robeson was too rattled to leave his room, but my brain was spinning. I went up to the rooftop bar and ordered a beer. I took a pull, closed my eyes and imagined floating in a tub full of bills the color of the jungle. Oh, man. I was so ever-lovin' tired of the short end of the stick, risking my butt for a lousy fourteen bucks a day, made lousier by the make-believe conversion rate. I had investments I wanted to make, opportunities that needed financing.

I had kept to the Pacific Rim, hoping this swell little war would stay that way. I was gambling the glowing volcano wouldn't blow just yet, despite the sweaty nightmares I still had about Korea and human-wave attacks. There wasn't enough ammo in all the ammo dumps in the world to take them all down, even in my dreams. Asia had put more than dengue into me. Indochina was its own fever, infecting with equal measures of love and hate.

The Viet bosses and the Cholon Chinese were buying exit visas for their kids to go to school in Paris and the States, while the parents were busy building up their own getaway stash. And everybody collecting green gratitude but me. They weren't the only ones who needed a flush future to relocate to when this show tanked. And tank it would. Just a question of when.

The French had long ago screwed the pooch in Indochina, and no one was going to outlast or unseat Uncle Ho. We weren't going to unfuck the future for these people. I could only look to unfuck mine. Bangkok, Vientiane . . . somewhere.

The sunset colors bled into the river and the tropical twilight turned quickly to night.

My brain was buzzing with the fortunes being made all around me, zips buying dollars for next to nothing and tripling their investments, bushels of cash being hauled out of Saigon, while I walked around with chump change, owning nothing but pieces of roadside greasy spoons, some nasty bars, and a steam-and-cream operation where vehicles got washed while dicks got stroked.

We were risking our necks out here, sucking hind tit while the Vietnamese elite were parlaying American tax money into sweet import deals that made them fortunes. We meant no more to them than the underpaid Buddhist bumpkins in the ranks of their army. We got to flirt with the Red Reaper and play tag with comrades in the woods so they could enjoy their overseas villas and mountain chalets in the hotter months. Fuck. What was it the VC called us—the war dogs of capitalism?

All that fucking dough. A generous hunk of which was getting paid to the enemy to buy safe passage for goods so that everyone involved could harvest more money: buy more, steal more. No such perks were coming my way. No Vietnamese was buying me immunity from Viet Cong mines or ambushes. They happily paid to keep the roads safe for their imported and looted American booty, but I didn't see anyone offering to pay the VC to make sure the Red Queen didn't plug me next. Us? We were useful dog soldiers, cheap and interchangeable, sent to far-flung shores to protect the empire.

The situation was ridiculous. The safe passage our allies bought for their worldly goods was helping finance the war being made on them *and me*. I was nothing but an *X* marked on a map overlay, a smudge easily rubbed out, another one just as easily penciled in.

I didn't have a life waiting for me stateside like Robeson, but I could make plans too. I just had to be able to afford them. I called Sergeant Flippi from the Majestic. "Flip" was a Georgia boy, a crazy fuck who'd come by his frayed nerves honestly in Korea, where we'd met. Loyal to a fault, but a sinister dude when he wanted to be. No one was better than Flip at getting over on somebody with just a whisper. When I raised him at his billet he said my timing was great: he had something he wanted to show me. Thirty minutes later he called me down to the lobby.

"Aloha, motherfucker." He flashed his dentures. Whatever he had to show me was making him jolly and red-faced. Right away he asked if I wanted a piece of the action.

"What kind of action we talking?" I said.

"You ain't gonna believe it. Come 'n' look fo' yo'self," he drawled. "Got it right there 'cross the street in pieces. But you'll suss it out quick. Come on, come on."

Flippi's prize lay under a tarp in the back of a three-quarter-ton Army truck. The Vietnamese driver slipped from behind the wheel and climbed up with us onto its bed to help Flippi pull the tarp away. Two long poles lay flat beside iron braces, and something that looked like what I'd seen on a fifth-grade field trip back in Philly—wooden stocks the Pilgrim fathers used to restrain minor lowlifes, imprisoning their wrists and necks while exposing the rest of them to public ridicule. Except Flippi's yoke had just a head hole, none for hands.

A large, heavy slab of polished metal lay on sandbags in the truck. Tapping it, Flippi grinned and announced, "A hundred 'n' ten pounds of steel."

"What the fuck?" I said, reaching to touch its gleaming edge.

"Careful. That baby's sharper 'n' hell. A giant razor blade. This all's one of them gen-u-ine portable guillotines the Frenchies used to keep the zips in line, suckin' on government opium pipes."

"Flip, you own this thing?"

"Nearly. Whaddya think, Ellie? The posts stand fifteen feet high once they're put together. Blade fits on rails in between. They lash the dude to the plank 'n' shove him—or her—under the blade head first. Close the neck restraint, unleash the blade. Drops seven feet. Whap! Bounces a bit on these springs that cushion the fall so's it don't damage the edge. It's a honey, no?"

"Friggin' sensational."

"Body rolls right into that chest there, head tossed in after. Lined with zinc, for the blood."

"Still works?"

"Smooth as the tits on a goat. We had it operatin' this afternoon."

"What's the plan?"

"I'm thinkin' folks back home will flock to see it. Newsmen, TV reporters. Everybody and his missus will want a gander. Lotsa publicity wherever we send it. Tailgate picnics, mall openin's . . . choppin' heads o' lettuce at county fairs? Maybe slaughter a few head at livestock shows. Could be we rent it to Hollywood."

"How will you get the rig stateside?"

"Simple. Returning military get free shipment of household goods, right? I'm rotatin' back to the world early next month when my tour's done. The struts, blade, and casket fit into a freezer I bought. I crate 'er up, ship 'er stateside with the spin dryers and cribs gettin' sent home by the married studs. Hell, my bunkmate is shippin' a Studebaker Lark two-door. My crate sails on the third. I fly home Monday the fourth."

"How much?"

"This baby will run me twenty-two hundred. It'll take another three hundred to grease its way home. I got two other investors at five bills a head. There's two shares left. It's a great deal if you've got the coin."

"You coming back anytime soon?"

"A week after New Year's. Should take delivery on the freezer by month's end. I got lots of leave comin' to me in the Zone of the Interior. I'm thinkin' Louisville, maybe Memphis."

"But you're taking the bonus bait."

"Signing on the line and takin' the re-up money, damn straight." Flippi beamed alcohol and adrenalin. "So whaddaya say?"

The blade shone like coin silver in the streetlight.

"You up for a little cumshaw?"

He eyed me, excited. "Whaddya got?"

"Laotian horse. Half a kilo."

"Hells bells, yeah. We can work out a little somethin'."

"Might have another deal for you too," I said.

"That right?" Flippi pulled the tarp back over the machine and told the driver to *di di* as we jumped down.

"Seems there's an oil company guy who carries protection money to the VC on the first of every month," I said.

Flippi lit a joint and passed it over. "How much Cong insurance we talkin' about?"

"Monthly installment runs around eighty thou." I took a toke and held my breath.

"Eighty large?" Flippi whistled faintly.

The dope whooshed out. "I'm thinking we might liberate November's payout before it falls into enemy hands."

Flippi took back the weed. "Relieve the oil dude or the VC doin' the collecting?"

"The oil dude's safer," I said. "Unlikely he'll have a chaperone. The company won't want witnesses to the transaction. They won't make a stink when we confiscate the payout, either. They'll likely write it off their books and let the matter lie. The Cong, on the other hand, don't look kindly on anybody screwing with them. I wouldn't want those fuckers on my ass."

Flippi raised both fists. "Beau-ti-ful! Either way, nobody's gonna go complaining to the law. Who delivers the dough re mi?"

"Some office flunky at Dutch Shell."

"Shell? That's good, that's good. Fat and rich."

"So you in?"

"Deny the enemy aid and comfort? Shit yeah. It's fucking patriotic."

"I'm a bit tied up right now. Think you could figure out who actually hands it off?"

"Piece o' cake. My replacement's already here. I'm breakin' him in. Otherwise I'm free for playdates."

I retrieved the heroin from the hotel safe and handed it over. Cranked, Flip whooped and did a country jig. This doped-up good old boy knew how to clog dance.

"Hoorah, Sarge!" he half shouted. "I'll see you on the first. Anythin' to make this little old world safe for hypocrisy."

CHAPTER TWENTY-FOUR

Mrs. Lacey called early to say the intel reports and classified traffic the ambassador had requested were waiting for us at the embassy. I kissed Nadja goodbye and fetched Robeson. When we arrived, Mrs. Lacey said a room had been set aside for us on the Agency's floor.

"Take the stairs," she said. "Don't let the innocuous signs fool you." She reminded us nothing classified was to leave the building.

I impressed on her that a Mr. Fred Tuttle needed to get airborne immediately. Mrs. Lacey posed no questions, simply jotted down his information as I spoke. "I'll see to it, Sergeant Miser." I loved this woman.

After the yokel on reception duty checked our IDs and found us on the authorized list, a Southern belle came out and escorted us to a bare office. The only decoration was a newly printed poster of Nhu in his uniform as Supreme Leader of his pistol-packing boy scouts, the Republican Guard. Had the Agency guys hung it up as a joke, or a prediction? A mountain of classified paper weighed down the lone steel table and two credenzas behind it, with more piles growing like termite mounds up from the floor.

"We don't need everything from the beginning of time," I said to her.

Eyes sparkling, she replied in Southern singsong, "This output is just October, and the month isn't even done yet."

"What's with the barrels?" Robeson asked, pointing to a pair of metal drums stenciled with skull and crossbones.

"You mustn't touch those," she said. "They're full of chemicals for destroyin' classified papers in the event of a hostile intrusion, or an emergency evacuation of the chancery." Her blue eyes circled the room, taking in the surfaces and the wooden floor laden with stacked paper. "It might be quicker just to strike a match. This raggedy buildin's a firetrap. Consider yourselves lucky all this isn't for y'all. Come this way." She took us into an adjoining room.

Lodge had okayed our seeing all traffic and intelligence reports related to the Red Queen. Which turned out to be nearly nothing: a thin file consisting of a silly survey put out by General Harkins's headquarters, full of malarkey about precautions to take against further attacks by Unit Eight. And a skimpy alert from Air Force intelligence reporting rumors of an "unidentified VC female" thought to be targeting American advisors in Saigon.

"Damn, Sarge," Robeson said, "CIA's keeping close enough tabs on the Red Queen to know how she did in General Lang, but somehow with all their fancy deception and gadgets, they still haven't come up with anything we can use to locate her."

"Or anything they're willing to share." I tossed both files aside. "We don't know how long before she aligns on her big target, and what've we got? These bullshit intel alerts, some itty-bitty bones, and a corner of an astrological chart Miss Blue's poking at?"

"There's her calling cards," Robeson said. "Find the printer, maybe he tells us who ordered them. Gets us a little closer to finding someone on her team."

"A long shot," I said. "But I'll give it a try."

"I keep thinking about her latest hit. Killing General Lang put the hurt on Nhu's cash operations. I get why the VC would want that. But the *way* she did him in seemed awful intimate, you might say. Personal."

I saw his point. I went back to the corridor and found the Georgia peach. "Could you get us anything you've got on General Nguyen Van Lang?" I said. "Recently deceased."

"Sure thing." She took down the name and this time returned with a meaty file. I took half of it and handed Robeson the other half.

General Lang came from a banking family. *Graduate of Infantry School, Auvours, France, 1948. Command Class, Dalat, '53.* Made general at thirty-seven. He had an office at the Directorate of Commercial Aid, housed in the Ministry of the National Economy. Another at the National Bank of Viet Nam. A desk and secretary at the Personalist Party headquarters. Like Tuttle said, General Lang managed untold public sums and reported only to Nhu. He'd been living high on the blood and bones of his countrymen when the Red Queen stripped him naked and killed him with a crystal dagger. Sounded like a fairy tale.

"I think I got something. Listen to this," said Robeson, waving his portion of the report. He ran it down for me.

Four years ago, in '59, Lang was province chief of Tay Ninh on the Cambodian border. Diem had sent teams of police into the provinces to root out suspected Communists among the Viet Minh Independence League veterans who'd returned home to the South after defeating the French at Dien Bien Phu in

'54. After the alleged Communists were identified, Diem's army officers sat as judges in traveling kangaroo courts, trying and sentencing them—to prison or death—on the spot.

Robeson said, "And the man in charge of the adjudicating and eradicating in Tay Ninh? Colonel Nguyen Van Lang. Ain't Tay Ninh where the Red Queen made her bones with those roadside ambushes before getting promoted to Saigon?"

"And the medallion she used to pin her card to his eye, Blue said it was the cap insignia worn by the Cao Dai army in Tay Ninh."

I circled *Tay Ninh* and *Cao Dai* in my notebook.

A Marine guard appeared and had me sign for a manila envelope from Mrs. Lacey. Inside, I found a note saying that Donald had personally escorted "Mr. T" to the airport and onto a waiting plane. He would soon be over the Pacific, winging east to Manila, on to Alaska and a connecting flight to Chicago. Good news for Tuttle, but his departure also meant the Red Queen had no more loose ends to tie up from the CIP report. She could turn her full attention to taking out the Old Fox—unless she decided to check us off her hit list first.

The envelope also contained a brief rundown on the truck bomb that had nearly done in Lodge and me. Best for last: a memorandum in Vietnamese from the interrogation of Prisoner Tam. Lodge's juice had worked.

The Vietnamese memo was ours to take away, her note said, so we carried it quickly to the office to Miss Blue, proud holder of a Michigan State Certificate of English Proficiency. While she began typing her translation, we read the MAAG incident report on the bombing that had mangled the ambassador's limo. They'd sent the explosive remnants to the state-of-the-art forensics lab the CIA had built for the Vietnamese police. The

arsenic sulfide and potassium chlorate mixture had been deto-
nated with a timer from an electric stove. Same with the second
bomb we'd heard go off as we evacuated the area.

"Y'all were damn lucky," Robeson said. "Timer was set for
the wrong-minute egg or you'd be scrambled, my man, and I'd
be wadin' in these troubled waters all by my lonesome."

Robeson went to Blue's desk and looked over her shoulder
as she worked. He frowned. "This comes from the director of
Service des Études Politiques et Sociales. Service for Political and
Social Studies. That sounds . . ."

"Like nothing," I said. "Like our Office of Public Safety.
Real innocent." I froze as the penny dropped. "But if CIO
doesn't have Tam and SEPES does . . . Shit. Shit, shit, shit."

Robeson made a face. "Seeps?"

Blue pointed to the report. "*Say pay*," she said.

I held up a hand. "Seeps, *say pay*, whatever. They're Brother
Nhu's Personalist Party's secret enforcers."

"Nhu's political party has its own private goon squad?"

"Yeah, and you better hope Governor Wallace doesn't get
wind of the idea."

"George don't need no secret police. Fucker's already got the
Klan and Bull Connor."

"SEPES has no American advisors," I said. "No outsiders
means it's the police force Brother Nhu trusts most. He even
uses them to spy on his own loyalists. SEPES recruits people
who've got accounts to settle with the Communists. If they've
got Mr. Tam . . . Nhu's thugs will bleed every drop from him
and take their time doing it. Shit."

We waited impatiently for Blue's translation, which took
nearly an hour. When we sat down to read it, she hovered
behind us, worrying.

*I, Ba Van Tam, am born 1933. Thirty years ago. Small
coast city of Tuy Hòa my home place. My father, a merchant,
is Leninist.*

*I twelve years old when world war end and Japanese
surrender. Hồ Chí Minh declare us independent but American ship bring soldier of French to Hà Nội to take back
everything. In Sài Gòn, British army arm Japanese prisoner
to keep order. French again recruit the puppet emperor Bảo
Đại to make government. I join Vanguard Youth and haul
provisions to fighters in jungle. Do this for several year until
I myself am cadre. At twenty-one I fight in north's mountains
at Điện Biên Phủ in the valley of the Nam River. We defeat
16,000 foreign legionnaire and take their surrender.*

*The north of my country liberated. In south, Emperor
Bảo Đại appoint Ngô Đình Diệm prime minister and
United States pick up fallen banner of France.*

*In January 1958, committee send me to Viet Cong unit
in my home region to remove enemies of revolution. Most
our comrade female. Police or soldier less likely stop and
question womens. None have proper identity paper, but
movement for female is smaller risk than for mans. We spy
on traitors the Party condemn. How live, work, pleasure.
Again and again. After many week, pick place and time of
assassination. More than month to plan each.*

*We three executioner stay underground. After time and
place chosed, we surface. Women comrade lead us to marked
person. Usually we shoot. One guilty man we confront and
announce people's sentence. It too hard. Better strike and run
away fast.*

*We execute sub-sector chief, two informer, police captain,
village headman, two hamlet chief, a judge, and three*

landlord. Eleven traitor. Take one year for liquidate these eleven. Verdict arrive to eliminate enemy number twelve: schoolteacher who inform on sympathizer and our agent. My comrade track her. Tuesday she linger in schoolroom, always. She to die Tuesday. We find her in empty student room. I recognize her—old classmate. She big with child— pregnant.

Not resist, not beg. With knife to throat, she ask we wait one month until birth. She swear she accept her sentence then. My comrade want me cut her throat, like we plan. Order is order. Punishment harsh if we fail. But order say execute one, not two. Baby kick, already in first year of life. I not follow plan.

Our political officer scream and rant for many hour. I must write confession. Say long apology for her escape. Five week passing. Two comrade go to learn where she flee. She waiting. Hire wet nurse for infant, lay out funeral attire. Letter to her parent and husband ready. Infant name Van Tam. My name: Ba Van Tam. They shoot her once, in side of head.

In Sài Gòn, lady assassin kill American officer. Despite old disgrace, commissar assign me to second team to assist in important assassination. Need replace one of three comrade who talk between lady and cadre. They no with her except when attack. Commissar say I to help her quạt mo.

I said, "What does that mean, Miss Blue? *Quạt mo?*"

She bit her lip. "It mean—" She showed us, fanning herself with her hand.

"His commissar wanted Tam to help fan her?"

"No, no." She slapped the air again.

I raised my hands in surrender. "I don't get it."

"It mean, fan fire."

"Help fan the fire. Stir her up?"

"Fan spirit of Queen, yes. Mean also, hide face." She raised her hand, fingers spread to mask her features.

"Got it. Motivate her. Help her hide."

I turned back to the interrogation report.

I can no face more killing. I flee. Surrender as hồi chánh. American captain treat me well. I tell fable, that I regular guerilla soldier. My host silent. I give more information. Hope he keep me. When no more story to tell, Americans ready me for Open Arms center. Police claim me instead. Threaten prison. Bring me to Sài Gòn to inquisitor—you.

Your beasts beat me with rod. Torture with thong around genital and throat, run electricals to my private flesh, whip with bamboo, twist with plier, drown me. I confess everything again and again. No matter. You not stop. Every second day take me from cell. Ask nothing—just strike and twist and stab. Animal answer my scream. You, sir, smoke. They break bone in my hand, in ankle. Cut tendon each leg to hobble me. I stoop, made old in a night.

Torturer dig at fresh wound. I scream, retch, swear, beg. I not have shame. You write all I utter. Nothing I babble enough. Not stop pain. After last torture, throw me into pit with ash and lime. Something dead in gut. I not to survive. They not stop while I alive.

Tomorrow another second day. You leave soon. After midnight workmen of you come and begin again. If Spirit merciful, it last time in this life. You want make of me a terrible ghost, cut something from me so I not find way to grave. Confuse. Make lost. No find grave. But I find you.

"Amazing that they gave us even this much," I said. "Imagine what they kept back."

"Poor bastard." Robeson chewed on a fingernail.

"You done good work, Missy," I said over my shoulder. "Real good."

"Sad story," Blue said, walking slowly back to her desk.

Robeson pushed the report away. Neither of us had the stomach to read it again. "He didn't give them so much as her real name."

"You really believe this is all they got from him? I don't buy it. You think Tam didn't give up a single name after all that?"

Robeson shook his head.

"They're holding back plenty. We need to question Prisoner Tam ourselves."

"Who do we brace for that?" Robeson said. "And where do you think they're holding him? Chi Hoa prison?"

"Too big, too busy. They'll keep him away from any pen full of US advisors. He'll be someplace where there's no long noses."

"What's left? Nhu's secret-police headquarters near the Xa Loi pagoda?"

"CIA's got advisors there too." I rubbed my forehead, my eyes. "What did Tam say about creatures howling while he's being tuned up?"

Robeson picked up the translation, searching for the quote. Blue looked up from the torn piece of the astrologer's chart she'd been studying. "Animal answer my scream."

"Thanks, doll. 'Animal answer my scream,'" Robeson repeated. "What would howl back at him? Another prisoner being tortured? Jungle monkeys? Squealing pigs? Maybe he's being held in a slaughterhouse. What's the closest SEPES shithole?"

I turned to Missy Blue. "You ever hear of P-42?"

"You no go," Blue snapped.

"So it's a real place?"

"No go," Blue repeated.

Robeson glanced at her. "Go where?"

"A little out-of-the-way spa run by Nhu's party police," I said. "Supposedly somewhere underground in the Saigon zoo."

"I thought that was made-up bullshit, like the Pacific island where GIs with super serious venereal diseases get sent to watch their dicks fall off and die."

"It real," Blue said. "You no go."

Robeson looked at her with concern, then back at me. "How do we do this? The only credential we got is from the National Police—standard-issue paper in three languages saying they should treat us kindly, let us pass checkpoints after curfew, and not interfere in our work. We can't just sashay up to the door of some slope stalag and politely demand to parlay with a prisoner being worked over in their dungeon."

"It worked in Da Nang."

"These SEPES boys don't sound like Da Nang night-watch yokels. And we don't have enough Vietnamese between us."

I turned to Blue. "Missy, would you—"

She looked terrified but slouched toward the door.

Robeson didn't look happy either. "If Tam's been here in Saigon this whole time," he muttered to me, "we didn't need to go to Con Son. That sentry'd still be alive instead of patrolling through my dreams."

"Us unfortune," Missy said, clutching herself like a mourner.

CHAPTER TWENTY-FIVE

I forewarned Captain Deckle's clerk about where we were headed and what we might have to do if SEPES took exception to us invading their turf.

We signed out two flashlights big as clubs and swapped our .38s for .45s—more bang, more bullets. We filled extra magazines, then set off in the open jeep, Robeson at the wheel, Miss Blue alongside. Clovis took us straight up Catinat to the cathedral and hung a right, heading northeast on the broad Thong Nhat Boulevard. A half mile later we were at the gate of the high iron fence that surrounded the Jardin Zoologique et Botanique.

Six cents' worth of coins bought the three of us admission to the grounds. We strolled toward the zoo, trying to look casual. With four pounds of warm gun up against the crack of my sweaty ass, I felt anything but. I just hoped the .45 wouldn't take my pants to the ground during a confrontation.

Blue took the lead. We followed a horde of schoolchildren and their escorts, Vietnamese women in Western dresses and teachers in raspberry *ao dais*. The path took us past a gazebo, a long stone dragon, and some boys diving off a wooden footbridge into a pond filled with swans.

A wedding party passed, the bride in red, heading toward a grove of red Japanese maples. Blue and the other Vietnamese visitors stood still, not moving a muscle or speaking. Blue looked worried.

"What's wrong, Sweetness?" Robeson said.

"Cross path wedding people bad luck."

Robeson laughed. "That's all we need."

When the wedding party was finally out of sight, we continued through immaculate gardens with wood follies, cactuses and bonsai trees, reflecting pools of lilies and lotus blossoms, trestles covered with flowering vines, shrubs sculpted in the shapes of wild animals. Birds dozed in cages decorated with wrought-iron curlicues and bunches of grapes. Kids ran around the zoo tempting the captives with sugarcane.

Nothing looked out of the ordinary.

We circled a sunken enclosure for black bears, ducked a python knotting itself in a tree, and came to a large fenced-in area of gibbering red-assed monkeys. How were we supposed to find a hidden clink in all these acres? It's not like signs pointed THIS WAY TO THE DUNGEONS.

"Animals answered his screams," I said. "Gibbons? Macaws?"

Robeson shrugged. "Could be any critter short of a snake."

"Big cat," Blue interjected, so confidently I wondered if she already knew.

She pointed to the tigers staring up at us from a large open-air enclosure below grade. One tiger was napping in the water of a large pool, his head resting on a dry rock. A huge turtle slunk along the bank. Other tigers lounged deep inside a cage at ground level. A handful of visitors stood watching one of the cats pace back and forth along its bars. Pausing, it peed in their direction. A young girl shrieked. The rest of the visitors laughed. Ignoring the puny humans, the huge creature resumed its prowling.

Robeson pointed with his chin toward a French-era building set in a grove of casuarina trees loaded with green flowers spiky as pinecones.

"You think there's a back way out of there?"

"Probably," I said. "Why?"

"Take a look at those guys stepping real lively like they got a serious destination. They sure don't look like no zookeepers to me."

Both men entering the building wore aviator sunglasses. One had on a jacket of thin Italian leather, the insane gestapo look Vietnamese special-branch policemen favored even in the heat. I looked at Blue. She nodded. Me and Robeson touched the extra magazines in our pockets to make sure they faced the right way for quick reloading.

"We stroll in that same door, real brazen," I said. Once inside, we slunk along a corridor that led straight back to a guard wearing a shoulder holster and sitting at a crude desk. He didn't look like an animal lover, any more than the guys we'd seen coming in.

In a shrewish voice I'd never heard before, Missy Blue announced we were there to interrogate Prisoner Tam. We held up our credentials. The guard popped to his feet and called out. Armed men appeared, Sten guns at the ready. One reached out a hand to frisk Robeson, who slapped it away.

Missy brashly kept talking. Robeson muttered under his breath to give me the gist: Missy was insisting we had clearance to question the prisoner. She pointed at me and said I had been sent this memorandum from the Personalist Party. On her cue, I casually flashed the SEPES interrogation report, pointing to the official signatures, which clearly startled him. Missy bluffed good.

A captain in a red beret stormed toward us, swagger stick under his arm. He read out the prisoner's name and number from the memo and announced to Blue that the man was no longer available for interview. No, he had not been moved elsewhere. He was dead.

"Oh hell," Robeson groaned. "Dead again?"

Blue insisted we would need to confirm this for our superiors. The officer gave a nod. Robeson shot me a look that said this was too easy. He was right. I got the distinct feeling they knew we were coming.

The guard manning the desk led us down a steep set of stairs into an airless underground labyrinth. The farther we went into the maze of passages the hotter it got. We smelled them before we saw them, packed solid in sweltering cells: men penned like chickens, jammed so tight they couldn't possibly all lie down or sit at the same time. They hadn't bathed in weeks or even months. Their latrine boxes smelled like they hadn't been emptied in days. Half-naked prisoners in tattered underwear stared blankly, lowing like cows as we passed. Some squatted with their wrists shackled to their ankles and then to a rod in the floor. The ones closest to the bars fanned stale air to others farther back. The fingernails on the hands that reached out to us were missing or black. Gagging at the stench, we went by like tourists in hell, not wanting to see, unable to look away.

Robeson said, "Tell me we're gonna get outta here as easy as we got in, bro."

"Oh, *now* you come with the 'bro.'"

"Damn, Ellsworth." Robeson's voice was hoarse. "Your leadership ain't inspirin' confidence."

"No way they're keeping us here—bro."

A crude sign outside a dim room read LA MORGUE. The

guard urged us to enter and like fools we did. Two bare bulbs hung above a row of draped bodies laid on packing crates almost the size of caskets. A fan barely disturbed the air. Something skittered behind the crates as we approached: a large bug or a small rat. The corpses were ripe, their decomposition accelerated by the tropical heat trapped underground. I lifted the sheet off the first body. It was not uncommon for the lips of the deceased to be cosmetically sealed to spruce up a corpse. But this guy's lips had been sewn shut while he was alive. I dropped the sheet. It was hard to think straight with demons leering from the shadows.

A civilian in a soiled white coat and apron entered behind us and introduced himself.

"He doctor for dead," Blue said through the hanky she held to her face.

"Ask him which is Tam."

The doc consulted his notebook and led us to the farthest body. He delicately pulled back the sheet from the face and torso.

"*Trời ơi*," Blue gasped, her voice coarse with shock.

"God in Heaven," Robeson croaked.

Was it even Tam? I held up my flashlight while Robeson compared the pulp of the formerly human face to the Polaroid snapshot the Psy Ops captain had taken in Da Nang.

"Whaddya think?" I said, mopping stinging sweat from my eyes.

Robeson squinted. "He's beyond fucked up."

"He Tam," Blue said, peering from behind her man.

How could she tell? The bludgeoned face was swollen and clenched, mutilated beyond reason. He had bitten through his lip in two places.

"Maybe you should turn away now," I said to Missy.

She didn't. I pulled aside the rest of the sheet, exposing welts and cuts and huge bruises all over his scarred flesh, strips of which were missing. Fluid and pink blood leached from everywhere. Most of his major bones looked broken. Bulges and discoloration covered him all over, even his dick, which stood erect and huge. It was red, yellow, black, purple, blue. He had been ripped up, taken apart, the mechanism completely undone. Pieces of him were destroyed or missing altogether. No way he could ever have been put back in working order.

"I seen a lot of nasty cadavers in my day," Robeson said, "including a boy roasted to death inside burning tires." Sweat dripped from his face, his arms. "Never seen nobody this wrecked."

Dread washed over me. No way were we going to let ourselves be detained in this hell. If we were challenged, it would be on.

The doc spoke again. Blue listened closely and interpreted politely, like we were at a diplomatic function.

"Doctor say family come on bus today, from Tuy Hòa. Collect body. He say prisoner die from beating." The doc nattered again. "Die of other prisoner beating."

"Ask him why the . . ."—I pointed—"the member is so large and hemorrhaged."

The coroner looked uncomfortable as she put my question to him. He said something, smiling broadly, and left the room.

"Let me guess," I said, "he remembered pressing business elsewhere?" Blue nodded.

Robeson said, "You okay, Miss Blue?" She looked gray, holding her hands tightly in front of her.

"*Dây thần kinh run rẩy*," she whispered. "Shake nerve."

Robeson took out his big pistol. He swayed from foot to foot and pointed it toward the man's privates. "That . . . that just ain't right."

I shone my flashlight where he was pointing. Something stuck out of the man's dick, glistening.

Robeson leaned closer. "Glass. Looks like glass," he said, voice gravelly. "A catheter?"

"What?" I snapped. "They fucking embalm him through his johnson?"

Robeson breathed heavily, his mouth open. "It's solid. A glass rod."

"Why in the hell'd they shove that in him?" I said.

"To get everything out of him."

"Nobody knows everything."

"The man must've wished he did," Robeson said, "when they snapped the rod."

CHAPTER TWENTY-SIX

Except for the penned-up prisoners, no one was around to wish us a fond farewell from Hades until we got to the top of the stairs. An armed party of six men and their leader had gathered by the duty desk, blocking the exit. Robeson made a noisy show of racking a round. I followed suit and we marched straight at 'em like they weren't there. Blue seemed to be mumbling a prayer as she trailed behind us.

Twenty steps from the not-so-secret policemen of the Personalist Party's finest, she started making terrifying moans. As we turned to look, she took the gold ring from her finger and threw it at the wall, keening like a banshee.

"So many," she cried out, hysterical.

"Many?" Robeson asked, perplexed. "Many what?"

"Ma đói! Ma đói!" She continued in fast, howling Vietnamese. I looked at Robeson.

"She's talkin' about hungry ghosts."

Blue pleaded with the unhappy spirits. Wrestling her purse open, she threw a handful of coins toward the wall, and another. Coins flew and bounced everywhere.

Every Vietnamese feared wandering souls. The cops yammered rapidly to one another and backed away. Blue laid into them, screeching. They started pulling loose bills from their trouser pockets and tossing them in the direction of the wall. Their leader shouted angrily, but two of the cops turned and bolted for the door, quickly followed by the other four, everyone but the leader. The door banged behind them.

Blue gasped and moaned louder. The boss walked, as slowly as he dared, out to the daylight after his men.

I bent to retrieve Blue's gold ring and coins.

"No, no," she called out, her voice shaky. "Better you leave."

The three of us emerged into the heat of the most beautiful ever-lovin' day I'd ever seen. Robeson held his arm tightly around Missy's waist. "You totally saved our bacon."

She looked confused, but leaned into his embrace.

As we passed the jittery SEPES creeps, Robeson grinned. "Go piss up a rope, pig swill," he said, with a rictus smile.

WE INFORMED CAPTAIN Deckle that it looked like we were never going to learn what else Tam had told his interrogators.

"Was there *anything* useful in the interrogation report?" Deckle demanded.

I tried to run through it in my head, barely able to think after what we'd seen.

"Maybe one thing," Robeson said.

"Yeah? What?" Deckle looked hopeful.

"Tam says he was assigned to her *second* team in Saigon. And then he says he was the replacement for one of her *three* go-betweens."

"Christ," I said, catching Robeson's drift. "We should have suspected."

"Suspected what?" Deckle said.

"The size of her operation. She kills three—four, counting General Lang—in what, less than two weeks? Tam said the legwork for just one premeditated killing took his discipline committee weeks. She managed *four* in half the time his group took to execute one traitor. How? Because it's three separate teams, not one team rotating roles. She don't have to rotate nobody."

"Damn," Deckle blurted. "We're thinking we have to identify which Old Fox she's going after. She could be prepping to take out both—and lining up on a third." Which could easily be me.

I shook my head at the scope of what we were facing. "Three death squads, three different cells, each one walled off from the other two. Each team sets up its own target. When they have the person, the place and the time, she activates that group, has herself delivered to the scene at the precise moment."

Robeson whistled. "Twenty years old and coordinating *three* assassination committees?"

I leaned on Captain Deckle for extra agents, arguing that she had way more people prepping her targets than we had hunting for her. And if Lodge was next, his existing security wasn't worth shit. We needed help guarding him if the ambassador was going to stay in one piece while me and Robeson were chasing her down. Plus a man to spare to get up to Tay Ninh.

"All right, point taken." Deckle folded and put out the word to three good investigators in Nha Trang to drop everything and report to CID in Saigon.

I swapped the .45 for my holstered .38 while Corporal Magid briefed us on the personal information he'd been able to gather about the first two murdered MAAG officers. Like Furth, both had recently been seen in the company of demure local women. Nothing definite. But I couldn't help wondering if, far from remaining hidden until the moment of attack, the Red Queen was moving anonymously aboveground, personally taking the measure of her victims, charming them, maybe even bedding them, as she made ready for their murders. Had she made them all come to her?

If that had been her play with the three MAAG officers and General Lang, it wouldn't get her anywhere with Cabot Lodge or celibate Diem, whose personal life was a zero; the only girl he'd ever wooed had signed on with a religious order and taken vows. A Bible was all that sorry soul ever curled up with. Diem only had eyes for the Virgin Mary and Lodge only for his wife. Neither one was a womanizer. She'd need a different tactic.

Robeson and I were too quaky to sit around the office listening to the captain stoke himself up to convey our revised assessment of the Red Queen's reach upstairs to Major Asshole. Missy Blue, Robeson and I went back to the Majestic. They disappeared into his room and I called up to Nadja's. Happily, she had retreated from her office when their air-conditioning failed.

We shared a quick, distracting shower. I badly needed to walk off my nerves, so we set out along rue Catinat, me in desert boots and drip-dry civvies doused with water, Nadja in canvas sandals and a forbidden thin sleeveless dress. The dress was plain, the bare-armed girl beautiful. I draped a soaked kerchief around her neck and tied one around mine. A rivulet slid down her skin and disappeared under the bodice. I traced its path with my finger as far as I dared in public.

Rue Catinat remained very French. Unlike other parts of the city, the sidewalks were intact, not pitted or cracked, and paved with small rectangular tiles. We moved gratefully into the shade of the tamarind trees that lined our route from the foot of the river toward the cathedral and the old Sûreté head-quarters, now VBI, where my sometime colleague Captain Ting was assigned.

I wanted to stop at Aspar printers to ask the Portuguese proprietor if he might be able to run off some cards.

"Business cards?" he said. "Calling cards?"

"Larger—the size of, oh, a playing card."

"We can produce invitations, announcements, note cards. No engraving, I am afraid."

"This wouldn't need engraving." I took out my wallet and handed him the death card I'd found in the jeep. He went pale.

"We . . . ah . . . cannot do anything illustrative. No four-color graphics."

Nadja peered at the ghoulish figure, obviously curious. "This appears to be only three colors."

"Monsieur, madame," he said, sweat beading at his hairline. "It is most illegal to own so much as an unregistered mimeo-graph machine. Our printing press, she is closely monitored." His brow furrowed. "To manufacture cards such as this is absolutely forbidden."

"Full decks of gaming cards, sure. But this would be only the one. A novelty."

The man held the death card by one corner like it was gonna burn his hand. "I can make no such piece for you."

Nadja said, "By chance, do you recognize the printer? Or perhaps the artist?"

"This is done on a letterpress, but I don't recognize the workmanship or the artist, no." He was clearly eager to hand it back.

Nadja tried a flirty smile. "Do you know of a printer who might be persuaded to do a job like this?"

"No, madame. No one would defy the president's morality decrees or wish to bring unwanted awareness in such times as these."

I thanked him and slipped the card back into my breast pocket. No doubt her cards had been run off in a printing shop deep in the Chinese district of Cholon where Diem's morality laws were meaningless. A shop I'd never be able to find.

We continued up Catinat. Every shop window displayed the obligatory photo of "beloved" President Diem. None of Nhu—yet. The kerchiefs around our necks were already dry. We ducked into the Thai Thach gourmet shop to drink in the air-conditioning and the rich aromas of imported French mustards and cheeses. We bought cold sodas in bottles and downed them quickly. Nadja held the sweaty glass to her cheek and told me about street vendors in Warsaw who wheeled a kind of mobile carbonation cart invented by Communist engineers.

"You get two choices," she said. "With raspberry juice or without. But you don't get your own individual glass. The cart comes with glass cups permanently attached by strings. After you've had your drink, the cup gets a quick rinse and it's ready for the next customer. We call the soda *gruźliczanka*. Tuberculosis water."

We snuck a kiss before reentering the stifling heat and crossed the wide median, making our way through the rows of motorbikes parked under its trees. A half-dozen blankets lay spread on the far sidewalk: a mini black market in canned goods and sodas. A crippled vendor displayed a few paltry loose pencils and cigarettes, but she also had V8 juice, hard to find in Saigon, asking about eight cents a can. I bought a few for Robeson and accepted the precious plastic bag she put them in.

A beggar sitting cross-legged on the shady sidewalk moaned

as he exposed legs covered with sores and extended what was left of his hand. I dropped some coins in the leprous paw, hoping he'd get out of there before the white mice found him sullying the fashionable street.

"C'mon," I said. Nadja nodded, hand to her mouth.

Near the corner Tran Thi Banh squatted beside her two young children. She was a regular, an ARVN wife living in the street, worried her husband would never find her again if she left Saigon. Her own possessions sat in a nearby doorway: a cooking pot, a ceramic brazier, two spoons, a few clothes for her and the kids. I bought both packs of Camels she had on offer for eleven cents apiece. They went into the plastic bag with the cans.

I could feel the heat penetrating the soles of my shoes even as kids passed us barefoot, heading to their napping places. My brains were steaming by the time we reached 213 Catinat, which housed the Indian and Filipino embassies as well as the august dental office of Dr. Nguyen Van Tho. I didn't like dentists, I told Nadja, but definitely endorsed Tho over the sidewalk docs who pulled teeth curbside for pennies.

Out of Tho's office strolled the unmistakable one-and-a-half-handed figure of CIA's bad boy, Lucien Conein. Conein looked straight through us, did an about-face, and walked casually back toward the cathedral. I turned and noticed a black Renault parked at the curb. A streak of red marred its shiny front hubcap: the not-so-private sign secret policemen used to identify themselves to one another. Nhu's undercover cops weren't even bothering to camouflage their presence. The car started up and rolled slowly in the direction Conein was walking.

"Who was that?" Nadja said. "And what happened to his hand?"

"You could say that he's another legit sort of shady guy." I explained that Conein liked to tell people he'd lost several fingers in a clandestine op, but in fact he'd lost them to the fan of a stalled automobile he'd been trying to fix on his way to an assignation with his best friend's wife. At least according to Radio Catinat.

Nadja and I turned back toward the Majestic. A second car, a Citroën Black Maria, sat at the curb, its rear hubcap also streaked with a splash of red, the driver smoking. A Westerner and a Vietnamese idled in the shade across the street, sweltering in the stupefying heat. I could see them reflected in store windows as they trailed us along the opposite sidewalk.

"Damn."

"What's the matter?" she said.

"Something I forgot I needed to pick up."

I took her to Rickard's gunsmith shop, where I bought a full-speed loader for my .38, which I pocketed, and a box of ammunition that I added to my plastic carryall. I had plenty of extra ammo back at the office, but you never knew when you might need some sooner.

As an afterthought, I asked Rick if by any chance he had a Vis Radom for sale. He opened a display case and brought the pistol out on a black velvet mat.

"A Polish gun!" Nadja exclaimed. "You are becoming a little fond of Poland, I think."

The piece was beautifully balanced, the pale grips comfortable. The gun felt good in my hand. I could see why the Red Queen favored it.

"You sell any of these lately, Rick?"

"Nah, can't remember the last time anyone picked one up."

Like printers, willing gun-sellers would be easy for her to find in Cholon. But not for me.

I slipped my pistol into the bag just out of sight, finger on the trigger. If needed, I could let the weighted bag drop away and raise the weapon in one motion.

Our shadows were waiting for us outside Rick's shop. The Asian man had crossed to our side; the Westerner remained on the opposite pavement. I mentioned them to Nadja, but she seemed unconcerned.

"Coming from what you call an Iron Curtain country, one is used to being observed," she explained. I wished I could be that calm; I was still shaky after the zoo.

I started to steer her toward the Aterbea, a small upstairs bistro near the Caravelle, then thought better of it. A public place with lots of Americans would be safer.

CHAPTER TWENTY-SEVEN

Nadja's face was flushed and her hand felt clammy. We needed to get inside before she worked herself into heatstroke. I urged her past the Caravelle's Sikh doorman in red uniform and turban. The Caravelle was Saigon's newest and biggest hotel, where the Australian and New Zealand embassies had their premises. At seventeen bucks a night, it was also the priciest, not that the guys at the bar in Jerome's were paying for their housing or booze. The serious papers and magazines took good care of their newsmen. Jerome's was the watering hole for all the big-shot journalists who'd come to hike through scrub and jungle or sit through the daily bullshit military briefings at the Rex Hotel, popularly called the "Five O'Clock Follies."

"Champs Elysées restaurant if you're hungry?" I said. "Or Jerome's Bar?"

"I have no appetite in this heat. Jerome's."

"How are you feeling?"

"Light-headed. Trembly."

I ordered us cold Cokes in frosted glass steins and checked the room to see if our tails had followed us upstairs. Didn't seem like it, though they could have switched off with another team. Jerome's was full of familiar TV faces in town to cover the coming coup, complaining loudly about the long wait for the action to begin.

I swigged my drink and licked my parched lips. Nadja sipped slowly from her stein, then took out a cigarette and lit up. She didn't like hypodermics, she said, and preferred to smoke her heroin. Easy to do in Saigon, where the smack was cheap and unusually pure. More important, it didn't give off an odor as it burned. You could smoke heroin in public, even in the spiffy, high-class saloon where we'd parked ourselves, and nobody would notice unless you fell off your barstool.

Nadja slid her fingers up my chest and extracted the card from my shirt pocket. Her glass stein went up again for another long sip, her eyelids dipping for a moment. She applied the icy glass to her forehead.

"Is this the calling card of the 'Lady Death' I've been hearing about?"

I nodded. "We call her the Red Queen." Helping myself to her funny cigarette, I took a long drag and handed it back, holding my breath.

"I see why you might. Perhaps your job is a little bit exciting after all," she said, her smile full of mischief. I shrugged, my lungs and cheeks full of her magic smoke. My heart rate slowed. For a moment, images of the nightmare morgue stopped flashing in my brain.

"Am I going to read about you in the papers when you catch her?"

Better than reading about her catching up with me, I thought. The smoke escaped from me in a smooth rush.

Coyly, she said, "What a story I'll have to sell then: 'My wild nights of love with the sheriff who snared the Viet Cong's infamous girl assassin.'"

She held my chilled glass stein to one flushed cheek, her own against the other, and closed her eyes. She looked blissful. I asked for a glass of ice water, dunked her kerchief, wrung it out and draped it back around her neck.

"Mmm, that feels—"

I smiled and brushed stray strands from her moist face. The heat and the dope had made her loopy.

She swayed and I grabbed her by the elbows. Sweat glistened on her upper lip and the pale skin above the low scoop neck of her dress. She smelled of talcum and whatever women sweated that made men woozy.

Nadja put down the steins, took another long drag and looked like she'd inhaled light. She was beautiful stoned and I told her so, which launched a complicated discussion of whether she was beautiful in my eyes because I was "trollied" too, or because she was? Or . . . The thread of possibilities slipped away.

I hoped Nadja might return to earth once she got some food inside her, but she barely grazed on the appetizers. Her eyes were like saucers. The bartender sold me a pair of sunglasses that somebody had forgotten and I stuck them on her cute nose.

"I shouldn't have taken you out in this heat. We should go. Bathroom first?"

"No need. All those drinks and I swear I don't need the loo."

I made her drink more Coke and helped her to the lift. If our watchers were in the lobby, they'd be expecting us to emerge from the elevator, so we got off on the first floor and took the stairs. The two men were seated on an upholstered silk couch, facing the elevator bank with their backs to the staircase. I slid Nadja into an armchair and took a seat at the small writing desk just behind the couch. Nadja began snoring. I had to work hard not to laugh. The sound was so aged for someone so young and beautiful.

I lit a cigarette and blew smoke over their heads. They didn't notice. I stubbed out the cigarette and asked the white guy for a light. He barely glanced up. Just patted his shirt pocket for his lighter, a snazzy little silver deal. He froze when he turned to find me at his shoulder, my hand in the bag on the writing desk, gun pointed at him.

"Thanks, pal," I said, as I bent toward the flame.

He signaled his Asian partner and made to rise. Nadja blinked herself awake and upright. She beamed at the Western dude like he was family. The Vietnamese guy leapt up, startled at being caught out. The senior man quieted him with a look and they left like normal citizens. Nadja followed me to the door, where we watched them cross Lam Son Plaza and walk past the National Assembly to their waiting Black Maria.

"At least they weren't armed," she said, not having seen the bulges above their ankles. "Who were they?"

"The Asian looked Vietnamese. The other one could have been anything."

"Guess his nationality," Nadja said. She sounded worried, or was it just the opium?

"Aussie, American, badly dressed Frenchman? Doesn't matter. They're all from the same place," I said. "Spookland."

"But what nationality did he look like to you?"

I took her hand. "Trouble, honey. They all just look like trouble."

We hopped in a taxi and were home five blocks later. As we got out, she whispered that the doorman was taking down the license plate of our cab. Did I think he was one of them too? I brushed back her hair and told her not to worry. Like all Vietnamese, Gai the doorman was always on the prowl for lucky numbers to play and she looked like someone fortune favored.

CHAPTER TWENTY-EIGHT

The envelope with the official seal of the United States had been delivered to the front desk of the Majestic by embassy courier. I brushed away the spots of fresh cockroach droppings that stained the fancy blue envelope. The matching card inside fit exactly, a handwritten dinner invitation to the ambassador's private residence, signed *Emily Lodge*.

Saigon had no television station, and barely a power grid or a telephone system. After three attempts, I gave up trying to get through to the embassy to *respondez*. I poured Najda into her bed and went back to the office to use the military phone.

Warrant Officer Rider and Sergeants Moehlenkamp and Francis had arrived from Nha Trang. I told Rider and Francis I'd be with Ambassador Lodge tonight, and assigned them to stake him out starting at 0600 the next morning, in the hopes her advance team might show itself as they clocked the ambassador's movements for repeated behaviors that would help them plan the Red Queen's attack.

"If we position ourselves right following the ambassador, I'm hoping Unit Eight will come to us. Like the Vietnamese say, 'The water is in the well.'"

Sergeant Francis shuffled a deck one-handed. "You've been in-country too long, Sergeant Miser."

"I'll notify the embassy Marines you'll be trailing the ambassador. Contact me or Robeson quick if you get suspicious about anybody in his slipstream."

I told them he'd almost certainly start his morning swimming laps at the Cerc, and also cautioned them: if they noticed a slight, attractive, demure young Vietnamese woman anywhere in the proximity of Ambassador Lodge, it might be the Red Queen herself.

I gave Moehlenkamp the Cao Dai military medallion Ting had slipped us, and told him to get up to the sect's headquarters in Tay Ninh City near the Cambodian border. "You're looking for anyone who can connect the medallion to a female sharpshooter from the region."

After Moehlenkamp left for the airport, I called Captain Ting to get his read on who might have been tailing me. I kept the question vague but he got the idea. He said he hoped we might perhaps run into one another soon—meaning he'd call to meet up when he knew something.

I returned to the Majestic, but it was still early, so I went upstairs to the roof where Seftas was already encamped on his usual barstool. "Sef" raised his chin, acknowledging me as he tapped ashes from his cigarette.

I checked my watch before taking a stool.

"Hot date with the honeypot?" he asked.

"Dinner at the ambassador's residence."

"Oooh." Seftas grimaced. "Dinner with the Man. Tread careful. Don't get dis-Lodged. He's racked up quite a body count. You realize you're dining tonight at the Richardsons' old place?"

"You're kidding."

"Richardson was sandbagged and barely gone from Saigon

when Lodge appropriated it for himself. A class-A power move lost on no one."

"Yeah: cross the ambassador and get shopped."

Seftas scanned the roof. "And with Richardson gone home to DC, there's no one left to object if Lodge wants to lay out emergency funds to back the coup plotters. Mr. Ambassador's free to goose the generals, offering fat overseas accounts and bona fide passports with visas along with the absolutely first-class escape routes if things don't work out when they storm the palace. Well, maybe somebody's objecting. The Dragon Lady's been giving newspapers an earful of poison, accusing us of conspiring with the Viet Cong, if you can believe it, to overthrow Diem. In the event of an attempted coup, she says certain Americans—meaning your host, no doubt—stand a good chance of being assassinated themselves. A not-very-subtle threat that he should not be encouraging rebellion."

"You buy it that Lodge is backing a coup?" I said.

"I do. Seems he has a direct go-between with the coup plotters. Name of Lulu."

I groaned. "Tell me they're not using Lulu's bordello in Vientiane to put their deal together."

"Madam Lulu's Peace Palace." Seftas snickered. "Secret meetings in a brothel, no one paying any mind to who's slipping in and out, everybody real discreet." He shook his head and smiled to himself. "Fucking ballsy if it's true."

A PAIR OF Marine guards waved me past the sentry box at the residence gate. The white stucco house looked like a modest mansion on Philly's Main Line.

An elderly male servant knelt on the grass, pouring salt into an old-fashioned ice cream bucket while a woman cranked the handle and churned. A lance corporal in camouflage utilities squatted next to them, advising. A new Air Force AR-15 lay across his knees. The old man looked up from his labors and gave me a toothy gold smile.

Gravel crunched underfoot as I tromped up the inclined driveway. A Marine in battle dress peered down at me from his balcony perch on top of the portico. On the raised patio at the side of the house, a woman sat watching the twilight fade. Behind her, French doors stood open to the evening. White blurs of blossoms wound around a trellis, scenting the oncoming darkness. Bats darted overhead, scooping insects from the air. A manservant lit large hanging coils that would smoke and smolder, keeping mosquitoes away.

I mounted the steps to the front door. A maid showed me to a sitting room, where a little green light pulsed to the music on the Grundig radio-gramophone as Louis Armstrong and his All-Stars blasted out their New Orleans rendition of "*Ochi Chernyie*" on the turntable under the raised lid.

Over the mantel hung a large painting of a very white woman lying very naked on a velvet couch, her pussy showing. An Italian gent was admiring it and asked if I didn't think the "craquelure" was fantastic. Looked pretty average to me.

Emily Lodge came through the French doors in a dress of tangerine colored Thai silk and introduced us to one another—Ambassador Giovanni d'Orlandi of Milan, dean of the Saigon diplomatic corps. And me, US Army gendarme, Detective Ellsworth Miser from Philly.

D'Orlandi shook my hand enthusiastically. "Nadja's young man!"

Emily Lodge looked momentarily confused until he

explained. "He's seeing one of ICC's loveliest young associates. A delightful Polish girl with a degree from London."

Emily Lodge gave me a knowing look. My secret was out. A servant girl offered us glasses of prosecco and spicy pork balls on a bed of banana leaves, usually served raw. Mercifully, these had been cooked. A male servant drew the curtains on the picture window and turned on more lights.

Ambassador Lodge came downstairs wearing pleated trousers, shiny loafers without socks, and a pink-and-yellow striped dress shirt. He shook my hand and embraced the Italian. Though ten years younger than Lodge, d'Orlandi looked older, plagued by a parasite that had made itself at home in his gut, he said, and quickly changed the subject.

We were led into yet another room, filled floor to ceiling with empty shelves. The Italian and I took armchairs; Emily and Lodge, the couch. A huge vase on a side table overflowed with snapdragons, daisies, and what looked like a version of my uncle's zinnias. From Dalat, Emily said. A houseman poured drinks and the two ambassadors got right into it, d'Orlandi working hard to make his host think better of President Diem.

"*Et tu*, Giovanni?" Lodge said with a laugh, but grew serious as he listened, shaking his head no. "Diem takes all our aid and refuses all our advice. Diem doesn't govern like a president. He rules like a patroon. The government looks like the Ngo family tree. Cousins, uncles, nephews. Anyone with authority is connected to Diem by blood or marriage. Competence seems an obsolete concept."

"Sir, this is Asia," I said. "Nobody trusts anybody outside of family."

"What would he need to do to rehabilitate himself in your eyes?" d'Orlandi asked.

"Do one thing we've asked him to. Any one. Washington pressed him for accommodation on the Buddhist question," Lodge said. "He insisted he would—and hasn't. Same with land reform. He doesn't budge. Or dissolve the Personalist Party and allow genuine opposition parties to form. Promises, always promises. Never action. We would especially appreciate it if the South Vietnamese actually took the field to confront the Communist threat. Instead, the units hunker in stand-down positions so they can dash to Saigon to protect Diem if and when there's a coup. He has taken the Special Forces we've paid for and trained and turned them into a private security force for his own family."

"The internal threats against his administration are real."

"True enough," Lodge conceded. "And most of them he's brought on himself."

"Diem needs help," d'Orlandi said.

"And we're ready to provide it. Washington is of a mind to bring in American troops. But Diem won't hear of it, even though his huge army is moribund and the government completely seized up. Frozen in mid-crisis while he burrows into the tiniest administrative details. Does this village get electricity? Does that hotel get a permit to build? You've seen the state of his office in the palace. Stacks of passports, waiting for his personal blessing because Diem insists on signing every one of them himself. Student visas rot on his desk so long the kids with free rides in overseas colleges lose their scholarships. Inexcusable. While guerillas gnaw at the country's guts and monks incinerate themselves in the streets, he busies himself with minor bureaucratic labors. He delegates nothing." Lodge was indignant. "One whole side of the office is lined with sideband radios he uses to order around his troops in the field. Some units have to report their positions to him every hour. That's bloody insane, never mind inefficient." He opened his hands in a helpless gesture. "We may have to disassociate ourselves if this goes on much longer."

Washington would bring Diem to heel or find another top dog to supply with money, coaches, combatants. I wondered if Diem's face would appear in the clouds.

D'Orlandi looked thoughtfully at his drink. "I am not sanguine about President Diem's chances of remaining in power. But I don't see a viable alternative."

Lodge smiled. "Our ambassador to India likes to say, 'Nothing succeeds like successors.' There's always someone to step into the breach. He needn't be perfect. He could hardly be worse."

Emily Lodge looked uncomfortable. Trying to distract her guest and husband for her, I said, "Have you heard about the magic fish in Quang Nam province?" All three shook their heads. "There's this gigantic old carp in a pond in Quang Nam. The local Buddhists claim the fish is a disciple of Buddha so the pond's become a pilgrimage site. The powers here in Saigon started getting nervous that hundreds of Buddhist pilgrims could easily turn into protesters, so Colonel Tung dispatched some of his Red Berets to Quang Nam."

"Who will rid me of this turbulent carp?" Emily said, laughing.

"The Red Berets sprayed the pond with automatic fire. Nothing. They covered the surface with bread crumbs to attract the fish, then tossed in grenades. The carp kept swimming. Believers started coming from all over the country to commune with the remarkable fish and drink the miraculous pond water, including ARVN soldiers. So government flunkies planted the story that the water was poisoned. Which changed nothing, except now the visitors started to protest the government's actions. They can't kill the carp, and they can't stop the demonstrations. My mama-san at the Majestic said it was an omen."

The Lodges laughed politely. The Italian commissioner didn't.

"Cabot's grandfather's dearest friend became a Buddhist monk," Emily Lodge told d'Orlandi, trying to lighten the mood. D'Orlandi apparently didn't find the image of a Boston Brahmin sitting cross-legged in a three-piece suit as funny as I did. He looked grim, whether from the trouble in his gut or the attitude of the American ambassador, I couldn't tell.

Seeing that her first attempt hadn't worked, Emily Lodge tried again. "Counselor Nhu," she said, "was very sweet with his wife last month at Tan Son Nhut."

"Oh, yes?" d'Orlandi said.

"Nhu and the children were seeing her off on her grand tour. Remember ours, Cabot?" she said to her husband, happiness lighting her elegant face.

"Good gracious," Lodge said. "We were in our twenties. Newlyweds."

D'Orlandi brightened. "You honeymooned in Asia, Emily?"

"We did. We were here, in Saigon, thirty-five years ago. It was enchanting." She and Lodge gazed at one another.

"*You* were enchanting," he said, and leaned over to kiss her on the cheek.

A gong announced dinner and he extended a hand to help her up.

CHAPTER TWENTY-NINE

Four places were set at the far end of a long candlelit table. Orchids bloomed on the serving counter laid out with shelled lobsters and an artichoke salad. A houseboy poured a French white wine. The first course was crab and soupe Chinoise.

D'Orlandi and Lodge did most of the talking over dinner while I daydreamed about the fancy meals I'd treat Nadja to when Flip and I pulled off our little redistribution of oil-company wealth. Seeing I wasn't following the diplomatic back-and-forth, Emily Lodge quietly surprised me with questions about my "young lady" and the difficulties of dating in a besieged city where the usual forms of entertainment had been outlawed.

"You're a fortunate young man," she said, "to have found love in this troubled place. Tell me, what's been the biggest obstacle?"

"Probably that she's a Communist."

She burst out laughing, as if I'd made a joke. Lodge and d'Orlandi stopped mid-sentence and looked over to see what had her so amused.

Dessert was homemade mango ice cream doused with Courvoisier, accompanied by dark-roast Vietnamese coffee from a highland plantation. D'Orlandi asked to speak with the ambassador privately.

Emily offered me port. No one had ever done that before. I pretended to ponder.

"Whiskey it is," she teased. "Ice?"

"Straight, please."

"Here you are, Agent Miser," she said, "neat." She handed me the heavy crystal glass just as the power failed. "Oh, how irritating."

Outside, Marines called to one another as they hurried to the perimeter. Emily began to light candles on a side table. Their flames flashed all around the room, reflected by mirrors on the walls behind them.

Blinking at the sudden glare, she said, "We're still settling in and I haven't had time to do anything about those mirrors."

"I wouldn't," I said.

"Why not?"

"They're eight-sided."

"They are, aren't they," she said, peering at them. "They're scattered all around the house."

"Buddhist clergy must have installed them. They fend off unhappy ghosts, I think."

"Ghosts. Really? Do you believe in ghosts?"

In Viet Nam, how could you not? I thought. "Vietnamese do, ma'am. Your staff does. Your servants and groundskeepers will leave if you remove the mirrors and disturb the spirits."

"I'll bear that in mind. Why would they think unhappy souls were hanging around the premises?"

"Something could've happened here."

"Something untoward? Here in the house?"

"Yes, or somewhere in the compound."

"I should look into that." She stared out into the darkness, sampling her port. "Did you know that Cabot resigned his Senate seat to go to the war?"

"No," I lied. I'd seen that in his file.

"Washingtonians were shocked. No one had done anything like that since the Civil War. Our sons were twelve and nine when he joined. He was forty-two. Assigned to an armor battalion in North Africa. So happy in his tank. I prayed he'd come home to us and he did. He was lucky; we were lucky. The thought of losing him now is more than I can bear." She faced me straight on. "President Diem has hundreds of bodyguards and thousands of soldiers at his beck and call."

"Yes."

"And you've seen what passes for the ambassador's security?"

"Yes, ma'am. I have."

"When we first arrived in Saigon, we had just one sleepy old man guarding our place. Freddy Flott and Mike Dunn were staying with us temporarily and appointed themselves our sentries. They slept on a rug in front of our door and took turns on watch, weapons at hand, until real guards could be arranged."

"You've got Marines now," I said.

"Yes, thank goodness." She tipped her head slightly.

"And I'm putting two good CIDs on his tail, starting in the morning."

"Thank you for that. I wish it could be twenty. I worry Cabot enjoys taking risks. He likes the exhilaration. Hates sitting at a desk." She glanced away. "I almost hope he doesn't try for the presidency. He'd loathe the administrative part."

"Yes, ma'am." I sipped the whiskey, almost as old as I was, and a lot smoother.

"You're pursuing the assassin who may be after Cabot and President Diem."

"Yes, ma'am, we are."

"She seems quite remarkable." Lodge didn't want her to worry; apparently she didn't want to worry him, either, and had let him believe she knew nothing. But if she already knew her husband was in danger, I saw no reason not to be direct.

"She gets it done."

"That's what scares me." She held her glass in both hands. "My husband likes you, thinks you're smart—and lucky for him."

I kept silent, a little surprised to learn he thought of me as a rabbit's foot.

The Italian ambassador and Lodge were returning. "Sergeant," she said, dropping her voice, "please do whatever you can to keep my husband safe."

It was almost nine-thirty, the ambassador's well-known bedtime. Ambassador d'Orlandi thanked the Lodges for their hospitality and departed. Emily retired as well, leaving me alone with the ambassador, who plied me with more whiskey and, taking a candle, led me onto the dark patio where the white blossoms shone in the dark.

"Your security detail lets you go outside after sundown?"

"They're all right with it as long as we don't have too many candles out here or silhouette ourselves against the glass doors when the power is on." He scraped back a wrought-iron chair and sat down. "Any progress on finding our comely young killer? Did the interrogation report help?"

"Some," I said. "Not enough."

"Any idea what she might have against a nice fellow like me?"

"It could be your suspending the economic aid program."

"How extraordinary. What's the connection?"

I considered telling him about Major Furth's damning report, the hucksters, the double-dealing importers, the siphoned monies, the laundering, the whole stinking mess. Then I thought better of it.

I said, "The MAAG officers she's killed all worked on the Commodity Import Program one way or another. The ARVN general she stabbed to death at the Continental was in charge of its finances. You're the official who shut it off."

"So the trail leads her to my door." He sipped his whiskey.

"Possibly. Yes, sir. That and your position. Your rank as the senior American in-country is more than enough to tempt her. She aims high."

"Speaking of aiming high, you should be aware that things are heating up in Saigon. CIA says an assassination attempt on Counselor Nhu was aborted at the last second earlier today."

"Nhu? Where did this go down?"

Lodge swatted his neck and checked his hand. "Just north of town. An attempted ambush of his Mercedes."

"The Red Queen?" With no love lost between Washington and Nhu, we'd never considered he might be the Americans' Old Fox.

"No. Strictly in-house. South Vietnamese army snipers, American trained. They had clear shots. But apparently they were called off."

"What spoiled it? Were Nhu's kids in the car with him?"

"No."

"A foreign dignitary?"

"No. Only he and General Don were in the limo. Don is Chief of the Joint General Staff but the title is hollow, like Big Minh's." He put down his glass. "Neither one actually commands anything."

I waved away a buzzing mosquito. "Do we know who any of these coup conspirators are?" I said, curious to see if Lodge would make me part of the *we*.

Lodge fluffed his open shirt, fanning himself. "The generals? No. I wish I knew. I only have the names of a few junior officers in the younger coup group."

With a go-between to the plotters in place, Lodge had to know exactly who all the leaders were. Then again, he'd never promised me candor. Just asked for mine.

"I think *we* know one," I said.

"Who?" Lodge raised his chin.

"The general sitting beside Nhu in the Mercedes."

CHAPTER THIRTY

Moehlenkamp called from Tay Ninh to say he might have a lead on the Red Queen. He was anxious for us to get there. Corporal Magid offered to drive us to the airport but got called into Deckle's office, leaving Robeson and me to hail a taxi out to Tan Son Nhut.

Air Vietnam and KLM prop jets were lined up single file, roasting on the civilian side of the airfield behind the international flights. First in the queue, an Air France Boeing, made its dash and took off, heading for Tokyo, then across the Pole to Paris, another fifteen hours away.

On the military side of the airfield, at the Thirty-Third Tactical, a bunch of Americans in khakis and civilian clothes stood alongside a mob of ARVN soldiers, all waiting to learn where the half-dozen US aircraft would be flying to. The only transport headed for Tay Ninh was a war plane pregnant with rockets and ordnance to be delivered onto Communist enclaves and two major supply trails in the border province.

A trio of bombers idled, engines churning, waiting their turn to power into the air. Ahead of them, a pair of overloaded jet fighters released brakes and raced down the strip to struggle into the sky. I called Captain Deckle on an Air Force phone circuit to report our lack of progress. He wasn't happy.

"There's a hundred and eleven vehicles at a rally point just north of you," he growled, "right near Bien Hoa. They'll set out for Tay Ninh in an hour. I suggest you get your asses over there."

In a pig's eye, I wanted to say. The road to Tay Ninh and the province itself were mostly Viet Cong, had been for years. Playing tag with the VC for ninety-nine kilometers through the Ho Bo woods or the Boi Loi forest could seriously deplete my personal quota of close calls.

"Captain, that's a sixty-mile trip. It's gonna take forever going overland. Accompanying armor will slow us up terrible. So will the fully loaded trucks."

"You'd make it there in three hours, four tops. Convoy's got air cover, gun jeeps, armored carriers mounted with fifties. Every eleventh vehicle's a tank."

"Sir, we'd eat road grit the whole way and spend four hours praying not to hit a goddamn mine. Besides, we haven't got a vehicle."

"Don't be such a candy ass," Deckle roared. "That road's loaded with US equipment and personnel at the staging point. Hitch a ride."

Right, like maybe on a tanker hauling aviation gas.

"We'll keep at it, sir," I said, and rang off before he could order us to join the f-ing convoy. A while later a snide Air America crew chief tossed a whole platoon of Vietnamese in battle dress off a short-hop flight and put half a dozen of us round eyes on his DC-3 in their place. The dinks pretended not to care but they had to be pissed at being treated like beggars.

As we climbed to altitude, Robeson tapped me and pointed to a long line of transports uncoiling far below: the convoy setting out for Tay Ninh, a gun jeep with a red hood in the lead, another with an orange hood last in line. The plume of grit that rose along its entire length would quickly turn the goggled drivers and escorts into raccoons.

I kicked back and closed my eyes. "I bet you're sorry we missed that ride."

"I am for sure shit glad we missed that sucky fucky ride."

We flew northwest toward the cul-de-sac that was Tay Ninh province, surrounded on three sides by Cambodia from which it had once been gouged, something the Khmer never forgot. Half an hour later Black Virgin Mountain loomed on the starboard side, and we banked sharply to avoid Cambodian airspace before landing in Tay Ninh City.

SERGEANT MOEHLENKAMP SAT at the wheel, next to the Presbyterian holy Joe he'd latched onto, me and Robeson in back. Circular bomb craters peppered the long stretch of road, some filled with water and ducks, others converted to rice paddies or mud baths for water buffalo. A dozen local women were using one to bathe in. Normally we would have commented on the view, but not with a padre on board.

Reverend Crawford was doing most of the talking. "There's a longstanding tradition of self-sufficiency in Asia where you build political and military muscle around a spiritual center, both to protect it and to maintain order in the community of believers. Here in Tay Ninh, Cao Dai was such a core," he explained as we bounced along the hard-packed road.

"The founder of Cao Dai was a huge fan of French culture— and of séances," Reverend Crawford went on, clamping a pipe between his teeth. "Back in the twenties this was. He started conferring with one particular spirit who eventually identified himself as Cao Dai."

"That means 'Supreme Being,'" Moehlenkamp said with authority, downshifting as we approached a checkpoint with a warning sign that read:

STOPPING THROUGH RED SIGNAL

DISOBEY MUST BE KILLED

"Damn," Robeson said, "does that mean they're gonna shoot us if we stop or shoot us if we don't?"

Laughing, Reverend Crawford waved to the guards and told Moehlenkamp to drive on. "Sometimes the séances called forth Victor Hugo," the padre said, "who'd dictate poetry—a good deal of it suspiciously anti-colonial," he added with a wry smile. "The late Chinese nationalist Sun Yat-sen joined them. Then a famous Vietnamese poet—"

"Trang Trinh," said Moehlenkamp.

"Right you are." Reverend Crawford grasped his shoulder, cordial and encouraging. "Thank you, Sergeant. The founder declared all three of them immortals of the faith, along with Joan of Arc, Shakespeare, the Virgin Mary, Muhammad, Moses, and a whole drove of other folks they worship as incarnations of the 'Supreme Being.'"

"That's some lineup," I said.

Moehlenkamp nodded. "There's some other real doozies. Tell 'em, padre."

"I won't remember them all." The Rev concentrated. "Let's see. Louis Pasteur. Did I already say Winston Churchill? Um, Napoleon, Thomas Jefferson."

"Lenin," Moehlenkamp volunteered.

"Of course. Vladimir Ilyich."

"You're pulling my leg," I said. "A Communist saint?"

"He's not puttin' you on," Moehlenkamp insisted. "Buddha, Confucius, and Jesus Christ made the cut too."

"I should hope," Robeson said, and quoted scripture: "He is before all things."

"And in Him all things hold together," the Rev finished.

"Is the founder still alive?" I asked.

"Nah," Moehlenkamp waved off the question. "He got bumped off by the Commies years ago."

"Who's in charge now?"

Reverend Crawford puffed his pipe. "The sect is in some ways organized like the Catholics, with bishops, cardinals, even a pope, although Diem deposed their pope and forced him into exile. But quite unlike the Catholics, Cao Dai's priests are both male and female. Women can rise as far as cardinals. They worship a Holy Mother alongside Cao Dai."

"Are we meeting with a lady priest?" Robeson asked, eyebrows raised.

"No, Sergeant." Reverend Crawford tried to relight his pipe, but the air rushing past us wouldn't let him. "We're having tea with a cardinal. He's become a friend. His memory is getting a little spotty but eventually it all comes back to him. You'll just need to be patient."

"You really like these Cao Dai," I said.

"Mmm." He held his hat in front of the pipe and drew in flame. "Hard not to be intrigued by them. They want to unite people of all religions in peace, and they personally eschew all luxury. They communicate with the departed ancestors of believers during their séances. I am reading my way through all the transcripts of these sessions. You can appreciate that Diem's law outlawing spiritualism has not been well received here. Cao Daists far outnumber Catholics in Viet Nam, but of course Diem and his fellow Catholics hold all the power." He puffed hard and the tobacco glowed.

Reverend Crawford directed Moehlenkamp along a dusty road into a huge bare plaza with a pink, green, and blue basilica at its center and people in white robes everywhere.

"The Great Temple of the Cao Dai," Reverend Crawford announced. He pointed his pipe at huge eyes painted along the building's sides and over the main entrance. "The all-seeing eye of Buddhism."

The crowd of Vietnamese men and women in white approached the main doorway in orderly lines. We followed at a respectful distance, the only Westerners in sight. Huge stained-glass windows flanked the sides of the building, each with an eye inside a triangle, like giant versions of the eye atop the Masonic pyramid on American dollars. Inside, hundreds of barefoot worshippers sat cross-legged in spotless white ranks on a white marble floor, facing two pulpits mounted on pillars at the front end of the large gallery.

"One pulpit is for men," the Reverend whispered, "the other for women."

"Fine-lookin' women," Robeson observed.

"The female clergy are all celibate. The men too."

Two rows of columns ran the length of the hall with enormous sculpted creatures in gaudy colors coiling around them: a bug-eyed dragon, a gigantic cobra, a scaly lizard. It looked more like a carnival back home than a cathedral.

"The colors just scream, don't they?" Crawford said. The sect was obviously more thrilling to the padre than his own Presbyterians.

Reverend Crawford led us out to a patio on the side of a small residence where he introduced us to a white-robed elder with skin like shiny parchment and a polished bald head. The cardinal showed us to a wooden table overlooking a modest garden and served us tea in white porcelain bowls with little clear ovals that the light shone through. Crawford eased him into conversation with pleasantries until the cardinal relaxed and asked us, in quite good English, how he might help.

Moehlenkamp showed him the medallion Ting had removed from General Lang's no-longer-seeing eye. The cardinal confirmed it was the beret badge of the sect's former military arm. "Until the newly appointed Prime Minister Diệm disbanded and co-opted the armies of the Cao Đài and the Hòa Hảo sects, we had fifty thousand in uniform, trained and armed. A force to reckon with. Our Cao Đài soldiers were given a wide berth; they managed to keep our region free of Việt Cộng until fifty-six, fifty-seven."

"This was at the very beginning of Diem's regime," Crawford added. "He used nine million of the original aid dollars he received from us to persuade Cao Dai generals they should lead their troops into the ranks of the new nation's French-trained army. Most of their soldiers were absorbed into the new force, but a good many also went over to the Viet Cong or fled across the border to Cambodia."

"This is quite true," the cardinal agreed. "Only a small group of retired Cao Đài military men is left. Less than a hundred elderly veterans."

Moehlenkamp said, "And with the Cao Dai army gone, Charlies in Tay Ninh go unchecked. They just walk into any old village and provision themselves like it's a supermarket. They got huge bases nearby."

"It's a young Viet Cong lady we're interested in, sir," Robeson said. "A sharpshooter, 'round twenty years of age."

"We have no one like that among us."

Crawford held up his palm, interrupting. "Perhaps not at

present, cardinal. But you did have. Those siblings you told me about? The brother and two sisters we spoke of."

"Ah. Yes, yes." The cardinal stroked his chin. "It's been some years. Remarkable youngsters." The cardinal paused, recalling. "The boy displayed exceptional prowess with firearms."

"His sisters," I said, "were they proficient too?"

"All three acquitted themselves extremely well with weaponry. They had been instructed relentlessly from an early age. Our old militiamen marveled at their skill. Like Japanese archers, they barely needed to take aim." The cardinal fell silent and sipped his tea.

"They were uncanny shots," Crawford prompted. "An old Cao Dai sergeant arranged a demonstration, you told me."

"Demonstration? Ah yes. The sergeant blindfolded the two older children while the younger girl hid behind an upright iron slab some thirty meters distant. The little one recited an ancient poem about an anvil. Her siblings had only her voice to guide their aim."

"How'd they do?" Robeson asked.

"All their shots clanged the iron on cue. Neither child missed. Each placed six shots dead center. Afterward, their younger sister fired a small-caliber handgun at a paper sign, accenting the letters." He shook his head at the memory. "The old sergeant awarded the little one his khaki beret with the medallion on it. She was never seen without it from that day forth. The old sergeant had no family of his own. He became like a grandfather to them."

"Can we talk to this Cao Dai sergeant?" Robeson asked.

"It's possible but not certain," said the cardinal, with a smile. "He passed over some years ago. Not a good death. He complains from time to time."

"And the older daughter, what was she like?" I said.

"Her mother's child. Quiet, self-contained. All three young-sters had a disarming innocence about them, quite in contrast to their weapons discipline."

"When exactly was this?" I said.

"They came to us the year the defeated French Expedition-ary Force quit Indochina and sailed for home: nineteen hundred and fifty-six. We understood their mother had been the con-cubine of an important man and sought a contemplative life after the turmoil she had known with him. She shaved her head, became a novice, and took vows. Only later did I learn that the notorious General Bảy Viễn had fathered the children."

"What became of the children?" Robeson said.

"Misfortune," said the cardinal, his face surrendering to memories. "Some three years after they came to us, I returned from a retreat to find the community in chaos. The province chief was rounding up former Việt Minh fighters. This was in fifty-nine." He paused, checking his recollection. "Yes! Four years ago. Our country's new president had issued a decree launching a nationwide *trừ gian*."

"*Tru gian*," I repeated, remembering the scrawl on the ven-geance card stuck in General Lang's unseeing eye.

"'Extermination of Traitors,'" the cardinal translated. "Law ten fifty-nine. A decree from President Diệm, unleashing a national campaign against any Communists and sympathizers among the old independence fighters, the Việt Minh."

"Signaling the arrival of Diem's dreaded night visitors," Crawford said.

"Here in Tây Ninh," the cardinal continued, "Diệm's field police swept in before dawn, surrounded the homes of those on their list and dragged them before military tribunals for immediate trial. The edict did not distinguish between nation-alists and true Communist ideologues. If they had ever been Việt Minh, the tribunals did not care whether they were Bud-dhists from the League for National Salvation, men of the Peasants' Associations, Socialists, or even Resistant Catholics. The accused were given no right to examine evidence, call wit-nesses, or appeal the instant verdicts. Some were sentenced to prison, many to death by beheading. And, sadly, there were no Cao Đài militia left to resist."

"The condemned," Reverend Crawford said, "were put to death on the spot with a portable guillotine."

"Horrific," said the cardinal, shaking his head. "The chil-dren's adopted grandfather, the old Cao Đài sergeant, was among them. The children were forced to witness his gruesome death. Naturally, this horrifying purge lost Diệm the loyalty of any surviving nationalists and earned his government the undy-ing hatred of all those affected—which was everyone." He made a futile gesture. "The children's mother was also among the accused."

"Had she fought with the Viet Minh?" I asked.

"No, no. The children's father, Bảy Viễn, had once sided with the Communists, but only out of convenience. In truth he was an opportunist, not at all a committed leftist, but he had made an enemy of President Diệm and was on their list, and hence so was his former concubine. Her association with the children's father was enough to condemn her. Our province chief ordered the local constabulary to escort the military policemen to her home. A large detail converged in the pre-dawn dark and encircled her house. Her son, all of seventeen, fired on them immediately, with shocking accuracy. Wounded five, killed two—in moments. Seven shots, seven casualties.

Until that moment the combat police carrying out the *trừ gian* had encountered no armed resistance; they panicked. Their senior man bravely tried to rally them as he rushed toward the house in a weaving run. He was struck in the chest, the third to die."

"Fully armed soldiers acting on orders to sow terror," Crawford said, "driven off by a teenager."

"The government agents were completely unnerved. They fell back and called for artillery, insisting that they faced professional combatants instead of a boy with a handgun. The shells came howling down," said the cardinal, closing his eyes. "Bursting into white tendrils."

"Phosphorus," Moehlenkamp said.

"Mmm. They set the house ablaze." The cardinal was visibly moved. "Such a shame," he said. "The mother was arrested as she dragged the older daughter from the flames, unconscious. Of the children, Mai alone had survived. The brave young marksman and his younger sister perished in the inferno. In the commotion of the mother's arrest, a vehicle bore the rescued girl to the hospital. Somewhere along the route she made her escape."

"How old was she then?"

"Mai? Perhaps sixteen. Her younger sister, eleven; the boy, seventeen or thereabout. The Cao Đài community rose up in outrage to challenge the tribunal. To everyone's relief, their mother, Madame Nguyễn, was quickly exonerated."

"Madame Nguyen still live here?" Robeson asked.

"No," the cardinal replied, sadly. "When we entombed her children's ashes she remained by the grave all night. She exhibited no rancor. Indeed, she seemed strangely calm. We found her body the next morning. She had taken her own life with her youngest child's aluminum pistol." The cardinal peered over the top of his glasses. "The tomb the three share is close by."

"Does Mai ever visit the family grave?" Moehlenkamp asked the old man.

"Not that I am aware. Though I'm told fresh blooms and offerings appear from time to time."

"And the province chief in those years," I said, "do you remember him?"

"Vividly. A deeply unpleasant person; truly a swotter. He rose to major general and died violently himself a short while ago. An automaton of a man. What was his name? It will come to me in a moment."

CHAPTER THIRTY-ONE

We followed Reverend Crawford and the cardinal to the grave where the family's ashes were interred above ground in a traditional Cao Dai crypt. A hand-tinted enamel etching of the mother and her children filled a polished oval set into the face of the tomb. I studied the image of the older sister. Impossible to know how good a likeness of Mai it was, or what those features might look like now.

The cardinal had brought a small bouquet of flowers and incense sticks. Moehlenkamp lit the joss sticks for the cardinal and Reverend Crawford. Palms clasped, the two clerics held the stems to their foreheads and bowed before anchoring them on the tomb.

Looking toward the eastern horizon, the cardinal spoke with regret. "She is an admirable woman. I pray she and her children transitioned peacefully to a better sphere."

"And this General Bay Vien?" I said. "The father, was he the one who taught them to shoot?"

"Indeed. From a very early age, he encouraged them to play with small-caliber aluminum pistols, light and pretty," the cardinal said.

"Baby rattles for the baby rattlers," Robeson said.

"Hardly that. They were good children. They worked hard

to please their father and win his heart. Their mother told me they expended countless rounds on ranges near Chợ Lớn and at Bảy's headquarters under the Y Bridge. When they were a little older, he took his son and older daughter hunting in the mountains."

"He instructed them well," I said.

"Yes. He taught them misdirection games and the small duplicities he had learned over a lifetime of illicit pursuits."

"Illicit?"

"The general, though illiterate, was a formidable thief. A bulldog of a man. Half Chinese, half Vietnamese, a cunning, consummate criminal. He taught them to stalk and to survive."

General Bay Vien, the reverend explained, had risen from bossing a small-time pirate gang to running the most efficient protection and extortion rackets in Saigon, and the Hall of Mirrors, the largest brothel and gambling hall in Indochina. Gold smuggling, opium refining, document forgery . . . he did it all. "Bay Vien had ambition but no use for ideology. Called it a toy for intellectuals."

"My hero," I said.

"Bay Vien became wildly rich, the toast of Saigon, even befriended by Emperor Bao Dai, who awarded him his second general's star and issued him the lease on the Grand Monde gambling complex and then the lease on another institution— the National Police."

"Wait," Robeson said. "The emperor handed control of the National Police to a mob boss?"

"Indeed," the cardinal confirmed. "Bảo Đại named the biggest racketeer in the country the head of law enforcement and all the security and intelligence services. Then sanctimonious Diệm came to power to cleanse the country of Communism and sin, openly threatening Bảy Viễn's lucrative vice empire. But in addition to controlling the police, Bảy Viễn had his own army, forty thousand strong, complete with artillery. He shelled the palace and engaged Diệm's brand-new Vietnamese army in deadly combat right in the middle of Sài Gòn."

The cardinal paused, almost spent.

"What happened to Bay Vien?" Moehlenkamp asked. "Any chance Mai is in Saigon with him?"

"General Big Minh happened," said Reverend Crawford. "Minh burned down the casino complex and the huge brothel. He struck Bay Vien's gun and mortar emplacements with artillery and outmaneuvered his battalions. Minh drove the survivors back into their old pirates' lair in the mangrove swamps of the Rung Sat and plunged in after them. He fought them for three months, brought out no prisoners."

"Big Minh killed Bay Vien?" Robeson said.

"No," the cardinal replied. "Bảy escaped by sea with his lieutenants and dozens of his women and their children. The French flew him to Paris, where he still resides. He left behind his decimated criminal enterprises, a son killed in the battle, and the three sharpshooting children he so prized."

Reverend Crawford mopped his brow. "And now his surviving daughter prowls the capital, seeking revenge on her family's enemies."

Robeson looked troubled. I leaned in close. "What?"

"What do you mean, 'What'? We're hunting Al Capone's daughter."

CHAPTER THIRTY-TWO

When we arrived back at the office to brief Deckle, Blue held out a note inviting me to a cinema in Cholon. Unsigned, but Captain Ting's scrawl was unmistakable.

Robeson and I snuck in during the first reel of an old black-and-white comedy. Cary Grant and a knockout blonde were gorgeous ghosts in evening dress, messing with a goofy sad sack in a tuxedo. Like all English-language films, it was dubbed in French, had Chinese characters running down the sides, and subtitles in Vietnamese streaming across the bottom. When the ghosts walked through something or somebody, the audience hissed and sharply drew breath, then giggled behind their hands to cover their anxiety and delight.

Robeson stood guard at the rear while I edged into the row behind Captain Ting. He offered me his cone of French fries.

"What's up, Captain?" I said quietly.

"You displease boss," he whispered back over his shoulder.

"Sorry to hear that." I wasn't sure which boss he meant, but like all the cops in the country, ultimately Ting worked for Nhu.

"Counselor Nhu not renew visa. Same-same Sergeant Robeson."

"What did we do?"

Ting turned his face half toward me. His teeth glowed like his white shirt. "Conspire against Việt Nam. Offend Brother Nhu. He have you investigate."

"Investigate for what?"

"Sacrilege. Crazy New Orleans voodoo murder."

"What voodoo? Whose murder?"

"Man on Con Son Island. Buried in arms of pig."

"Who's investigating? Your guys?"

"No we. CIO and SEPES. For Colonel Tung." Ting leaned back and whispered, "Colonel *người hủi*. You understand?"

"Yes," I said, not surprised. Ting was calling the head of the Red Berets and SEPES a leper. Street slang for a cop best to stay away from. Like we didn't already know. Tung had started his life as a servant of the Ngo family and now served them as chief enforcer and extortionist.

"You and Sergeant Robeson must take great cautions about your person."

"So the surveillance on me and my girl the other day on Catinat—was that part of Tung's investigation?"

"They say you make plot with Communist."

"For fuckssake. She's a secretary. She works for the ICC."

"Not exactly."

"What do you mean?"

"She Polish State Security."

"WE'RE IN THE crapper now, Mr. Miser." Robeson and I sat on his balcony, nursing beers. "Nhu's SEPES operators are some mighty twisted dickheads. And they know I killed that sentry." He took a swig from his beer can. "I'm officially scared shitless, Ellie."

"You got company. We're not living right."

Robeson pressed his temples. "I swear I ain't gettin' lynched in no human zoo. God, are you sleeping after seeing the way they did Tam? I'm not." He took another swallow. "They wouldn't do that to Americans, right?"

"Right." I didn't sound convincing. "But this ain't about the sentry, Clovis."

"You think finding Tam in that shithole dungeon is why they're really on us?"

"That—or Major Furth's report," I said. "We've gone poking around lots of places Nhu doesn't want us."

"What the fuck do we do? We can't exactly hop the next flight out like Tuttle."

"*Xin loi*, bro."

"'Sorry about that!' *Sorry* about that?"

"Okay, okay. We tip our friendly night manager to let us bunk in any vacant room when the guest is away. If nothing's vacant, we double up and alternate between our rooms. Maybe set up some cots in the office. Crash at the Rex. We don't sleep in the same location two nights in a row. And no sleepover dates with your Malaysian honey out by Tan Son Nhut. You're easy pickings there."

"Got it," Robeson said, reluctantly. "So much for the nights. What about while we're out and about the world in broad daylight, doing our jobs? It's not just Nhu's goons after our scalps. The VC let us know they were pissed off at us for talking to Tuttle. How long before they figure out we traced the Red Queen back to her family?"

I shrugged. "What can we do? Stay alert. Drive dodgy. Never leave the jeep without kids keeping watch. Pay 'em extra so they don't let anyone leave us a surprise in the gas tank. Carry an extra piece."

"Cannons shackled to my ankles and a .38 on my hip does what? How about we do like Special Forces and President Diem—hire us some Nungs?"

"If somebody's of a mind to take us out, it won't matter how many bodyguards we rent. Need be, they'll kibosh us with an undetonated Air Force bomb and poof, we're gone. Wouldn't be enough left of us to fit in a tea bag."

"I guess we can't put on flak vests and steel pots and hide in some bunker until our tour is up." Robeson crushed his empty beer can. "Or hole up at Hotel Duc. What a number ten situation."

"Look at the bright side," I said. "We got skin in the game now."

"Yeah, our foreskins."

I didn't tell him what Ting had said about Nadja. He already had enough worries.

THE NIGHT MANAGER said he'd find Robeson an empty suite to crash in. I found Nadja in her room, her sleeping body cocooned in mosquito netting. I double-locked the door, stripped off my clothes in the bathroom, and stood under the shower, eyes closed, letting the lukewarm water stream over me.

I wrapped a sandalwood-scented bath towel around my middle like a sarong and went out on the balcony for a cigarette. On a merchant ship docked across from the hotel, a Victrola played a slow familiar rumba, "Bésame Mucho." A couple danced on the canvas cover of the cargo hatch like it was a giant fight ring without the ropes. Either they hadn't gotten word of Madame Nhu's ban on social dancing or they didn't care.

Illumination rounds lit up the sky across the river. I thought about the first time I went back to my uncle's place in Pennsylvania after my hitch in Korea. I sat on the front porch like I had as a kid and willed the lightning strikes to march closer and closer, until the cracks of thunder shook the house. But a lightning storm and a few brews at the VFW hall on a Saturday night just didn't cut it. I knew eventually I'd come back for the real brimstone.

Ducking inside, I lifted the netting and slipped in next to Nadja. She stirred, and I stared at her. Her bright red hair, almost black in the dark, fanned out across the pillows.

Nadja stretched. "You came back."

"Yeah, I'm back."

"Mmm. Learn anything new on your case?"

"Not much that can help us."

"Too bad."

"I did find out who was shadowing us along Catinat."

"Mmmm. Who were the rozzers?"

"Most likely a Vietnamese from the Central Intelligence Organization and his American advisor."

The lazy breathing stopped. Both eyes opened. "Why were they following us?"

"Keeping tabs on our capitalist-Communist conspiracy."

"*Yob tvoyu mat*," she cursed.

I said, "Are you really an appointments secretary at the ICC?"

She shifted onto her side, facing me. "No."

"Do you type?"

"Not terribly well." Her breasts pressed against each other. "Sounds like I've been rumbled."

I stretched out next to her. "What exactly do you do there?"

She rolled onto her back, her eyes on the ceiling. "I'm kind of a border collie. Diligent, obedient, well trained. Faithful to my masters. Not very popular with the sheep. I watch my fellow Poles at ICC, make sure they don't fraternize with Westerners and dutifully return home when their time outside is up. As long as they respect the limits and no one defects, they get to stay—and I get to stay."

"Your masters, who are they?"

"The Interior Ministry's Security Service. *Służba Bezpieczeństwa.* SB-nicks they call us, when they're being polite."

She closed her eyes.

"We didn't just happen to meet in the bar that night," I said.

"No."

"Your bosses," I said, "wanted . . . what?"

She opened her eyes and turned to stare into mine.

"To follow the progress you American military policemen were making, get information on the likelihood of the Red Queen being discovered by you . . . and stopped."

"Why?"

"So my masters could report to their masters, I suppose. They don't exactly say."

"Do they pass your information on to the Viet Cong?"

"I don't think so, though I can't be sure. What I report flows in one direction only. Warsaw. Then Moscow."

"Why would the Russians want the information?"

"I'm sure they worry that she might get through the palace defenses and eliminate Diem."

"Wouldn't that make their day?"

"North Vietnamese hardliners and their Chinese mentors would be pleased. The Russians, no. The Maoists want baby revolutions. They applaud the Cubans for fanning the flames in South America and Africa, and the Vietnamese for inspiring peoples' wars of liberation in the rest of Indochina and Algeria."

"But not the Russians?"

"No. The Soviets don't want Diem removed. They want protracted negotiations with Hanoi. Everything kept as is."

"No wars of liberation."

"They're still rattled by coming so close to Armageddon last year over their missiles in Cuba. They don't particularly wish to find themselves underwriting a long war in Indochina. They appreciate Diem's resistance to the introduction of actual American combat units into Viet Nam and that he rejects US impositions on the country's sovereignty. He leans in the direction they prefer to see things go."

"Which is?"

"Toward a deal with the North that will avoid an all-out conflict which the United States would inevitably join. At least that's what my deputy commissioner says each time he returns from Hanoi bearing confidential messages for the South Vietnamese from their cousins in the North. My boss and the French ambassador have informed Diem they are ready to act as intermediaries at a moment's notice. They may be doing it already. I haven't seen my boss since he left for Hanoi."

"What do Ho Chi Minh and the North Vietnamese want from the deal?"

"A reunified Viet Nam," she said. "All of us gone. Your lot and our lot."

"So while we're financing the fight against Communism, Diem and Nhu are ready to negotiate with the North. If Uncle Ho plays it right, he could win the whole thing without having to fire another fucking shot."

"Do you care?"

"Me? I like all the cards face up, knowing where all the players stand."

She laughed. "Please, this is Viet Nam."

"Getting this close to me, was that your assignment?"

"No, and they mustn't find out or I'm in trouble."

You and me both, I thought. I said, "Then why are you with me?"

"Same reason you're with me. Don't make me say it. We'll only feel worse. Not that it matters at this point, given our situations. D'Orlandi may find it adorable that we are romancing, but my overseers in Warsaw would shut us down in a second if they thought it was serious. Sounds like your superiors would be none too pleased either." Nadja brushed her hair away from her eyes. "Mrs. Lodge may think you are lucky, but this may be the end of it—us."

I closed my eyes. *Lucky.* I'd been alone with Emily Lodge in her living room when she said that.

Nadja drifted off. I slept too, holding her fingers close to my cheek, my arm across her waist. It wasn't a very restful night. When I awoke she was gone.

CHAPTER THIRTY-THREE

I went down to my room and pushed open the shutters to take in the dawn traffic on the river. A rust bucket was tying up at the dock where the couple had danced on board the merchant ship the night before. A small ferry crossed upriver, carrying a few cars and a bus with cages lashed to its roof. Freighters were moored midchannel, surrounded by small, nimble wooden craft that moved around the ships like insects, lining up at floating docks beneath the steel hulls to cart away portions of their innards. Booms swung cargo nets over the sides and lowered sacks onto their decks. From what Tuttle had told us, at least half the skiffs and sampans would push west into Cholon where their valuable loads would vanish.

My civvies were hanging neatly in the armoire but still damp. I carried the pants and shirt on hangers to the balcony to hook on the awning. The tropical heat would finish the drying in minutes. In the bathroom, I lathered up my beard and lifted the razor to my face. The morning sun bouncing off the mirror hurt my tired eyes and I opened the medicine cabinet to shift the angle. The reflected light caught the rod that held up the plain white shower curtain behind me, illuminating something shadowy where it met the wall. Razor in hand, I carefully peered around the curtain, hoping it wasn't a snake.

A fat old Russian fragmentation grenade was tied to the bar. Four pounds of hash-marked iron. The thinnest of lines ran from the pin to a shower-curtain hook. The cotter pin's split ends were straight and even. They'd probably shortened the fuse too, to make it go off right away. The slightest tug on the curtain would draw the pin out. Hell, a wrong breath, a slamming door. I'd never hear it go off.

Heart in my mouth, I reached up and crimped the ends of the pin so it couldn't slide out and detonate the fucker, sending shrapnel in all directions and turning me into a colander. With the pin secured, I sat down on the toilet lid and forced myself to breathe steadily. My hands shook worse than Lodge's. If I had come home to my own room and showered here last night instead of at Nadja's, there would have been no morning light striking the mirror to reveal the silhouette. I stuck my hands in my armpits and bent at the waist. No way was I going to shave the way my hands were shaking. I sure as shit wasn't getting in that shower. I sponged off best I could and got dressed.

I asked the front desk where they'd put Robeson for the night so I could warn him, but they said he'd already gone out. I also learned that Mama-san Kha hadn't shown up for work yesterday while we'd been up in Tay Ninh. Some day hire had serviced the room. Whoever had taken her place had primed the booby trap. The clerk blanched when I showed him why Monsieur Franchini might not want to put her on the payroll. He assured me she had not returned. But neither had Mama-san Kha.

I HAD A pretty good idea I'd find Robeson at the Melody Bar on Catinat, one of his regular joints, not mine. Black enlisted men had claimed the Melody as theirs. Whites and Asians weren't welcome, and most definitely not military cops. I got a bad vibe when I walked in but Robeson's greeting tamped down the hostile attitude coming my way.

On the sound system, an accordion wailed a zydeco stomp. Robeson's doing, I assumed. He retrieved Bloody Marys for us from the bar and we took a corner table.

"Rough night?" I asked.

Robeson gave me the stink-eye. "The promised suite didn't exist. I cooped in Seftas's room. He's escorting some admiral around Cam Ranh. Where the fuck were you?"

"With Nadja." I waved away the sleepy girls sashaying toward us. "Better a bad night in Sef's room than waking up to this," I said, placing the Russkie grenade on the table. "Found it in my shower, rigged to go."

"Holy shit."

"Better check your john and all your equipment when you go back."

"Goddamn!" Robeson said. "Ting sure waited until the last fuckin' minute to warn us. You think this is a South Vietnam-ese message or Viet Cong?"

"Take your pick. Whose cage have we rattled more?"

Three bloods came up on me, bristling. "Don't get comfort-able, honky," the shortest one spat. "What the fuck you think you're doin' in here?"

"I'm integrating your saloon, asshole." The anger helped push down the fear making its home in my gut.

Robeson held up a palm. "We'll be gone in a minute, Ty."

"See to it. The cracker ain't welcome." But when they saw what lay on the table between us, the brothers backed off.

FRANCIS RADIOED THE office. They'd spotted a tail on

Ambassador Lodge going from the Cercle Sportif to the embassy after his swim and breakfast. If there'd been other trackers before now, they'd been switching off so repeated appearances wouldn't give them away.

"But this guy definitely showed up a second time."

"Is Beantown there?" I said, meaning, was Lodge at the embassy?

"Affirmative. Heading off in half an hour."

"Understood. Meet you at your location in ten. Out."

Robeson and I hauled ass.

Looking spiffy in a tropical suit and pale blue shirt, the ambassador was just leaving the embassy when we arrived to take over from Rider and Francis. Lodge's car pulled out first, hood pennants flying. The Marines' armored jeep fell in immediately behind. The jarhead riding next to the driver held his Thompson machine gun at the ready. Both were in utilities and had on steel pots, flak vests, harnesses with ammo pouches, canteens, and first-aid kits. They had to be hot as hogs.

We kept a few vehicles between us and the ambassador. A bare-headed skinny young Vietnamese on a pale green Vespa, plaid shirt—the guy Francis had spotted—was riding the escort jeep's fender. Early twenties, black hair, real thin, average height, looking like a thousand other Saigonese on motor scooters rounding traffic circles to peel off onto other streets. But I could see why Francis had called: the unhurried, nervy way the guy drifted through the traffic, never quite catching up with the limo, at times even casually hitching onto the back corner of the gun jeep to be towed along without effort. He was almost teasing us.

When Lodge arrived at the gate of the Mac Dinh Chi cemetery, the Vespa rider paused to light a cigarette while the ambassador and a dozen dignitaries walked toward the sea of white headstones. A Marine guard carried the wreath Lodge would place at a point overlooking thousands of legionnaires' graves.

Brushing the hair from his eyes, the slight young man straddled his Vespa, revved the machine and resumed his ride, heading west. We followed at a discreet distance straight down the boulevard.

"Damn." Robeson slapped the wheel. "This good idea ain't gonna be so good in a minute," he said, seeing the stalled traffic ahead. "We need to get ourselves some hogs."

"Oh, yeah. I'm sure Captain Deckle will be happy to requisition us some Harleys."

The Vespa rider turned and studied us. After a minute, he dropped his cigarette and calmly threaded the lane between the flanks of standing vehicles, working his way forward until he disappeared in the crush.

"We finally found one of her scouts," I said.

"More lost than found," said Robeson, glumly.

ROBESON DROVE BACK to the Majestic to sweep his room for surprises. I took the jeep and headed for the embassy. At the chancery, Mrs. Lacey greeted me with her usual smile and good spirits. I asked for a few minutes with the ambassador.

"He's just gone in with Mike Dunn and Colonel Conein," she said, motioning toward the shut door, "but he's been wanting to get hold of you as well. Can you come back in twenty minutes?"

I went down to the windowless CIA reading room to see if they had any files on a Mai Nguyen, and, while I was at it, asked for a look-see at their eyes-only file on General Don, the passenger in Nhu's Mercedes whose presence had saved Nhu from assassination. The Georgia peach apologized that they had nothing on Mai, but promptly delivered the dossier on the general.

Born in France to Vietnamese parents, raised in Rome, the

intel read. Highly respected French army officer. His Vietnamese wasn't the best, it said, but he spoke good English and perfect French and Italian. CIA was unsure of his loyalties. The report called him an "opportunist" close to both Nhu and Nhu's biggest critics.

During the war, General Don wound up in a Japanese prison with another young Vietnamese officer—Big Minh. Lodge's tennis buddy and General Don were the best trained field commanders the South had, but at the moment all they commanded were their aides. The two were plotting a coup, using someone codenamed "Lulu" as their go-between with the US Embassy, just as Seftas had said.

The geniuses in Washington were regretting that choice. They'd grown uncomfortable with Lulu's freelancing. They wanted a new liaison, someone who'd just listen in on the plotters and report back, not take an active hand—a conduit, not a co-conspirator. But the skittish generals would only deal through Lulu. And Lulu wasn't the madam of the namesake brothel in Laos, or even female.

During the Second World War, Don had befriended a French-born American with a Kansas City twang who'd served in the French army until France surrendered, then escaped to the US, returning with the OSS to help the Resistance. He'd parachuted into China and joined with French-trained Vietnamese like Don to drive the Japanese from their homeland. His underground codename: Lulu. The same Colonel Lucien Conein huddled with Lodge in the ambassador's office, the lone CIA operator Lodge appeared to trust.

I wondered if Lodge and Conein ever met at Lodge's residence. I hoped not. I now knew for certain it was infiltrated with VC, and likely with Counselor Nhu's snitches as well. If Nhu had learned how close Lodge was to the coup-plotters, he'd be only too happy to have the Red Queen take her best shot at our esteemed ambassador. The Saigon regime's hands would be clean, American wrath would pour down on the Communists, and undoubtedly the bounty of the Commodity Import Program would resume flowing into Saigon.

Twenty minutes were up. I returned to the ambassador's floor and Mrs. Lacey showed me right in.

In the middle of the gloom sat Lodge in his crisp blue shirt with a rose-colored tie, hair parted perfectly above his furrowed brow. His cuffs were rolled a little above his elbows the way WASPs liked to wear them to show they were laboring as manfully as their Pilgrim ancestors. The .38 and the big Magnum had migrated closer to his reach. He looked happy as hell.

"What did you need to see me about?" he said.

"We've seen the Red Queen's scout tailing you, sir. Confirmation you're being prepped."

Lodge frowned uncomfortably. "How would you rate my chances of surviving if she gets a clear shot?" he asked.

"Nil to lousy."

"What do you suggest?"

"Mix up your routine. Stop swimming the same ten laps of breaststroke at the Cerc at exactly the same time every day. When you do swim, have them clear the pool for you."

"That's it?"

"Hardly. Stop walking in the street. You're a head taller than everyone in Saigon. You can be seen for blocks."

"There's not much I can do about my height."

"No, but you can stop going into crowds, shaking hands, accepting gifts from strangers." I gave him my sternest stare. "You're predictable and vulnerable—a perfect target."

"Direct as always, Agent Miser." He looked sheepish. "But I'm afraid I can't avoid any of those activities at the moment. We need public opinion with us." He turned his gaze toward the window. "I hope you realize how much I'm trusting you, Sergeant."

"We all make mistakes."

Lodge flat-out guffawed. "You have some brass."

"You wanted it straight, you said."

"I do. It suits my purposes." Lodge massaged his shaking hand.

"The Red Queen may already be closer to you than we thought. Your staff in the embassy residence is infiltrated."

"By Viet Cong? You're sure?"

I nodded. "Odds were always good your house staff was compromised, but now I have confirmation."

"How do I go about culling them?"

"I need you to do exactly like I say."

"Go on."

"Those eight-sided mirrors around your residence . . ."

"You told Emily they ward off spirits."

"They do. And all Vietnamese fear unhappy ghosts."

"Sergeant, you urged her to leave the mirrors where they were or risk upsetting the staff."

"Correct. Which is why you need to have your Marine sentries take them down right away."

"Remove the mirrors?" Lodge's eyebrows shot up. "Wouldn't that be rash?"

"Yes. Do it right away, today. And make sure the maids and cooks and gardeners all see it happening."

"You want them upset."

"Yep. Panicked if possible. Most will bolt. Have 'em stopped at the gate."

"Okay. We create an incident. Then what?"

"A few won't take off. They'll be rattled but they'll tough it out, make like they're too loyal to run. Pay those off and have Marines immediately escort them from the compound. Don't let any of them back, not for anything."

"The ones willing to stay, they'll be the plants?"

"Mostly, yeah. This may not flush 'em all out, but for sure it'll improve your security."

"And then?"

"Have Buddhist priests standing by. Right after you clean out the ranks, have the priests reposition the mirrors and conduct their rituals. The staff has to see the ceremony for themselves or they won't come back."

"And what after that?"

"Double the guard."

Lodge stood up to convey the instructions to Mrs. Lacey for Emily, and then turned to me.

"Sergeant Miser, on Saturday President Diem will take the salute of his armed forces at the Vietnamese Independence Day celebration. I have to attend. Given the excessive security precautions, I'm not too concerned for him—or myself. But on Sunday, Emily and I will be with him in the mountains, dedicating a nuclear reactor."

"A what, sir?"

"I know, who would put a nuclear anything in the middle of a guerilla war?" Lodge sighed. "We would, of course. I'm assured the reactor's applications are all very peaceful, none of its byproducts useable in an atomic weapon. In any case, South Viet Nam's world-famous physicist is flying in from Paris to inaugurate it. Emily and I have to attend. And Nhu is pressing hard for me to accompany Diem immediately afterward on an inspection tour of the Strategic Hamlets program in the Delta.

After which I'm expected in Washington for consultations at the White House."

"You don't want to do that, Ambassador."

"Go back to Washington?"

"Go into the Delta."

"I may have to."

"The lower Delta is Communist, the middle portion almost as solidly red."

"You mean it's theirs at night?"

"Night, day—doesn't matter. It's theirs."

"But the Delta . . . it's vital. The country's rice basket."

"Yes, sir. And all of it Viet Cong."

"Really?" Lodge didn't sound convinced. "Surely Saigon wouldn't concede all that population, all that harvest land."

"The Delta's been in the red column since the forties. It's not worth risking your life to visit a place the South Vietnamese haven't held in decades. Tell 'em you've got a fever."

"I'm not happy to hear it." He pinched his bottom lip, thinking. "The first day I was here I was warned the Ngo family had a plan to bump me off during a faked VC attack at a strategic hamlet. I'll do my best to beg off. In any event, while I have you here . . . President Diem has advised me that the inn where we had planned to stay in Dalat is too remote to be safe. He insists we stay with him at one of his villas. Emily would consider it a personal favor if you'd accompany us Sunday as part of our protective detail. And after what you've just told me, I concur. We would all return late afternoon Monday."

"Of course, sir."

"Excellent," he said, and looked pleased.

I didn't mention that I wouldn't consider myself much of a rabbit's foot anymore, not after this morning's shower surprise.

CHAPTER THIRTY-FOUR

Missy hustled us over to her olive-drab typing desk where a plastic map case held the torn paper fragment of the astrograph I'd found by Major Furth's café chair. She pointed to the colored impression in the corner containing a few broken Chinese characters.

"Chop of fortune-teller," she said.

"Chop?" Moehlenkamp looked bewildered.

"Stamp," Robeson said, getting excited. "Missy means part of the astrologer's signature block."

"A rubber stamp?"

"Stone," he said, "but same idea, yeah."

The chop on the torn paper was incomplete, but when Missy Blue slipped a whole unsoiled chart under the scrap, the Chinese characters lined up fucking perfect. God bless her, Blue had tasked her informants across the city to gather every astrologer's chart they could and tried them all until one aligned. She had found the fortune-teller. The Red Queen's scout had easily slipped through our net, but Blue had found her spotter. If it wasn't for the pounds Robeson had on me, I would've kissed her right there.

Blue held out foolscap with an address and a name: Huyen.

"Fortune-teller is a . . . *sourcier*," she said in French.

I looked to Robeson for help. "Sorcerer?"

"Diviner."

"Huyen is a *đồng cốt*," she continued, "a medium."

"So he talks to the dead, like your Gran," I teased Robeson, who glared at me.

Predicting people's futures was officially banned, but Missy Blue said Huyen still received petitioners privately twice a week and held a séance around ten in the morning on those days.

"Which days?" Robeson said.

"Each Tuesday and Friday," Missy answered. "Séance happening today."

THE SÉANCE WAS on the second floor above a tinsmith's shop in Cholon. Our arrival seemed to disturb the many handsome male assistants who fluttered about the room. Seeing us, they immediately went blank and stupid and tried to back us out the door. But it was too late: they had already accepted money from Blue, so we joined the others who had come to consult the spirit intermediary.

A quartet of musicians seated on the floor played Asian violas and drums. Two others sounded gongs, while a young man sang to warm up the crowd clapping in rhythm and singing along.

Huyen, the medium, was in his late thirties, dressed in a mandarin's white tunic covered with intricate dragonflies embroidered in silver thread, and draped with necklaces. An elaborate white headpiece was wound tight around his head like a turban. Huyen's face was powdered white, his lips artificially red, eyelashes and eyebrows blackened. Sashes and gold-link belts hung from his waist and clinked when he moved. Long silver earrings brushed his shoulders. He shimmered as he did little dance steps to the music.

Behind Huyen a giant breakfront glowed with candles set among porcelain figurines, small statues of elephants, carved dragons, live flowers, ornate boxes, and tiny orange and yellow electric lights. A shelf held sepia photographs surrounded by offerings of fruit and bouquets and more candles. Panels of Chinese calligraphy, some wooden, some silk, flanked the altar, covered the side walls and even decorated the ceiling. Blue-and-white jars crowded together, filled with boughs of peach blossoms. Robeson and I were the only Westerners other than a young Nordic type sporting a bald spot encircled by pale brown hair that made him look like a friar. Friar Boy was bickering with two of Huyen's assistants, who seemed to object to his camera. With hand signals and rapid Vietnamese, they made it clear that photos were not allowed. He tried to pretend he didn't understand but finally stopped shooting when they covered the lens with their hands. He pulled the camera toward him and snapped its leather case shut.

We sat down on the bare floor, our backs against the wall. Blue sat between us, doing the play-by-play. A striking male assistant circulating through the audience asked who we wished to contact.

"His grandmother," I said on impulse, indicating Robeson. Blue interpreted. "Does the medium speak English?"

The minion smiled his apologies. "Speak French, no English."

Huyen looked nervous as hell. Was he concerned about the gods and ghosts from the underworld who would soon be sharing his body and soul? Maybe the Red Queen's bird dog just wasn't keen on having Americans snooping on his business.

An assistant announced that Master Huyen was a follower of Princess Liễu Hạnh, the Supreme Goddess, mother of all things, who empowered his second sight. The medium took a seat on a sea-blue cushion propped on a low platform, closed his made-up eyes, and smoked.

Blue quietly said, "*Tình cảm*," and something else to Robeson I didn't catch. Robeson leaned around her and explained. "Mister Ghost Guy has a 'sentiment for men.'"

I nodded. Common enough among mediums in Viet Nam.

"Did ya catch that assistant?" Robeson asked. "The young stud?"

"Which one?" I said. "They're all young studs."

"The busybody that was hassling the guy with the camera. He looks a lot like the spotter on the Vespa playing tag with Lodge's security convoy." He tried to find the kid again to point him out to me but he was gone.

The string quartet struck up another song. Huyen stood up, smiling, and joined in. His bright red lips parted in a laugh. I started. His teeth and gums were fucking black, the pink tongue a shock.

Gongs sounded. Assistants brought forward a beautiful set of long oars so Huyen could stand in the stern of an imaginary boat and punt while the musicians played. He and the audience crooned something that sounded sentimental. Joss sticks burned, turning the air dusky. Huyen's eyes closed again, his face growing blissful. Assistants stepped forward and bundles of crisp new piaster notes replaced the oars. Huyen spread the notes in his hands like playing cards and turned his back to the audience seated on the floor. Still singing, he held the bills aloft and tossed them high over his head. They dispersed in the air, fluttering down on the people, who squealed with delight, happy that it was raining dough, excited that they'd soon hear from their loved ones.

Huyen resumed his seat on the cushion; the band played on. Assistants covered his head with a long red veil and invited the ranks of otherworldly beings to appear: sun goddess, moon goddess, the Goddesses of the Four Palaces, the Thirty-Six Spirits, and some goddess who shored up heaven with stones, Missy said. A gong sounded.

The master, Blue whispered, was praying for somebody's protection from spirits, for another's prosperity, for a woman's recovery from illness and good health for her daughter. Huyen moaned slightly, sinking deeper into trance.

Something rose under the red mesh. The veil opened to reveal a catlike woman, a summoned goddess who called for the souls of the dead to approach. The departed spirits could hear but had no voices in this world. They borrowed the medium's to speak to the relatives seated lotus-style before her.

A young man in the audience said he didn't want to be haunted any longer by the unhappy ghost of his father. The goddess conveyed the list of gifts the son was offering and bargained with the patriarch to leave his son in peace. It wasn't clear whether the ghost took the deal.

The red veil closed. Gongs clanged. The attendants chanted and helped Huyen settle. The veil peeled back again and another female spirit appeared. This one was older and a little dotty. She carried a heartfelt message from a mother to her grown son in the crowd. Tears and emotion flowed from her kneeling child, granted a few precious moments before his mom's soul departed forever. Their talk went too fast for Blue to translate. The veil fell shut. Gongs clanged once more.

When the veil parted the third time a higher being sat before us, basking in her goodness. An angel without wings. More messages flowed: family news and apologies, warnings and laments. People seated near us wept, laughed, implored, thanked. The final exchange brought a widower to tears. The red curtain closed and reopened quickly.

At my request, Blue loudly announced in Vietnamese that I wanted to speak to a fallen soldier—an American major who had died days earlier in Saigon with a diviner squatting at his feet. This didn't so much as raise a flutter in the master lost in the mists. Huyen was someone else, somewhere else. The goddess addressed me in singsong Vietnamese. Blue looked pale and puzzled.

"She say angry soldier come. Not American. Warn you, leave Việt Nam."

"Angry soldier" was vague enough to mean anybody. I figured the crafty medium was just trying to scare me off his patch and off the Red Queen's trail, but Blue seemed certain the vision and warning were real.

A jaunty goddess appeared next, bearing a message from an elderly woman, who spoke directly to Clovis: *"Don't suspicion that fine young thang. You seek huh' out and beg fo'giveness, y'hea?"* Robeson just about jumped out of his skin on hearing the voice of his dead granny coming out of the medium's mouth, berating him about some girl he'd wronged back home. From the look on his face, he knew exactly who she was talking about.

The veil closed and Huyen slumped, head bowed. The quartet kicked in with loud, twangy music and nasal singing. The audience of Vietnamese leapt to their feet, chattering excitedly. Friar Boy held his Leica high over their heads, trying to get a picture as they milled around him. We three pushed through the crowd toward Huyen. The red veil lay atop an empty cushion. He was gone.

Robeson and I raced downstairs to the street. Huyen had

disappeared, if he had come that way at all. Missy Blue came down with Friar Boy and reported that the assistants had vanished almost as quickly as their boss.

"*Fantastique, non?*" the friar said to Miss Blue in schoolboy French. He wanted to take a group picture with us, using the camera's timer *automatique*, he said.

"Get fucked," Robeson muttered, craning to see up the road, still rattled by the surprise visit from his gran. Friar Boy clutched his camera to his chest.

Blue gave him a broad Western-style smile, with teeth, and he relaxed. The smile vanished and she growled, "Need photo," leaving him confused but intrigued. In exchange for Blue's accepting his invitation to lunch, he rewound the film and handed over the cartridge.

"You wait," Blue said to the friar. She turned to us, hand raised toward the stairs. "You come."

We followed her back to the apartment where not a soul remained, living or dead. She led us through the kitchen to Huyen's small quarters, furnished with a slatted wooden bed, a stepstool, a modest Chinese cabinet and not much else. The cabinet contained no playing cards with skeleton ladies, only some red veils like the one that had draped him in the séance. I held one to my face. Gardenia.

A narrow armoire behind the door held completely ordinary pants and shirts. Small piles of underwear rested on the bottom. Next to them lay some piaster notes folded in quarters—something Vietnamese commonly did with money they carried—and a dozen postcards with different views of the outside and inside of Gia Long Palace, including Diem's personal suite.

An eight-by-ten manila envelope held a contact sheet with four rows of small black-and-white frames edged by sprocket holes. The scene in all twenty shots was a clay tennis court and two tall opponents: General Big Minh and Ambassador Lodge. At the net, I could make out the frog-faced General Xuan and the lethal Captain Nhung. In the last few frames, I could see myself in Robeson's ill-fitting seersucker jacket. Two large prints showed the ambassador in the street surrounded by an adoring crowd. The exposures on a second contact sheet showed Cabot Lodge swimming, walking, conversing with diplomats at a reception, and a few frames of the ambassador's empty residence.

WE GOT FRIAR Boy's film developed in a hurry at the information office in the embassy and had them run off multiple prints of Huyen decked out in his regalia. Robeson hand-delivered prints to the embassy's security staff and Marine detachment.

We didn't have the manpower to track Huyen on our own. I took a bunch of the snaps upstairs to share with Donald CIA, along with Huyen's address, although I doubted the medium would go back there anytime soon.

"Hard to tell what he looks like under all that getup," Donald said, squinting at the elaborate costume, the black gums and teeth. He asked if he should pass the photo to the Vietnamese plainclothes police.

"Not yet," I said. "If they pick him up, we'll never get to question him. But it's likely he's been her spotter at every killing and that he'll try to get close to Lodge soon. We found these in his rooms, too," I said, and turned over the contact sheets.

Donald whistled and said he'd pull out all the stops. "I understand you've been inquiring about a Mai Nguyen. May I ask who that is?"

I told him. We both knew it wasn't much to go on in a

country where half the population shared the surname Nguyen, but I sure enjoyed the look on his face when he realized us Army cops had come up with intel nobody else had.

Back in my room at the Majestic, Robeson made straight for the balcony. The photographer had taken Blue to lunch at the floating Chinese restaurant moored on the river just south of the hotel. Robeson looked worried. Turned out Friar Boy was a Danish doctor with Lutheran Relief, not to mention very, very white. Robeson stared south for nearly an hour, leaning out from time to time to get a better view. Just as I was about to tell him not to "suspicion the fine young thang," he bolted past me.

"Blue's coming back from her date with Aryan boy."

Robeson tossed himself on my bed and struck a nonchalant pose. The elevator cage crashed open and Blue appeared at my door.

"Well, Sweetness," Robeson drawled, "how's the albino?"

"Food good, kiss numbah ten," she said, screwing up her face.

CHAPTER THIRTY-FIVE

Enormous portraits of Diem festooned the fronts of buildings all over town, announcing Viet Nam's Independence Day. The palace was celebrating without the public. Citizens weren't allowed anywhere near the festivities. Even the troops that would parade past the president and his honored guests would carry empty rifles on their shoulders. Nhu and Colonel Tung were taking no chances.

With Diem and Lodge safely on a reviewing stand surrounded by throngs of military, Robeson and I went to find Mama-san Kha. We followed directions from the front desk at the Majestic and drove past the north end of town. We knew Mama-san Kha lived alone. Her husband was long dead. She had already lost one son to the war; another was serving in I Corps somewhere near the Demilitarized Zone.

Robeson steered with complete confidence along narrow, twisting dirt lanes that eventually turned off onto a bumpy track. He wrestled the jeep through the deep ruts past a huge garbage dump, where smoldering piles of trash sent up swarms of embers. It reminded me of the coal fields I'd seen as a kid in Pennsylvania, where every once in a while fires that had been burning underground for years would break through to the surface.

We found ourselves stuck amid a pack of half-starved dogs wrestling over scraps. A gaggle of women and kids and hobbled men with sacks picked through the smoky refuse, squabbling over empty number ten cans. With their labels stripped off, the cans shone like bright steel. Since the VC could turn anything into a weapon or tool, scavenging was officially illegal, but the two lone Vietnamese guards smoking outside their crappy shack showed no interest in enforcing the regulations. There were too many pickers, too much garbage. Robeson craned his neck, looking for someplace to turn around.

A pair of bored American MPs sat on the hood of their jeep, shooting at rats with their .45s. They hooted when they popped one, sending it flying across the smoking hill of filth. The other rats just continued about their business.

The haze from the burning rubber and trash made my throat raw and stung my eyes. Another shot sounded. A mangy mutt yelped, mad with pain. The terrified dog dragged its useless back half in a circle, mewling and whimpering. The pack of wild dogs descended, snapping and baring their fangs at each other between tearing at the half-paralyzed mutt. The MPs whooped and broke out some C-rations.

Robeson turned us around and drove us back out.

MAMA-SAN KHA'S SHANTY neighborhood had no yards, no open spaces, hardly even a path to walk along. No other vehicle had followed us, so we chained up the jeep and then spent almost an hour picking our way through makeshift shacks built from shipping crates and roofs made of "tinnies"—crushed soda cans. By dumb luck we came upon a kid who understood who we were looking for and brought us to an old man using a spent artillery shell for an anvil. He led us to her one-room hut,

constructed from wooden pallets she'd bullied us into scroung-
ing and roofed with corrugated metal we had cumshawed.
Given how orderly she kept our rooms, I shouldn't have been
surprised that her place was neat as a pin, its hard dirt floor
swept clean.

Her raw wooden coffin sat in the middle of the room. The
old man removed the bowl of rice and three incense sticks set
on the lid to keep the corpse from rising. Her body lay wrapped
in a blanket and a bamboo mat. Dead from a fall, the old man
informed us nervously and left.

"Poor Mama-san," I said.

Most likely they had leaned on her, trying to coerce her into
cooperating, and she refused. Once she knew what they were
after, they couldn't risk her warning us.

"Somebody put her down 'cause she wouldn't participate in
icing you."

I kneaded my forehead. "And there's fuck-all we can do
about it."

"Look," Robeson said, his face screwed up as he sniffed at
something in a plastic bag. "A foot of boa meat. She certainly
didn't spend no eight piasters on a snake dinner, come home
and off herself."

"Congratulations. Suicide successfully ruled out."

A tiny ceramic Buddha sat on a shelf with no altar. In a tin
can next to the makeshift stove in the corner, we found nuggets
of C-4 explosive. Looked like she had burned pinches of it to
boil water as we might've in the field.

We undid the shroud and saw discoloration at her throat.
Robeson lifted an eyelid.

"Asphyxiation," he said.

Whoever had strangled her, the Saigon police wouldn't be

investigating her death. The poor died here every day without ceremony or attention. For that matter, a couple of long nose GIs getting shredded wouldn't have stirred them either.

I pointed to the gold chain around Robeson's neck and beckoned for him to give it over.

"How am I gonna keep my cross on?" he whined, even as he unhooked the chain. "I'm in serious need of protection at the moment. I wanna be wearing that whenever I flush my commode to make sure it don't blow my ass off."

"She's leaving town. She needs gold in her mouth so she'll have some purchasing power when she gets wherever she's going. I'll get you another chain."

"Yeah, okay. Girl's traveling light. She needs funds."

I lit a joss stick and held its smoking stem to my forehead like a respectful mourner. I stuck it beside a few others in the crappy vase and dropped the gold chain next to the Buddha. Robeson added some cigarettes and hundred-dong notes. I tossed on some more.

Even with the boy's help, it took some time to locate our jeep. Robeson undid the big lock, unchained the steering wheel, and swept the vehicle for explosives while I souvenired the kid a pack of cigarettes and three American greenbacks. He took off like one of the miniature deer the well-off in Saigon kept as lawn pets.

Robeson started the engine. "Who's gonna set the scales right for this?"

I shook my head. The bitter joke around Saigon was that there was a street named 'Cong Ly'—'Justice'—but it only ran one way.

CHAPTER THIRTY-SIX

Robeson and me spent the night at the Brink Hotel. Sunday morning early I slipped away to the Lodge residence and escorted them to the airport. We got there before everyone except General Don, who had come to see his president off to Dalat. The general and Lodge huddled while I checked the interior of the presidential plane. Diem arrived. Son of an emperor's grand chamberlain, the country's first president waddled toward us in a double-breasted white suit. With his hair marcelled to his oversized head, he looked like a portly duck next to lanky Cabot Lodge.

"Mr. Ambassador," he said in English.

"*Monsieur le Président*," Lodge replied.

An infantry captain in summer whites and gold sash called the presidential guards to attention. As we passed between the facing ranks of guards in palace white and gold, they rendered a rifle salute with scarce new AR-15s. Given their weathered faces and black berets, they were unmistakably Nungs, the hard-as-nails tribal mercenaries from up near the Chinese border. I'd never seen Nungs in such fancy uniforms. Basic black was their thing, not white duds with gold epaulettes and trim.

Diem and the Lodges boarded first, followed by the scowling Mr. Vy and Mike Dunn. I brought up the rear. The flight took us over the mountains and across the plateaus of the Central

Highlands. It should have taken an hour to reach the resort town of Dalat, but Diem insisted on a detour to Dao Nghia so he could show off a strategic hamlet, part of Brother Nhu's bullshit strategy to deny local support to the Viet Cong. Diem wasn't going to let Lodge take a pass on inspecting one of these new artificial villages, in reality a spiffed-up concentration camp where farmers, removed by force from their ancestral lands, were locked away behind barbed wire. The "villagers" had to show ID and get groped coming and going. Today they lined up to welcome us with smiles and little yellow silk Vietnamese flags on sticks, waving like happy robots. Treated like inmates, they'd sneak away first chance they got.

A seven-course lunch followed, served on fancy place settings brought from Gia Long Palace. The fingers of Diem's hands were stained yellow with nicotine from his incessant chain-smoking, but he didn't touch any of the liquor. I recognized the type. There were wannabe priests like him in every firehouse and police precinct in Pennsylvania. Well-intentioned, overcommitted, on the side of the angels. Except this one was a dictator. Diem was easy to underestimate. Everyone knew about Diem's overflowing prisons, the political rivals he'd iced. But it was hard to imagine this roly-poly schlub pulling the Montblanc pen, fat as a cigar, out of his breast pocket to sign death warrants. Diem might have dedicated the country to the Virgin Mary, but the wrath of God still came upon him, I supposed.

After lunch we headed for Dalat. Mountain forests and sleeping volcanoes passed beneath us as we circled the one-time colonial hill station where the French went to escape the weather in the lowlands. The houses looked unreal, like Swiss chalets set down on evergreen slopes. We landed after three. The air smelled of pine and wildflowers. It was sixty-four degrees but we shivered like we had come down in the Arctic.

The important passengers got in an oversize black Mercedes and drove off: Diem and the Lodges in back, Mike Dunn and the town's mayor on the jump seats. Mr. Vy and I followed in a Land Rover. An armored car led the way and another brought up the rear, .50-caliber machine guns at the ready.

The president stopped to personally point out primitive Montagnard houses of wood and thatch sitting on posts high off the ground. The normally bare-breasted tribal women had been provided USAID bras for the sake of Diem's prudish modesty. The Western underwear looked absurd and shameful.

We stopped at the Nhus' mountain retreat, a huge new mansion with cathedral ceilings, surrounded by arbors and flowering gardens. Ivy rose in wide columns on either side of the entry. The three youngest Nhu kids were in residence, enjoying the Olympic-size swimming pool in back. The oldest daughter was abroad with their mother. As their uncle, the president, warmly greeted each child, I could tell from Lodge's expression that in spite of himself the ambassador, like his Catholic assistant, Mike Dunn, was growing a little fond of Diem.

Toward evening, Diem hosted dinner at his own villa. Two rings of sentries stood guard outside; Mr. Vy and me, inside. I eyed the help, but they were all longtime retainers, which made the host and guests relax; me and Mr. Vy less so. We both knew the VC had people everywhere, among the young servants and the old retainers. So did Brother Nhu. I wondered if Mr. Vy had any idea Nhu was having him watched.

The mayor of Dalat and his wife, Mrs. Lodge and the ambassador, Mike Dunn, and the president of South Viet Nam shared an elegant meal. Mr. Vy and I sat at opposite ends of the room, eating off trays.

Most of the table talk was in French. After the town's mayor and his lady left around eleven, Mike Dunn, Diem, Cabot and Emily Lodge stayed up, switching to English. I heard Diem mentioning the Commodity Import Program and saying to Lodge that he didn't think he could continue to govern if it wasn't restored soon. The ambassador didn't offer any assurances.

"In a subversive war," Diem said, "one should expect all sorts of unpleasant surprises from one's enemies, and sometimes also from one's friends. With or without the aid, I will keep up the fight, and I will always maintain my friendship toward the American people."

The president lit a cigarette with a Dunhill lighter that looked like a gold Pez dispenser. I fired up a Camel and snapped shut my Zippo. Lodge asked about the president's personal security measures. Diem assured him he was perfectly safe and in complete control of both his government and the armed forces.

"Yes, we hear you are keeping busy with prophylactic measures."

"Counselor Nhu advises that to make an omelet of a threatened coup," Diem said, "one must crush the eggs. Smash them before they hatch, n'est-ce pas?"

Lodge urged Diem to consider keeping Madame Nhu abroad permanently. The president shook his head no, explaining what a respected position she held in the family as its only mother. He, Brother Cẩn, and Archbishop Thục were all childless bachelors. Given Madame Nhu's four children, her role in the family's future was central. She needed to remain close.

"Of course, I understand," Lodge said politely, sounding resigned.

I was out on my feet, praying they'd turn in, when the ambassador took a last crack at swaying Diem. He raised the president's mishandling of the Buddhist crisis and implored him to implement a change in approach he could report at his upcoming meeting at the White House.

Diem disagreed, saying it was no different than the Negro crisis in the States, that he had ordered his brother to use force against the southern Buddhists just as President Kennedy had ordered his brother to impose the government's will in the American South. Except, he said, the Vietnamese government had not used snarling dogs and fire hoses and cattle prods to restore order. Crazily, Diem seemed to believe the Kennedy brothers were the ones who had turned the dogs and fire hoses on Negro demonstrators.

Lodge didn't even attempt to challenge this cuckoo reasoning and bid Diem a friendly goodnight. One-thirty chimed as I walked the couple back to the guest house, a huge colonial villa. A contingent of ARVN soldiers were camped around the building.

I went in first. The place was an icebox. A fire had been laid in the stone hearth in their bedroom. I checked to make sure it was only paper knots and wood, opened the flue and set a wooden match to the kindling. When the flames rose, I put the screen in place, turned back the purple silk quilts on their bed and checked the rest of the place thoroughly. One room was filled with the slipcovers that had obviously protected all the furniture before the Lodges arrived. Clouds of mosquitoes rose as I disturbed the pile. I retreated and closed the door.

Lodge headed straight for bed. Emily invited me to join her for some tea. We made our way to the kitchen, where she put water on to boil.

"You were right about the ghosts at the residence," she said. "It does have an unhappy past."

The other embassy wives had told her that the previous tenants, the Richardsons, hadn't been able to hire any staff at all at first, because the villa stood on the grounds of a French prison where the Deuxième Bureau had secretly tortured political prisoners. During the war, imperial Japanese occupation forces had found the place handy for particular interrogations and summary executions. Then after Tokyo surrendered, Ho's Viet Minh had used it for storing and questioning prisoners. Few who were detained there in any era emerged the same at the end of their stay, if they emerged at all. Over the decades, hundreds had suffered torture and endured bad deaths on the grounds.

"It's the Times Square of ghosts," I said.

The kettle whistled. She quickly found the strainer and loose tea, which she tossed into a plain blue teapot. The boiling water brought out a wonderful aroma.

"While Cabot was at the parade yesterday, I did as you instructed about the mirrors," Emily said. "It caused a terrible ruckus among the staff when they came down. We couldn't enlist any Buddhist monks on short notice but our ancient cook recommended a ritual specialist who came immediately with his assistants and set to work, using nothing more than a veil and some joss sticks jabbed in a flowerpot. There was no need to understand the language. The ritual was . . . extraordinary. We were mesmerized, witnessing an invisible transformation we absolutely felt. Everyone was moved by his incantations. Everything went splendidly until one of the Marines took a Polaroid picture—whereupon pandemonium struck. The camera upset our staff no end. Watching the instant picture develop set them off even worse."

She produced the photo from an envelope in her pocketbook. The Polaroid was slightly blurry and oddly colored. No ghosts, but chilling nonetheless. On one side of Emily Lodge, in headdress and earrings, wearing eyeliner but no other makeup, stood Huyen. On the other, his assistant, the young man on the Vespa.

"He quieted the Vietnamese really masterfully," she said, "and then completed the ritual. The groundskeepers and house staff meekly returned to work."

I nodded. I didn't want to upset her. As casually as I could manage, I asked if she would let me keep the Polaroid temporarily. Though slightly surprised, she agreed. We warmed our hands on the tea and bid each other goodnight.

I decided my room was too far back from theirs, so I took the bedding to the front room and laid a fire. The dry wood roared when set alight. From my valise, I unpacked a stubby grenade launcher and its big shells, half of them buckshot, the rest grenade loads. If anything went down tonight, it wasn't going to happen quietly.

I lay down in my clothes, one hand tucked in my armpit, the other gripping the launcher.

MONDAY MORNING WE got driven to the war college for the ten o'clock dedication of the Mark II reactor. After long-winded speeches, rods were pushed and pulled to gin the thing to life. Diem declared the reactor would churn out 250 kilowatts forever. Lunch followed, and a quick closed-door session between Diem and Lodge. From Lodge's expression, I could tell Diem wasn't giving an inch. Whatever sympathy he had felt for Diem the day before was evaporating fast. At five o'clock, we were back in the air, on our way to Saigon.

When we landed, an embassy Marine handed Mike Dunn a note from Mrs. Lacey letting him know his wife and two kids were en route from the States. I leaned into the back window and told Dunn he had to arrange for the immediate dismissal of the cook at the embassy residence. I showed him the Polaroid of Huyen, explained who he was, and insisted that the cook who had enabled his access to the residence had to be fired and evicted under guard. The Polaroid needed to go directly to Donald.

Robeson picked me up a few minutes later. After the sleepless night I'd had in Dalat, I passed out in my clothes and didn't wake until first light.

I FOUND A note from Flippi on my desk: *Just a reminder, son. Friday's the first of the month. Payday!!!* The fool had signed it *Jesse James*.

The bottom radio in our stack of sidebands piped up, reporting a bombing, American personnel possibly involved. Robeson and I acknowledged the call and rushed off to investigate, worried that the Red Queen's Unit Eight was changing tactics and going for bigger body counts.

Just a small incident, the white mice informed us when we arrived—a ball of *plastique* rolled into a Chinese restaurant. Shattered glass lay everywhere. The place reeked of splattered food and flesh. A woman dusted with debris slumped so far forward in her chair she was folded in half, forehead to the floor. Almost silly looking, like an upside-down doll, except she was stone-cold dead. Her breakfast companion remained in his seat, alive and unblinking, not registering anything being said to him by the ambulance attendants taking his vitals.

"Nooo *Mỹ*, nooo *Mỹ*," the plainclothes dick kept repeating, meaning no Americans. We nodded and left, grateful not to have to wade through body parts looking for pieces of US personnel to bag up.

CHAPTER THIRTY-SEVEN

Corporal Magid said "Donald," no last name, had called for us several times while we were out. Said it was important.

I tried several times to raise Donald on the phone but couldn't get through, so Robeson drove me over to the embassy. After checking with Mrs. Lacey to make sure the residence cook had been fired, we went to find Donald.

"Picked up your soothsayer this morning," he announced, real casual, like my sending him the Polaroid had nothing to do with it. "He was cooped outside Ambassador d'Orlandi's, right next to MAC-V on Pasteur. Some balls, right? Lodge was there for a private parlay. Found a camera on Huyen too. Just had these developed."

He spread some prints on the desk: Lodge dining with fellow diplomats at the Caravelle, walking amidst admirers, arriving at d'Orlandi's door.

"Trouble is, we can't have a candid talk with the soothsayer. The Agency's just been ordered to back off, drop everything, not pursue the Red Queen matter further. So what the hell do we do with the guy?"

Robeson's eyebrows rose in surprise. "Who ordered you to stand down?"

"Ambassador Sab-o-tage himself. New priority. Our intel and Air Force intelligence says the coup is coming in the next forty-eight hours. Pacific Command in Hawaii has a naval task force standing off the coast prepared to evacuate dependents as needed."

"What's this, the third or fourth time we've heard that warning?"

"Yeah, yeah," Donald said, "the coup's always forty-eight hours away until the generals find themselves in 'equipoise,' as Lodge likes to say. And then nothing. Which is why my money's on the Red Queen touching up Diem before the mutineer generals ever get their shit together. But I've got a direct order. Which means if there's information to be had from Huyen, you'll have to get it out of him. We're to dispose of our catch and step away."

"Fuck," I said. They were the interrogation experts, not us.

Donald gave us the address and scribbled a note. "I'll radio ahead. Present this and they'll give him over. Better you get him than the slopes. They'll just waste the asset, pun intended."

We bolted downstairs and vaulted into our jeep.

"I don't get it," Robeson said. "Why would the ambassador muzzle CIA? Especially since he's in her sights? Whether she's coming for him next or saving him for later, she's coming."

"I'm not so sure he minds her gunning for him. Takes him back to his war. But the coup is close. The drawbridges are going up. Soon it'll just be us CIDs out here with Miss VC Assassin and the SEPES creeps from *The Crypt*."

We tore ass over to the little Ton Nol Hotel, screeched to a halt and jogged briskly into the humble lobby. Ton Nol wasn't much of a hotel, just two small floors above a narrow reception area. CIA had commandeered the entire second floor. We found Huyen in a back room with a view of the alley, immobilized on a slat-board bed, handcuffed and his arms lashed together at the elbows for good measure. Eyeliner did nothing to conceal the dark circles of fatigue, or the sudden look of terror at seeing us again. The agent in charge read Donald's note and said, "Knock yourselves out," as he handed over the keys to his cuffs.

We took custody, put an extra fatigue shirt on him to cover the restraints and hustled him into the front seat of the jeep.

"What do we do now?" Robeson said.

"Grill him."

"I'm not sure I have enough of the lingo to do that."

"You're not gonna be discussing philosophy. We just need the who, where, and when. He speaks French. Your French will be enough."

Robeson jabbered questions at Huyen as I drove. The man gave up nothing.

The clock was ticking. We couldn't ride around all day with a sullen, cuffed Vietnamese prisoner in the front seat of an open jeep.

"What are we gonna do with him?" Robeson said.

I had an idea. I drove toward Tan Son Nhut along the long parched stretch of tarmac where the poorer locals liked to picnic on weekends, through Soul Alley where Robeson went sometimes to shack up with his Malaysian girlfriend. We turned in to the line for the airbase. Jets were screeching into the air every thirty seconds. The MPs waved us through. I drove to the far end of the field and the 120th Aviation Company at the back of a small warehouse that Flippi had turned into a repair shop for helicopter engines.

Flippi's buddies told us he was finishing up processing for

his departure, but due back any minute. They pointed us to his work area at the rear where engines sat on blocks or hung suspended from a frame made of steel girders. The airfield's siren announced high noon. The mechanics knocked off for chow, leaving us alone in the large space.

"What're you intending to do?" Robeson said. "Take him up in a Huey for a little heart-to-heart in the wild blue yonder?"

I shook my head. I was counting on Flippi. The rest of us faked hard-assed nasty. He was the real thing, a mean fucker ever since Korea when the gooks had slithered into our lines in the pitch-black, freezing night and slit the throats of half the GIs asleep in the two-man holes. Flip had awoken next to his dead best friend. He was never the same after that, never took another prisoner. If anybody needed terrifying, those eyes could do it.

"Hey, you guys come to see me off in style?" Flippi said, walking in, giddy at the prospect of a nearly two months' leave stateside with his re-up bonus in his pocket.

"Couple days, Ellie," he said in a stage whisper. "You ready?"

He gave me a meaningful look in case I'd forgotten our Friday appointment with the oil company bagman and his eighty thousand beautiful dollars.

Afraid he might say more in front of Robeson, I quickly explained our situation. I worried he might not appreciate my hitting him up for a tough favor so close to the end of his tour. But he lit up. Flippi was hot to test-drive his machine, he said, but no way was he erecting the whole thing again. The blade alone would have to do.

"You've got it here?"

"Hell, yes." He gestured grandly, like a ringmaster presenting a prize elephant.

A narrow box of thick rough wood rested on a pallet, covered with a drop cloth he pulled away with a flourish. Flippi released the unsecured sides of the crating and they fell flat, kicking up dust as they struck the concrete floor. The blade stood upright, an enormous axe-head.

"Can't resist looking at her," Flippi said, grinning at the business end of the killing machine. "Gotta close up the crate soon, though. Ships in a few days. It's going by sea. Me, I wing home on Pan Am with round-eye ladies bringing me cocktails all the way across the fucking Pacific."

Flippi took charge of our prisoner and shoved him facedown onto a large empty worktable on big metal wheels. He pushed the table under the girders and trussed Huyen's ankles to his arms until the man looked like a chicken wing. Hooking a fat cable to his fancy knot, Flip ran the line up to a motor-driven pulley attached to the steel beam resting on the girder frame overhead. When he hit a big red button, Huyen flew toward the ceiling, screaming. He yowled a second time when Flippi held down the black button, dropping the prisoner to eye level. Flip and me wrestled the blade into position under the dangling fortune-teller until it was close to Huyen's gut. Wiping his brow, Flippi switched on an air compressor real loud.

I gave Robeson the nod to ask Huyen again where the Red Queen was hiding. Robeson yelled the question in French. Huyen didn't answer, just stared at the hundred pounds of bright, sharp steel beneath his abdomen. He started wheezing and gasping for air.

"Let's give him a practice swing on the trapeze," Flippi shouted. I pulled back on Huyen's bare shins, lined him up and let go, hoping we'd calculated right. He whined in a high pitch as he flew forward over the blade, moaned louder still as he swung back over the sharp steel, straining to arch himself away from it. He couldn't tell how close he was. Actually, we couldn't either.

I caught him at the knees and held him while Robeson repeated the question. He said something in Vietnamese and then in French. Robeson looked at me and shook his head: the man wasn't answering the question. Flippi cackled like Igor and let out the cable a few inches, dropping Huyen closer to the blade's edge.

Flip took the cover off the zinc-lined basket and removed a cabbage. He dropped the head of lettuce onto the blade. It sheared in half instantly. The compressor howled.

"This combination slicer-dicer," he barked. "If Junior here don't spill his guts—it will. Ha ha!"

An unmuzzled jet engine screamed as it sped a warplane down the closest runway. The deafening sound completely overpowered your senses, your brain. The jet leapt into the air, straining to outrun its unbearable eruptions. How was it Flippi and his crew weren't all deaf and crazy?

Flippi recovered the cabbage halves and shoved the smaller one down the front of Huyen's trousers like a codpiece, hooting with glee.

"Let him swing free this time," Flippi shouted, "back and forth." He lit up a stogie. The cigar smelled like a cat's ass burning. "Let 'er rip!" he yelled, pumping the air.

I let go of the feet, hoping again Flip had judged the height correctly. Huyen swung past the blade and back like a pendulum. I pushed him to add some altitude and he shot over the silver blade a second time, moaning as the edge nicked his trousers and the cabbage.

Flippi cackled. "Looks like we got slaw."

Huyen went rigid. I caught him by his ankles and eased him to a halt. If he didn't have a heart attack, I might. "Ask him again where the Red Queen is," I yelled in Robeson's ear, my pulse racing.

Robeson put it to him, looking a little ill. The fortune-teller answered in rapid French.

"Says he don't know nothin'."

I signaled. Flippi made a show of pulling out the cabbage like it was a magic trick and lowered our prisoner one more link. The blade was just touching his shirt. As I drew him back it slit the cloth. Huyen hummed high-pitch panic. The next swing would cut him for sure. How deep, none of us knew. Flip dropped him an inch more. Another jet engine raged into the air.

"If I let go of him it'll be nasty," I yelled.

"Aw," Flippi whined. "Let me skritch 'im a little." He revved the compressor higher to cover any screams.

CHAPTER THIRTY-EIGHT

Robeson helped me pull Huyen back by his ankles.
"Use her real name," I said to Robeson.

"Où est la camarade Mai Nguyen?"

Huyen's eyes jumped from Robeson to me to Flippi to the huge blade.

"Tell him he's gonna sing soprano if I let go."

Flippi reached for him and Huyen blurted out a long declaration, rapid-fire.

"He's never met her, only sees her as she rides up. His job is simply to occupy her targets. He was instructed not to look at her or learn her face in case he was ever captured."

"When does she strike next?"

"Perhaps in a few days, 'as conditions ripen,' he says."

"Who else will aid her? How many cadre?"

Robeson put the question to him and interpreted. "Swears he's not included in the plan this time. Doesn't know how many comrades will partake. Those who participate in an action only ever learn their own parts. Their orders come only from her. Nothing is shared between the other comrades."

I didn't believe him. "Where do you assemble before an attack?"

Words tumbled out. Robeson summarized.

"They rendezvous at the site only on the actual day. Instructions about where and when arrive just minutes before, so they must rush to get in position." I doubted that, too. He'd been her spotter. He'd have known all the attack sites well in advance.

"How are you told the next target?"

"A picture arrives by ordinary mail. We memorize the face and begin studying the man's habits."

"Has the team received the American ambassador's photo?"

"Yes."

"What are her plans for the ambassador?"

"Same as Diem."

Huyen's face darkened as the blood settled in his head and upper torso. He looked faint.

"What? Make him say it," I insisted. Robeson did.

"*Assassinat,*" Huyen croaked.

"You were in the American ambassador's villa. Why?"

Huyen looked horrified. Was there nothing we didn't know?

"Scouting the premises, he says. Casing the place."

"Is that where they are planning to attack him?"

Robeson shook his head no as he listened to the answer. "More likely when Lodge swims. Possibly when he walks in the street."

"And if Lodge changes his behavior?" I said.

Robeson translated: "He won't change. He will swim. He will flirt with the crowds."

"Did you receive pictures of President Diem?"

"Just postcards of the palace. He says he was sent to take exterior pictures. They all know what Diem looks like."

"Who is to be struck first?"

"*Qui est-elle pourchasse maintenant?*"

"*Le président de la République. Au palais.*"

"She's hatching a plan to kill Diem at the palace."

"What about Lodge?"

"Après Diệm."

"'After Diem,' he says."

I wasn't buying half of what he was telling us. For all her skill, how could they pull off an attack on Diem in the heavily guarded palace? Huyen was blowing smoke up our asses. But I still had hopes he could lead us to Mai.

"Why did she leave him out of the plan this time?"

Huyen went on at length; Robeson summarized. "He says he was compromised by our attending his ceremony, and immediately dropped from the team. He's been ordered to leave the city."

Bullshit. He'd been scouting Lodge's residence, shadowing him at d'Orlandi's place just this morning. Could we trust any of what he was saying?

His eyes rolled up. I signaled Flip to let him down. Robeson carefully unhooked Huyen.

"Damn," Flip complained as he took away the blade. "If he'd only held out a little longer. I ain't never gonna get to slice any meat."

He shut off the compressor and pulled me aside. "You got my note?"

"Yeah. You found the bagman?"

"Easy as pie. Followed him home the other night. Lives on Boulevard Norodom. Right near the Dutch Shell HQ, that big Nazi-looking building with all the columns and pedestals."

"Sure. Number fifteen."

"Right. Company housing is at number seven. There's three white mice permanently parked, two of 'em moonlighting, the third on regular police duty."

"So we steer clear of the white mice in front of the apartment complex."

"Right. We exit the other way, past the offices, follow the bagman to the drop site." He took me by the shoulder. "Meet me at sixteen-thirty in front of the shipping company next door to your hotel." He slapped my shoulder and went to repack the blade in its crate. "Friday is payday, boyo."

Robeson had cut the truss, freeing Huyen's arms and the tethers on his ankles. I tossed Robeson the keys to the cuffs. Huyen collapsed into a chair. I reversed a chair and sat down facing him, my arms resting on the back. We were all drenched. Robeson filled a metal cup with water from my canteen and doused Huyen with half of it. Huyen gulped down the rest and held out the cup for more.

"What do we do with this guy now?" Robeson said, looking at his watch.

"Pop him and make the captain happy."

"Jesus, no!" Robeson exclaimed.

"You need to stoke up beforehand?"

Robeson shook his head. "I'm not down with that. No way. Can't we just cut him loose?"

"He helped ambush three of our people. His comrades killed Mama-san, tried to kill me. Don't be stupid. The man's hardcore. Let him go, he'll fly straight back to her and tell her what we know. Odds are, we're both already on the comrades' hit list. You wanna move to the top spot?"

"I ain't shootin' the man," Robeson protested.

I gulped down more water while I considered the options. Better him than us, I wanted to say. "Okay. I'll tell you what. You tell him he's gotta run for it, not go to his place, not say goodbye. Leave Saigon right now, leave Viet Nam like his commissars told him to. Hop the bus to the border. Just *di di mau.* Because as soon as we let him loose, we're giving his name and picture to Colonel Tung at SEPES, and to the VBI, the CIO, Nhu's Special Branch, the lot. If he sticks around, he'll be a guest in one of Nhu's spas before nightfall. Make sure he understands that." I smiled over at Huyen. "We'll let him cool down for a while so he don't look so wrecked. Flippi can take him to the bus."

After Robeson translated, I sent him to get us more drinkable water and pulled Flippi aside. "I hate to lay this on you, but the kid won't go along with disposing of him."

"What do you need me to do?"

"Let the kid think you're taking Huyen to the bus and, you know, take care of him, quiet like."

"No problemo, boss. I'm happy sending any of them to their ancestors. Tell your captain I'm available, always. You know, like Paladin on TV." He dropped his voice low like an announcer's. "Have portable guillotine, will travel."

"Careful. I'm guessing he understands way more English than he lets on."

"Don't worry. His will be a real quick trip to the workers' paradise."

CHAPTER THIRTY-NINE

The door opened on its own when I knocked. Nadja was packing.

"Changing rooms?"

She shook her head. "You didn't get my message? A car is coming for me. I'm being recalled."

"Because of me?"

She shook her head again and resumed pulling clothes from the wardrobe. "One of the Polish secretaries went missing," she said. "Turned up in Hong Kong with her Canadian swain. They'd gotten married. She's defecting."

"That's not your fault."

"If someone slips out of the collective grasp, the fault is assumed to be mine."

"You in big trouble?"

"I'm being posted to Tallinn."

"Where the hell's that?"

"The Soviet Republic of Estonia. On the Baltic Sea."

"Behind the Iron Curtain," I said.

"Pretty town. Lots of black bread. Blood sausage at Christmas."

She laid the folded blouses in her suitcase and sat down on the bed. I joined her.

"Maybe it's better that it happened," she said, "before we got involved." She leaned her head against my shoulder.

Hell, I thought we were involved. The weight of my disappointment surprised me. Not that I'd been ready to offer marriage and sanctuary, like the Canadian groom had done. Pretty sure she would have said no if I had.

Nadja stroked my arm. "We were never going to be allowed a private peace in this backwater war. I told you—one side or the other would have put an end to us soon enough." She touched my cheek.

"I haven't much by way of a parting gift," she said. "Just a little something. Seek out a Mr. Ma Tuyen in Cholon. He can help you."

"Who is this guy?"

"He's the unofficial mayor of the Chinese district. A businessman, an exporter. Among many other things."

I kissed her deeply, feeling passion and pain well up. "Stay," I said. "Let's make a run for the border. Phnom Penh? Vientiane?"

She smiled indulgently as if I was a child proposing something adorable and absurd, a picnic on the moon.

I CALLED RIDER to let him know we needed to locate Mr. Ma Tuyen for a sit-down, then headed to meet Robeson at Cheap Charlie's. Coup gossip over breakfast was at fever pitch. Everybody agreed mutiny was near. Who would launch the challenge? was the only question. I half-listened and concentrated on my sautéed asparagus and poached egg while Robeson and Blue concentrated on one another. Now that Nadja had checked out of the Majestic and out of my life, their mooning was the last thing I needed to see. I fed my face without enjoyment and the three of us drove over to CID.

The whole city was lethargic. Nothing like the usual scramble in the streets.

CORPORAL MAGID CALLED me to the telephone. Rider for me, being deliberately vague on the open line. "That person you asked me to find? There's a guy says he can take us. Remember the place we ate overlooking the water? See you there in fifteen."

I gathered up Robeson. We parked the jeep in care of the street kids at the Majestic and walked a few blocks south to the Nautique, a sad little yacht club that happened to have a first-class restaurant with a waterside dining patio overlooking the Chinese Canal where it joined the Saigon River.

I spotted Rider's white-wall haircut with a little tuft of sun-bleached hair up top. He was sitting at a table beneath a flagstaff flying the club's blue-and-white yachting pennant. We made sure we had clear sightlines before we sat down.

Rider had ordered us three cognacs, Bisquit Dubouché. In the tiny marina below us a couple of sleek sailboats—what passed for yachts at Saigon's yacht club—bobbed alongside the floating dock. A junk slid toward us, its hinged masts lying flat. Rider stood and raised a hand to shade his eyes. "Our ride's here. Let's go."

"Already?" Robeson said, his head coming out from behind the menu. "Damn. They got lamb and veal flown in from Paris." He downed his cognac in one gulp.

We followed Rider down the incline to the dock. At the tiller of the junk stood a thin gray-haired Eurasian in a creamy white shirt open at the collar. He was barefoot, his pant legs rolled up.

"I have been asked to bring you to my employer," he said.

The junk nudged the dock's rubber-tire bumpers on the starboard side. Robeson and I stepped across the gap, Rider close behind us. The lone Chinese deckhand pushed us off. We pulled away under power, the diesel engine huffing black exhaust. The vessel hadn't looked like much from shore, but up close you could see how solidly built it was, the tropical hardwoods varnished smooth. The Eurasian guided the junk west along the canal.

He was called Stephan, he said. A precise fella, judging from his well-ordered boat and the skillful way he maneuvered the crowded waterway choked with sampans. Many of them were covered with thatched shelters, charcoal cooking fires smoking in their sterns. Wooden planks, perched between the sampans like sidewalks, clacked as we passed.

Shacks crowded the shore too, their backs jutting out over the rank water on wooden posts. Stephan slowed the engine as we eased past the floating slums teeming with half-clad kids and their grandparents.

We sailed beneath a bridge that smelled of mildew and wet straw. The junk slowed as we trailed a wooden barge, thirty feet wide, laden with sacks piled twice the height of a man. A rice-treatment plant oozed large, slow swirls of milky waste into the putrid water. Naked children on the banks pointed and shouted at us. Smoke from distilleries and factories bit our throats. A flat-bottomed sampan slid past with two women standing in the stern, each punting with an oar. The sampan rode low in the water, loaded down with bananas, green jackfruit, and shiny orange papayas, as well as crates of live ducks, the squawking heads protruding through holes on top.

We passed under a steel and concrete bridge, ten yards wide and long as a football field, that loomed over an island dividing the waterway. Stephan took the right channel, taking us ever deeper into Cholon.

Vietnamese spoke of the Chinese quarter like it was a minor section of Saigon, but Cholon was a city unto itself, with a million souls crowding its dark alleys and neon-lit streets. Cholon was where Saigonese went for meals, gambling, assignations and other earthly pleasures; a haven for secret societies, the most private clubs, and the Viet Cong.

Stephan expertly swung the prow, easing the junk to a stop against a pier where sampans were giving up their cargo. The air was filled with the sweaty sour smell of ninety-pound men humping hundred-pound sacks of rice, coffee beans, and tea. Stephan led us from the waterfront onto a street teeming with bicycle rickshaws. I hoped he would hail some for us, but he pressed forward on foot. Buildings six feet across and one or two stories high butted one against the other for blocks. Their fronts, open to the street, were businesses where artisans and merchants plied their trades: hammering tin, butchering meat, treadling sewing machines, dispensing herbal remedies. Home was at the back or on the second floor. The few three-story buildings had verandahs at the top.

We passed through a street of tile shops, then stores filled with elaborate baskets nested one inside the other. Over an open storefront a single neon Chinese character glowed lucky red, tinting the white marble counters of the butcher shop and the cooked fowl hanging alongside strips of dried pork. A thick wooden chopping block was getting a good workout as civet cats paced a wire cage, waiting for their starring role in somebody's dinner.

Rounding a corner, we entered a street lined with

pornography shops and brothels. A huge green Heineken sign, topped by its iconic red star, gleamed inside a saloon. Unlike Vietnamese, the Chinese stared openly at us, talking and laughing as they ate curbside at counters, on balconies, and squatting beside glowing braziers.

A wide alleyway along the backs of identical one-story buildings had us splashing through puddles and scrambling over crates. The path narrowed beneath tarps and plastic sheets that blocked out both sun and air. "The Casbah's got nothin' on Cholon," Robeson muttered as we zigzagged through the labyrinth.

We came on a small candlelit temple blackened by filth and smoke, filled with folk idols—homeless gods abandoned for bigger religions, yet still worshipped. This was deeper in Cholon than I'd ever been, nowhere near Cheap Charlie's, or the enlisted men's billets where we'd go to shoot pool. Oddly, I felt safer than I had in days, knowing that our path through the dense district made tailing us almost impossible.

We followed Stephan into a building filled with neatly stacked hundred-pound bags of rice, each stenciled with a long-stemmed flower, the courtyard out back piled high with more. Our escort directed us through a crude hole in a common wall into the shop next door and then through another breach into a third building and a fourth. The last portal had an actual door monitored by two hard-faced Nung guards who ushered us into a large shuttered hall, tiled and cool.

Sunlight from the rear courtyard illuminated a red-and-gold ancestral altar. Candles flickered in red glass cups and joss sticks burned in a gold incense holder next to votive offerings of fresh fruit and reddish banknotes printed with historical scenes and costumed figures.

Beautiful calligraphy panels hung on either side of the altar. A lacquered wooden screen depicted an ancient mountain inn overlooking tiers of rice paddies that climbed the steep hills. From the ceiling hung a dim bare bulb and a blue flag embroidered with a folded umbrella.

Stephan introduced us to our host, a small Chinese man with a high forehead framed by receding gray hair, stylishly dressed in an Italian linen suit and precisely knotted black tie.

"Welcome. My name is Ma. Won't you be seated?"

Miniature armchairs circled a low narrow slab, more bench than table, on which rested five blue cups and a teapot glazed a deep red. Beside it sat a game board with small wedge-shaped tiles etched with Japanese characters. A beautiful orchid in a shallow bowl arched over the table, its purple blooms edged in black.

We took seats. Mr. Ma saw Rider admiring the umbrella flag. "A family heirloom," he said. "The ensign of brigands once headquartered near Hà Nội on the bay of Ha Long."

Mr. Ma poured us tea. He nodded toward the board game. "Do any of you play *shōgi*?"

"Japanese chess?" Rider shook his head. "No."

"The board looks bigger than ours," I said. "And I don't recognize the pieces."

The *shōgi* board was square, nine rows by nine. Twenty flat pieces sat in three files on each side: nine in the first, only two in the second, nine in the last.

"You call it Japanese," Ma said, "but of course it was Chinese first. It is sometimes called 'the generals' game.' When enemy pieces are captured they are not removed from the field. They are recruited by the generals to the rival's side. Turned, if you will."

"Very Asian," I said.

He smiled, but his eyes were unmoved. "Yes, our attitudes are different about such matters. They say this rule of adaptation pays tribute to a mercenary who chose a change of allegiance over execution. After a point, any form of surviving is winning, is it not? One does what one must. So," Ma said, leaning back, "you are the noted policemen giving chase to the talented Viet Cong assassin. I understand you have apprehended the medium on her team. Did he divulge her location?"

Mr. Ma seemed keen to hear the answer. He moistened his lips, his eyes hard and serious above the rim of the teacup. I shook my head no and wondered how the hell Mr. Ma knew about the capture of Huyen.

"A shame. The astrologer is her mentor and second in command. Having been raised among the Cao Đài, it is perhaps natural that she should seek the aid and counsel of a medium. Huyen tried to scare you off and ordered your elimination when you did not heed the warning."

Mr. Ma's confidence eased my mind about consigning Huyen to Flippi. But it also made me wonder again if anything the medium had divulged could be trusted.

CHAPTER FORTY

M r. Ma sipped his tea. "I hope I can be of some help to you."

"But you don't know her whereabouts?" I said.

"No doubt she's here, somewhere among Chợ Lớn's million souls. Our labyrinthine hive cloaks her activities, as it does those of our own organizations and cartels. We all avoid Sài Gòn's official scrutiny."

"Nhu's secret police must be looking for her here," I said.

"Of course, but security services do not function well in Chợ Lớn. It's what makes our quarter attractive to libertines and lovers of privacy."

"I can't help wondering why you'd want to help us catch her," I said. "These days most people are mortified by President Diem. They want to see the back of him, not protect him."

"And he certainly hasn't dealt with you Chinese any better than with the Buddhists," Rider added.

"True. Diệm thinks we Cholonese are a threat. We control eighty percent of trade in this country, not at all to his liking. The Vietnamese resent our business acumen. They never object when he issues us ultimatums."

"Ultimatums?" Robeson said.

"To assume Vietnamese names, not display Chinese characters

on our signs, to assimilate. Those who refused were no longer permitted to deal in textiles. Or mill rice, sell meat or fish, charcoal or petroleum, or so much as own a modest grocery. But still we resisted. For a time, at least."

"How did you resist?" I said.

"We withdrew our funds, closed our accounts. The currency tumbled. Everyone quickly saw how precarious the country's economy was without our participation. They backed off. Yet Diệm kept insisting: conform or else. When we didn't follow his precepts, he imposed fines, arrested and harassed us until we were worn thin."

"So in the end you complied," Rider said.

"Cosmetically. We chose to survive. I suppose our sympathies generally lie with our brothers in China, regardless of their unfortunate political enthusiasms of the moment. Peking wishes independence for *all* of Việt Nam, and to have Diệm ousted. Recent indications are that your government desires the same fate for him."

"You don't share that wish?" I said.

"Actually, no, Agent Miser." Mr. Ma refilled our cups. "Diệm is a curious person, quite unlike most Vietnamese. He trusts only his Catholicism, thinks God wants him where he is. Like Mao, he insists on the superiority of his beliefs to the exclusion of all others. Yet, these foreign attitudes notwithstanding, he is our only viable option in the present circumstances. If he is removed, our enterprises will cease."

He took up his cup.

"Mr. Ma," I said. "I'm sorry, but I don't completely follow."

"I just mean trade is our *raison d'être*. Chợ Lớn means 'big market,' aptly enough. It has endured Vietnamese royalists, Japanese fascists, French colonialists . . ." He held up his hands in mock alarm. "Marxists, even tourists. Despite our reluctance about Diệm and his government, it's important to us that he remain in power."

"Why?"

"Simplicity itself. If he manages to stay at the helm, USAID and American military aid will continue, the commodity imports will inevitably resume and business will proceed apace. If he is ousted, and in the ensuing chaos Communism prevails, all American aid will cease and our many investments will be no more. Our enterprises will be appropriated by the state. Regrettably, many signs indicate we are slipping toward that eventuality."

"What signs?" Robeson interjected.

"The generals and colonels are dangerously close to reaching consensus on their plot." Mr. Ma crossed his arms. "Meaning the end is approaching. Yesterday, in Nha Trang, General Đôn met with Diệm's beloved young General Đính. Even as we speak, they are closeted again at a private club not far from here."

I said, "You think General Dinh would turn against Diem, the man he considers his second father, who put general's stars on his shoulders and made him military governor of Saigon?"

Mr. Ma offered around a bowl of small oranges, taking one for himself at the end.

"The impetuous general already has. You may not know that Đính recently proposed himself for a third star and a bigger job—minister of the interior. Diệm rebuffed these ambitions, laughed in the arrogant young man's face. General Đính ran off to Dalat to nurse his bruised ego. It seems a prominent astrologer had been hired to put him up to making that silly proposal, convincing Đính the time for his promotion was propitious. The generals knew Diệm's refusal was inevitable, and thereby delivered the rambunctious egotist securely into the arms of the rebels."

"They played him," I said.

"Most expertly. His vanity is notorious. He already fancies himself a national hero, and travels with his own personal photographer to document his every exploit. Now instead of rushing to Diệm's aid, Đính's forces will prevent aid from reaching him. Yet Nhu still believes young Đình is busily preparing the false coup that Nhu devised: a sham Viet Cong 'uprising' here in Sài Gòn that would need to be mercilessly crushed by Đình's forces to save the nation, returning Diệm to power as the only one who can provide law and order. Regrettably, in the melee, American homes would be pillaged, and many lives would be lost, your ambassador's among them."

"You're certain Dinh has defected? That this pretend uprising isn't about to happen?" Robeson said nervously.

"I am. The coup, when it comes, will not be the charade Nhu expects. It will be real." Mr. Ma offered a dish of lychee nuts. "We in Chợ Lớn can only hope this latest coup will fail like all its predecessors. Meanwhile, the Red Queen poses an even more imminent threat to the president. Unlike the generals, she does not vacillate."

"The planets aren't lining up well for Diem," I said.

"No." Ma's expression grew serious. "Which does not bode well for us either. We Chinese have been here for many generations. We do not wish to have to uproot, to reestablish ourselves somewhere else. Our elders find the prospect of beginning again especially discomfiting."

"So Cholon is for Diem," Robeson said, "not for Ho Chi Minh."

"Neither, actually. President Diệm and Uncle Hồ are purists; one chosen by God, the other by history. They have intolerance and certainty in common, convinced as they are of their own worth and goals. Both men are heliocentric believers in the One True Way. To achieve their ends, they are ready to sacrifice themselves—and us—as needed. Neither has much interest in the well-being of our mercantile colony, except to the extent that we temporarily provision their followers, equip their armies, and replenish their treasuries."

"You want to be neutral," Robeson suggested. "Like Switzerland."

Mr. Ma smiled slightly. "We want to trade. We are traders."

"I can see that the Communists would kick Westerners out pronto, but you . . . don't they need you?"

"We too would be shown the door, I assure you. Chinese conquered Việt Nam a century before Christ was born and stayed as unwelcome overlords for a thousand years. Vietnamese do not forget. In their eyes we are nearly as foreign as you. Meanwhile, we play for time. Which is how I hope you will help us."

Mr. Ma stood up and unrolled an architectural drawing of a large building. He spread the schematic across the ancient bench, anchoring the corners with smooth black stones he took from around the orchid's base.

"I may not know where the Red Queen is now. But I have a good idea where she will be soon. You recognize the structure?"

"Gia Long Palace. Diem's office and residence are there"—I pointed—"on the second floor."

"Exactly so. And here"—he tapped the opposite wing—"are the Nhu family quarters."

"Huyen told us Mai planned to attack Diem at the palace," I said. "But unless the entire palace guard is infiltrated, how the hell would she get in? Or out?"

Ma smiled. "You will be particularly interested in this addition, built last year."

Mr. Ma's manicured fingers touched the main floor on the palace schematic, then traced two lines from the building's wings to the middle of the palace garden.

"What is that?" I tilted my head to try to make it out.

He rotated the blueprint carefully so we could see it better. "Six rooms, two point two meters high, made of reinforced concrete with steel doors ten centimeters thick. Twelve feet underground."

"A bunker."

"Precisely, Agent Miser. Twenty meters in length—sixty-five feet, built at a cost of two hundred thousand dollars. Ventilated and air-conditioned. Bombproof living quarters with amenities, a full pantry, water, a well-stocked Frigidaire made in Ohio. Telephones and shortwave radios to keep in touch with commanders in the field. Teletype machines, a map room with charts showing where government units are deployed. All of it safely four meters below the flower beds."

"Is this shelter secret?" I said.

"Sadly, no. It took the architect half a year to excavate and build. Entrances from either wing of the palace descend to the passageway to the shelter. Two tunnel entrances lead down to it from blockhouses on the palace grounds. All that construction couldn't be hidden. This construction, however, was."

He unrolled a large thin sheet of translucent paper and positioned it on top of the plan. A structure on the overlay intersected the tunnel from the western corner of the bunker, snaked underneath the grounds of Gia Long Palace, its wall and encircling security fences, and continued for several blocks, past the modern building being erected in place of the bombed-out palace, the vestige of last year's failed coup, finally curving into the parkland across from the building site, where it stopped.

"A hidden extension," Ma said. "In a corner, where the

corridor makes a turn of ninety degrees, is an entryway disguised as a blank wall. The secret addition ends in the park underneath what looks like a groundskeeper's shed, not far from the Cercle Sportif. Diệm and Nhu have not shared the fact of its existence. But I'm afraid that in spite of their efforts, the extension is no longer secret."

"Mai has these plans? You're certain?"

"I am. Her copy of the overlay came from a Communist sympathizer on the construction crew. I bought this one from the architect's assistant. One million piasters for the plans and his silence."

"Seven grand," Robeson said.

"A small enough price. The plan and its overlay offer Miss Nguyễn Mai a clear path to the palace itself, or the shelter they'll retreat to in the event of a bombardment like the one that destroyed the old palace." He rolled the map and its overlay together and slid them into a tube. "I pass the baton to you," he said. "The next leg of the race is yours."

"Why give this to us and not to Nhu's secret police?"

"Because these days it is most uncertain who is interested in Diệm's well-being, other than you gentlemen. Including Counselor Nhu."

We started toward the door, but he raised a hand to stop us. "Before I forget, I should give you a word of warning. You may wish to consider a change of quarters once this is done. Mathieu Franchini, the owner of your hotel, is Bảy Viễn's financial advisor in Paris. Mr. Franchini and Mai's father are close friends."

"God damn it," Robeson and I muttered, almost in unison.

Ma smiled. "A price will be exacted from us all before this is over. Please do call again."

CHAPTER FORTY-ONE

Stephan dropped us at the yacht club wharf as swiftly as he had swept us up. The junk pushed out into the Saigon River and raised its masts, the sails bright red.

The three of us walked to the Majestic and unrolled the plans across Robeson's bed, passing a bottle of Jack Daniel's back and forth.

"This is the first time we actually know where she'll stage before she strikes," I said. "The water is in the well."

"So she sneaks into the tunnel extension from the park entrance—in the shed," Rider said.

I said, "How is she gonna get through all the rings of protection in that freakin' castle to get at the Old Fox?"

"Maybe she doesn't have to," Rider said. "The palace might be impossible to breach, but that bunker's not big enough to hold a lot of guards. Once Diem's hunkered down, waiting for the mutiny to be over, she just needs someone to open the bunker door."

Robeson held out the bottle to me. "The VC are like ticks. Every Vietnamese unit in the country is infiltrated. The palace guards must be, too. When the time is right, the bunker doors open, and she and her cadre slip in and cap his ass."

We cooped together in Robeson's room. In the morning, we

carried the plans to Captain Deckle's windowless office at CID and spread them across his desk.

"We're going to need eyes on the shed around the clock to spring this trap," I said.

He didn't argue. "You can have Sergeants Moehlenkamp and Francis. Mr. Rider too. Assign them and Sergeant Crouch to whatever you and Robeson need done."

"Yes, sir."

I trusted Moehlenkamp and Francis. Crouch was a lazy no-account but Rider was a no-nonsense warrant officer, reliable and steady. He outranked Crouch and could keep him in line. I hoped the six of us would be enough to take on the Red Queen's Unit Eight.

"For God's sake," Deckle admonished. "Don't fuck this up, Miser. She's a better shot with a handgun than all of you put together. Make your peace with that right now. You've got the advantage with rifles. Use it. Take her down first, and then you can get into a pissing contest with her comrades." Deckle looked us each in the eye. "Between her Tay Ninh ambushes and Saigon, she has sixteen kills to her name. I don't want any of you added to that score. Understood?"

I told Moehlenkamp and Francis to change to fatigues, grab their carbines and two T-11 radios, and meet us out front. We unlashed our jeep and set off through traffic slow as lava. Robeson loaded our carbines as I drove. At Gia Long Palace, we passed through the outer perimeter. Red Berets in battle dress stood guard along the building's iron fencing, which was fronted by coils of barbed wire seven feet high. More Red Berets patrolled the grounds behind them.

At either end of the palace garden we found the concrete blockhouses that hid the outdoor entrances to the tunnels from the palace grounds. We casually followed the westernmost tunnel's underground route, tracing it along the surface until we reached the approximate point of the secret extension, and from there tracked it into Parc Maurice Long.

Robeson was the first to spot the shed near the bridle path, though we drove right past like he hadn't and parked at the Cercle Sportif. Sergeants Moehlenkamp and Francis stayed with the jeep while Robeson and I casually walked toward the windowless brick structure standing amongst a few shrubs and a sparse stand of tamarind trees heavy with pods. Young American girls trotted by on the bridle path aboard small horses, their polished riding boots gleaming. Chattering like starlings, they broke into a canter under the alleyway of tall trees.

A heavy wooden bench faced the door of the shed, framed by a burst of purple bougainvillea. Between us and the shed, rubber trees were flanked by two mounds of earth, each almost eight feet high, probably built from the excess soil snuck out of the excavation and quickly landscaped with short palms and multicolored lantana to blend into the park. The two hillocks formed a small saddleback. That would be our observation post.

Real nonchalant, we paced off the distance from the saddleback to the shed: a hundred and twenty steps; about a hundred yards. Maybe fifteen yards less to the bench. We sat down and made like we were admiring its thick mahogany, making sure nobody was paying us any mind before we walked to the shed and stepped inside. The space was very tight. A trapdoor occupied a quarter of the floor. Gun out, Robeson lifted the lid. I shone my flashlight onto steps leading down into the dark well and the tunnel extension. Nothing moved.

We spent a while just strolling in the park, trying to spot

any cadre doing reconnaissance like us, but all we saw were children walking across the parkland to and from the Cerc.

Satisfied there weren't VC nearby, we retrieved Moehlenkamp and Francis and escorted them to the hillocks to set up between the overgrown humps. We left the guys there to caretake until Robeson and I returned at 7 P.M. for the first twelve-on twelve-off shift.

"**The ambassador's pushed** back his departure for Washington again," Mrs. Lacey lamented, tucking away strands of hair that had gotten loose. "The White House is getting antsy. They keep cabling."

Embassy personnel in ties and shirtsleeves kept popping in to pose pressing questions and get Lodge's signature on documents before he left for the States. The plane sent to fetch him was still idling on the tarmac, manned and fueled. Lodge was stalling. Like everyone else in Saigon, he didn't want to miss the showdown.

A deputy exited Lodge's office and Mrs. Lacey got us in to see him. The ambassador seemed distracted, almost irritated to hear that we had a good line on the Red Queen's next move. He had no time to listen to details. When he said, "Good work, Sergeants," he certainly didn't sound like he meant it. We were out of there in under a minute. *Fuck you*, I thought.

Robeson complained: "We're busting ass to protect his ass and Diem's, and he blows us off?"

"Well, if it's any consolation, from here on we're looking to protect Diem's ass. Lodge's ass is on its own."

We stopped by CIA, ostensibly to thank Donald for sharing his asset with us. I figured that if I let slip I was now as pissed at Lodge as he was, I could hit him up for some Agency weapons. "Sure thing," he said, and led us to their arms room, stocked with three long racks of Czech, French, Swedish, Russian, and Swiss rifles. All sanitized: no markings, no stamps. We each took three Swedish Ks with collapsible wire-hanger stocks, far superior to the Uzis they resembled, and far better military rifles than the carbines we carried. Straight blowback, not much recoil, they wouldn't dance off the target and were even easy to control on full automatic, which we'd need if we were going to impede the Red Queen's accuracy.

I tried balancing the rifle by the pistol grip and tall magazine column. No good. I unfolded the stock and braced it against my shoulder. Much better.

"What's the rate of fire?" I asked Donald.

"Twelve rounds a second. Effective range is about three hundred yards. Her pistol isn't going to be much use beyond a tenth of that distance. Accuracy falls off fast after twenty feet. Thirty feet'll be her outside limit."

"Then we'll certainly discourage her from gettin' any closer," Robeson said drily.

We took eighteen long coffin-box magazines apiece, loaded with thirty-six 9-millimeter rounds. Heavy mothers, especially once we added the full mags. We slipped the long magazines into their leather pouches and shouldered the slings. Robeson went back and appropriated more magazines, tossing them into his duffel, and passed me extras as well.

"In case she brings all three teams of *Kamaraden*," he said.

THE WHOLE CITY felt desolate. Anticipating a coup that kept not happening was making everyone listless. We parked on the grass a quarter of a mile away, shackled the steering wheel, and humped the seriously loaded duffels toward the blind. Luckily

there weren't any cops or troops around to see us cross the
bridle path and disappear into the foliage.

Moehlenkamp and Francis lay hidden in the ferns under
enormous leaves of young palms about as tall as we were. We
crowded into the position, the giant fronds looming over us.

"This is way overpopulated in here," Robeson complained.

"Keep it down," I whispered. I handed the guys their Swedish Ks, which they were happy to get.

The hillocks afforded cover and some protection. But when
the shit hit the fan, the parkland's open terrain wouldn't be
much help, I thought. Distance was our only real advantage,
besides the Swedish K's rate of fire and power. If we did our
job right she'd be using a water pistol against a fire hose. Once
she was down, I was pretty confident we could handle the rest
of her team.

"If we have to engage, we tap her first," I whispered. "If she
walks into the kill zone, we drop her. I'm hoping her comrades
will scatter when they see her fall and realize the firepower
they're facing. Got it?"

Francis and Moehlenkamp nodded.

Above us, the sky was losing light. A yellow insect landed
on Robeson's arm, another one on Francis. My knee throbbed.
It started to rain lightly, but the palm leaves kept us pretty dry.
I peered beneath the fronds to study the silhouette of the brick
shed. I was parched, my throat scratchy. My canteen was sitting
at Flippi's. Robeson passed me his and softly sang one of his
favorites, a song he'd learned from his gran.

*"There's a girl in the heart of Maryland / With a heart that
belongs to me. And Mary-land was fairy-land / When she said
that mine she'd be . . ."*

"Sergeant Miser," Moehlenkamp whispered, "you think

somebody's gonna wonder why these bushes are singing in American?"

"Okay, listen up. Moehlenkamp, you and Sergeant Francis crash in my room at the Majestic tonight. Put Rider and Crouch in Robeson's. Tell them to relieve us at oh seven hundred tomorrow. All of you sleep in shifts. Keep the T-11 transceiver on. We'll report every three hours to the CID office and you guys. So stay alert. If the Red Queen's team shows up, we'll need everybody to come quick. Drive all the way in, use the jeep for cover."

"Keep your boots on," Robeson said. They left in the dark. The mosquitoes found us immediately, the nasty little vampires drilling through my civilian socks and feasting on my ears. It was going to be that kind of night: scratching and watching, half asleep.

OTHER THAN THE bugs, no one showed the slightest bit of interest in us or the shed for the twelve hours we cooped in the blind. But neither of us slept. The bugs kept Robeson occupied. Thinking about Nadja kept me awake. Seven o'clock the next morning Rider and Crouch took over. "Which room are we gonna sleep in?" Robeson asked. "Yours or mine?"

"I'm going to rack out in my own bed by my own self."

Maybe not the safest choice, but I needed privacy. It was the first of the month. Me and Flippi had our rendezvous with the bagman that afternoon. I figured the snatch would go pretty quick. We weren't due back to the blind until nightfall— assuming she didn't show earlier. Spreading *Stars and Stripes* on the bed, I quickly oiled my toss-away piece and wiped down the magazine of the 9 millimeter before reinserting it.

Despite my fatigue, sleep didn't come easily. I was dozing

fitfully as the noon siren went off. When I roused myself a second time, it felt like five minutes had passed, but it was after three. Just over an hour to the linkup with Flippi. Liberating the VC money was going to be sweet but it would've been a lot sweeter to spend it with Nadja.

I showered quick, dressed in fatigues with no rank stripes or name strip and pulled on my boots. The phone rang. I answered, expecting Robeson checking in or Flippi checking up, but it was Mrs. Lacey. She said the ambassador had seen President Diem that morning with our supreme leader in the Pacific, Admiral Felt. Afterward, Lodge had escorted Felt to the airport and seen him aboard a military jet for the nineteen-hour flight to Honolulu. Then he'd gone back to his residence. He wished to see me, she said. Oh, and would I do Mrs. Lodge a favor and pick up some fruit on the way over. "Durian," she said, and rang off.

The plotters had committed. The coup was on.

CHAPTER FORTY-TWO

"Fuck," I muttered when the line went dead as I tried to reach Flippi. I threw on my harness, grabbed the ammo pouches and Swedish K, and banged on Robeson's door.

"What 'n the hell," he yelled. "I'm sleeping."

"The coup-de-fucking-la is on. Meet me on the roof with your guns and gear."

I didn't wait for the elevator. The rebels might cut the power any second. By the time I reached the roof, I was panting and swearing never to smoke again. Low-hanging rain clouds hovered over the terrace and the city. No vehicles or pedestrian traffic moved in the streets. Columns of marching rebel troops stretched out along the empty boulevards, trudging single file along barren sidewalks. Robeson joined me at the railing and pointed out they were all wearing red neckerchiefs.

"They got on their away colors so they can tell who's on their side."

Firing broke out somewhere: a crackling exchange of small arms followed by a lull. We stood still, listening. The *tok-tok* of machine guns turned into another ripple of gunfire.

"What's going on?" said Seftas, coming up to the rail.

I pointed to the lines of troops snaking through the city. "Change of command."

Red and white tracers crisscrossed a few blocks away as loyal and rebel soldiers fired at each other.

"Oughta be blue tracers too," Seftas commented. "That would be appropriate for an American production, don't you think? I mean, shit, we've armed all sides in this clusterfuck."

A bleary-eyed Australian appeared, naked to the waist. He said he was hearing army rebels had taken the naval headquarters on the river while truckloads of pro-Diem soldiers reinforced Gia Long Palace, firing along the empty boulevards as they pulled into the palace grounds. I tried using the bar phone to call our captain but that line was out of commission too.

"Damn," Seftas said. "The guys at the Rex must have a front seat on the action. Their roof looks right over Gia Long." The Aussie asked Seftas if he wanted to go over there. "Hell, yeah," Seftas said, excited as a kid offered seats behind home plate. The two took off.

A T-38 buzzed the palace. Another banked to fire rockets and cannon at the presidential guards' barracks half a mile on. Anti-aircraft guns fired back from the palace roof. One Vietnamese gunboat loyally shot at the rebel planes from the river just below us.

The electricity went out. It was a quarter to four. I told Robeson that Lodge wanted us at the ambassador's residence and we hauled our T-11, Swedish Ks and ammunition downstairs to the jeep. Robeson jumped behind the wheel. Lines of rebel troops marched past us going north and slightly west toward the palace. We drove toward the ambassador's villa, passing red-kerchiefed troops aboard trucks and sitting atop armored personnel carriers. The town was locked down, the sidewalks bare.

I checked in with Captain Deckle on the T-11 as Robeson drove. The captain said the barracks of Colonel Tung's Special Forces were under attack. At that moment every navy gun on the river cut loose with cannon and anti-aircraft guns.

"What the hell are they firing at?" Deckle roared.

At nothing as far as I could tell, I said. A meaningless show of support for whichever side was ahead.

The captain rattled off what he knew. All over the city Americans were stranded at their jobs and trapped in their residences. Big Minh was at the civilian radio station, announcing the "removal of the autocrats Diệm and Nhu" who had caused American economic aid to be cut off, without which the Communists would win the war. Robeson and I looked at each other slack-jawed. Of all of Diem's offenses, Big Minh cared most about Diem's killing the golden goose.

The pops and cracks of small arms increased as we drove. Moehlenkamp got on the horn and reported he and Francis were stuck at the CID office, waiting for rebel troops to finish moving past in force. Looked like it was going to be a long wait.

Machine guns clattered, letting off ten-round bursts. A mortar thumped coming out of its tube and exploded seconds later with a *crump*. The familiar sounds excited me.

We arrived at the ambassador's villa to find a dozen embassy Marines in civvies, heavily armed with riot guns and tear-gas grenades. Leathernecks were deployed all over the house and garden, guarding the Lodges against the latest rumored threats: an assassination attempt on him, a kidnapping of them both.

Inside, Mike Dunn and some of the other staff were busy on the phones and civilian sideband radios. A Marine communicated over a field radio while Lodge was on a regular landline telephone, talking to the American liaising with the plotters—Lulu. I was impressed the residence had working phones at all. Courtesy of the plotting generals, no doubt. Mike Dunn hung up and filled us in. The ARVN generals and colonels, he said, had met for their regular Friday lunch at the officers' club near the Joint Chiefs' headquarters. Police carrying submachine guns had detained the officers inside. General Big Minh announced the coup d'état and gave them a simple choice: stand to join the rebellion or remain seated. The few who stayed in their seats were promptly arrested. Those who stood had to sign their names to a declaration of rebellion.

Lodge took another call and turned to face the shuttered windows, receiver clamped to his ear. He wedged open the slats of the blinds at eye level to look out as he listened. Over his shoulder I could see black smoke rising from the general direction of Gia Long. Tank and artillery salvos boomed. Reports streamed in: the rebels had seized Tan Son Nhut airport and the Ministry of National Defense. City phone lines were inoperative. The post office was taken: the coup plotters controlled all cable traffic. The arms cache at the National Police headquarters was theirs too. They'd declared a 7 P.M. curfew.

I looked up at the wall clock. Four-thirty. Shit! Half of eighty grand was slipping through my fingers. I consoled myself thinking chances were the handoff had been canceled on account of raining bullets.

A handsome child dashed through the room, pursued by an amah. Mike Dunn's Chilean wife and twin boys had been invited to lunch by the Lodges and were now houseguests for the duration. The boys had been out on the tennis court collecting geckos in tennis-ball cans, their dad said, when to their delight an ARVN M24 tank rolled by and fired its 75-millimeter gun, the compound's first confirmation that the rebellion was in motion. The available flak vests and helmets were way too big, but the Marines strapped them on the boys anyway—on Emily and Fran Dunn, too.

The Marine radio operator reported sixteen tanks converging on Gia Long, but not yet firing. Another gyrene rushed up to Lodge and said, "Sir, President Diem's on the phone for you."

Robeson and I followed the ambassador and Mike Dunn to the dining room, which was a shambles: paper strewn everywhere, radio squelch blaring. In one corner a Marine on a sideband kept repeating the same call: "Wizard Six, this is Whiskey Tango One. Come in please . . . Wizard Six, come back . . . Wizard Six, are you receiving?"

Mike Dunn picked up the extension in the hall to record the ambassador's conversation with President Diem. Somebody turned down the Vietnamese radio station that had defiantly been playing forbidden rock. Diem spoke so loudly that Lodge had to hold the receiver away from his ear.

"Some units have made a rebellion," Diem was saying. A Marine jotted it down. "I want to know, what is the attitude of the US?"

"I do not feel sufficiently informed to tell you," Lodge bullshitted. "I have heard the shooting, but I am not well enough acquainted with all the facts. It is four-thirty A.M. in Washington and the US government cannot possibly have a view."

"You must have some general idea," Diem insisted. "I need the protection of the US Marine teams aboard the Seventh Fleet standing off the coast. I need them to come protect the palace."

"I am unaware of any such Marine units."

"Mr. Ambassador, you are talking to the president of an independent and sovereign nation. I want to do what duty and good sense require. I believe in duty, above all."

"Sir," Lodge said, soothingly, "as I told you only this morning, I admire your courage and your great contributions to your country. No one can take away from you the credit for all you have done. You have certainly done your duty. I am worried about your physical safety. I have a report that those in charge of the current activity offer you and your brother safe conduct out of the country if you resign. Had you heard this?"

"No," Diem said.

"He sounds completely deflated," Dunn whispered.

"Mr. Ambassador, will you stop the coup?"

"That is not in my power," Lodge said.

"What would be your advice?"

"You are a head of state. I cannot officially give you advice. But as a friend, someone concerned for your health, my suggestion would be that you think seriously about getting away. If I can be of help with that, I am prepared to send my driver and my close aide, Mr. Dunn, to escort you to safety."

Lodge looked to Mike Dunn, who nodded assent. Better you than me, I thought.

"He is known at the palace and would ride in the front seat of my limousine with the chauffeur. The car will fly embassy flags. I am confident he could get through the standoff and escort you safely away."

"*Non*," Diem said. "No. I will not flee."

Lodge looked grim, the worry in his voice apparent as he upped the offer. "An American crew and fueled plane are waiting for me at the airfield. It's a comfortable plane appointed in a manner appropriate to your position. It will carry you to the

Philippines and on to any country of your choosing. France, Italy . . ."

Diem didn't bite. "I will only leave this country if it is the wish of my people. I will never leave at the request of rebellious generals or of an American ambassador. You have no right to make such a request of an elected sitting president. Your government must take full responsibility before the world in this miserable matter. I am the President of the Republic of Việt Nam. I will never desert my people," Diem said. "You have my telephone number."

"Yes. If I can do anything for your physical safety, please call me."

"I am trying to re-establish order." Diem rang off.

None of Diem's forces were coming to his rescue, Mike Dunn said, not Nhu's Republican Guard, not even Madame Nhu's women's auxiliary. Not General Dinh's troops either. The coup generals barely trusted one another and the hotheaded young General Dinh not at all. All river ferries had been moved to the far shore. If Dinh had a sudden surge of old loyalties, his tanks were stranded on the other bank.

Lulu called to report that Diem had tried to telephone the Red Berets' commander, Colonel Tung, who had been detained at the officers' luncheon. Big Minh put the colonel on the line. Tung apologized to Diem. He couldn't help. The Special Forces were no longer under his command. He was a prisoner with a gun to his head. The call was cut off.

Running secret police squads and keeping dossiers on all the army's top officers hadn't won Colonel Tung or his Special Forces any fans among the generals. Captain Ting wasn't the only one who thought he was a leper. Tung had smeared reputations and sowed distrust while serving his president. Big Minh's bodyguard, Captain Nhung, had loaded Colonel Tung and his brother into a jeep and driven them to a wooded corner of the headquarters, Lulu said, where he made them kneel on the lip of their own graves. Captain Nhung showed them two new notches on his knife before he shot them dead.

"Nhung's taking out Big Minh's trash," Robeson muttered. "This ain't gonna be pretty. Payback's a beast."

LULU CONEIN REPORTED that the head of naval operations, a Diem loyalist but well liked by his fellow officers, had been executed on his way to his own birthday lunch. "Revolution's messy," Lulu said.

Conein had to be right there with the mutineers in their war room to have all this so quick.

The rebels knew Diem would stall, waiting for reinforcements, still thinking this was a part of the false coup to flush out traitors, that all he had to do was sit tight and wait for Dinh. So Big Minh had phoned Diem and put dashing General Dinh on the line to reveal his duplicity and drive home Diem's hopeless situation with no loyal "son" coming to rescue him. With a string of curses, the young man told Diem to come out of the palace or die. Big Minh took the phone again to add further intimidation. Diem hung up on him, only to call back, full of conditions. Minh would not negotiate. General Don got on the line to offer Diem safe passage out of the country, nothing more. Despite all the firepower amassed around the palace, Diem would not surrender. Big Minh was flabbergasted. He gave the president five minutes. Diem hung up and the palace defenders answered the ultimatum with gunfire.

Lulu Conein was calling again. Big Minh had made all the generals tape-record declarations about participating in the mutiny, and was having their statements broadcast over civilian radio. There could be no backing out, no denying they'd participated.

Mike Dunn confirmed to Conein that two helicopters were standing by on the eighteenth green of the Saigon Golf Club, ready to serve as getaway transportation for the top-dog mutineers just in case. Which meant the conspirators weren't yet sure if the coup would succeed. And if they had to flee, Big Minh had informed Conein he would be coming with them. Conein had skin in the game now too.

"Sir," a Marine announced, "twenty more rebel tanks are converging on the palace. The ones already in position still aren't firing." With that amount of firepower amassed, they could afford to wait for Diem's surrender.

We followed Lodge upstairs through the master bedroom and onto the portico over the entry. Smoke continued to rise in the distance, no doubt from the presidential guards' barracks. There was a commotion at the gate as the relatives of Lodge's Vietnamese staff crept onto the grounds looking for safe haven. A Marine advised Lodge to leave the balcony. Two neighbors were firing tracers at each other, settling some private beef. We followed Lodge inside. Mike Dunn's twin boys were playing foxhole in a big cast-iron bathtub.

"Hell," Robeson muttered to me, "with the pasting the rebels are about to give the place and no General Dinh coming to their rescue, Diem and Nhu will go to ground in the bunker. The perfect time for the Queen to slip through the secret tunnel."

He was right. The brouhaha outside was perfect cover for her to make her move.

"Let's get out of here."

Whatever Lodge had wanted from us was lost in the hubbub. We were needed elsewhere.

CHAPTER FORTY-THREE

I raised Captain Deckle on the T-11, told him why we thought she'd be striking soon, and that we needed everyone at the emplacement. He said the rebel troops had quarantined the American offices along rue Pasteur, including MACV and CID. Investigators Francis and Moehlenkamp weren't going anywhere. That meant there would just be four of us. God help us if she brought the house.

Despite the absence of traffic, we were forced to drive an ever-widening circle to skirt the fighting concentrated around the palace and the guards' barracks a thousand yards farther down Thong Nhat Boulevard. At each intersection we'd catch signs of combat on parallel streets: splintered trees, shattered windows, walls pocked by gunfire.

It was starting to rain again as we rolled into the parkland. There was supposed to be a full moon but the sky was dark with clouds, except for the light flashing continuously over the palace roof. Small arms crackled from the direction of the palace. A howitzer barrage tugged at the air in our lungs.

Rider and Crouch made room for us to settle in. Besides the Swedish K, Rider had brought his M14, the long gun we carried in Korea. A cloud of smoke drifted toward us, smelling of cordite and something creosote-sweet. Two waiters in white shirts and black bow ties jogged past, trying to escape the fighting or obey the curfew. An ambulance klaxon wailed, stopped for a minute, and howled again as it sped away.

Diem's presidential guard and the Red Berets were having a bad time, but it didn't sound like they'd be surrendering anytime soon. The battle was deafening. We had to shout to hear each other.

"Sounds like fireworks at Tet," Rider yelled, nodding in the direction of the palace.

"They were never this excited to be fighting when we was advising," Robeson shouted back.

The conflict ebbed and surged. We rubbed at the cramps in our legs, gazed out through the fronds and waited. A bicyclist pedaled across the soft turf. One of her scouts? We followed him with our gunsights until he exited the park. A clutch of civilians hurried through the oncoming dark, followed by a dozen little kids carting burlap bags filled with spent brass scooped from under the guns, hollering for joy at what the scrap metal would fetch.

The warm rain misted us. Robeson and I guarded the front; Rider and Crouch, our back. I hoped like hell the mortars and tanks didn't overshoot their targets. We were easily within range. I exhaled slowly, trying to bring down my racing pulse. A block or two away people were fighting for their lives and over in our valley we were bored and anxious.

Jasmine hung in the air. Robeson sang "The Twist" soft and slow, like a lullaby. I wanted to lie down and close my eyes for a week.

The rain eased up and we caught glimpses of the moon. Rider tapped me and pointed. A lone rider on a dappled horse, all in black, was clopping steadily along the sodden bridle path in our direction, a nutcase out for an evening's canter in the middle of a coup.

As they drew closer, the speckled horse grew skittish from the battle noise. Robeson was the first to cotton on. "The Queen's arriving."

Rider flipped off his safety. "Party's on."

She looked elegant in a long-sleeved top and loose pants, cone hat tied under her chin, hair trailing behind her tethered only with a scarf tied in a simple loop. Brazen, I thought, as she left the bridle path and guided her mount toward the shed.

Heavy ordnance popped and boomed a few blocks away, lighting up the sky. Stray rounds buzzed high over our heads, scooting through the treetops, knocking down branches. I scanned the park, looking for her cadre. They could already be in place, waiting patiently to pop out of spider holes in the ground like they had roadside in Tay Ninh.

"Mr. Rider," I said, "watch our rear. See if you can spot her comrades."

She dismounted lightly, untied her hat, undid the ribbons around her hair and her waist. The panels of her black *ao dai* dropped down over the black pants. Her horse shifted uneasily at the steady gunfire and explosions. She patted his forehead and touched her own brow to his. The horse settled slightly. With her back to us, she undid the saddle and let it slide to the ground. Tossing the reins over the withers, she turned him back toward the bridle path and slapped his flank. The horse galloped off, heading for home.

No horse, no Vespa. How did she plan to get away? Did she expect to slip into the tunnel, execute her targets, and walk back out into the night? Fearless, this one, I thought. Relying on sheer guts rather than numbers.

Why not, I supposed. In the bunker it would likely be just the two brothers and a bodyguard or two. With her skills, she could surprise them and emerge, disappearing into the blacked-out city as easily as she had vanished from General Lang's hotel. Our job was to keep her from entering the tunnel.

The Red Queen turned, taking in her surroundings, giving us our first real look at her. Even at ninety yards, her easy grace and manner were arresting.

"The confidence of the righteous," Robeson whispered.

Lady Death took in the inky landscape, staring right at us.

CHAPTER FORTY-FOUR

The foliage had done its job. She hadn't spotted us. She bent to get something from the saddle on the ground, strolled to the bench ten yards from the shed, and sat down, her back to us. Her long black hair shone in the explosive flashes.

"What the hell?" Crouch growled. "What the fuck's she waiting for?"

"She's just waiting for the rest of the team to arrive," Robeson said.

"Maybe." Then it dawned on me—finally—what her plan must be. "I take it back," I said.

Robeson hissed. "Take what back?"

"She doesn't need a collaborator on the inside. She's not going in through the tunnel to find Diem in the bunker."

"Whaddya mean?" Robeson said. "She's here, ain't she?"

"The palace is gonna fall. Who's gonna rescue them? Even if he wanted to help, Dinh's boys are stuck on the other side of the river, remember? When Diem and Nhu realize there's no help on the way, they'll bail."

"They'll quit the bunker—and come sneaking out of that shed?"

"Shit, you might just be right," Crouch drawled. "Making a run for it in the middle of the bedlam would be their best chance."

"And her best shot at nailing them," I said.

Robeson nodded. "So she's waiting to pop whoever comes out of that shed. The good news is there's nobody else here but us friendlies. Four of us and only one of her."

"So far," Rider corrected.

Crouch turned to me. "Where are her little Victor Charlies?"

"Close by, most likely, waiting for word from inside the palace that Diem's making his getaway."

Robeson said, "Then we better hurry up."

"Yeah," I said, resigning myself. "We gotta move on her now." I cursed her, nerving myself up to take her on. She's Viet Cong, I told myself, proven lethal many times over. Was there any point in capturing her? We'd have to hand her over to the Vietnamese. They'd break her a millimeter at a time, extracting vengeance for every drop of blood she'd spilled. Instead of being relieved that she'd come unaccompanied, I almost felt bad for her. There was nothing for it but to descend without warning, close on the enemy and kill her.

"Rider, stay and cover the back. Make sure none of her people roll up on us unannounced. Sergeant Crouch, loop left; flank her. Sergeant Robeson, on me. We go straight at her."

Safeties clicked off.

"The palace fighting is noisy as fuck," I said, "but don't shout and risk alerting her. Remember, her weapon is only accurate to thirty feet. We're ninety yards from where she's sitting on the bench. We advance to where we're forty yards from her, then we light her up. I count off the paces. I fire first."

"Better zap her quick," Crouch said, his voice antsy and resentful. "There's nothin' but flat ground in between us and her. If she spots us—"

"Once more: we go to within forty yards of her on the bench and I fire—me. First."

Pumped, they nodded, except Crouch, who was flipping his safety back and forth, looking aggrieved.

"Suppress her fire," I said. "Hose her. Don't let her get off any clean shots. Okay, spread and go. Maintain your intervals."

We edged over the slight rise, slipped down off the higher hillock and fanned out as we moved from the greenery into the open, wire gun stocks against our shoulders. Four rifles against a sidearm. No contest, I kept repeating to myself as I paced off the distance down from ninety yards. Eighty . . . Seventy . . .

The incessant firing around the palace lit the night sky. We moved steadily. Still counting. Sixty yards . . . When the fighting slackened for a moment, the light from the muzzles stuttered, like flashguns going off. We looked like a silent movie, our motions jagged.

Fifty . . . I gave a hand signal to get ready—three paces to go. And then fucking Crouch fired. Blasted his entire clip at her: thirty-six rounds, three seconds. She dropped to a knee and shoved the bench over as the slugs flew at her.

Three shots flashed back at us. Robeson buckled. The side of my face burned. My ear was bleeding. Mother of God. She'd hit two of us in an instant, in the herky-jerky dark. If it had been steady daylight we'd be dead.

She fired four times more. Crouch emptied another whole magazine in the second it took her to reload. My eyes teared. I loosed three-shot bursts in her direction, aiming the tracers. Robeson, flat on the ground, stitched the bench. We smothered her. She fired again.

Crouch poured on more from the left flank. Tracers zipped by as Rider, in the blind, fired single rounds from his M14, trying to snipe her.

Our bullets peppered the shed, the bench. The ground

geysered dirt around her. She couldn't raise her head but fired at Crouch and pivoted to me. Crouch unloaded a third magazine at her. She went limp.

No return fire.

Our gun barrels smoked in the misty drizzle. Crouch dropped to a knee, afraid to approach any closer. I crept forward. Nothing. I walked with more confidence. Crouch came up alongside me, rifle trained on her, when the shed door opened.

Out of the bougainvillea stepped the unmistakable silhouette of Mr. Vy, carrying a large case. Behind him, two priests in cassocks. From their height and postures I recognized them right off. The taller priest strode arrogantly past Mr. Vy, ignoring the tipped bench and body like they weren't there. He signaled to a car coming toward the shed out of the inky night, headlamps dimmed. The shorter priest waddled after him like a duck. Not a word to us. We were invisible.

Mr. Vy walked calmly toward the Red Queen, extended his arm and snapped off a round. The body jerked. He stepped closer, bent slightly, and fired again, this time at her head—*pop*. We stood there like fools, dumbstruck.

The car pulled up and the pretend priests got in back. Mr. Vy hoisted the heavy valise into the trunk and got in front, the driver sliding over to let him take the wheel.

Crouch spat in the direction of the retreating automobile. "You're fuckin' welcome."

ROBESON WAS GIDDY with adrenaline. His right pant leg oozed blood from his groin all the way to his boot. I made him lie down, using the bench to elevate his leg. Rider knelt and ripped open Robeson's pant leg to apply a field dressing. I held a flashlight on his thigh and a bandage to my mangled earlobe, grateful she hadn't torn my face off. Rider pressed a dressing hard against Robeson's groin.

The firing around the palace grew louder. Red tracers whizzed by overhead, shearing off high branches around us and making the soaked trees smolder.

"How bad?" Robeson said, high as a kite, flirting with shock and laughing, happy to be alive, terrified to have been in the Red Queen's sights.

"Not bad," Rider answered. "All meat." The first dressing was already soaked. He lifted it off to apply another and froze. "Shit."

"What?"

He leaned close to me. "Nicked his scrotum too."

"Am I gonna die, Ellie?" Robeson moaned, trembling like he was cold, sensing all the blood exiting. "Sweet God in heaven."

"Clovis," I barked. "You'll be fine."

I sent Crouch to hustle back to the blind to radio for a medic. Rider pressed a second bandage against Robeson's crotch but Robeson kept tugging at it.

"Stop messing with the bandage," Rider snapped, "or I'll tourniquet your dick."

Crouch waved from the blind and mimed that the T-11 had taken a hit. We had no commo. I made driving motions. "Get the jeep!" He gave me a thumbs-up, jettisoned his helmet and harness, and ran.

"This is payback for the sentry and the pig, ain't it, Sarge," Robeson sputtered.

"He's delirious," Rider bitched and stuck him with a syrette. He painted M for morphine on Robeson's fatigues with a bloody finger and a second one on his forehead for good measure. The rain smudged both in an instant.

The palace fighting surged again. "Has the bleeding stopped?" I shouted in Rider's ear.

He shook his head no, still pushing down on the bandage. Even in the din, I heard Crouch roaring toward us like a madman, pedal to the floor. He fishtailed through the bridle path and was on us in seconds.

I helped ease Robeson into the back as they made ready to race him to the naval hospital by the rail station. Thank God, it was close. Rider jumped on ass-first, feet dangling over the side, still pressing the bandage hard. "Send somebody back for me," I shouted and the jeep sped away, rooster-tailing mud.

I COULD FEEL blood dripping onto my shoulder from my torn ear. An inch to the right, the round would have cracked open my skull. I slumped down next to the Queen. We had risked ourselves to stop her and she had hurt us bad, yet I felt oddly defeated that she'd failed.

Her cloth saddlebag held extra clips and the Queen's calling card. I slipped the card into the breast pocket of my fatigues and retrieved the Radom pistol from under her hand. Beneath the translucent grip was a familiar picture of a seated woman surrounded by her three children.

Uncapping my flashlight, I illuminated the Red Queen's face and sucked air. Blood seeped from her cheek, her lips, teeth. The bullet to the back of the head had exited through an eye and taken part of her cheek, its flesh now hanging loose. There'd been no call for those shots from Diem's bodyguard. I hated Vy for needlessly disfiguring her. She was no longer the elegant Red Queen in the flowing *ao dai*. I reached to straighten her tangled, bloody hair. All of it came away in my hand.

CHAPTER FORTY-FIVE

A wig—the hair beneath it just as black but shorter. No longer a Queen, now a One-Eyed Jack. It took only a moment to see she'd been both all along: the innocent angel shooting Americans dead with unreal skill, and the swaggering rider trailing Lodge to the cemetery; the tender beauty in the photo Furth carried in his wallet, and the fey young assistant standing next to Emily Lodge in the ambassador's residence.

I looked again at the photo under the Radom's grip. The Red Queen was not Mai Nguyen—Mai, like her younger sister, must have perished in the inferno in Tay Ninh. The teenage brother was the child who had survived. Already wanted by the police, he must have saved himself by slipping away disguised in his sister's clothes. Mr. Ma had told us Huyen was the Red Queen's mentor. No doubt Huyen had helped him perfect the illusion, adding gesture and movement to transform his young innocence into female beauty. Captain Ting thought the young lover who siphoned the life out of General Lang had vanished like a *qui*. But while Ting's men were looking for the Red Queen, she had simply walked away unnoticed as a man.

Yet in my imagination, the Red Queen was still the daring heroine striking down her enemies with impossible shots. Without mercy or remorse she'd drained every last measure of life out of the man who had brought hellfire down on her beloved family. And she'd almost had her vengeance on the self-righteous holy Joe who'd ordered the exterminations. She hadn't counted on us lying in wait to ambush her. If it hadn't been for Mr. Ma, she could easily have killed Mr. Vy and Nhu and the Americans' Old Fox, President Diem, even escaping to ambush Lodge another day. The Reds would have hung her image in some hall of heroes and proselytized youngsters with stories of her daring.

I closed the remaining eye and covered the face. I cut away the *ao dai* down to the padding underneath, took the shoes and the bloody wig, shoving it all into my rucksack. My brain was nearly too fried to function, yet I knew I didn't want the Red Queen mutilated any further or ridiculed in defeat. I retrieved a blanket from our emplacement and wrapped the body tightly, head to foot.

The fighting slacked off a bit. The siege would ratchet up again when more ammo arrived for the attackers. In my exhaustion, I wondered if anyone defending the place knew that Diem was no longer there. But of course they didn't or the fighting would have stopped.

I crawled back into our position and lay down under the fronds. Protected by the dark, I fell asleep in seconds. I didn't stir until a tremendous roar of howitzer blasts banged my chest like a drumhead. Those had to be going directly into the building. Tank guns and .50s spit streams of bullets into the masonry, shredding doors, windows, defenders. Mortars lobbed rounds, artillery boomed. I lay on the crest of the hillock and watched the continuous lightning halo the palace like searchlights at some Hollywood opening.

The gas tank or ammo in an armored carrier touched off

and blew straight upward in a flaming ball that topped the
roofs.

Rider reappeared with the jeep. "They stopped the bleeding," he shouted into my ear. "They're transfusing and
stabilizing Robeson before surgery."

I nodded and breathed easier.

We loaded the wrapped corpse on board and drove along
utterly empty streets. Rider said a Catholic colonel named
Thieu was leading the assault on the palace and "gettin' it
done." Clever of the Buddhist generals to have a Catholic make
the direct assault, he said.

WE LEFT THE anonymous body at St. Paul's Hospital morgue.
I dropped Rider at the Majestic and headed to the embassy
residence to report. It was a little before five and dimly light.
The dozen Marine guards were still at their posts, groggy after
their long night. A pair of them greeted me with shotguns leveled.

"You're back," said the corporal.

"No keeping me away," I replied.

The muzzles dipped and the jarhead waved me past the gate.
Another set of leathernecks guarded the front door. I found
Mike Dunn inside, bleary-eyed and still working the phones.

Dunn told me about more phone calls between Diem and
General Don, more attempts to bargain. Don reminded Diem
of the many opportunities he'd had to change his ways, the
fortunes his family had made at the expense of the country.
Diem expressed no remorse. He wanted to exit in style. He
expected appropriate transport, time to collect his personal
effects, and deference accorded in keeping with his position:
he wanted an honor guard.

Like the rebel generals, Conein and Dunn assumed Diem was telephoning from the palace. I explained I had seen him leave during the night, after we thwarted a VC attack on the escaping president. Dunn came fully awake and rushed me upstairs to inform Lodge. Coup or no coup, the ambassador had turned in at his usual hour, but was now back on the portico, taking in the eruptions of the fighting. I delivered the news that Diem was in the wind.

Head bent, Lodge ordered Dunn to convey the information to the Joint General Staff headquarters. No thanks, no nothin'. He barely looked at me. I started to tell him about the Red Queen but stopped myself.

Dunn got right on the horn with Conein, who was still with the generals, and asked him to alert General Minh. Shaking his head, he hung up.

"Big Minh refuses to believe Diem's not in Gia Long. Minh called the palace and spoke with the president a number of times."

Fool, I thought, the connection was patched through the palace switchboard to wherever they were hiding out in the world, something they must have planned long in advance. At a quarter to six several reports came in that the palace defenders had run up a white flag, then shot and killed a rebel captain who'd come to take their surrender, whether by accident or out of malice nobody knew. But the siege was over, and rebel soldiers were already ransacking and plundering the building. Madame Nhu's collection of silk negligees and her husband's stock of liquor went first. China and curtains were being carted away, along with a black marble sink and pink bathtub.

"To the victor the souvenirs," Dunn quoted Conein saying, as a grinning soldier skipped by Lulu wearing a mink stole, his buddy draped in one of the tiger-skin rugs lifted off Madame Nhu's floor.

They were totting up casualties at the palace while Big Minh stood by in full dress uniform with a felt-topped table prepared to take Diem's signature of surrender in front of the press and the world. His troops searched every corner. No Diem. No Nhu. South Vietnamese soldiers lay dead and wounded from attacking and defending an empty palace. Sacrificed for nothing. Standing in the debris, cheated of his moment, made to look a fool, Big Minh grew furious. Having lost face, Conein reported, Big Minh had raced back to his headquarters in a rage.

Lodge's other aide, Fred Flott, had just volunteered to go to the palace to verify Diem was missing when Diem telephoned. Lodge stepped to the phone. Dunn and I got on the extension.

"Where are you, Mr. President?" Lodge said.

"At St. Francis Xavier Church in Chợ Lớn. We have attended mass. Our confessions have been heard. We have received absolution and taken communion."

"What can I do for you, sir?"

"If you send a car we would avail ourselves of your earlier invitation to leave. You mentioned a plane at Tân Sơn Nhứt."

"Ah," Lodge said, pinching the bridge of his nose. "I'm afraid there's a complication. The closest long-range aircraft available is a KC-135 in Okinawa."

Dunn and I exchanged a look. The aircraft he'd originally offered, the one sent to take Lodge to Washington, had a luxury interior. Wasn't it still on the tarmac, fueled and waiting? Certainly General Harkins's plane was there. What Lodge was saying was nuts. Why would he send a head of state into exile aboard a Stratotanker, a flying gas station designed for aerial refueling?

"We can't get that plane here until tomorrow," Lodge went on.

"I see."

"Mr. President," Lodge said, "I have to step away for a moment." He handed the receiver to Mike while he went to a different phone in the living room. Was he calling Lulu to pass along Diem's whereabouts?

Mike Dunn was speaking with Diem in English. Diem said he and Nhu had driven to the home of a Chinese trader in Chợ Lớn, a Mr. Ma Tuyen, who had served them tea and soup, sheltering them until morning, when they'd driven to church for early mass.

Dunn covered the mouthpiece and said, "Ma Tuyen is chief of the five associations that control the Chinese districts. He's supposed to be Nhu's connection to the Cholon drug syndicates that help finance the military and Nhu's enormous army of secret police snitches."

I nodded but didn't mention that Mr. Ma and I were acquainted.

Mike's two boys came barreling down the stairs, fingers cocked, shooting with loud *bang*s as they roared through, barely keeping their oversized flak jackets in place.

Diem spoke: "Time has run out for us. It is the day after All Saints, second of November. The Feast of the Dead."

The ambassador was coming back.

"Dies irae," Diem said. "Dies illa." He rang off.

Dunn and I exchanged a look. We both recognized the Latin. I'd learned it as an altar boy at St. Monica's: That day is a day of wrath.

Colonel Dunn extended a hand toward Lodge. "Let me take the embassy limo. They're twenty minutes away. Big Minh isn't onto them yet."

"I'll go with you," I said, and took up my weapon.

"Your plane is still on call, sir," Dunn said, barely keeping the plea out of his voice. "We'll take him and Nhu straight to Tan Son Nhut. We'll see them to Manila."

"No." Lodge brushed off the suggestion.

"Sir?"

"We can't get involved."

Flott said, "Washington doesn't want him setting up a government in exile anywhere in the Pacific region."

Dunn blinked nervously. "I don't understand."

"That's the latest word from DC," Flott went on. "Diem must fly nonstop to Europe or to South America."

Dunn held his forehead like he was pushing back the thoughts also rushing through my mind. "Big Minh is livid," he said. "There isn't time to line up an asylum country to accept them. They'd be safe with us in the embassy until we finalized something. Left out there they won't last long enough for a plane to come get them."

Lodge stood firm. Diem was off his mandarin's throne. The ambassador no longer needed him to cooperate about anything. I remembered Lodge's firm handshake with Big Minh over the tennis net. Lodge would be dealing with his tennis partner from here on. Diem's day was over.

"They'll kill him," Dunn said.

"We're not to get involved," Lodge repeated.

The broken pieces kaleidoscoped together. In exile, Diem and Counselor Nhu would be a liability, endlessly intriguing to regain power. The pair needed to go permanently. And whatever happened to one of them needed to happen to both.

Dumb me. When the mutineers' resolve had seemed to waver and it looked like a coup might never happen, Lodge had pulled CIA back from pursuing the Red Queen. He'd tried to delay our search for her too, taking me away to Dalat, diverting us with a summons to the ambassador's residence. With the coup looking shaky, he needed her in the game. She was the fallback play. If the rebels did not screw up their courage and act, he needed her to be able to do her worst unimpeded.

Had Diem died at her hands, Washington would've been privately relieved and publicly blameless, as innocent as the diplomat well known to be next on her to-die list. Robeson and me, we were pawns who advanced too far. We should have come off the board sooner.

CHAPTER FORTY-SIX

The Dunn kids turned in their steel helmets and flak vests and surrendered to their mother for a bath in the iron tub that had been their trench. The coup was over, the regime officially toppled.

At his rooftop apartment atop the Italian embassy on rue Pasteur, Ambassador d'Orlandi could finally conclude the lunch he had sat down to the previous day when ministers from Diem's cabinet had appeared at the embassy door begging for asylum. Getting his government's official consent would have taken too long, so he'd invited them in for a meal where they'd officially be safely on Italian soil. The lunch had lasted all night.

Lucien Conein was exhausted. Before the coup, Lulu had managed to keep his involvement with the mutineers cloaked by meeting in secret with General Don at their mutual dentist's office on rue Catinat and other equally innocent locations. Conein had requisitioned funds from the Big Rock Candy Mountain and kept his personal safe stocked with neat 250,000-piaster bundles. He'd arrived at the conspirators' headquarters with five million piasters in cash to pay the coup forces and cover condolence payments to families of any soldiers who died in the attempt. No doubt the promise of cash had given courage to any officers who remained on the fence.

When Conein heard the press was on its way to the rebels' headquarters, he retreated quietly to preserve his anonymity in the affair. He went home to relieve the Special Forces team that had been protecting his wife and infant daughter in his absence. But before he got the chance to finally close his eyes and sleep, the embassy abruptly rousted him.

Upsetting intel had reached the White House. They wanted President Diem's status confirmed. Conein hustled back to the Joint Chiefs' headquarters. Diem and Nhu had taken poison, he was told. Did he want to see?

See?

Their bodies were out back.

Fuck no, Conein did not want to see their corpses or play any part in certifying their deaths. Although he had helped launch and finance the coup, he wanted no overt connection with it, most especially not with this ridiculous cover story of self-murder. The fairy tale of two devoutly religious Catholics committing suicide was patent nonsense, soon demonstrated by a published photo showing them badly mauled, their hands tied behind them. The Red Queen would have been quick. Whoever had done this had taken his time.

The generals' story changed immediately. The new version was that Nhu had provoked the stone-cold assassin Captain Nhung into a murderous fury, causing him to shoot both men and stab them repeatedly. Given how pissed General Minh was at the brothers for refusing to surrender at the palace, it seemed a safe bet his longtime bodyguard hadn't just flown into a white-hot rage but carried out the killings coldly and deliberately, on Big Minh's orders.

The brothers' death certificates were designed to humiliate. Both were demoted to posts they had held under the

French: Diem to province chief, and Nhu to chief of library services.

News of the deaths spread like wildfire. Saigon's streets erupted in celebration. Buddhists were triumphant. Homes of Diem's supporters were looted, his mouthpiece newspaper trashed and set on fire. White mice scrambled to trade their tell-tale uniforms for less conspicuous clothing. Crowds that had been made to salute Diem's portrait publicly tore it to shreds on the steps of the National Assembly. The headquarters of Madame Nhu's Women's Solidarity Movement was burned to the ground and an overzealous mob toppled the statue of the Trung sisters, beloved Vietnamese heroines, that the Dragon Lady had commissioned for six million piasters—with the sisters' faces looking suspiciously like her own. Dance halls rolled out their dance floors and filled with forbidden tangos, raucous rock 'n' roll blared from the bars, and political prisoners were set free. Dr. Phan, released from Con Son, was draped with garlands and carried through Saigon on the shoulders of his students.

ALL SMILES, LODGE took congratulatory calls in his office, doors flung wide. Colonel Dunn eyed his boss basking in the compliments and broke out a bottle.

"Quite a finish for the country's first chief executive," he said, pouring bourbon for us both.

I didn't speak.

"To fucking gangland murder," he said, raising his glass. I raised mine in kind.

A grinning consular official entered Lodge's office next door and offered hearty congratulations. Mike rose and eased the interconnecting door closed, shutting out the scene.

"Hallelujah," he said, raising the bourbon to his lips. "They're dancing a jig in Hanoi."

Big Minh and General Don had also shown up with some of the rebel generals, he said.

"Lodge didn't want to receive them," Dunn murmured, "lest they look like happy conspirators reporting their success to their mentor and protector."

"The winning team celebrating with their coach," I said.

But in the end the ambassador couldn't resist the shared moment of triumph. The generals confirmed that shutting down CIP had bolstered their cause. Lodge restarted the economic aid then and there, even upped it by twenty million bucks.

The word back in Washington was that President Kennedy was deeply upset, his cabinet still divided and full of misgivings. But not Lodge. Not a bit. The death of the Ngo brothers was unfortunate. But in a coup, he said, "order cannot be guaranteed everywhere." The press and the public in the States were as much behind him as the people in Saigon. The ambassador wasn't sweating the second-guessing and backpedaling going on in DC. Aftermath and consequences be damned. He had taken decisive action and was receiving the praise and thanks of citizens everywhere.

Come Monday, Cabot Lodge got his conference room back when the Buddhist monks he had been harboring left the chancery free men. On Lodge's orders, Fred Flott flew to Dalat on General Harkins's C-54 to collect the Nhus' three younger kids and accompany them to Saigon. Their mother wanted her children sent to her in Los Angeles, but Washington had no interest in offering the family asylum. Lodge ordered Flott to escort the children to Rome, slowly.

The embassy improvised travel documents that Ambassador

d'Orlandi gussied up with visa stamps. Three hours after arriving in Saigon, the youngsters and Flott were on a commercial flight bound for Italy, flying the long way round, making five stops en route in the hope Madame Nhu would be drawn out of the United States to comfort her grieving children. In Rome, Flott surrendered the kids to their uncle, the archbishop, and Madame Nhu finally left the US to rejoin them, declaring that "all the devils of hell are against us." Then she demanded a visa to return to the States to raise some hell of her own. Request denied. Mike predicted she'd never set foot on American soil again.

Although Lodge lobbied for a proper burial, the bodies of Diem and Nhu had become political footballs, taken first to the Joint Chiefs' headquarters to be interred like executed Colonel Tung and his brother, but quickly moved to the morgue at St. Paul's Clinic, only to be transferred to the basement of the Joint Chiefs' headquarters and from there into anonymous graves on the HQ grounds, their burial attended only by a Catholic priest and Diem's nephew and niece. No stone or marker. Instead, a slab of concrete was poured over their graves to make the spot inconspicuous and keep it from becoming a rallying point for loyalists.

Saigon got back to normal. The race track, brothels and dance halls reopened. Korean and Filipino cover bands arrived to blast the latest rock 'n' roll hits in the clubs and new bars along rue Catinat, called more frequently by its newer Vietnamese name— Tu Do. The port's berths once again filled with unloading ships. Goods and materiel resumed arriving—and vanishing.

The rest of life soon reverted to the usual, too. Buddhists took to the streets to protest discrimination and started immolating themselves again. Rocks and sticks once more flew at the white mice and combat police huddled behind their round wicker shields. Demonstrators were again beaten and imprisoned. The poor cluttered the streets, sleeping rough. Kids pestered and bullied us for cigarettes and money, pushing against our pockets to try to make something fall out.

Mike Dunn and I met up to exchange scuttlebutt in the bar in the Caravelle. Mike asked after Sergeant Robeson. I told him Clovis was in Tokyo, recovering from his second surgery. He had managed to avoid getting evacuated stateside and hoped to recuperate in Japan, which meant he might make it back to us in Saigon instead of being reassigned elsewhere. In the meantime, Rider had teamed with me to hold down Robeson's slot at CID and keep his bed warm at the Majestic. I did tell Mike the worst of it, that Robeson had lost a testicle and it was uncertain the other was functional.

"Does his girl know yet?" he said.

Before I could answer, he was called to the phone. I ordered a cosmopolitan and thought about Flippi. Him I'd told no one about. When I hadn't shown for our first-of-the-month payday venture on the day of the coup, he'd proceeded alone. I only knew he'd successfully liberated the extortion money when I saw the package he'd left for me at the front desk. Thirty-eight thousand fucking dollars in hundred-dollar bills, and a note scribbled on Majestic stationery. *Sorry you missed the party. Piece of cake.*

Thirty-eight grand, it felt like a million—the most money I'd ever had in my hands at one time. I sent Flip a postcard: *Thanks for the swell party favor.* When I didn't hear from him, I put in an international call to some basic training instructors we knew back in the world, hoping they had a clue where he was holed up, partying hard with his thirty-eight large and the extra twenty grand for re-upping. Had anybody sighted him?

Oh yeah, a pal confirmed. He had turned up in Nashville with his household effects. Or most of him. He'd been found in the freezer, bagged in plastic inside a long, zinc-lined casket. The head was missing, but it was Flippi all right.

The goddamn fool. Had he gone and done exactly what I'd said not to, taken off the Viet Cong collector instead of relieving the oil company guy of the money? Or was this payback for the other favor I'd asked him to do, disposing of the medium, Huyen?

After a last drink, I swayed home to bed for a troubled night's sleep. At breakfast, Seftas and I were both wearing sunglasses. He said there were signs that Henry Cabot Lodge might be going home early. Praise for his courageous work in Viet Nam had erupted in a groundswell of support back home that was carrying him toward the race for the White House.

Lodge was being touted for nomination even though he claimed he didn't want to run. Everywhere he went in Saigon, he was greeted by Vietnamese admirers with cheers of "Vive Capa Lodge!" I saw him one day outside the Rex Hotel pressing the flesh and basking in the movie-star treatment. People were smiling and bowing, laying mementos on him, asking for his autograph. Applause burst from the crowd as he waved a last time and turtled his head getting into the limousine. Emily, getting in the opposite side, saw me and came over. She held my face to kiss my cheek. "Don't be a stranger," she said.

Three weeks after the coup, JFK got lit up in Dallas by an ex-Marine rifleman. Lodge flew home to stand in the ranks of the official mourners. The newsreel at the Kinh Do theater felt like it came from another planet.

Early in the new year, a junior general named Khanh pulled off a second coup, ousting General Big Minh and the other top conspirators. An admirer of Diem's, General Khanh hated them for killing the Old Man, yet the new coup was almost bloodless.

Almost. Detained along with the ousted generals was Big Minh's bodyguard, Nhung, recently promoted to major. Under questioning, he admitted that he had executed both President Diem and his brother, and later even approached Associated Press chief Malcolm Browne looking to sell photographs of his handiwork.

"Unfortunately," Seftas said, "Major Nhung grew distraught and committed suicide in his cell."

"Shoelaces? Belt?"

"Shot himself in the back of the head is what I heard."

As for the US Military, the Big Green Machine was clearly rumbling into life. Sef raised his glass to clink against mine. "It's on, baby, it's on."

"You mean we ain't gonna wind it down by next Christmas?"

"You wait," he scoffed. "Marines are gonna wade out of the surf some morning, and the Hundred-and-Worst will unass their cloud wagons and drift down on their silky chutes like angels."

"You really think this fucker is ratcheting up, not down?"

Seftas leaned toward me. "See that contractor at the end of the bar? His company is bidding on a job to lay eight hundred miles of undersea cable between Nha Trang and the Philippines. That sound like any of us are getting booted anytime soon?"

"Well, that's good, then. But it's beginning to remind me of Korea. 'Can't win, can't lose, can't quit.'"

The next morning I caught a chopper to Tay Ninh and met up with Reverend Crawford, who took me to the cardinal. I explained whose ashes I was carrying. Early in the afternoon while the province dozed, we added them to the family crypt. We placed offerings of fruit and flowers, lit joss sticks, touched them to our foreheads and stuck them in a small vase next to a candle. When the ceremony was over, the padre and cardinal walked away, talking. I slipped the Radom pistol under the white chrysanthemums and followed.

AFTERWORD

The bodies of Ngo Dinh Diem and Nhu were exhumed in 1965 from beneath the blank concrete slab that marked their graves behind the Joint General Staff's headquarters. They were moved to Mac Dinh Chi, the beautiful antique French cemetery in the center of Saigon, rich with elaborate sculptures and tombs of the famous, as well as the simple headstones of legionnaires.

In 1968, the government granted permission for an annual graveside memorial service. Three years later, on the eighth anniversary of Diem's death, thousands gathered. Cabinet ministers attended, an army general offered the eulogy. Latin prayers were recited at the basilica and a requiem mass was held.

Less public was President Thieu's involvement. A year prior to this commemoration, he had invited a Cao Dai medium to summon Diem's ghost. Thieu was the Catholic colonel who—at the insistence of the top Buddhist generals—had led the assault on the Gia Long Palace, a fact Diem's ghost knew only too well. Thieu asked what he could do for the deceased now.

Diem's spirit complained that he was trapped by the Mac Dinh Chi cemetery's encircling wall. A short time later a thirty-foot-long breach appeared in the western wall of the graveyard.

In 1983, the brothers' remains were shifted again when the

victorious Communist regime condemned the cemetery as a colonial relic, insisting that Vietnamese claim their kin and that the French government repatriate the bodies of their soldiers. Abandoned monuments were bulldozed and the field made into a park.

Diem's body was reburied with his brother's at Lai Thieu, a town northeast of Saigon. They were entombed near their brother, Can, and their mother. With the blessing of his brother, Brother Can had ruled Central Viet Nam as a dictator. After the coup, his land had been found to contain dungeons and mass graves. Can pleaded for asylum, but Lodge sent Lucien Conein to turn Can over to the new government for trial. He died by firing squad. Of the six Ngo brothers, the eldest was buried alive (along with his son) by North Vietnamese Communists, and three were executed by South Vietnamese. Diem's monument bears only his baptismal name, Gioan Baotixita— Jean Baptiste. Nowhere does it identify the crypt as that of Ngo Dinh Diem, first president of the Republic of Viet Nam.

ACKNOWLEDGMENTS

My thanks to Viet Nam veterans for their help, encouragement, and shared memories: Robert Klett, Colonel Karl Hopp, Juris Meimis, Lenny Goodstein, Richard Stolz, Harry Pewterbaugh, George Ruckman, Ellsworth Smith, Dr. Douglas Bey, Tom Glenn, John Lathnin, Captain Fred Heather, Gene Hale, Kendrick Forrester, author Shaun Darragh, Robert Shookner, Special Forces Major Jim Morris, Jerome Gold, and the irascible Samuel Garrison.

And the civilians to whom I owe so much: Karen Palmer, Charles Ruas, Aleks Rozens, J. R. "Rip" Westmoreland, Stuart Fishman, Ira Pearlstein, John Thomas, Francis Karagodins, David Moehlenkamp, Michael Guinzburg, Sonia Rivera, T. Glenn Coughlin, Sister Y Panh, the Saigon Kids, Harrison Shaffer, and author Kathy Dobronyi.

I am much indebted to Takashi Oka for allowing me into his private files and reportage and to his daughter, Megumi Oka, for making that possible. Many thanks as well to Tom LoPiano, Jr. of Hansen & Hansen Arms & Antiquities on the Old Post Road in Southport, Connecticut, for so generously sharing his wealth of knowledge. Also to Lady Borton in Hanoi, and David Lloyd Sinkinson of Ho Chi Minh City, once called Saigon.

And my undying gratitude to Jeanne, for putting up with it all—and me. It couldn't happen without her.

A NOTE FROM THE AUTHOR'S WIDOW

Aposthumous publication is always bittersweet. Juris died suddenly in November 2018, not knowing that his third novel would be published, much less by the house he had co-founded with Laura Hruska in 1986. It's hard to imagine a more fitting home for the book.

My thanks on behalf of Juris go, of course, to Laura's daughter, Bronwen Hruska, who took over the helm of Soho ten years ago and is, in Juris's own words, "deeply intelligent, wonderfully candid," and—his highest praise—"swell." And although Juris didn't know Juliet Grames would become his editor, he had long ago rightfully deemed her "brilliant." My personal thanks go to both of them as well the rest of the Soho crew, especially managing editor Rachel Kowal, who was endlessly patient with me even though I am, as Juris loved to remind me, a publishing "civilian."

In the early days of Soho, Juris, always a contrarian, went against conventional publishing wisdom by starting a line of international mysteries that were at once compelling stories and windows onto the history and culture of the places they were set. That was certainly his aim with *Play the Red Queen*. As with his earlier novel, *Red Flags*, Juris wanted to "bear witness," as he said, to an underreported aspect of the Viet Nam war: the "elaborate, even treasonous corruption—and our complicity in it." Exposing this part of the story of Viet Nam was his way to honor his fellow veterans; the Vietnamese people whose lives were so often at the mercy of those in power; and his beloved Montagnards, the indigenous peoples of the Central Highlands, where he served.

Juris said that Viet Nam had marked him for life. In the end it marked him for death as well, through the toll Agent Orange took on his heart. Given the subject of *Play the Red Queen*, his final novel, it's a terrible irony that the aerial spraying of Agent Orange—known first as Operation Hades and later, when that name presented a public-relations challenge, as Operation Ranch Hand—was initiated at the request of none other than President Ngo Dinh Diem.

Jeanne Heifetz
Brooklyn, NY
September 2019